By Katharine Ashe

The DUKE

A Devil's Duke Novel

Katharine Ashe

AVONBOOKS

An Imprint of HarperCollins*Publishers*

Excerpt from *The Prince* copyright © 2018 by Katharine Brophy Dubois.

THE DUKE. Copyright © 2017 by Katharine Brophy Dubois. All rights reserved. Printed in the United States of America. No part of this book may be used or reproduced in any manner whatsoever without written permission except in the case of brief quotations embodied in critical articles and reviews. For information, address HarperCollins Publishers, 195 Broadway, New York, NY 10007.

First Avon Books mass market printing: October 2017

Print Edition ISBN: 978-0-06-264172-4
Digital Edition ISBN: 978-0-06-264173-1

Cover illustration by Ann Kmet

Avon, Avon & logo, and Avon Books & logo are registered trademarks of HarperCollins Publishers in the United States of America and other countries.
HarperCollins is a registered trademark of HarperCollins Publishers in the United States of America and other countries.

FIRST EDITION

17 18 19 20 21 QGM 10 9 8 7 6 5 4 3 2 1

To my dad (with the angels).
To my husband.
To my brothers.
And to all the good, kind, compassionate,
loving men out there.
You are my real-life heroes.

CONTENTS

Come what might she would be wild, untrammeled, free.
—JAMES JOYCE, *Ulysses*

Rule, Brittania! Rule the waves:
Britons never will be slaves.

JAMES THOMSON (1740)

Prologue

The Plan

April 1808
Willows Hall
Estate of the Earl of Vale
Shropshire, England

*A*t the advanced age of eight, Lady Amarantha Vale announced to her elder sister, who was her closest companion, that she would not marry for wealth, title, or land.

"For what will you marry, then?" Emily replied.

"Love, of course," Amarantha declared, adding, "Silly." But she did not blame her sister for obtuseness. Emily had been betrothed since birth and had no choice in the matter. Obviously she hadn't given it any thought.

Amarantha had. She had given it lots and lots of thought. Moreover, from the stories her father read to them about the great heroes of yore, she knew precisely which sort of man would steal her heart.

"He will be frightfully strong and fearsomely brave,"

she said. "He will have blue eyes that sparkle like the sea, golden curls that shine like the sun, and shoulders so broad that he could carry a mountain upon them."

"To support all of that magnificence he must also have legs like tree trunks," Emily said, turning the page of the book their father had lent her that morning.

"Oh, yes," Amarantha said, knowing her sister teased. But she never minded teasing when it was done lovingly. "He will be gentle and kind, too, especially to small children and animals, and always chivalrous with ladies. And he will be generous. He will give away his riches to anybody who needs them."

"That will be impractical. How will your family acquire food and shelter?"

"With my dowry, of course. And when that is spent I will take in sewing projects, like Fanny Butterworth in the village does."

"Sewing?" her sister said skeptically. "You don't even like to embroider."

"That doesn't matter," Amarantha said, blithely waving away the obstacle. "I will do whatever necessary so that we will be happy. Anyway, I will have some time to do those sorts of things when he is off leading his men to victories against the enemy."

"The French, presumably."

"And any other villain that crosses him. He will ride a magnificent white steed, which will gallop valiantly into battle. And he will enjoy making snowmen."

"A horse making snowmen will be a sight to see, for sure."

Amarantha laughed, flopped onto her back, and stared at the crisscrossing branches above, which were dotted with new green leaves unfurling from their winter's repose. It was springtime and even the air sang of expectation. "He will travel all over the world and get into all sorts of wonderful scrapes and adventures."

"Won't you accompany him on these adventures?"

"When I'm able, for I will have infants to care for. We will have six children. But he will definitely accompany me on *my* adventures."

"I think I am beginning to like this paragon."

"Good. Because we will always prefer staying at home, so you must visit often, and our sisters too. And he will love his mother and father as much as I love mine."

"It sounds like a fine plan, Amy." Emily looked up from her book. "But you know that Papa will choose a husband for you, as he will for our sisters as well."

"I will ask him not to." Amarantha jumped up, scattering the grass braids she had fashioned with fingers full of energy. She stepped out from beneath the shading branches. Mama always said direct sunlight made her freckles even more numerous. But the warmth of the spring day felt so good and she was simply bubbling over with anticipation. Her bridegroom wouldn't dislike a few freckles, after all; he would love her too much to care about that sort of thing. "I will choose him myself, and I will know him the moment I see him."

"How?"

"By his smile and kind words and good deeds."

"He sounds like a veritable Prince Charming."

"He will not be a prince," Amarantha said, stretching her arms out at her sides. The sun in her hair was like a wild dancing of flames. "He will be an angel. My angel. And I will love him and no other with all of my heart until the day that I die." She twirled, faster and faster on bare feet, until the trees and grass and sunshine blurred.

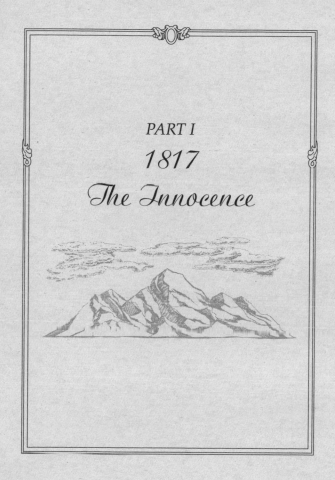

PART I

1817

The Innocence

Chapter 1

The Departure

August 1817
Willows Hall, Shropshire

Dearest Daughter Emily,

A companion has been hired! The ship has sailed! Your sister has gone!!

I am beside myself and have told your other sisters that if they ever so much as glance at a preacher, their father will disown them. How unfortunate That Man resembles the man in her childhood Plan!! If only he had black hair and a dark countenance, our darling Amarantha would never have glanced twice at that unsuitable Mister with his wretched Mission! I would curse golden curls entirely if not for the delightful lemon wash Sally prepares for my toilette, which has superb effects on mine.

Amarantha's suitors are deeply vexed. Upon

hearing the news, Lady Witherspoon's poor Eustace wept into his tea and experienced such a disturbance of temper that he did not leave his room for two full days. Sir Roger announced his intention of sailing after her at once. (Your father felt it necessary to remind him how last summer at the punting party he became ill from the rocking of his boat, which Sir Roger explained was due to taking four lemon custards that day rather than his usual three.) Lord Brill's poem "Destitution Upon the Loss of a Strawberry Flower," which I enclose here, speaks for itself. Yet I fear none of their manly tears will bring her home!

I also enclose a message to you from your father. How devastated he is to have lost not only you to London, but also now our beloved Amarantha to the wretched colonies!

I shall cry myself to sleep tonight and spend the entire sennight in bed with the draperies drawn, taking consolation only in the knowledge that Manchester is governor of that miserable island now, and his duchess is exceedingly stylish, despite now being a colonial. Our darling Amarantha simply must cling to her for guidance.

Do come up to the Hall soon. We are at quite a loss now and a visit would cheer us.

Grosses bises,
Your Devoted Mama
Encl.

Dear Emily,

Your mother is in high distress, as are your sisters and indeed the entire household. When Mr. Garland sailed two months ago I felt certain that, in his absence, Amarantha would swiftly come to her senses. Yet she remained steadfast. I am persuaded that the novelty of it all deserves some credit; she has always been my most dauntless daughter. I have little hope that Garland will make her truly happy. But I have every faith that our intrepid, big-hearted Amy will nevertheless wrest happiness from whatever adventure she throws herself into.

With Affection,
Edward "Papa," Seventh Earl of Vale

10 October 1817
The Queen's Hotel
Kingston, Jamaica

Dear Emmie,

This is not at all as I anticipated! But I will try to describe it.

The people seem English, yet how different from in Shropshire! Everywhere one sees great excess beside great want. Modestly prosperous gentlemen and gentlewomen wear monstrous loads of fashion—even as Mama and Papa do! Yet I have seen others so poorly clothed that they lack shoes. The hotel manager says the latter are slaves and cut sugar cane in the fields. (Without shoes?!)

In fact it seems that most people one encounters here are slaves. I remember now that you told me this would be so, but how remarkable to actually see it! Some of the sailors aboard our ship and servants at the hotel, however, are freedmen. When I asked the chambermaid about this she said that some freedmen have shops and land, and that even the pastor of her church is a freedman. (Despite your attempts and Papa's to teach me of the world,

I had little notion of any of this before. How much I have now to learn!)

My companion, Mrs. Jennings, thinks the gentry here are puffed up like mushrooms. She is nevertheless eager to visit with them. (She adores gossip and is very silly.) Several have already called on us here.

The Duchess of Manchester sent an invitation to stay with her until the wedding, which I declined. My darling Paul says it would be unsuitable for the fiancée of a humble missionary to reside at the governor's mansion.

As to the island, all is lush and verdant beyond imagining. The heat is astonishing. There are glorious mountains and beaches with the whitest sand I have ever seen. Here are fruits I did not know existed before two days ago: guava, mango, pine-apple, and "bread fruit." They are all delicious. (Mrs. Jennings dislikes them and demands marmalade.)

The port itself is astonishing. The bay is filled with every sort of vessel and everywhere there are people speaking in so many tongues that one's head spins. The greatest sight is the Fairway. *Her captain and crew are heroes of an important battle (I do not recall which—you know I am a wretched study at History!). It is a spectacular sight: the Union Jack flying proudly from the mast of such a magnificent ship in the lapis waters of this world so far from home. In truth, I never understood the vastness of our empire until now.*

All is not entirely alien. My darling Paul's church is blessedly quaint, although somewhat austere. He promises to make me known to the parishioners as soon as I have regained my bearings on land. I told him that I do not suffer from lingering "sea legs," so he needn't have concern. It was adorable how he

*blushed then, and implored me to lower my voice.
I believe the notion that I have legs gave him pleasurable pause! I do not shrink to tell you, sister,
that it is thrilling to be admired by a man in such
a manner.*

*(I am still astonished Papa allowed me to come
here. He is the most generous, most kind, most
wonderful father in the world!)*

*A footman has just told us that a storm will arrive
tonight, but that we must not fret, although we are
across the street from the quays, for the hotel is
tightly caulked. How singular of him to alert us to a
storm, and how clever to know when it will happen.*

*Beyond the windowpane I see there is now great
activity at the docks. Rather than put this letter
in the hands of the footman, I will walk to post it
myself. Mrs. Jennings says we must not venture
forth without Reverend Garland's escort, but he
has not yet come today and I simply must escape
this confinement—or by the time he finally does
call I will surely be in ill sorts. Also, I packed only
one pair of boots. I should not like to cover them in
mud when I walk to post this after the rain.*

With all of my love,
Amy

P.S. The Battle of Rappahannock River!

Chapter 2

The Storm

*H*e saw her for the first time ever in a storage cellar with rain slashing at her face, standing atop a crate, struggling to fasten a window, and the first words he heard from her lips were, "Damn and blast it to Hades!"

Before he could duck his head beneath the lintel and move forward, she turned to him, eyes the color of clover-leaves and lit like lightning.

"Don't gape, you big column of shark bait," she shouted. "Help me!"

A blast of wind struck the building and the shop above them shuddered. Her grip slipped over the window latch.

Gabriel shoved his shoulders through the narrow door-way and in three strides crossed the room. The wind blew hot and punishingly hard through the opening, but she did not release the latch. Covering her hand with his, he drove the frame shut.

The building moaned, and Gabriel found himself look-ing down upon a nose both freckled and wet, lips both lush and damp, lashes both long and dripping, and cloverleaves that had gone entirely round. Her features were English, fine, and not unattractive. After five months at sea, he would have been one sailor in a million to resist following the trail of rainwater down her pale throat in which her pulse beat visibly to the gown laced tight around her collar, sodden, and clinging to her curves.

Sweet curves.

"Remove your hand from mine and your eyes from where they have fallen out of your head," she said in such an altered tone that he barely heard it below the groaning of the walls and the pounding of the rain. Rather, the pounding of his pulse.

Too long at sea.

He removed his eyes and then his entire self. Stepping back, he offered his hand for her descent from the crate. She lifted a single brow.

"I beg your pardon," he said roughly, withdrawing his hand once again.

She grasped her sodden skirts and climbed nimbly down. "You are pardoned, Shark Bait. This time."

"Lieutenant," he corrected.

Swiftly scanning the room with those eyes that even in the murky light of this day were like the green of Highlands mountains, she untied the ribbons at her throat, removed her dripping bonnet, and tossed it atop a barrel.

"Have you got a handkerchief?"

He reached into his waistcoat and proffered the square of linen. She glanced at his outstretched hand, then at his face, then at his hand again, and did not move forward.

"You are a giant beast of a man, aren't you?" she said.

"So I've been told." He set the linen on a crate and backed away, curling his fingers into his palm that had easily encompassed her whole hand.

Taking up the kerchief, she unfolded it with trembling fingers and wiped the rainwater from her face. Wind and rain battered the building in frenzied fury, filling the tiny space with sound.

"I wonder how you go along aboard a ship." Her gaze passed up and down him anew. "The crown of my head is barely to your chin yet I found the quarters aboard our ship frightfully cramped. Unless naval ships are much more spacious, you must spend every day bent over."

"Aye, but only the part o' the day belowdecks."

The lush lips twitched.

When she withdrew her gaze to look about the room, he felt the loss of that reluctant smile in his chest like the loss of air.

Nonsense. He was muddled with exhaustion from preparing the *Fairway* for the storm.

This storage room beneath the shop was minuscule, heavy with heat, and packed with sacks of rice and grain, barrels of sugar and ham, wooden parts for furniture, skeins of silk, boxes of nails and other tools, and even one small keg of gunpowder. She strode the circumference of it, rounding him, and then halting where she had begun. The wind blasted against the shop above and she tilted her face upward to peer at the ceiling that hung an inch above his head. Biting her lips between her teeth, she drew a hard breath, and then looked at him again.

"I suppose you have experience with storms of this sort," she said.

Not of this sort. But spots of pink sat upon each pale cheek now. She had tucked her hands into her soggy skirts to hide their quivering. She was making a valiant effort to conceal her distress—more valiant than many a sailor he'd known.

"'Twill blow over soon enough, lass."

"That was a lie," she said, a dart forming between her brows. "Why did you lie to me?"

"I didna—" He bit back his retort. But his patience was

frayed. There had been no sign of the *Theia* entering the harbor, though he had stood in the downpour until the swells were rising so suddenly and steeply over the quay he had finally been obliged to shelter here. And now this: a sharp-tongued English girl with the manners of a stevedore. Gabriel didn't care much for social niceties. But a man wasn't made First Lieutenant of a ship of the line at twenty-three by failing to mind his tongue.

Minding his behavior was another matter entirely.

He bent his head and a stream of water cascaded from his hat brim. He glanced at her through the waterfall.

"Would you be fretting if I remove my hat?"

The cinnamon spots that trailed over the bridge of her nose and across her cheeks crinkled together to make one big cinnamon blotch. "Why on earth should I?"

He set his hat upon a crate. Wrapping her arms about herself she watched him closely.

"Well?" she said. Some of her hair had escaped the knot at the back of her head and clung wetly to her brow just as the fabric of her gown clung to her hips and legs.

Copper hair striated with gold.

Softly rounded hips.

Long legs.

The damn pulse in his head was a snare drum. He knew men whose cravings for feminine flesh got the best of them when they finally came into port. He had never been one of those men. Women weren't to be enjoyed like a randy stallion taking a mare, rather with as much appreciation as a man savored a tumbler of fine brandy, or a sublime piece of music, or a painting by an Italian master—a Michelangelo or Botticelli.

Sweet curves.

Her garments were fine, her speech cultivated, and she was old enough to know that her damp gown was not in the least modest at present.

The stallion was winning.

"'Twill be some time before the storm passes," he said in too husky a voice. "'Tis miles wide."

The brilliant cloverleaves popped round again.

"Miles?" Beneath the freckles and agitated flush, her skin was smooth—cheeks, brow, hands. She had not been in the islands long, and she was little more than a girl.

After nearly a decade at sea, Gabriel could barely remember boyhood.

"You've just arrived?" he said.

"Two days ago on the *Camelot*."

Gabriel knew it. As first officer on one of His Majesty's finest ships of the line, it was his responsibility to know the merchant vessels that docked at English ports.

"No one warned you o' hurricanes?"

"No." She had remarkable features: mobile and bright and expressive. "Should they have?"

"'Twill be hours still." And it would leave a mighty mess of destruction.

"How many hours?"

"No' till morning."

With a long inhalation, she released her arms from about her chest.

"Then we should make ourselves comfortable," she said with newly crisp decision and swept him with another perusal, lingering ever-so-briefly on the medals pinned to his coat. "If you can. You are as wet as I, yet you look like a toy soldier, standing there so erect and unbending. I suppose sailors are accustomed to being soaked through, of course."

"If they're bad sailors, aye."

Pleasure flared in her eyes. "Now, make yourself useful and help me search these crates for a woolen shawl or blanket. For I *am* soaked through." She set to her task on the nearest crate, but the lid was nailed shut and her fingertips strained at the wood.

He went to her side. Scent arose from her damp hair and skin. She smelled like a memory.

He withdrew the knife from his coat and pried open the lid.

"It seems that you are useful after all," she said with a half grin that abruptly turned something very sharp in his gut and made him want to tell her the truth. Urgently. All truths. Truths about the hurricane and truths about the depths of the sea and the stars in the heavens and every one of the sins that made him a beast indeed.

"Lass, 'tis as likely as no' that before this night is o'er, the sea will top the wharfs an' swallow this building."

"And we in it."

"Aye."

"I see." For a moment she said nothing. "After we find blankets we should look for a deck of cards or a backgammon board in these crates. For if we are to die tonight, we had better enjoy our final hours on earth, hadn't we, Shark Bait?"

"Lieutenant." He could not look away from her eyes. Black clouds without blotted the tropical sun, allowing only the most reluctant light into this room, yet her eyes sparkled.

Backgammon. She had the body of a siren and the innocence of a girl.

"You've a disliking for sailors, it seems," he said.

"The officers aboard the *Camelot* confined me to my quarters for the entire duration of the journey. They said it was not suitable for me to be atop, but I think they simply did not want me to witness them drinking the day away every day."

More than likely they did not trust themselves with the pretty little siren wandering about.

"I think you are trying not to smile, Shark Bait. Will you attempt to deny that sailors drink excessively?"

"No."

"So, you understand the reason for my dislike."

"Because hardworking men are fond o' spirits?"

"Because they refused to share their spirits with me."

They found blankets woven of soft wool and tins of biscuits. They had no lamp, which Gabriel said was for the better, and she accepted that without comment. As the storm lashed the shop above and water trickled through the seams of the window, and darkness fell, they found a cask of new rum. She said that she had never tasted rum, and asked if, being a Scot, he preferred whiskey. He replied that he did, but that any grog in a storm would do. She smiled so readily, as though her lips were more accustomed to smiling than not. Despite her obvious breeding, there was no maidenly modesty in her frankness. It was on the tip of his tongue to say that over both whiskey and rum he already preferred her.

She discovered sugar, which he added to the rum to make it more palatable for her, and she sipped warily. As the daylight waned and she explored the contents of crates and barrels, she darted glances at him—frequently. She spoke with ease but she came no nearer to him than necessary.

When the black night consumed every last wisp of light she ceased speaking. As the hurricane shook the walls, Gabriel settled onto the ground with his back against a crate. Closing his eyes, he made himself picture the *Theia* bobbing violently at anchor in some nearby port, its decks flooded in foam but its crew and officers tucked into some terrestrial haven.

No time left for repentance.

He had thought he and Jonah would have plenty of time. Sailors perished every day at sea, but somehow he had believed them untouchable.

Invincible, Gabe. That's what the storytellers will say of us someday. Invincible.

In the heavy darkness, her scent came to him again. Like home. Not the mossy grass of the mountains of Kallin, nor the wildflowers that carpeted the hills of

Haiknayes. She smelled of woodland fir: crisp and warm and rich.

The room rattled and he felt her settle silently at his side.

"How did you come to be here in this cellar?" she said very quietly. She was close to his shoulder, closer than he had anticipated.

"I was watching for a ship. You?"

"I walked to post a letter and got caught up with exploring. Everything here is so different and interesting. I was far from the hotel before I thought to turn around." She made a sound that might have been a sigh. "I failed to heed the warnings."

"Dinna fear, lass. 'Twill be morning before long."

"You are lying again, Shark Bait." Then he felt the pressure of her body against his arm, her shoulder leaning in. "But this time I don't mind it."

He did not move. He could not move. He wanted her bone and flesh pressing against his so simply. Perhaps in these final hours that had come far too soon in his life, God was offering him mercy, a moment of innocent pleasure after all the moments of sinful pleasure he had seized.

Something bumped against his leg. Then her fingers slipped beneath his hand. Her clasp was unhesitating, her fingertips brushing across his palm then pressing tight against his knuckles. Palm to palm with her, he strove to breathe and his heartbeats flew at twelve knots.

"You are lying to comfort me," she said, "so that I will not dwell on how we are about to die."

"Am I?" Only thin wooden walls and ceiling separated them from death, and yet the touch of a girl's hand was all he cared for now.

"You are," she whispered clearly and softly beneath the storm's scream. "It seems that I will be obliged to reconsider my poor opinion of sailors. One sailor, at least."

Blindly he turned his face to her. He was in fact a beast of a man, and she was a little thing that he could crush with a single arm, and he knew he should not be holding her hand, not even in this circumstance.

He bent his head closer. "Aye?"

She did not reply and her hand remained snugly in his and the night raged on.

Chapter 3

The Aftermath

12 October 1817
The Queen's Hotel
Kingston, Jamaica

Dear Emmie,

There has been a tremendous storm, a hurricane. Yet now the rain and wind have gone entirely and the sky is as gently still as on a Shropshire summer day. But the harbor still churns and all on land is in upheaval. Mrs. Jennings will not allow me to leave the hotel unless accompanied by my betrothed, who has not yet called although he sent a note with a boy yesterday morning to assure himself of my safety.

Instead I will tell you of the plans for my wedding day, which, because of events, has had to be postponed . . .

ORDER OF COMMAND

By Order of the Lord High Admiral of the United Kingdom and Commander of the Atlantic Fleet, you are required to take command of the Theia, *with all the rights and responsibilities attending, and to carry out, and to cause your crew to carry out, any and all Orders by Superior Officers, barring none.*

Given on board the Fairway *at Kingston Harbour, 15th October, 1817, to Gabriel Hume, Hnble, from this moment forth Commander of His Majesty's Frigate* Theia.

Chapter 4

The Captain

*A*marantha stood before the hotel parlor window, peering at the people rushing to and fro. Her fingertips drummed.

"I cannot remain another minute inside," she said to her companion, Sarah Jennings, whom her parents had hired for the journey to Jamaica.

"You cannot go out into that melee, my lady."

"Everybody is busy except us. There must be a hundred and one things I could do to help."

"You will only be in the way." The widow was plying the needle to a linen cap.

"In a fortnight I will be the wife of a man of the cloth, Mrs. Jennings. I cannot rest in idle comfort while everybody else labors."

"Reverend Garland's note indicated that he will call on us the moment he is able. Until then we must remain here."

The hotel was damp and making Amarantha's temper

damp too. Outside, the tropical sun bathed everything in heat. Even yesterday morning, as she had found her way from the dry goods shop to the hotel entrance, the sun had already been baking the carnage: uprooted trees, parts of buildings, lifeless livestock, broken furniture, torn sails and tangled rigging, and pools of water everywhere. Now that landscape was a whirl of activity.

"I cannot wait here," she said decisively, moving to the doorway. "I will go out now and find someone to lead me to the mission."

"My lady, you must not—"

Grabbing her bonnet and a parasol, she threw open the door and stepped out into the sunlight.

Before the hotel was less a proper street than a morass of detritus from both sea and civilization. Everywhere people were at work picking through the remnants of buildings, heaping refuse into great mounds, and sweeping and scrubbing and hammering. As she headed in the direction of the mission, nobody even noticed her.

Not far away, where a small building had been only days earlier, amongst the rubble an elderly Englishman with a deeply tanned face and hands was tending to the wounds of a cluster of people, most of them brown-skinned, including some sailors she recognized from the *Camelot*. For several minutes she watched, shocked as the people crowded about him, some bleeding and others weeping, but all polite as they requested his aid. The doctor moved from one wound to the next without even looking up.

Moving to the edge of the crowd, Amarantha held the parasol high and said quietly, "May I pass through?"

They parted for her, swiftly returning hopeful eyes to the doctor.

"—then reapply the salve and rebind the wound," the doctor was saying to a mother holding a wailing child in her arms.

"Doctor," Amarantha said, "I am Amarantha Vale. I am staying at the hotel—"

"Dr. Hill will tend to you at his practice, miss. I've others to care for here."

Amarantha stood for a confused moment, looking about at the people waiting for treatment. Then, abruptly, she understood. While she wore fashionable jonquil muslin, the people around her were all dressed simply and plainly. Dr. Hill must be treating persons of means.

"Oh, no, sir," she said. "I am not injured. I have just arrived in town and have no home or family here yet." It felt odd to say that. "May I be of use to you here?"

He peered at her more closely.

"Somewhere in the wreckage here, Miss Vale, is a medicine cabinet. You will need two able-bodied boys—those two. Find the cabinet and bring it here. Then I will need your assistance."

They found the medicine cabinet beneath the ceiling that had fallen on it. While digging it out, she asked the boys about the doctor. In English she barely understood, one of them said that Mr. Meriwether had been a ship's surgeon but now treated slaves and sailors living near the docks. When the medicine cabinet had been moved, she sent the boy to the hotel with a message for Mrs. Jennings. Then the surgeon bade her assist in arranging pallets on the ground for the most seriously wounded.

Mrs. Jennings appeared, hovering at the edge of the makeshift sick-house with a laced kerchief pressed to her nose.

"This is not suitable activity for a lady of your delicate years. Your parents will be shocked that I have allowed this."

"My parents would not bat an eyelash at this." Only a slight exaggeration. "And I am far from delicate. I spent my childhood racing from one adventure to the next."

"My lady, *this* is hardly an adventure."

"Mr. Meriwether needs help," Amarantha said, shifting tactics. "It is the work of God."

In Shropshire when she had discovered the angelic Reverend Paul Garland preaching in that church beyond the border of her father's estate, he had warned his congregation that the life of a missionary was not for the faint of heart. The notion of sailing off to a foreign land had so thrilled Amarantha that she had fallen in love with his crusade on the spot. When, after a month of courtship, he told her that he must finally depart for the West Indies, and asked her to join him there as his bride, she had not hesitated to accept.

And yet, never in her wildest imaginings had she expected this. The injured that sat on the ground awaiting the surgeon's care seemed to have nothing but the clothing they wore. As people searched among the patients for their loved ones, cries of joy with each reunion and wails of despair from others filled the sticky air that smelled of mud and brine.

"Will you help me?" she said to her companion.

"I most certainly will not. I will remain here and wait for you to remember yourself," she said, and sat stony faced with disapproval on a pile of rubble.

Amarantha offered her the parasol then decided not to worry about her. She was far too busy.

It was a long, long day.

"Miss Vale, you have overtaxed yourself," Mr. Meriwether said as the evening made shadows across the cluttered street. "You must go home now."

"But there is so much still to do. So many people!"

"You are exhausted, and I cannot have my only nurse fall ill."

"Do you not have a regular nurse? An actual nurse?"

"Eliza left for the interior yesterday to see to family. Now, do go and rest, child."

Returning to the hotel on sore feet, with blistered

hands, aching arms, and a gown stained in things she didn't want to think about, Amarantha had only one ear for Mrs. Jennings's complaints. For her companion had spoken rightly: this was no mere adventure. Her entire world had changed. In comparison to the suffering she had seen in a single day, her mother fretting over megrims seemed so foolish.

She entered the foyer with a full head and uncomfortable heart.

"My lady," the footman said. "A gentleman called for you earlier."

A spark of happiness pierced her befuddlement. "Reverend Garland?"

"It was an officer from the *Fairway*." He proffered a calling card.

The crisp rectangle of ivory cardstock bore two sentences in clean, bold script: *A backgammon set is purchased. I will hold you to your promise.*

Nerves tumbled into her empty stomach.

In the small hours of the morning, in the blackness of the shop's cellar as wind beat at the walls, they had not spoken of the storm. Instead they spoke of unimportant things: the impressive variety of bolts in a crate she had opened, the most effective methods for tying a secure knot, the challenge of choosing the perfect Yule log at Christmastime, the unfortunate occasion when at age ten she had opened a gate before taking note of the ram on the other side of it, the curious practice by which naval lieutenants wore a gold epaulette on only one shoulder rather than on both, her profound appreciation for all shades of red despite the color of her hair, the first instance in which he had accidentally walked into a door lintel, and whether winning at backgammon required true strategy or only good luck.

Concerning the last, she argued for luck, he for strategy. Laughingly she scorned his position on the matter, to which he replied if she were so confident, then she must be able to beat even an officer trained to naval tactics in a mere game of backgammon. She promised him that she could—easily—and that if there were any light she would on the spot.

But there had been no light, not until hours later when she had opened her eyes to discover silence all around, that they were alive, and that she had slept, her cheek pressed to his shoulder, her hand still tucked in his.

Standing now in the hotel foyer, filthy and unsteady, Amarantha flipped the calling card over and learned the name of the man with whom she had survived the most terrifying hours of her life: Lieutenant Gabriel Hume, Royal Navy.

She cast the card into the hearth. She was shortly to be wed to the Reverend Paul Garland. It was everything she wanted. There was no place in that scenario for the acquaintance of a naval officer. More importantly, there was no place in her soul for the agitated excitement that had filled her when his hand entwined with hers and the big, hard strength of him became an anchor to her during those endless hours.

Resolved to forget about that night entirely—*and him*—in the morning she set off with an objecting Mrs. Jennings for the hospital.

"You are a good girl, my lady," Mr. Meriwether said. "But your young reverend will be unhappy with both of us if I allow you to help me here."

Mrs. Jennings had obviously told the surgeon about her. With an odd, papery disappointment coating her enthusiasm, she engaged a guide and walked with her companion to the mission.

The storm had damaged the church and the modest house attached to it in which Paul lived, the house that was to be her castle after their wedding. Men were clearing the debris.

"There is nothing for a woman to do here, dear lady,"

Paul said with grateful eyes. "Continue assisting Mr. Meriwether. In condescending to do God's work among the
poor there, already you are showing my parishioners an
exemplary model of Christian femininity."

Amarantha suspected that exemplary Christian femininity did not include spending the night with a sailor and
never telling a soul of it.

Returning to the makeshift hospital, Amarantha found
three more volunteers taking Mr. Meriwether's orders, all
of them from other churches, two brown-skinned. Their
tasks were many: fresh water to be fetched and boiled,
linens to be collected for the washerwomen, instruments
to be cleaned, and bandages to be changed. When the
others weren't looking, Amarantha took the hand of a
weeping patient and held it snugly, confidently, as a naval
officer had held hers for hours, helping her find courage
within the depths of her fear.

The following day the surgeon's nurse, Eliza, arrived.
A woman of about sixty, she had a dark brown complexion and spoke with the accent of the island. Yet, unlike so
many others aboard ship and in town, Amarantha could
entirely understand Eliza's English. With a breath of profound relief, she went from patient to patient with her,
taking instruction on how best to help.

"I am grateful for your patience with me, Eliza, despite
my mistakes."

"I was your age when I tended my first patient."

"Did Mr. Meriwether teach you all of this?"

Eliza chuckled. "No. My mother taught me healing,
and the patients themselves, and their families. Listen to
them as you listen to me. In time you will learn too."

That evening she returned to the hotel exhausted,
wrote to Emily, and collapsed onto her bed. Her fingernails were torn, her hands raw, and her hair a halo of un-
tamable frizz, and the hotel laundress had to apply bleach
to her gown and linens.

Yet in the morning she awoke with renewed energy. She had never felt so *useful*.

The quays seemed particularly busy, and at the hospital she heard that ships laden with supplies from other islands had begun arriving and unloading tools, timber, and laborers. Among the arrivals was a naval vessel, *Theia*, which limped in with one of its masts broken, sails torn, and half its crew lost in the hurricane, including every officer except the surgeon and second lieutenant.

The night of the storm, wrapped in darkness, her companion in the cellar had told her of the *Theia* and its second lieutenant, who was his cousin. Hearing the news of the officer's survival now, Amarantha felt a pang of regret that she would never have the opportunity to tell Lieutenant Hume how glad she was for him.

Each time she remembered his big hand around hers, his hard shoulder against which she had slept, his rumbling brogue, and the shadows in his beautifully dark brown eyes, an agitated little dance of nerves started up in her stomach.

Never seeing him again was for the best.

SHE HEARD HIM before she saw him.

"Good day, Mr. Meriwether," he said not five yards away, and she jerked her head around.

Smartly dressed in naval blues and whites, and attended by another officer and a half a dozen sailors, he stood straight and tall, surveying the sea of pallets as the surgeon approached him.

"How may I help you, Captain?"

Captain?

"I present to you *Theia*'s surgeon, Mr. Boyle. He an' these men are at your disposal till *Theia* sails."

"At my disposal?"

"His Grace the governor has requested it. Put my men to work, sir."

"This is a godsend! We are in need of a roof over these patients' heads."

"You'll have your roof by fortnight's end."

"Thank you, Captain. And may I congratulate you on your new command?"

He nodded curtly then gave his men orders.

Forcing herself from paralysis, Amarantha finished wrapping linen about her patient's hand. Her heartbeats were far too quick. She kept her head down and face averted, and when she heard Mr. Meriwether bid the captain goodbye, she said two silent prayers of gratitude: first for the sailors Captain Hume had lent to build the roof, and second for his leaving. He had not noticed her, and now he would not, for surely he would not return. His ship's refurbishment would be his first priority.

Walking to the hotel later, Mrs. Jennings was all praise for the navy. But the following day, when new acquaintances called for a cozy gossip, the praise turned to shock.

"Captain Hume's reputation is nothing short of scandalous," one woman said in hushed tones.

"Scandalous?"

"Oh, yes." The silk flowers on the gossip's bonnet jiggled as she whispered, "He and Lieutenant Brock are known *carousers* and *libertines*."

Mrs. Jennings gasped. "But with such a reputation, however did he win a command?"

"His skill and bravery are not to be doubted," the gossip said with another knowing tick of her head. "But I suspect that his noble rank has done him no harm."

"His noble rank?"

"He is the son of a duke. Second son only, of course, and Loch Irvine is a Scottish title. Nothing to compare to your charge's lineage," she added with a glance at Amarantha, and discovered both Amarantha's and her daughter's eyes on her.

"What is a libertine, Mama?" the gossip's daughter said.

"Good heavens." The woman's cheeks colored. "It is not for a gently bred girl to know such things, or to eavesdrop on her elders' conversation. Forgive me, my lady," she said to Amarantha.

But after their callers departed, Amarantha asked her companion the same question.

"You must forget you ever heard the word," Mrs. Jennings said firmly.

"If I am to be the wife of a man responsible for the eternal souls of other men, I must at least know what names to put to the earthly sins that bedevil them."

Mrs. Jennings's lips pinched.

"Consider this," Amarantha said. "If you do not tell me what a libertine is, I shall be obliged to ask it of one of the other volunteers at the hospital."

As though she sucked on a lemon, Mrs. Jennings told her.

"If Captain Hume returns to the sick-house," her companion concluded, "you must remain as far from him as possible."

This warning seemed wise to Amarantha. Given her ridiculously quick pulse when he was near, she had little doubt that a weak woman could easily be caught by the lures of such a man.

Two days later, as she carried a heavy pot of water, she discovered him blocking her path between pallets.

"Allow me." Without awaiting her response, he took the pot. His hands brushed hers and the madness of nerves that Amarantha had been pushing away for days returned in a wild rush.

"Where to?" He had a deep voice, which seemed a bit hoarse now.

"There." Her tongue could manage no more syllables. She went ahead of him, stomach tight and cheeks hot. As he set down the pot she knew this fever must be her punishment for seeking comfort from him that night—from mortal man. Only now did it occur to her that throughout that entire night she had not said a single prayer.

Not the ideal behavior for a woman betrothed to a man of the cloth.

The captain bowed. "Ma'am."

She nodded. "Shark Bait."

His smile was roguish, as appealing as the rest of him, and as confident as he had every right to be. It horrified her. She horrified herself. Only a sennight into her life as a missionary, and already she had sins to confess.

"How may I be o' service to you, lass?" he said in the rumble that had soothed her terror through an endless night.

"I have no authority here." She attempted an attitude of crisp dismissal. "You have spoken with Mr. Meriwether. You must already know which task most requires attention."

"Aye," he said, his gaze dipping to her lips. "An' I mean to give it my most devoted care."

It was too difficult meeting those dark eyes that seemed to see inside of her to where she was still trembling from the storm—and from waking lodged against his side. Instead, she took up a tray of surgical instruments and said, "You are too forward, sir."

"I'm a sailor, lass. When I see a thing I want, 'tis only forward I can go."

"I am not a *thing*. I am a woman."

He was no longer smiling, rather studying her face, slowly: the curves of her lips, the angle of her cheek, consuming each lash across the inches. Finally he looked into her eyes.

A thousand spaces hollowed out beneath Amarantha's ribs. She had never seen it before, never felt it, but some instinct in her recognized it in his eyes: animal desire—thick and hot and powerful.

She made herself speak.

"You are doing God's work here, and I commend you on your devotion to seeing to the comforts of others."

"Lass." The brogue caressed. "We both know God's got naught to do with the reason I've come here."

It was alarming and shocking *and pleasurable* to feel his dark gaze on her. *Too pleasurable*. It could not continue.

"I am engaged to be married. To the Reverend Paul Garland."

With the hint of a half smile, he said, "No' for long."

He strode with nonchalance from the hospital as the surgical instruments in her hands made soft, tinny music dancing upon the tray.

The following day he came again.

"There are no pots of water to carry at this time, Shark Bait."

"Give me another task," he said, smiling a bit.

Obviously he required a set down firmer than a statement of her disinterest.

"That man must be turned," she said, nodding toward a patient.

"Turned?"

"To prevent bedsores," she added, repeating as though she were an expert a lesson which Eliza had taught her only that morning.

Without comment, the naval commander went to the cot and, with careful strength, performed the task. From the distance, she heard him speak quietly to the patient, and the man's responding chuckle.

She could hardly breathe.

Returning to her, and standing just a bit too close, the captain bent his head.

"I've sewn wounds an' swabbed decks after battles since I was thirteen, lass."

"Then what can I do to frighten you away?" she said, outrageously.

Now he smiled fully.

"Give it your best." Upon that, he departed.

That night she folded her hands, clamped her eyes shut against the image of him, and prayed that he would not return the following day.

He did not.

The day after that he did. And regularly thereafter, performing every task she required of him, and not only in the hospital. Upon Mr. Meriwether's request, he went to the nearby church to summon the vicar to a dying patient's bedside. When Amarantha was obliged to do an errand he escorted her through the busy streets, and then carried whatever packages she gathered.

No one seemed to think this remarkable. The hurricane had turned the world upside down, and everyone worked to put it to rights. And, quite simply, people deferred to him. He was the youngest naval commanding officer anybody had ever heard of.

"How do you come to captain a naval ship at such a young age?" she asked as she finalized a purchase of timber the surgeon had made, with which the *Theia*'s crewmen would build cots for patients.

"'Tis a modest command, lass."

"How modest?"

"Fifty-six guns."

"Even I know that there is considerably more to captaining a naval ship than the ability to count its cannons, Shark Bait. Everyone says your promotion is impressive."

"Everyone?" He studied her so singularly sometimes, as though he cared about the words she said as well as the thoughts she did not speak.

Except for her father, no men ever listened to her. Her suitors in England had seemed most interested in telling her about their carriages or the poetry they had written. When Paul asked for her thoughts on a matter, it seemed he liked to hear his thoughts supported, which she did;

he knew much more about everything than she did, and as her husband, he said, it would be his duty and joy to shape her mind.

Aside from their disagreement about backgammon, the captain seemed disinterested in convincing her of his opinions on anything. But this probing into her head with his gaze made her feel always at the edge of a cliff.

"The other volunteers have said it," she replied honestly. "Even Mr. Meriwether remarked on it."

"War an' mishap have thinned the Atlantic o' good men. Lad," he said to the lumber seller's boy who waited beside the cart piled high with planks. "Assist her"—he gestured toward a woman burdened with packages nearby—"an' you'll have a coin."

The boy scampered off and the captain in the Royal Navy, son of a duke, took up the cart handles and pushed the load toward the hospital.

"Thinned?" she said, walking at his side.

"Tragedy was the mistress o' my command, lass."

Amarantha doubted this simple explanation. He had a brusqueness of manner with merchants, planters, and seamen alike that distracted from his youth. There was no fluidity to him, no sophisticated charm that could be credited for his easy command over other men. He was tall, powerful, and physically formidable, despite the hollows of his cheeks and lean waist. His speech was often abrupt. Occasionally he was awkward, surprising others with unexpected questions, or departing a place suddenly. This only seemed to lend to his authority: it was clear that his manners arose not from a desire to please, rather from utter confidence.

Sometimes when he arrived at the hospital especially late in the morning, his eyes were red and his movements unusually deliberate. On these occasions the women gathered at the washbasin whispered of his scandalous habits.

On a morning Eliza was to take medicine to a sick

patient at home, Mr. Meriwether unexpectedly required her assistance in surgery. Amarantha volunteered for the errand.

"It is a lengthy walk," Eliza warned.

"I have barely been beyond town yet. I welcome the opportunity to explore."

"You cannot go alone."

"Captain Hume must escort her," Mrs. Jennings said from where she sat folding clean linens, the only chore she would perform. "He is, after all, of noble blood, and a gentleman."

He was not, however, a predictable gentleman. As they walked the narrow road, Amarantha's boots got trapped. Drawing her feet from the sucking mud, she investigated the path. It promised even greater peril ahead.

"I must return with a horse and cart, if an idle horse and cart can be found."

"Afraid to wet your feet?" he said.

"To ruin my only boots. The cobbler is sufficiently occupied supplying shoes to those who lost everything in the storm. But I have slippers at the hotel." She inched toward the mud.

"I'll carry you across."

She laughed. "It seems you have something in common with my sister. She enjoys teasing me too."

"I'm no' teasing."

Butterflies alighted under her ribs.

"You would *carry* me? As though I were a helpless invalid?"

"A princess."

"Oh, then absolutely not."

"Absolutely?"

"It would not be allowed!" she said with mock archness. "That is, I don't know any princesses personally, but it is my understanding that they are obliged to live by any number of rules, and I'm certain one of those rules must be that they cannot be carried by a lowly sailor, not even to save their boots."

"I see," he said, smiling. "Only by Prince Charming, I assume."

"Of course." She laughed again and felt positively light enough to *fly* over the mud. He had a manner of looking at her with his entire attention, as though she were the only soul in the world. It made her unsteady.

Dragging her gaze away, she took a renewed step toward the mud, prepared to sink to her ankles and ruin the hem of her gown as well.

He came to her side.

"You'll wear these." He proffered his boots. His trousers were rolled above his ankles.

Amarantha knew it was wrong to stare but she did anyway. She had never seen a gentleman's bare calves. The muscles were starkly defined. The sight of them did things to her insides: hot, wicked things that made her face flame and her throat grow dry.

"Oh—But—I cannot," she burbled.

"Yet you will."

The boots were enormous and she swam in them with each footstep, holding her skirts aloft from the mud.

"In some cities," he said, strolling along comfortably despite his bare feet, "'tis all the rage for women to wear men's oversize shoes an' toddle about like children new to walking."

"You might have seen much more of the world than I, Shark Bait, but I am not a *complete* fool. I recognize a taradiddle when I hear it."

"Shame there's no portraitist here to paint you in all your glory now."

"You were obviously truant from your lessons the day they taught gentlemanly flattery."

He laughed easily and she felt it all the way to her toes inside his shoes.

On the way home she paused before the last turn in the road and told him that she must redon her own shoes.

"People will not understand if they see me now," she added.

"I gave your shoes to the woman to clean an' polish," he said.

"But she is already fully occupied nursing her husband! You should not have done that, not for—for . . ."

He offered her the smile she never saw him show others, a private, contented smile.

"Not for me," she said firmly, willing him to understand.

"Lass, she'll have payment for it."

Amarantha had no response. The house had been entirely bare: no jar of grain, no salt fish, not even a manioc root in the bin. Since the devastation of the storm, famine had come to the poorest on the island who could not afford the expensive foodstuffs brought on ships, and beggars were everywhere. In offering the woman compensation for this small task, he offered her dignity.

Amarantha felt the most urgent need to take up his hand and kiss it.

She did not.

She removed the boots and walked in only her stockings, feeling his gaze on her the remainder of the way and loving it. She had a horrible suspicion that she was falling in love *with him*, which was not possible. She had found her angel in a tiny church in Shropshire. This big, rough man with shadowy eyes and a bad reputation could mean nothing to her.

He was not the marrying sort. The women at the hospital said it in moments of idle chatter, and Mrs. Jennings's new acquaintances confirmed it. An established bachelor, Gabriel Hume had mistresses in every port. He liked women, drink, and game, and was never seen in a church, reformed or Anglican.

Amarantha suggested that perhaps he was Presbyterian, as most Scots were.

"My lady," the gossip said, "by all accounts, he is not even *Christian*."

"My maid heard that he attended a *heathen* service at the Abbott plantation," another woman said in a hush.

"No!" another gasped.

"But I thought the slaves on the Abbott plantation were Baptists," a third woman exclaimed.

"One in the same, of course," the gossip said with a dismissive flip of her hand.

Amarantha was skeptical. She knew the hospital volunteers from the Baptist church to be good, decent Christian women. As for Captain Hume, he was unusual, but surely the admiralty would not promote a heathen to the rank of captain. So she asked him about it.

In reply he smiled the gentle smile she was coming to believe was more natural to him than the roguish grin.

"Seems to me, lass, there should be more to religion than church walls," he said only. "An' more to faith than rules."

She did not know what to make of him. He seemed as indifferent to the scandalized whispers of the gossips as he was to the deference of those who admired him—a friend to all yet an intimate of none. In his company she felt light and fevered at once, excited and unsettlingly *right*. Despite his initial vow to undo her betrothal, he asked nothing of her and seemed content with friendship.

But occasionally, when she saw him watching her, she knew she was lying to herself to justify the time they spent together. At those moments she saw in his eyes the same desire that she had seen there the first day.

She was playing with fire—not the contained flames in a hearth, but the unbridled bonfires she had loved at harvest festivals back home—dangerous yet so beautiful that she wanted to stand as close as she could.

As her nurse had warned her on those festival nights, girls who played with fire got burned.

Chapter 5

Lords of the Ocean

"*W*here've you stashed the good whiskey, Gabe?"

"Majorca," Gabriel mumbled, staring at the navigational chart. He had been staring for an hour and his eyes were blurring.

"The good whiskey is in *Majorca*?"

"Tunis." He followed the curve of the route with his fingertip. "Majorca to Tunis . . . What in the—"

"Captain!"

Gabriel lifted his eyes to his cousin.

"Aye?" he said, but his head was still in the charts. At his admiral's suggestion he was studying these in particular, and an account of apprehending Barbary pirates near Gibraltar too.

It made no sense. *Theia* was thousands of miles from the Mediterranean, awaiting the arrival of the northern oak that would be her new mizzenmast. These charts were a test designed for him to prove that they had not made a mistake in assigning such a command to a man so young.

"What do you want, Jonah?"

"The good whiskey. Trouter kept it in this cabinet." Jonah tapped the tip of a navigation divider to the small cupboard door.

The captain's quarters on the *Theia* were not large, but they were well-appointed. And *his*. Five weeks of command as yet, and he had spent none of them under sail, instead commanding his crew in building, sewing, caulking, polishing, and reprovisioning.

And watching an extraordinary girl being extraordinary.

"'Tis run dry," he said, and returned his attention to the chart spread over the table.

"Run dry? The good whiskey has *run dry*? I beg your pardon, Captain, but who are you and what have you done with my cousin?"

Gabriel rubbed his temples with thumb and fingers. Tossing his measuring stick onto the map, he circled the table, opened the cabinet, and pulled forth a bottle.

"The no' good whiskey," he said, shoving it into his cousin's palm. "'Tis all I've got. I'll send the boy in the morning for more o' the good."

Jonah eyed the bottle. "Why not send him tonight?"

"Because I've no' the time to drink whiskey at present."

Jonah stared at him. Then he took up two glasses, set them on the table, and poured a dram in each. Tossing himself into a chair, he lifted his glass high.

"To the memory of Gabe Hume, the companion, the brother, the finest scoundrel this side of the Atlantic, the man I once knew and admired. May he rest in peace. But I highly doubt he will, not surrounded by all those flames." Jonah looked over the armrest at the floor, as though peering into hell.

Grabbing the other glass, Gabriel took the chair across from him. Studying the chart for hours hadn't gotten him answers anyway.

"What's got you out of sorts, cousin?" Jonah said, sipping the whiskey and crinkling his nose.

"I'm no' out o' sorts, you landlubbing sponge," he said, not drinking. He'd no need for a muddled head. "I've work to do."

"So much work that you cannot enjoy a glass of whiskey on a balmy tropical night?"

He said nothing to that. He had allowed Jonah to entice him into drink only four nights earlier. He had awoken with the devil of a head and—after seeing to ten different tasks on his ship—nearly missed the opportunity to accompany the prettiest girl on the island on a stroll out of town.

The prettiest girl anywhere.

She had walked down the high street in *stocking feet.* Not even the molls he'd known would do that. But she had not batted a cinnamon eyelash at it. Between wearing his boots where others could see and stripping her feet for any ogler's enjoyment, she had chosen to strip.

She had the tiniest ankles. But strong calves. Everything about her was a study in contrasts: vivid eyes and tresses, yet a voice that could soothe a man in an agony of pain, as he'd seen her do at the hospital; blithe disrespect for propriety, yet a firm sense of commitment; a quick, brilliant smile, yet a wariness with him that drove him mad with frustration.

Like a wild creature that had been caught but not tamed, skittish of man yet intrigued, she danced just out of his reach.

He wanted to touch her. He needed to touch her. Days spent in her company, the need distracted him to no end. And nights—nights, it was all he could think about, her delectable little curvy body in his hands, under his mouth, *beneath him.*

He wanted inside her more than he had ever wanted inside a woman before. And he had imagined every possible scenario for making it happen—

"How is the English gentle-maiden?"

Gabriel blinked.

His cousin lifted a blond brow. "Thinking about her again?"

Thinking. Fantasizing. *Panting like a dog*.

"She is . . . unusual." Exceptional. Like no woman he had ever met, certainly no woman of her pedigree. Yet she was hardly more than a girl—a girl who had been hurled into chaos in an alien land and responded with the courage of a weathered sailor and an endless supply of affection for people she should never even notice.

And she was so damn pretty he couldn't make himself stop staring.

And the way she looked at him sometimes, as though if he offered her any part of him she might nibble it . . . or lick it . . .

Judas.

"Unusual." Jonah snorted. "Unusually wrong for your head, that's what. Odd's blood, cousin. I've never seen you so preoccupied with a skirt. It is positively unnatural for men like us."

"Men like us? By that do you mean naval officers with a thousand an' one responsibilities or former naval officers with nothing to do but drink an' borrow my money?"

"Right! Remind me of my place. As though I could ever forget that you won *Theia* or that you sit a step closer to a title than I."

"No' a step closer, cousin. A life." Gabriel wrapped both hands around the glass and stared into the amber liquid. As many times as he had wished his brother across the world—anywhere else but tormenting him—he never wished his father gone.

"An unworthy life, in your brother's case." Jonah scoffed. "And two lives closer for me, of course. But I wouldn't want you dead anyway, not so that I could be duke. Whose whiskey would I drink? Though I suppose if I were laird of Kallin and Haiknayes I could afford to buy my own."

"Aye." Gabriel smiled.

"You miss it."

"Hm?"

"Haiknayes."

"Aye."

The rolling emerald hills and magnificent medieval fortress that belonged to the Duke of Loch Irvine in Midlothian were the only place on earth he would rather be than at the helm of a ship. Haiknayes had been a boy's adventure palace, with its high stone walls fashioned of granite, its battlements from which an arrow could be shot far enough to lose sight of it, and its secret nooks to hide in when his brother came searching.

"Crime it can't be yours," Jonah mumbled. "She never played favorites, I know, but I suspect your mother would've rather you had Haiknayes."

"The dukes o' Loch Irvine have been masters o' Haiknayes—"

"For centuries, I know. Blast tradition." Jonah swiveled the remainder of the whiskey in the bottom of his glass. "No land for you. You, Captain, shall live out your years on the sea instead, and die an old victorious salt. Heroically, of course."

"Writing my epitaph already?"

"Not until I've drunk up all your whiskey." Jonah grinned. "Gregory's hired me."

Gabriel sat forward. "As land agent?"

His cousin nodded. "He's eager to return to England. He said if I made the place productive, he would take me on as partner."

"Now this deserves a toast. To my rapscallion cousin, now successful Jamaican planter."

"I hope so. And I'll repay the gold I owe you as soon as I've got it at the ready."

"No, you willna, you penniless mongrel." Gabriel set down his empty glass. The debt he owed Jonah was far greater than any number of borrowed coins: the debt of his life, won thirteen years ago, the day his mother died. Alone on the docks at Leith, a skinny, weak lad far from his father's abstracted grieving and his brother's coldness, blinded by tears he could not show at home, Gabriel had not even heard the youths coming. But he had felt their hands. And the straps that had tied him down. "You needn't ever."

"You cannot refuse me an outing now, can you, Captain?" Jonah gestured to the bottle on the table. "A bottle of the good whiskey, in my honor."

"Aye, but I've a pile o' papers to read."

"And nocturnal dreams of an English maiden to hurry to, no doubt."

"Rule your tongue concerning the lady, cur, or I'll cut it out."

Jonah laughed. "This is a first. What is it about this girl that's so special, Gabe?"

Gabriel looked out the window toward the quay. "Have you ever considered how fine an' fragile females are? Their bones. Even the heartiest o' them, so small." Small enough to break with a single hand, as his brother had done to a maid—a girl who, his brother said, had grown too outspoken for a woman, who had it coming to her.

"To a giant fellow like you," Jonah said, "all females *are* small."

"'Tis a cruel, jesting God that made these creatures so strong within, so resilient, yet so inferior in form."

"Bloody hell, Gabe," Jonah exclaimed, standing abruptly. "The English maiden is having her way with your head. You sound more like a poet than a sailor."

Gabriel cocked a grin. "Canna a man be both?"

"When he's pining over a girl?" Jonah's lips twisted. "If he's a Scot, I suppose." He went to the door then looked over his shoulder. "It is only pining, Gabe? It isn't more? Is it?"

"'Tisn't pining. 'Tisn't anything, Jonah. She's a pretty

girl. 'Tis all." A pretty girl who turned him inside out. A pretty girl he wanted to touch more than he had wanted anything in a long, long time.

Ever.

Blast it. What in the hell was he thinking?

He took up his hat.

Jonah's face lightened. "Coming out after all?"

"Aye." The chart could wait. "'Tis time to show me if a landlubber can hold his drink as well as a seaman."

"I'll wager you a bottle he can," Jonah said.

"I will welcome that wager." And with it temporary oblivion in which he might, for a few hours, forget that she was another man's.

HE DID NOT touch her. Ever. So close their hands came many times, but never actually meeting. It seemed, in fact, that he took great care *not* to touch her. Except when he had teased about carrying her like a princess, he never even offered his arm to her.

This tantalizing stasis suited Amarantha poorly. Every day the respectful distance kept by the object of her increasingly reckless desires made her mad with frustration. She desperately needed advice, but letters were months crossing the ocean. In any case it was not safe to put her feelings on paper: someone other than Emily might read them.

Seeking out the comfort of her betrothed's company, Amarantha found none. Preoccupied with restoring the church and the homes of his parishioners, Paul had little time for conversation.

"But it has been weeks since the storm," she said. "How many homes have yet to be repaired?"

"Do you doubt the extent of my responsibilities?"

"No, to be sure!"

"One cannot quantify the measure of a soul's needs, my lady."

"Oh. Yes. I see." But she didn't really. She was discovering that she was entirely inadequate for her future role as the wife of a minister. She intended to learn, though. She would make him proud. "How many parishioners have you?"

"The faithful include five free families—"

Only five! Amarantha hid her surprise.

"—two English families, and fourteen enslaved souls, only two of whom are a married pair, of course."

"Why do you say *of course*?"

"Slaves are not permitted to marry. Their masters consider them property. One does not marry one's cow to one's bull, does one?"

"But they are men and women!"

"Indeed. Men and women whose lives are dictated by those who care nothing for the eternal soul, only for gold."

"Oh. Then . . ." She knew *nothing*, but she didn't much like being continually obliged to admit her ignorance to him. "What about the couple in your church? How did they come to be married?"

"Recently I had the honor of joining them together in that holiest of bonds."

She gasped. "But haven't you now put them in danger of punishment?"

"Better the whip of man's displeasure than the scourge of God's wrath."

To Amarantha, this did not seem like a good moment for opaque metaphors.

"I don't entirely understand," she said yet again.

"Of course you don't, dear lady. You are still young. But as both your minister and husband—"

Not husband yet.

"—it falls to me to teach you about that which your mother, in her feminine humility, spared you."

Her mother's *humility*? Every room at Willows Hall boasted three mirrors so the lady of the manor could admire her beauty from all angles.

"The unfortunate situation of this God-loving man and woman," Paul continued, "due to tasks demanded of them by their master, is to be continually thrown together, often in isolation from others. The man confided this to me. He assured me, however, of the purity of his feelings for her. I counseled him that rather than sin they should wed. Then, as man and wife, they would risk only the pains of the strap, but never the terrors of eternal damnation. He was able to convince her of the wisdom of this, and they were married in secret but in the full presence of God."

Amarantha's stomach churned. She ducked her head. The courage they possessed in order to be true to both their love for each other and their faith awed her.

But in her months on the island she had seen the punishments masters meted out to slaves for even minuscule offenses. The choice between love and mortal peril which this man and woman had been forced to make horrified her. How could it be right to demand that of any person? How could it be *just*?

But she understood so little about everything! She knew even less about plantations than she did about religion.

One aspect of the story, however, she understood perfectly. For in her five weeks on the island, she had gained knowledge of the sort of temptation—*the agony of longing*—that could drive a woman to endanger her mortal soul. That *she* had been permitted to choose any husband she wished, yet now she ached *for someone else*, made her thoroughly sick.

Shame coated her cheeks with heat.

"Should I not have spoken so plainly, dear lady? You needn't fear to displease me by saying so. Only allow me pride in a wife whose natural modesty causes her such discomfort."

Good Lord, he believed her *embarrassed* by the sensual details of the story! Even her horror and shame put on a false face.

How could the longing be sinful when it felt like heaven?

Flushed cheeks, be damned. She lifted her head.

"You and I are alone together now," she said. "Mrs. Jennings is not in the house. She went into the church. Are *we* not now in danger of sinning?"

His hand twitched away from hers.

"I am a man of God," he said.

"But you said that man, the member of your church, is God-loving too."

"*I* am a minister of Christ."

"You asked for my hand," she pressed. "I believed then that you found me attractive, even appealing. Do you still?"

"My lady—"

"Do you?"

"I consider myself the most fortunate of men to have such a lovely wife."

Not. Wife. Yet.

"Since my arrival you have called on me thrice each week. Now I think that perhaps you are afraid to call on me, but that you will not admit that fear to me." Just as she admitted nothing to the man who stirred such desperate desire in her. "Are you?"

"My dearest lady, how weary you must be of waiting for your life here to begin! But how patient you are with me. You are a treasure."

In fact she was an immodest wanton. And the worst of it was, she did not feel as though she were still *waiting* for her life to begin—rather the opposite.

But she could be better. She was no longer a child. Months ago, insisting to her father that she knew her own heart, she had made this choice. She must see it through. She would, no matter the temptation. In comparison to those who lived and died at the whim and will of others, she had nothing to complain about. Nothing to long for.

"I do not deserve your praise," she said.

"This natural humility will only inspire more of my praise, of course. I ask of you only a sennight more. By then every member of my little community will be safely resettled." He gazed at her through golden lashes. "And, consider, my lady: you cannot wish to speak the most important words of your life in a church without walls."

He left her with promises to return tomorrow for longer. Yet each time he called, his visits were brief.

Another sennight became a fortnight as his church repairs continued, while each morning she awoke even fresher and more eager for her day than the day before.

It frightened her.

"Allow me to work with you at the church." She needed to be away from where the captain might find her. A church seemed the safest spot. "You must be able to find some task for me there."

"Mr. Meriwether says he cannot spare you," Paul said, patting her hand. "I'm sure your lovely smiles cheer the patients enormously."

"You spoke to Mr. Meriwether?" she said in surprise, not bothering to mention that she spent her days at the hospital doing far more than smiling.

"Have you already forgotten our conversation at the house? I have waited months to have you at my side."

At his side. Not *in his arms*. While every hour she dreamed of having the muscular arms of a bronzed naval captain *around her*.

"This delay pains me more than it does you," Paul said.

She doubted it. Her selfless fiancé could not possibly now be experiencing the confusion that she endured each day as her pulse sped awaiting the captain at the hospital, or when she would encounter him on the street or in the market, or—*God forgive her*—when she volunteered to do errands that would take her near the *Theia*'s berth.

Each day she clamped down on her contrary feelings,

hiding them from all. The shame she would bring to her betrothed if anyone suspected—the hurt she would cause him—were unthinkable.

Newly determined, she began to avoid the captain when he came to the hospital, inventing tasks that would keep her close to the other volunteers. Then he would do something wonderful—like take a child onto his shoulders and stroll to the docks for a tour of the *Theia* while the child's mother went under Dr. Meriwether's scalpel, or sit with a dying sailor for hours until the man breathed his last, or simply lift his gaze to her and smile the smile that he reserved for her alone—and she would forget her noble goals and tumble back into confusion. And the agony of pretending that she was actually what everyone believed her to be grew.

Chapter 6

Awaken as the Beloved

When the Duke and Duchess of Manchester invited Amarantha and her betrothed to attend a supper gathering, she accepted eagerly. Praying that the company of people like her parents' friends would jolt her out of the insanity her thoughts and feelings had become, she dressed in her prettiest gown, allowed Mrs. Jennings to arrange her hair, and with new hope climbed into the carriage.

On the ride to the governor's mansion Paul fidgeted.

"You seem unhappy," she said. Perhaps Mrs. Jennings had told him of the time she spent with the captain. If so, she would admit to her mistake in becoming friends with such a man and she would not return to the hospital. It would be over. *Over.*

"I am."

Fear and relief and a thick, painful sadness mingled in her throat.

"With me?"

"No, dear lady." He squeezed her hand. "But I cannot like socializing in this manner with those who are still ignorant of the message of grace that I am bringing to this island—I and my colleagues."

Slowly she released her pent breath, and it struck her that his manner was now so different from the bright-eyed enthusiasm of those days in Shropshire.

"But the duke and duchess are Christians," she said. "They cannot wish to withhold salvation from anyone, can they?"

"When we first met, you knew little of the labor to be done in God's vineyard," he said, his eyes full of benevolence for her. "Yet now, less than a year later, you speak as though born to this life."

"If I am to be the wife of a missionary, I must speak thus." For the first time the *if* seemed to taunt her.

"Amarantha, these fashionable people," he said, "they do not wish slaves to become Christians. They fear that if enslaved people taste spiritual freedom, they will want to eat at the table as well."

"'To eat at the table'?"

He offered a patient smile. "That they will demand emancipation. Since Parliament ended the trade, rumors are rife on plantations of the imminent arrival of full abolition. With all the upset to order in the parishes since the storm, planters' fears are even greater. It is the reason for the new curfew on slaves, which of course has made the repairs on my church such slow going."

She had heard the other volunteers at the hospital speaking of these matters, and she recalled Emily and their father occasionally discussing abolition. Now it seemed reasonable. If all souls were equal in God's reckoning, why shouldn't they be equal in man's reckoning too?

"Won't they demand emancipation?" she asked.

"Possibly. Only last year in Barbados a large number

of them claimed freedom from their masters. It could happen here too. But just as in Barbados, they will not be granted it, and that is for the best."

"For the *best*?"

"Dearest, the negroes' souls must and will be saved. It is my greatest hope. But they will never rule themselves."

"Why not?"

"They are incapable. Like children and women, they lack the full capacity for reason and therefore the ability to govern themselves rationally. It is our mission to lead them to God. After that, God alone will determine their fate."

Like women.

Every day at the hospital that she awaited a man who made her heartbeats skip, but who by all accounts was a libertine *and who was not her betrothed*, she proved that she easily allowed her weakest instincts to overcome her rational mind.

Yet she knew women of reason. Emily adored museums and lecture halls. Their father, a man of rank, wealth, and education, respected his eldest daughter's intelligence immensely. From the time they were tiny girls, he had read to them stories about the female warriors and stateswomen of history—Cleopatra, Boudica, Queen Elizabeth—later encouraging them to read everything in his library. Granted, it was Emily who had enjoyed actually reading the pages. Amarantha had liked to listen to her sister read aloud, but the hills and pastures always called so powerfully that attending closely had sometimes been difficult. Even so, she had learned that not all women lacked reason, not even all women in her family.

And since she had arrived in Jamaica, Emily had sent her excerpts of writings by abolitionists that made it clear the issues surrounding emancipation were hardly simple. Yet her fiancé's ideas were so stark, as though they had nothing to do with actual people. *With the human heart.*

What's more, Eliza, who was both a woman and black, managed the busy sick-house so capably—patients, their families, volunteers, and industrious sailors—that Mr. Meriwether was able to devote himself entirely to surgery.

Amarantha descended from the carriage bemusedly.

Although not as large as Willows Hall, the governor's house with its magnificent white columns and elegant twin doors was impressive. Lights blazed from windows and the music of a quartet filled the humid night with magic. Amarantha enjoyed the jaunty tunes that the fiddlers and pipers on the docks played each evening as the sun set and the melancholy airs the sailors sang while working. But with her mind so unquiet, the cultivated familiarity of the duke and duchess's mansion dressed up for a party felt customary, warm, and delightfully gay. It felt *safe*. Shrugging off her musings, she entered the drawing room with a smile.

And came face-to-face with Gabriel Hume.

She lost her breath. She lost her senses. She had not anticipated this—him—*in her world*. She hardly knew what she did or said. Perhaps she nodded or curtsied when her hostess introduced her to the other guests.

"Lady Amarantha, I believe you are acquainted with Captain Hume from your work at the sick-house," the duchess said.

Acquainted seemed such a wrongfully innocent word to describe the feelings he created in her like wind created a maelstrom. His uniform was sharp white over his muscular legs and rich blue across the expanse of his shoulders, the medals on his chest gleamed, his rather long black hair was neatly combed, with a single satiny lock curving over his brow, and his stance was the erect posture about which she had first teased him. At least half a head taller than every other man in the room, he was the model of military strength and virtue. Only his eyes revealed him: dark, glittering with candlelight, and replete with hunger as they swept her from the bejeweled combs fixed in her hair to the toes of her satin slippers.

"How generous you have been, Captain," the duchess said, "to lend your crewmen and surgeon to the paupers' sick-house when the refitting of the *Theia* must have your first attention."

"'Tis no' generosity, ma'am," he said. "I saw a need that required attention."

He was not speaking of the hospital's needs. He was speaking of *her*, as he had done that first day.

She did not enjoy the party. She endured it. Throughout the evening her heart did not cease its quick, uneven tempo. To avoid being obliged to even look at him, she threw herself into conversation with other guests. Yet she knew where he was at every moment, as though her flesh sought his across the space. And she heard only him, as though her senses were attuned to the frequency of his voice alone. She felt brittle and too hot, like heat lightning crackling above a parched field.

Finally the hours of torture ended. Head aching, she tumbled into the carriage.

Paul patted her hand and rested his golden curls back against the squabs.

She twisted her kerchief between her fingers. "Do you despise those socialites even more thoroughly now?"

"I admit myself pleasantly surprised. And I have secured potential patrons for the mission school I wish to establish at the docks for freedmen sailors. It was not entirely the hardship I had anticipated."

Guilt weighed on her. What a great man he was to always be sacrificing his own happiness for others. And how wretchedly weak she was to desire another man so much that it hurt.

Later, on her bed in the room she shared with her companion, she could not sleep, replaying each moment of torment during the party in which she feared she would reveal herself—to Paul or to *him*—either would be horrible.

For she was certain of one thing: he was playing with her.

He *knew* she was betrothed. A man of honor would respect that. He would not look at her as though he would consume her. He would not seek her out and make her wild with wanting him. She was a game to him, only a momentary amusement for a careless hedonist.

She must clear her head of him *now*.

Rising as first light turned the blackness to hesitant gray, she dressed silently and went out of the hotel. No one yet stirred on the high street. Soon it would be bustling with activity; repairs from the damage the storm had wrought were slowly restoring the port town to its former beauty.

The damage the storm had wrought in her heart, however, was only worsening.

Crossing the street, she headed for the docks to walk away her fidgets, to exhaust herself so that she could return to her bed and a few hours of sleep before she was expected at the hospital.

When the captain appeared from the shadows she did not start or stumble. She knew it was he before she could even see him clearly in the darkness. She thought perhaps she would be able to recognize him anywhere, in her sleep, certainly in her dreams. Some part of her had known he would be waiting for her.

He stood entirely still as she passed him by. A narrow corridor between wagons stacked with barrels to be loaded onto a ship beckoned. She went into it and he followed.

He did not seize her or embrace her or do any of the lascivious acts that she had heard scoundrels were likely to do to maidens. Instead he halted at the other end of the wagon, yards away. Through the murky predawn she saw him rake his hand through his hair.

"*That* is the man you're to wed?" he said.

Her tongue crimped into a useless knot.

"*That*?" he repeated. "That pale, pompous, falsely pious excuse for a—*That* man?"

She hardly knew how to respond. He waited for her to speak into the silence cushioned only by lapping water and the familiar squeaking of ships' riggings.

"He is none of those," she finally managed to utter, and wondered that this was happening, that she was standing in the darkness alone with a young man who was a stranger to her family, and aching so deeply inside that she could hardly breathe. "How dare you—"

"You canna marry him, Amarantha." He said her name for the first time. The syllables in his rough brogue sent sublime pleasure through her.

"I will marry him. As soon as the church is rebuilt." Her fiancé's reason for postponing their wedding sounded ridiculous now. "I will be his wife," she said because she needed to hear it.

He came to her. Yet still he did not touch her. She looked up into the shadows of his eyes; they swam with the same confusion that swirled in her.

"Marriage to him will kill you." His gaze covered her face, one feature at a time.

"You must have seen him before this," she said.

"Aye."

"Then why are you saying this to me only now? Did you speak with him last night?"

"I didna speak. I listened."

"To what?"

"To the music o' your voice as you told them all about the hospital an' about the people you've come to know there. With every syllable, your pleasure was as bright as the light o' the candles burning around you. You spoke with affection an' with your heart."

Amarantha felt dizzy.

"An' you spoke like a man."

Her cloud of bliss burst.

"What do you mean by *that*?"

"You spoke your mind, lass."

"Oh." *Oh, no.* She had been so agitated, she hardly recalled what she had said.

"You spoke with intelligence an' knowledge," he said with an almost-smile. "An' fearlessness. As always."

Upon a painful leap, Amarantha's heart pounded back to life.

"Always?"

"Aye." His eyes narrowed. "An' I listened to him interrupt you an' speak over you an' belittle what you've done." He swung away and his fingers scraped through his hair again, disarranging it further. He had thick, gloriously black locks, and she did not wonder that women eagerly gave their favors to him, despite his many ports. To be allowed to run her hands through his hair as he was doing now might convince her to wait for him months on end too.

"That prim, superior son o' a—I nearly throttled him. I'd like to take his lily-white neck between my hands an'—"

"Stop!" Her hand was at her own throat, her other palm over her mouth. In all of the hours, all of the weeks that he had made her laugh and long for him, she had never expected he could be *this*. It frightened her.

It thrilled her.

He pivoted to face her. "He doesna deserve you."

"But you do? A man who could wish to harm another man in such a manner?"

Alarm flashed on his face. And abruptly, in the eyes that had seen war, she saw vulnerability.

He came to her again, swiftly this time.

"No," he said. "Never if it would displease you."

"It *would* displease me if he were harmed." The words shook a bit. "And . . . if you harmed anyone, I think it would displease me," she said brazenly. "Rather, I know it would."

"I've harmed plenty o' men, lass."

"Of course you must have. You have fought in battles."

"No' only in battle. In cold blood. In hot blood. With drink in my head at times, an' at others clear as rainwater. You were right to think me a beast. I am—a monster o' a man, damned a dozen times over by what I've done willingly, gladly. An' I've no apologies for it."

She swallowed across the thick scald in her throat. "I see," she whispered.

"I would give it all up to have you."

She closed her eyes. *This* was what she had been waiting for in her heart.

"Why—" Seizing the courage that had propelled her over vast hills and through dark woods and across an ocean, she opened her eyes. "Why have you not touched me since that night?"

"If I touched you even once," he said quietly now, like the rumble of an oncoming storm, "I wouldna be able to cease."

She could hardly breathe. "You do want me."

"More than I have ever wanted anything."

The laughter of pure joy burst through her lips. "I am not a *thing*."

"Aye. You're a woman. An' I thank the Almighty that he made you so." He smiled with such unguarded pleasure she nearly threw her arms about his neck and gave herself to him there, between the wagons, with dawn upon the harbor and the cries of gulls in the sky.

"You thank God?" Her lips would not be still; they smiled, and she laughed again. "I thought you were a heathen."

"Basking in the light o' an angel." In the burgeoning day, she could see his face entirely now, the boy who had had death and responsibility thrust upon him, who had embraced it, and who could still gaze so tenderly at her.

"A fallen angel," she whispered.

The roguish smile returned. "My favorite sort." The brogue was a seductive caress. It sent heat skittering into every crevice of her body. She balanced on the balls of her feet to be closer to him—his face—his lips.

"What shall we do next?" she said.

"You've told me I'm no' to throttle him. So you'll be needing to take matters into your own hands."

She was certain she should not feel this elation. She wanted him to kiss her more than she wanted to breathe. She wanted him to throw caution to the wind and seize her in his arms and make her his.

"I'll no' kiss you, lass," he said. "No' until you are no other man's."

"How did you know that I—"

The gleam in his eyes sealed her lips. By all reports he had kissed many women. Certainly he would recognize when a woman was longing to be kissed.

He backed away.

"Do what you must," he said, lengthening the distance between them with easy, confident strides now. "Then come find me." His smile was wide. "I'll wait."

She watched him disappear around the corner of the wagon at the very moment the sun crested the *Theia*'s mainmast, and in a glorious shower of gold and pink the day broke.

Chapter 7

The Promise

*A*marantha could not sleep. After breakfast, with nerves in her throat but certainty in her steps, she walked to the mission. She would make a clean confession and beg Paul's forgiveness. He would give it. He was fair-minded and compassionate. And if he could not give her his forgiveness, she already knew that she did not deserve it.

Arriving at the church, she was told that he had ridden to an inland village for the day.

Anticipation deflated, she returned to the hospital. With her nerves stretched as tightly as her lips, which would not cease smiling, she lavished her bubbling love onto the patients and waited for the captain to appear.

He did not. But her disappointment soon turned to appreciation. It was best for them to remain apart until she had spoken to Paul. That the naval officer showed this restraint proved his character. The thought gave her such pleasure that when the eternal day finally ended, her excitement overcame her frustration at Paul's untimely journey. Again she barely slept.

At dawn, a maid woke her and whispered that Captain Hume awaited her in the parlor. Swiftly she pulled a gown over her head and flew down the stairs.

The stiff propriety of the furniture and the very walls of the room made seeing him alone now jarring. He did not suit the modest setting. He was a great, powerful man who needed the sky above and the sea nearby. Despite his neat naval uniform, indoors he seemed almost feral.

"Where is Mrs. Jennings?" he said.

"Still asleep," she said, suddenly ridiculously shy. "She requires at least thirty minutes to dress." Her tongue felt awkward. "I did not wish to keep you waiting."

"You wanted no one to see me here?"

"No. I—That is to say, why *are* you here? At this hour? Is it not because you are cautious of being seen calling upon me?"

"I've received *Theia*'s orders. She is to put to sea today."

"Today?" She started forward involuntarily. But she caught herself up and her heart was beating too hard. "Is this not sudden? Where are you bound?"

His eyes were troubled. "'Tis confidential, lass."

"But—"

A pot rattled in the kitchen nearby. The open parlor door gave them no privacy.

"Follow me," she whispered.

Behind the hotel, the ground floor of a shop remained empty and boarded up. Closing the shop door almost entirely, he came to her in the single strand of light that remained. His gaze swept over her face.

"Have you broken it off with him?"

"I haven't yet found opportunity. Yesterday morning he traveled to the interior. When he returns today I will tell him. But I . . . I cannot bear to imagine . . ."

"What is it?" he said.

"I cannot bear to imagine the days without you here."

A gentle smile pulled at the corner of his mouth.

"I will think o' you every one o' those days, lass. An' I will write."

"You mustn't!"

His brow dipped. "No?"

"This society is too small. Someone would certainly discover it. If a letter arrived for me from—"

"A man o' my reputation." His voice sounded hard.

"From a man who is not my fiancé. I would be shamed. And—and he would be shamed."

"He."

"He is a good man. He is not perfect, but neither am I. I cannot hurt him, not like that, not publicly. You understand, don't you?"

He only studied her eyes, then her cheeks, then her hair.

"Tell me you're no' teasing," he said.

"Teasing?"

He bent his head, casting his eyes into shadow, and his chest rose on a hard breath. "Playing games with a man's heart."

"With his—?"

"Mine." It was a growl.

"No!" she said on a gasp. "No."

But she had done so with Paul. Not intentionally. Yet now it all seemed so clear.

"I could not—" She stumbled over the words. "I *could* not play a game. Not now." She looked directly into his eyes. "Not with you."

"Lass—"

"I want you to write to me. But you *must* not."

There was barely an inch between them but she was not afraid. The shape of his lips entranced her and made her fingers long to stroke them. In so many weeks she had memorized the hollows of his cheeks, the contours of his neck, the sinews in his hands, and the desire in his gaze on her. She could smell the sun on him, and she longed to touch it, to *feel* it on him. She was wicked, wanton, and aching.

"Promise me that you will return soon," she said.

"My ship goes where the admirals send it."

"Then quit the navy."

He smiled, and a sob filled her throat. Desperation swelled within her.

"Return soon," she whispered. "Give me your word."

"Aye. You have my word. But I'll have something from you now as well."

Her stomach roiled. *What a fool she was.* But she had, after all, expected this. Paul preached that the devil conquered hearts by donning attractive guises and leading men into carnal sin. Since women were even more easily duped, a woman of virtue must be ever-vigilant to guard against temptation.

Obviously, she had failed at *that* task entirely.

"What do you want?" she said, but she already knew. She wanted it too. She wanted his arms about her, his lips taking hers, the thrill of him all over her. She wanted him encompassing her and it made her weak inside.

"To touch your cheek."

Her eyes popped wide. "That is all you want?"

"No," he said quite seriously. "'Tis all I'm asking."

She stifled a moan. Heaven could not be so cruel to have created him, to allow her only moments of him, and then to steal him away.

"Yes," she whispered.

For a moment neither of them moved. Then she felt the heat of his hand, and the brush of his fingertips came like a whisper across her skin. Tingles skittered down her neck.

Holding her breath, she looked up into his face of angles and shadows that was more beautiful to her than anything else she had ever seen. His eyes were dark, his gaze upon her fevered. *Wanting her.*

His palm cupped her cheek and her breaths stopped. His hand was so large, so strong, yet he held her gently. His fingertips at her hair sent pleasure in more tingles down her throat and into her belly. The soft slide of his thumb along her jaw was the sweetest caress—*too sweet.* She could not remain still. Her lips parted.

He touched her there, on her lip, stroking, barely a caress. It tore the air from her lungs. She struggled for more air, with a gasp then with a long sigh. He caressed again and she was liquid, fire. Her heavy eyelids closed and she felt him everywhere, across her lips and in the deep core of her where she ached so fiercely now. She wanted him to touch her and touch her and never cease.

"Wait for me," she heard him whisper. "Dinna marry him." The raw heat of his words came against her brow. "Wait for me."

Her throat had closed entirely. She nodded.

Abruptly, he released her. His footsteps were hard and swift crossing the shop's floor. She opened her eyes and was alone.

She walked to the rear door, her chest a tight morass of loss. Leaving the shop, she went to the path behind the hotel that wended toward a cane field, then into the field. As she passed along the rows of decimated stalks, dry sobs collected in her throat.

He would not return. Not for her. She understood this as well as she had ever understood anything. Nine weeks ago she had known little of men of the world. She did now. She had heard all the gossip, the whispers.

Libertine.

Carouser.

Not the marrying sort.

Slowing to a halt amidst stalks broken by the hurricane, she let her tears fall silently. She did not believe that a gift of two such perfectly sympathetic hearts could be false. She *felt* it. And he, who might have demanded anything of her at the last moment, who might have asked her to give everything, had asked only to touch her cheek.

When he touched her, she had felt his trembling.

That afternoon in the port, the departure of the *Theia* was like a festival, with musicians on the docks and a great send-off of cannon blasts from the fort. A ship once believed to be dead had returned to life, just as the island would again. Everyone in town came out to celebrate. The sun shone, *Theia*'s banners snapped on her masts, and as her sails filled, the spectators cheered and applauded.

Amarantha could not enjoy it. She bought split coconuts from the vendors and carried them to the hospital where she gave the sweet milk to the children and the bright flesh to the men to cut up with their knives. Mrs. Jennings told her that Reverend Garland had called in her absence, but Amarantha found herself too occupied with tasks to walk to the mission. She wrote a letter to Emily, confessing that she had made a mistake and that she would book passage on the next ship home. But she tore it up.

On the third day after the *Theia*'s departure, Paul again called at the hospital. He seemed more tired than ever. But their wedding was imminent, he announced. In his restored house of God they would soon become man and wife.

"I will be especially glad," he said, "when you are no longer spending your days in this place."

"But I enjoy my work here."

"Despite the secret you have been concealing from me? Yes, Mrs. Jennings finally informed me."

Nausea slithered through her. "The secret?"

"I am not happy that you have practiced this deception with me. But I forgive you for doing so. The young often make mistakes."

"I—"

"Your father always indulged you so thoroughly, you believe every man to be as indolently honorable as he." He squeezed her hand. "You cannot possibly understand the rapaciousness of most men."

In shock, she managed to find her tongue.

"You are generous to forgive my—my *mistake*." It hurt to say it. "But it needn't affect my work here now."

"Of course it must. My wife cannot spend her days under the same roof with a man living in sin with a woman, their claims to marriage notwithstanding."

"But—Their claims to marriage? I don't—"

"God sanctions marriage between likes. It hardly matters that these colonials turn a blind eye to liaisons of this sort. Mr. Meriwether's unsuitable marriage cannot be condoned. After our wedding you may not return here."

He did not know.

But her relief lasted only moments before she took his meaning. When he left, she went directly to Eliza.

"It was love at first sight," Eliza said. "Mr. Meriwether and I married while he was still going to sea. It was years before he returned here permanently, after the birth of our second child. It can be a challenge to love a sailor," she said with a chuckle.

Love, children, fidelity of decades, and a humble life devoted to caring for those less fortunate than themselves: yet Paul believed the surgeon and his wife lacked virtue.

Paul Garland was not the man she had thought him to be. Twelve months earlier, in that white church surrounded by sparkling snow, she had heard him preaching all about love and she had invented a fantasy. That she had so blindly believed in that fantasy now appalled her.

Gabriel Hume had been no more than a fantasy too.

She understood herself now. It was simple: she had needed relief from the suffering around her. So she had created the profound attachment between them, imagining the violent, hedonistic sailor some sort of hero, a Prince Charming who would sweep her off her feet and make every moment of her life an adventure of passion and laughter.

He had left her.

In her heart she knew that if he wanted her—*if he loved her*—he would have found a way to remain, or he would have taken her with him. And the most damning evidence: he had never asked for her hand. Instead he had tempted her in secret, pretending friendship, even charity, because she was too foolish to insist that he mustn't.

With new resolve to never again make such horrible mistakes, she returned to the hospital the next morning.

Mr. and Mrs. Meriwether greeted her with momentous news: because of the sailors' excellent carpentry, the sick-house had been given permission to become permanent. They wanted her to assist in the venture.

It was the answer to her prayers. She needn't run home to Willows Hall. Instead, she would make an entirely new start here where she was finally finding her place. She would forget *him*—someday. But even then, Paul Garland would not be her future.

As though she conjured him, her fiancé appeared.

"The repairs to the church are complete," he exclaimed, grasping her hand. "The house is eager to receive its mistress. Amarantha darling, we will marry on Friday."

She tried to pull her fingers free. "I—"

"Forgive me. But I must call you *darling*, for you are that to me."

"I have work now. Will you return here at dusk and walk with me to the hotel?" However difficult, the deed must be done. A new life awaited her.

"Of course!" He chuckled and released her hand. "Go about your bandaging duties, my lady. I shan't require your undivided attention until Friday, and every day thereafter," he added with a soft smile.

She returned to her usual tasks, dreading the end of the day.

At midday, when Mr. and Mrs. Meriwether took their lunch in the shade of the office, and the other volunteers left for their homes, Amarantha visited each patient, moving quietly from cot to cot, feeling brows for fever, holding a hand here and there, and refreshing compresses. Lifting her head to stretch her neck, she saw Jonah Brock across the street.

From Mrs. Jennings's friends, Amarantha knew that after the hurricane, when the *Theia* limped into port, Mr. Brock quit the navy and took a post on an inland plantation. With a reputation no less shocking than his cousin's, but without the advantage of noble rank, in the months since then Mr. Brock had rarely ventured into town. Only once had he passed by the hospital, and another volunteer had been quick to point him out to Amarantha.

Now from the other side of the sun-drenched street he watched her and, through subtle signs, made it clear that he wished conversation with her.

She could imagine only two reasons for it: he assumed she would be an easy conquest and had come to take up where his cousin had left off, or he had word from the captain. The violent disparity of the two reasons proved she had not yet rid herself of insanity. She was wild for news of him.

While she awaited opportunity to leave the hospital, Mr. Brock remained, idly lounging in the shade. When finally she was able to walk to a nearby fruit stand, he arose and followed her inside.

He was not what rumors had made her expect. Attractive, gentlemanly, and entirely sober, he waited for the fruit seller to leave the shop's interior before approaching her.

"My lady." He bowed elegantly. He extended his hand. Upon his palm was a sealed letter. "This arrived by naval post boat this morning, enclosed in a letter to myself from my cousin."

The letter bore her name.

"Forgive my presumption," Mr. Brock said. "Knowing something of the nature of your acquaintance with my cousin, I sought you out to give it to you immediately."

Seizing it, she snapped open the seal.

The contents of the letter nearly sent her to her knees: he would return for her soon; they would be wed by special license in a church, before God and man; she must only wait, as she had promised him.

Pressing her knuckles against her lips to stifle the joy she wanted to shout to the world, she managed to speak four shaking words: "When will he come?"

Face drawn, Mr. Brock told her that his cousin would never come, that this was the last letter his cousin would ever write. Two days earlier the *Theia* had been ambushed by bandits, its crew decimated, its commander killed.

Captain Gabriel Hume was dead.

PART II

1818

The Pact

Chapter 8

Courses Set

24 January 1818
Kingston, Jamaica

Dear Emmie,

He did not perish. He is alive.

This afternoon, hearing the news from the gossips, I could hardly contain myself: I was so full of both joy and anguish. In silence and secrecy for a month I have mourned him. Yet he lives!

When I asked about the bandits, the gossips peered at me as though I were a child inventing stories. There were no bandits. Instead the women whispered of his mistress in Montego Bay with whom he spent his last nights on the island—nights during which I waited for him, longed for him, and—like a trusting child—loved him.

I know now that it was all a lie. He was merely sporting with a gullible girl—for amusement's sake,

I suppose, for diversion. Or perhaps he did care for me, yet apart he swiftly forgot me.

His ship now crosses the ocean, they say, although no one seems to know to where it is bound. Wherever it goes, I should take no interest in it. He is not mine to miss. He never was.

Oh, Emmie—Am I wicked to pray for his safety, or merely foolish to do so when he has dealt me this hurt? I know it is the latter—yet still I pray. How unguarded, how simpleminded I have been. And how foolish I am even now to wish this a terrible dream that will vanish upon waking.

I am all confusion, knowing that I have done wrong, that I do wrong still, yet unable—unwilling—to end my own unhappiness. For then, it will truly be over, and that I cannot yet bear.

(25 January)

Last night I wept myself to sleep, hiding my tears from my husband. Today, however, I am changed: wiser, more sober. Papa once warned that my heart trusts too swiftly and too deeply. I did not understand the warning then. I do now, for a naval officer has taught me a fine lesson: to believe a man's words and deeds rather than my heart's desire.

I will never make that mistake again.

—A.

July 1818
HMS Theia
Lat. −34.35, Long. 18.46

The hull heaved to starboard and rent the already deafening cacophony of thunder pounding the heavens, and rain pounding the deck, with a creak to send a sailor's heart scurrying to the soles of his feet.

Captain Gabriel Hume, commander of His Majesty's frigate *Theia*, having had no functioning heart to speak of for seven months, stood with legs braced hard and hands tight about the wheel, and closed his mouth and nose against the sea that rushed over him. His arms and back burned with the strain as, with a mighty groan, his ship righted herself then plummeted into another swirling green gully.

"Foremast'll go first, Cap'n! Mark me words!" shouted his bosun over the roar of the storm. Strapped to the mizzen with a rope, he had refused to go below as Gabriel had ordered.

Another wave rose portside, a flash of lightning illumining hills of water all about. Forcing his sixteen stone against the helm, Gabriel drove it, cutting the prow toward the oncoming swell. It burst against the hull, a river of foam and black flooding the forecastle. As *Theia* dipped again and he hauled the wheel back, the eerie crackle of wood snapping came to him through the clamor.

"There she go—!"

His bosun's next words were lost in thunder.

But the foremast held, rain cascading from reefed canvas in waterfalls.

"The next one'll take her, Cap'n!" his bosun shouted. "Mark me—"

"Blast it, man!" Gabriel hollered. "Bind your flapping lips or when we're through this I'll sew them shut!"

"Aye, Cap'n!" his bosun replied over the rain beating at the quarterdeck. "But the gods have it in for us this time!"

"'Tis no' the gods that sent this squall," came through his gritted teeth as a wave rose. Tilting, *Theia* began her slow roll into the trough.

Gabriel pulled the wheel, every muscle and tendon and bone strained to snapping. Through the thunder came the howl of a wild animal. As the swell crested and his chest throbbed with agony he knew the sound was coming from his throat, his mouth.

Eighty-four men.

Eighty-four men under his command. Men given into his care alone.

And one vengeful storm.

Ten months earlier he had cheated a hurricane. The devil apparently was not satisfied with the punishment he had already been dealt for that.

He threw his strength against the helm.

"You'll no' take any o' them, you son o'—"

A wall of sea swallowed the forward half of his ship and a spar flew at him from the darkness. Pain exploded in his head.

When he opened his eyes, he was falling with the helm. With a tearing of every muscle in his body, he fought, pulled, pushed to his feet, slipping in icy water, righting himself, struggling against the fog between his ears.

"You've got it right, Cap'n," his bosun burbled, water-logged now. "This ain't the gods. This storm be Satan himself come to carry we all home."

Funnels of water streamed from the ink above. Lightning snapped, showing the sailor slumped against the mast. Thunder like cannon blasted the wind. Gabriel closed his ears against the devil's madness. His exhausted fingers slipped on the wood.

No.

Not *yet.*

Not his ship.

Not his crew.

"What do you want, then?" he called out, clinging to the pegs as the lash of rain against his cheeks and hands washed all but savage audacity away. "What'll the Prince o' Darkness have from me in return for these men's lives?"

A spear of lightning split open the blackness from

cloud to deck, and a barrel tied to the railing burst into flames.

"All right." Gabriel watched the fire sputter out beneath the rain. "You're listening. Excellent!"

Wind swept over the deck. He pressed his shoulder into it and held the helm steady. But he could feel the weakening, the end of his strength coming finally, with no end to the storm in sight.

"You already know what I want!" he shouted into the fury of Hell.

The only thing he wanted.

"Now, you bastard—"

Portside, a curtain of black arose, darker than the foam, darker than the rain, a towering mountain of ocean. Beneath the screaming wind Gabriel growled, "Let's make a deal."

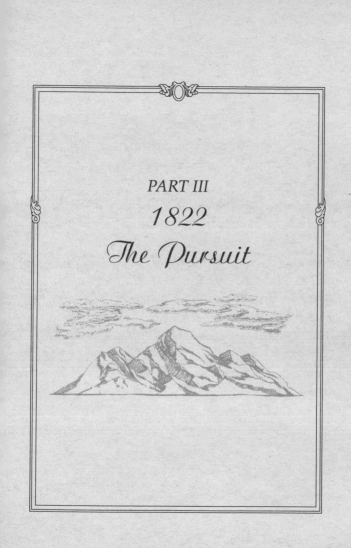

PART III

1822

The Pursuit

Chapter 9

The Dark Lord

19 March 1822
Kingston, Jamaica

Dear Emmie,

I sail tomorrow, but not to England. Months ago
my dearest friend Penny—sister to me here in your
absence—sailed to Scotland. She gave no warning and left no explanation to even her family, only
a message written, I believe, in distress, insisting
that she had good reason to go. I had intended to
travel directly home after preparing the mission for
its new pastor, but now instead will follow her in
hopes of discovering the astonishing haste for her
journey.

I say astonishing, for this is entirely unlike her.
Penny's character is more steady than volatile,
more thoughtful than impulsive, and more responsible than mercurial. (Paul regularly reminded

me that she and I were perfect foils.) I must go after her.

I will miss Eliza and Mr. Meriwether profoundly, for they and Penny made this island home to me. It is the desired state of a missionary's heart: to never become so happy in any terrestrial place that one's attention strays from the hereafter. It is a very good thing, then, that I am no longer a missionary's wife.

With love,
Amarantha

May 1822
Port of Leith, Scotland

*D*espite the Scottish chill that burrowed beneath her clothing and under her skin, Amarantha had discovered that port towns were alike in at least one particular: spending coin was the fastest route to learning anything useful.

"If you be wanting information about a pretty girl traveling alone," said the proprietor of the eighth pub as he pocketed the shillings she laid before him, "you'd best be asking Mrs. Eagan up at Kirkgate."

A madam, surely. Where sailors sojourned, there were always women to serve their needs.

"Isn't that quite a fine neighborhood?"

"Mrs. Eagan's callers no' be the sorts to trawl the docks seeking company, lass."

Even after five years that word—*lass*—still pinched at the back of her neck. Only one man had ever called her that.

"I see." Penny would not have willingly sought shelter in a brothel. But if she had been desperate, or frightened . . .

Amarantha set off.

Mrs. Eagan's house was a modest, Georgian-style building with amphorae overflowing with flowers by the entrance. A footman escorted Amarantha to a pretty parlor that revealed the madam's fondness for cherubs: chubby little nudes decorated the papered walls, the ceiling, and the mantel.

She smiled. Paul would be horrified that she was seeing this.

But her grin faded swiftly. She had displeased him so constantly that she hardly remembered his face in an attitude of pleasure—except on one occasion, the grand finale to four years of lies.

"Miss Foster?"

Amarantha started. She still hardly recognized her false name, Anne Foster. But it was necessary. Anonymity had already allowed her to search for Penny in places where an earl's daughter or missionary's wife would never go.

Mrs. Eagan stood haloed by the gilded door frame. Neither plain nor beautiful, with sweeping brows and straight black hair, she seemed entirely regular.

"*Mrs.* Foster, actually," Amarantha said.

"I am Loretta Eagan. What brings you to my home? It cannot be your husband, for at present there are no men in the house except my footman, and he is neither handsome nor wealthy enough to attract a woman of your beauty."

"You needn't flatter me, Mrs. Eagan. I have not in fact come here looking for a man." She extended her hand.

The madam's grasp was light but it lingered.

"I entertain guests in this parlor, Mrs. Foster. If you have come here seeking work, we must remove to my study for that conversation."

"I do not seek work here." A cherub seemed to wink at her.

"You smile," Mrs. Eagan said. "But you do not smile in derision."

"I don't, in fact. But how do you know it?"

"On occasion I welcome into my home women of your quality."

"Oh? I imagined your callers were—"

"My clients are indeed gentlemen."

"I don't suppose you hire these women as housemaids and such?"

Mrs. Eagan's smile was knowing. "Some are bored in their marriages. Others are confused. Some seek pleasure they are not allowed at home. And some seek forbidden adventure." Her gaze traveled over Amarantha's figure. "Have you come here seeking adventure, Mrs. Foster?"

"No."

"Are you certain?"

"Oh, yes. I have had my fill of forbidden adventure." *Once.* Enough to convince her to never seek it again. "Enough for a lifetime."

"Then what of your betraying smile?"

"I was imagining what my husband would think to see me here."

"No doubt that you are a woman of passion."

"No doubt." *The hypocrite.* "But I have not come here to speak of me. I seek a friend who disembarked three months ago from a merchant ship. A dear friend. A sister, in truth, through my late husband's family."

"How intriguing that a moment ago you spoke of him as your husband only."

"I have had only the one."

"A woman of enterprise can possess more than one husband in a lifetime."

Not this woman.

"Mrs. Eagan, I was told that you take a particular interest in pretty young women who arrive alone in Leith."

"I do, if they are well-spoken and free of disease. Is this friend also of your quality?"

"She is well-spoken and English, with the accent of

those raised on the island of Jamaica. At the time she left home she was in excellent health."

She seemed to study Amarantha. "How young?"

"Twenty-seven."

"I might have encountered her." Moving to a sofa, she draped herself upon it. "But I typically take little interest in mature women. For *he* does not take any interest in them."

"He?"

She laid a beautifully rounded arm upon the sofa's gilded back. "The Devil, of course."

"The—I beg your pardon, did you say the devil?"

"Have you come from the colonies so recently, Mrs. Foster, that you have not yet heard of the Devil's Duke?"

"It seems so." The mantel cherubs grinned. "Is this devil a client of yours?"

"Come, make yourself at ease and I will tell you."

Amarantha perched on a satin cushioned chair.

"Last autumn a girl from Edinburgh disappeared abruptly," Mrs. Eagan said. "She was eighteen, attractive, modestly educated, and pious, the daughter of a tradesman of no particular social distinction but comfortable income, and a maiden. Her name was Cassandra Finn."

"Was?"

"Three months later, another girl disappeared. This time it was a laborer's daughter, also lovely and young, but unlike her parents she was schooled."

"Well-spoken too?"

The madam nodded. "And betrothed to be married to a man who would lift her from poverty into respectability. Her name was Maggie Poultney."

"You have twice said 'was.' Are Miss Finn and Miss Poultney now deceased?"

"The Edinburgh police believe they are." Fingernails painted crimson stroked the gilded wood. "Cassandra Finn's abductor—"

"Abductor?"

"—left no trace of her behind. But Maggie Poultney's cloak was discovered. Drawn in chalk on it was a peculiar symbol: a star with three additional symbols at three points."

"How curious." Amarantha shifted on the soft seat, impatience jittering in her empty stomach. She had not traveled all the way to Scotland to hear tales of runaways and occult symbols. "Mrs. Eagan, I wonder if I could describe to you my—"

"And blood, Mrs. Foster."

"Oh. On Miss Poultney's cloak?"

"Yes."

"Why do the police believe that a devil abducted them?"

"They found the cloak at the edge of his property. Several months later, another girl went missing. Her name was Chloe Edwards. From the gentry."

"The police have not yet discovered the whereabouts of the three girls, I assume?"

"Four girls. Again, the discovery was at the edge of his property. This time it was her lifeless body."

"Good heavens." Amarantha folded her hands. "I believe I understand now your interest in young, lone women. You wish to protect them, don't you?"

"To warn them, Mrs. Foster. And to teach them how to withstand the dangerous allure of the unknown."

Amarantha could not believe that she had sailed thousands of miles from her husband's church to sit in the parlor of a *brothel* in which young women were cautioned to avoid temptation.

"Mrs. Eagan, who is this man whom the police believe is perpetrating crimes, and why do you call him the Devil's Duke?"

"Not only I. Everybody."

"In Leith or Edinburgh?"

"In Scotland. Even London. His infamy has spread far beyond Edinburgh."

Not to Kingston. But news traveled slowly across the ocean.

"Why has he such a dramatic name?"

"Surely it is obvious. He is the devil incarnate, living alone, eschewing society, speaking to none, plotting evil deeds, and then in the dark of night venturing forth to destroy innocence. The name suits him ideally."

"Interesting. The devil I have heard preached in pulpits always seems remarkably *active* in people's lives, encouraging them to bad behavior." That devil had been one of her husband's favorite topics, especially when he was vexed with her. "But I suppose the double *D* has a pleasantly alliterative ring to it. What of that other part of the name? Why do they call him a duke?"

"Because he is a duke."

"A duke? An actual *duke*?"

Her hostess nodded.

"A titled lord?"

"Yes."

"The police and everybody in Scotland believe a peer of the realm to be an abductor and murderer of maidens? Because the body of a young woman was found near his estate?"

"Not his principal estate. Rather, the property he owns in Edinburgh."

"Mrs. Eagan, for five years I lived on an island about which English people regularly tell stories of heathen rituals and dark magical goings-on, none of which I ever actually witnessed. Nor has anybody that I know. It is all hearsay and exaggeration of matters that outsiders do not understand. Englishmen adore believing in fantastical stories."

"These are not stories, Mrs. Foster, nor fantasy. There is proof."

"A symbol written in chalk on a cloak?"

"The same symbol is carved in stone on the lintel of the gate of the duke's castle. That castle is quite close to Edinburgh."

Emily's dear friend, Constance Read, was the daughter of a duke whose estate was near Edinburgh. But surely a man of the Duke of Read's stature would not be mistaken for a criminal. On the other hand, Amarantha's pious missionary husband had in fact been a cheating bigot.

"You asked if the Devil's Duke was a client of mine," Mrs. Eagan continued. "He never was. But I have made his acquaintance. A year ago, I was hostess at a dinner party for a gentleman of means in Edinburgh. The duke was a guest that night. Mrs. Foster, you have never seen a man more suited to villainy. He is handsome in a dark, formidable manner, and powerfully formed. He spoke to few. Throughout the evening he studied all of us as though he had particular use for each person at that gathering, as though he were surveying his prey in preparation for the black mass over which he would preside later that night."

"This party occurred before the first of the maidens disappeared?"

"Several months before Cassandra Finn's disappearance."

"And did he?"

The madam tilted her head. "Did he . . . ?"

"Did he host a black mass that night at which he sacrificed some of your party guests?"

Her nostrils flared. "Jest, if you will, Mrs. Foster. He is a dangerous man."

"Mrs. Eagan, you have succeeded: my curiosity is now thoroughly aroused. Will you tell me the name of this dark lord whom everybody fears so greatly?"

"But of course." Her fingers stroked the elaborately carved edge of the sofa again. "He is Gabriel Hume, the Duke of Loch Irvine."

Chapter 10

The Devil

*A*ll of the air got trapped in Amarantha's throat. Then, upon a gasp, a great ball of laughter barked from her mouth.

She snapped her lips together.

"Mrs. Foster, are you unwell?"

It had been so long since she had last laughed, she hardly knew.

"Mrs. Eagan, *you* now jest, do you not?"

"I do not. Why would you say so?"

"I was once acquainted with the present Duke of Loch Irvine. It was before he came into his title, to be sure, but only five years ago. Unless his character has altered beyond recognition in those five years, there is nothing more absurd than the notion of that man as a twisted demon, except perhaps that he is a recluse who shuns society."

"Yet both are accurate."

"I cannot believe it. You claim that all in Edinburgh and Leith do?"

"Everyone."

"Astonishing. Is there *no* one in this region who knew him before the girls disappeared?"

"Until last summer, he had been absent from Scotland since boyhood, although there is some disagreement concerning the age he departed his family's home."

Thirteen.

After she learned that he had not perished at sea, she had never sought news of his naval pursuits. She knew nothing of him except his unexpected accession to the dukedom, which she had read about in *The Times* when it reached Kingston.

"This is a busy port town," she said, "and he was a naval commander. Someone here must have known him before."

"He owns two vessels that sail from these docks," the madam said pacifically. "But the crew of both keep apart from others."

"I daresay hundreds of men arrived here last year, any one of whom could have done these crimes. Or it might have been a criminal who has lived here his entire life. Perhaps several criminals, each who committed a separate crime against the unfortunate girls."

"Do consider the symbol carved on the gate at Haiknayes Castle," Mrs. Eagan said, "and its appearance on Maggie Poultney's cloak, which proves the connection. The lairds of Loch Irvine have always made their home at Haiknayes."

"That symbol could certainly prove Miss Poultney's interest in the castle," Amarantha conceded. "But hardly the Duke of Loch Irvine's guilt."

"You seem to have a keen interest in defending his innocence, Mrs. Foster."

"I am expressing doubt, yes." The young man Amarantha had known in Jamaica had been no model of propriety, but she refused to believe him a vile abductor and murderer of innocent maidens. That he had gently, won-derfully *seduced* Miss Poultney, Miss Finn, and Miss Ed-wards, and that afterward the girls had fled their homes in heartbreak and shame, was however entirely likely. "The police have had ample time to place the blame on him. They must be doubtful too."

"They recently accused another man of the murder, but they swiftly released him. They had, after all, found her body near the duke's property."

"I did not know he had a house in Edinburgh." They had rarely spoken of their families or homes. Those ten weeks had been singular, at once fiercely thrilling and de-liciously intoxicating, a time-out-of-time idyll. Even her heartbreak had defied reality.

You were right to think me a beast.

At the time she had not believed those words. Instead she had believed his lies. She was, she had discovered, a very poor judge of a man's character when her heart was involved.

"Despite your acquaintance five years ago," her host-ess said, "perhaps you do not truly know the Duke of Loch Irvine."

Without doubt.

She scooted to the edge of the chair.

"Mrs. Eagan, will you tell me if you have encountered my friend, Penelope Baker? She stands two inches taller than I. Her complexion is light brown, her hair is black and curly, and she has eyes the color of amber."

"I am sorry to disappoint you, Mrs. Foster."

Amarantha stood. "Thank you for your time."

"I regret that I cannot help. A woman never enjoys sending a caller away unhappy." She offered a smile of feminine understanding.

"Oh, I do not go away from your home entirely down-cast. Your story of the Duke of Loch Irvine has had quite the opposite effect, in fact."

"I beg your pardon?"

"It is horrible that the girls' families are suffering, and I grieve for them, truly. But you have just told me Gabriel Hume is now believed by all to be a villain. That this rumor is surely false has no effect whatsoever on how thoroughly satisfied it has made me. Good day."

The walk back was short and as she reached the docks the sun was turning the canal a glittering gold color. She purchased rolls and ale, and carried them to the blacksmith shop.

Corporal Nathaniel Hay sat on a stool by the forge, his single weathered hand wrapped about a poker handle, prodding the coals. A fellow passenger aboard ship, he had kind eyes that had drawn Amarantha to him, only to discover that he had served under her father's command at Yorktown decades earlier. When he learned she was traveling alone, he had insisted on accompanying her.

"I have bought dinner, and it is nearly hot!" she said.

Taking up a lamp, he followed her into their temporary flat, two rooms behind the blacksmith shop. Watching him settle uncomfortably at the bare table, she recognized his silent suffering. In four years at the hospital, she had seen plenty of the chronic troubles of men and women who spent their lives laboring.

"I have been to a brothel," she said as she unwrapped the food and set the larger portion before him. "Now, you mustn't scold. It was a very elegant brothel. A passerby would never know what debauchery goes on inside it."

"That's a comfort to hear, my lady," he said, the creases about his eyes deepening.

"You mustn't ever speak without sincerity, Nathaniel. It is a sin."

"Did your husband teach you that?"

"And many more useful lessons. I'm certain I shan't exhaust all of them before we must eventually part." She bit into the roll and nearly moaned. To her starved senses, even this simple fare tasted marvelous. She had come no closer to finding Penny today, yet she felt a lightness of spirit that she had not enjoyed in months. Years. *Five years.* "What did you do today? Stir the coals of caution all throughout my absence?"

"You're as clever as the colonel."

"Not at all. Also, my father is much handsomer."

"I won't believe it."

"But it is true. My mother and father's five youngest daughters are all polished guineas too."

"And your elder sister?"

"Emily is pretty, but more importantly, she is brilliant, just as Papa. Oh, how *good* it is to speak of them." Paul had never liked to hear about her family. "Thank you, Nathaniel, for allowing me to trust you." She reached out and touched his hand.

His brow knit. "Have you written to Lady Emily yet?"

She snatched her hand back. "No."

"You should seek your family's help."

"I cannot." She had tried to write to her sister, yet always the words were garbled. Too much had happened to explain in a letter. She had changed. This—being alone, anonymous—was easier. Uncomplicated. She could pursue Penny without interference. "They will demand that I return home."

"You should."

She cleared her throat. "How did you pass the afternoon?"

"A boy called for you."

"Nathaniel! Why didn't you tell me this immediately? Who was he?"

He shook his head. "Just another urchin looking for money from the lady who'd doled it out at the pub."

"Which pub?"

"I gave him a coin and sent him on his way."

"Good grief, *which pub?*"

"The Blue Thistle."

Beyond the window night had fallen.

"It is too late already. I will go at first light."

"You won't go then either. 'Tain't safe for a lady. And you're looking peaked."

"Peaked?"

"You haven't slept a full night since we arrived, seems to me. You should take better care of yourself, my lady."

"I do not understand," she said, standing, "why I cannot seem to impress it permanently on my mind that all men feel the need to control women's actions. Even good men." She went to the doorway between the two tiny rooms. "I understand that you wish to keep me safe, Nathaniel. But I do not need safety." Only answers.

THE FOLLOWING MORNING Amarantha counted the remainder of her coins: a dispiritingly quick task. Paul had not allowed her to keep money. He thought her too irresponsible to make proper use of it.

Leaning her brow against the shelf above the brazier on which the kettle heated, she closed her eyes to relieve the pressure behind them. In her marriage she had been more fortunate than many women. Paul had never beaten her. He had never spoken disrespectfully to her when in the company of others. He had given her a comfortable home and just enough liberty to work several hours each week at the hospital.

She had been so grateful to him for allowing her to continue that work, despite his disapproval of Mr. and Mrs. Meriwether. When she discovered that he had done so only in order to hide his liaisons with his lover, Amarantha had not wept or screamed. Instead, she had walked the two miles to Penny's house, and found there warm, welcoming embraces.

Paul had regularly insisted the rumors that Penny was his father's daughter by an enslaved woman were false, that his father had never been unfaithful to his mother. Yet after his death she learned that he had lied about that too.

A scratch sounded at the door. She opened it to a grubby little boy.

"G'day, miss!" He snatched his cap from his head. "I be Rory Markum. My da's place be the Blue Thistle you came by yesterday."

"Oh, do come in, Mr. Markum! I am preparing my breakfast. Will you share it?"

He blushed to the roots of his matted hair.

"I've already took breakfast, miss. Mum dinna like to be spreading anybody's secrets. But after you left she said as you spoke respectful an' honest, she took a fine impression o' you. She sent me over here to tell you the lady you be looking for, Miss Baker, stayed a sennight with us at the Thistle."

Relief washed through Amarantha.

"She was—"

"Like you described her to Mum. The very image!"

"Do you know where she went after she left you?"

"She told Mum she was off to Edinburrah to find the devil," Rory declared.

A frisson of unease tickled Amarantha's belly. "What devil?"

"The Devil's Duke, o' course!"

The simplest explanation sufficed. The female population of Leith and Edinburgh had been whipped into a frenzy of anxiety with stories of missing maidens and bloody cloaks. Surely the pub mistress was as gullible as Mrs. Eagan.

When the boy left, Amarantha packed a satchel with necessities, tucked three of her five remaining coins into Nathaniel's bedroll, and donned her cloak. A blacksmith by trade, Nathaniel had already made himself at home in the pub nearby and in the smith's shop that kept this little flat warm throughout the damp nights on the Firth. She could not drag him with his aching joints the two miles to Edinburgh.

Nathaniel was a good man, and too observant: she was in fact not feeling her best. But she would never again allow any man's demands, even kindly offered, to impede her.

Sliding her notebook into the satchel, she paused, then opened the volume and drew from it a folded paper: a letter written to Emily but never sent. For five years she had kept it as a reminder to her unwise heart.

Unfolding the page, she stared at the words her trembling hand had penned, the ink smudged by her hot tears.

> *He did not perish. He is* alive.

A wave of emotion arose in her, an echo of the excessive feelings that had propelled the writing of those words.

> *Am I wicked to pray for his safety, or merely foolish to do so when he has dealt me this hurt? I know it is the latter—yet still I pray.*

She had continued to pray for months after that, guilty for the secret she hid from her husband, yet justifying it as piety, as though the Eternal Almighty had not known precisely the root of her prayers. She had only ceased praying for Captain Gabriel Hume the day she discovered God had given her another soul for whom to pray, a precious new life wholly in her care.

Nine months later, she had ceased praying to God entirely.

> *Papa once warned that my heart trusts too swiftly and too deeply. I did not understand the warning then. I do now, for a naval officer has*

*taught me a fine lesson: to believe a man's words
and deeds rather than my heart's desire.*
    I will never make that mistake again.

Yet she had, throwing her affection and good intentions into her marriage. Youthfully naïve, passionately
innocent, and so easily tossed to the heights of pleasure
or hurled to the depths of misery, even in the midst of
heartbreak she had sought happiness. And love.

No longer. Five years older, she was much wiser. And
the lessons her marriage had taught her—lessons in
dampening her emotions and mistrusting her desires—
could never be unlearned.

She wrote a swift note to Nathaniel. With rumors of
abducted women flying about, she would not give him
cause to worry.

For her own sake she was unconcerned about the diabolical duke. Gabriel Hume had long since stolen the innocent girl in her. If the Duke of Loch Irvine were, in
fact, the demon people believed him to be, she among all
women in Scotland had nothing to fear.

Edinburgh, Scotland

A dozen naked women gazed languidly at Gabriel.

"The roof is leaking again," he mumbled.

"I beg your pardon?" his companion replied, obviously
surprised.

Gabriel scratched his fingertips across his two-day's
growth of whiskers. Awakening from the old dreams
this morning, he had been too unsettled to hold the razor
steady enough to shave.

*Cloverleaf eyes fevered with desire. Tresses like fire
and sunshine. A smile that stripped him of all but the
hunger to taste her. Laughter that unhinged him and shot
his body through with hot, hard need.*

He had awoken with a head full of confusion and a cock so eager to please it ached.

He scraped a hand over his face again. How she could remain so beguiling in his dreams after five damn years, he'd no idea. Probably because he was an idiot.

He knew the reason for the dream's return, though. News of the death of Paul Garland had arrived in Leith aboard Gabriel's ship a fortnight ago. Every night since then he had dreamed.

The dreams had never really *ceased*, not entirely, not in five years. He had simply gotten accustomed to them coming a wee bit further apart.

Focusing his eyes again on the letter, he reread the final lines.

"The roof is leaking again," he repeated. "Worse than before."

"It is not," Ziyaeddin replied. "The roof of this house is perfectly adequate."

"An' they've need o' more sherry barrels." Crumpling the page in his fist, Gabriel blew out a breath and raked his fingers through his hair. "The fifty barrels I'd Courtenay send up from Spain a year ago cost the better part o' the quarter's income. *Judas*, the place will suck me dry an' those females will still be asking more o' me."

"Ah, Kallin. Again." The young man shook his head. "How you can stand there in the midst of these"—he gestured to the paintings lining the gallery—"and grumble about leaking roofs and sherry barrels, I cannot fathom. Although perhaps the inner beast is in fact awake, merely caged in ducal cares."

Gabriel dropped his hand. "Inner what?"

"*Suck you dry*? Honestly, Your Grace, if you had not been such a fine naval commander, I would think you entirely lacking in intelligence."

"Fortunately, Your Highness, a man dinna require intelligence to understand idiot innuendos."

"True. Now, which of these do you prefer for your study?" Ziyaeddin nodded at the array of paintings. "There is no space on these walls for the next. One must go."

Gabriel perused the canvases hung the length of the gallery. Daylight shone through the windows, but the late afternoon was rainy and the room dim. Employing few lamps in his studio allowed his houseguest to paint in natural light while securing privacy.

That privacy came more easily now that all of Edinburgh believed the man who owned the house to be a diabolical ravisher of maidens.

Gabriel had not actually lived in this house since returning to Edinburgh. No purpose in keeping an entire staff for the mammoth place when he had used it to entertain only once in three months. The hired house in Leith was small, required few servants who could carry stories to newspapers or the police, and it was close to the docks.

"You've smudged the features o' every one o' them," he said, stepping closer to the nearest painting.

"Not all features," the prince clarified.

"Only the facial features." Gabriel gestured toward the canvas. "Who is this one?"

"I do not know." Ziyaeddin spun a long, thin paintbrush between his fingers. "I have no interest in painting portraits. Only in studying the human form."

"An' your models, what is their interest in it?"

"It is a harmless game to them, innocent dallying with the devil. They believe I am you and they enjoy it."

"They've never seen your face or heard your voice?"

"I go and come from the house at Leith cloaked, and remain covered during the sittings."

Gabriel returned his attention to the painting. He peered closer. "I think I danced with her at that ball."

Ziyaeddin chuckled.

It loosened Gabriel's chest a bit. The exiled prince had

no pleasures except his art. His ploy to entice models to his studio in this house had taken advantage of the rumors that circulated in Edinburgh, rumors that identified Gabriel as the so-called Devil's Duke. It was a clever ruse, and successful.

"Wasn't that the ball at which you lost the heiress to that other fellow?" Ziyaeddin murmured around the pointed end of the paintbrush between his teeth. "The heiress you never actually intended to wed."

"Didna I?" He studied the next picture, yet another nude woman reclining on a divan. Ziyaeddin's talent was prodigious: even without facial features, each woman was at once alluring yet subtly distant.

Memories of an English maiden—her soft, damp skin and scent of desire—threatened the edge of Gabriel's sanity.

"Tell me, my friend," Ziya said, "what did you hope to gain from your brief courtship of Lady Constance Read? The friendship of the heiress's noble English friends, or perhaps of her ducal father?"

Gabriel hid his grin. "Do they teach court intrigue to young princes in your kingdom, or do you learn it by trial and error?"

"Error, obviously on my part," Ziya replied with a tap of the brush's handle. "You admit to intrigue?"

"No intrigue." Constance Read's friends were powerful men with interests throughout the seas, men who would rebuff a stranger, but who might partner with a man nearly betrothed to an intelligent woman they admired. "I had hoped to court her friends who are in trade." It had been a gamble from the outset, and had come to nothing.

"Therefore you courted her? You truly are a barbarian, Scot."

"An' you are a prince without a crown, Turk. Which o' us is the worse, do you imagine?"

The young man's smile was slow.

Moving to the window, Gabriel looked out onto the rainy village that flanked one side of his property. So close to both palace and castle, it was tiny, no more than six shops built a century ago to serve this house in which the lairds of Haiknayes resided while in Edinburgh. Now a flare of brilliant orange shone through the blacksmith's doorway.

In thirteen years at sea, the only creature comforts Gabriel had ever missed were the great big blazing fires that had burned in the massive medieval hearths at Haiknayes.

Five years ago, with a head full of arrogance and blood full of heat, he had dreamed of taking Amarantha Vale there—actually *taking* her, before the great hearth—stripping off her delicate garments, caressing her skin that glowed in the firelight until she moaned, doing away with her maidenhood to the music of her pleasured cries, and then making her his again till, exhausted, they fell asleep entwined on the fur rug there.

That a randy, youthful fantasy was the principal reason he had not yet moved to Haiknayes, although he had been master of it for two years now, was most certainly his greatest idiocy yet.

The estate was barely twenty miles distant. Now its lands were in poor condition. Distracted by his studies that had tempered the grief of losing his wife, his father had allowed Haiknayes to languish. Fortunately the castle itself was in better repair than the land, still full of the modern comforts his mother had installed to make it home.

If he could afford to restore Haiknayes to its former glory, he would in an instant. But Kallin required every guinea he could scrape from four merchant cargoes a year. His gambit to court Constance Read's wealthy friends had not worked. He simply must find more funds somewhere.

He turned to face the young prince.

"How would you like to move to Haiknayes?"

"The fortress?" Ziya replied. "You intend to sell this house, don't you?"

"I am giving it thought."

"What about another heiress? I understand that Britain is seething with wealthy gentle-maidens seeking noble titles."

"No more heiresses for me." No women for him, period. Not while his head was still full of a memory.

"Then I shall do as Your Grace wills it." The prince bowed in regal assent.

Gabriel laughed and started toward the door.

"Leave the house on occasion, Ziya. At least go to the park."

"Why? What is in the park?"

"None o' these"—he gestured to the paintings—"an' more o' the real thing."

"You cannot convince me that naked women cavort about in the parks of Edinburgh."

"No. But you can invite them inside an' take care of the clothing fairly quick. Devilishly tricky, all those buttons and fasteners, but no' impossible. 'Tis all in the wrist."

Ziya tapped the brush handle to his fingertips again. "I believe the idiom of this land that most suits now is the pot which calls the kettle black."

Gabriel grinned. "I'm off to London."

"Not to Kallin to repair the leaky roof?"

"Not yet." While his original partner, Torquil Sterling, had lived, Gabriel had not been involved in the mercantile side of their joint venture. The man that had taken on Tor's role after his death, Xavier Du Lac, coordinated it all now from Portsmouth. Since Xavier's brown skin and Haitian origins rendered negotiations with some Brits tricky, they had agreed that Gabriel would pursue business opportunities as well. It was either that or endanger Tor's most cherished project: the community of women currently residing at Gabriel's Highland estate.

Kallin needed money. Selling this house or Haiknayes, in which his mother had made homes full of laughter and joy, would be his last resort. But no woman would supply the funds needed. He had far too many females in his life already.

Chapter 11

The Journey

24 May 1822
Portsmouth, England

Gabriel,

Regrettably I must convey the news that the house in Edinburgh has burned down. Z. was in Leith at the time and has no notion how the fire began, but the possibility that it was arson concerns him. He has removed to Haiknayes.

Enclosed, find the most recent communication to arrive from Kallin. Of particular interest: Miss Cromwell has made plans to put up two dozen barrels of gin.

—Xavier

July 1822
Edinburgh Infirmary

"My clothes, at long last!"

Amarantha eagerly received from the nurse the gown, stockings, shoes, and cloak in which she had arrived unconscious at the hospital eight weeks earlier.

"I began to believe you would never restore them to me," she added with a smile as she pulled the gown over her shift.

"If you'd no' attempted to escape before you'd fully healed, we'd have allowed it afore," the nurse said, buttoning her gown, "Though we do wish you would remain, Anne. You're a fine nurse."

"A better nurse than patient, I daresay." She laughed.

"'Tis good to see you smile, child."

"I had no reason to smile before today." Only dreams from which she awoke each morning muddled and confused. "Except your kindness." Amarantha threw her arms about the woman and hugged tight. "Thank you."

"Be off with you, Anne Foster," the Scotswoman said upon a sniffle. "Or we'll be keeping you after all."

Amarantha's throat was thick. After years of marriage to a man who never bothered concealing his disapproval of her while boldly lying to her face, the kindness of strangers in this gracious country made her watery.

With nothing but her clothing, and coins that the nurses had scraped together as a parting gift, Amarantha departed. After so many weeks of rest, she felt remarkably well, and beyond a single errand this morning, she had no plan, only information. The advantage of being forced to remain confined to bed for weeks was that she had had ample time to read through the hospital's cache of old newspapers kept for kindling. She now knew quite a lot about Gabriel Hume.

He had been in the Mediterranean Sea commanding

the *Theia* when his brother perished in an incident in Leith and, a month later, a longtime malady finally overcame his father.

He was indeed elusive—even reclusive.

He did not reside at Haiknayes Castle near Edinburgh, which had been empty for years.

He spent most of his time traveling, yet no one seemed to know to where. Some suggested Kallin, but that estate was sufficiently remote that no one had ever confirmed it.

He almost never went into society. Since inheriting the title, in fact, he had done so only once: in March, while Amarantha had been crossing the Atlantic, in Edinburgh he had briefly courted the beautiful heiress Lady Constance Read, but it had come to nothing.

And, finally, he had never denied any accusation leveled against him.

Two months ago—on the very same day strangers found Amarantha fevered and insensible, and brought her to the poor hospital—an Englishman had confessed to abducting the third missing girl, Miss Chloe Edwards, and to the murder of the fourth girl. Nevertheless, Edinburgh's newspapers continued to call Loch Irvine the Devil's Duke. After all, Maggie Poultney and Cassandra Finn were still missing, and the duke's house in Edinburgh had mysteriously burned to the ground on the night of Miss Edwards's rescue. While the villagers around that house insisted he had not been in residence for years, few heeded them. Most believed that the demonic duke had retreated to the countryside, where he was busy perfecting his mastery over the dark arts.

Setting off toward the toll road, Amarantha managed to walk halfway to her destination before she was obliged to rest. Continuing on more slowly, she was still a distance away when she fully understood what she was not seeing: his house.

She had one clear memory of the day eight weeks

earlier when she had fallen so ill: standing before the duke's house, staring up at its three stories of austere Palladian elegance and marveling at how the young man she once knew had, in five short years, gone from naval commander to duke to infamous villain.

Reading about the fire had not prepared her for this.

Charred and black, the stone foundations arose from the grass and moss that had already grown up around them like huge fingers of tar from some underground well. The little village huddled forlornly now, even in the sunshine.

Amarantha's heart beat unevenly. It seemed not months but a lifetime ago when she had left Mrs. Eagan's house with a wide smile, thrilled that the world believed him to be a villain.

What did the world believe her to be now? A poor woman, alone and friendless? Certainly not the daughter of a wealthy earl or the widow of a righteous missionary.

No one. She was no one. She had been gone from home for so long, they all probably thought her dead. No one would even know if at this moment she simply ceased to exist.

After Paul's death she had sought anonymity. She had *needed* it—needed to no longer be the woman she had tried so hard to transform herself into, all to suit him. She had needed to be someone else, even no one else.

Now she truly was anonymous, an island, bound to none.

Walking toward the shops, she found all but two locked. At the door of the blacksmith's, a burly, elderly man with reddened skin opened to her knock.

"Well now, lass," he said with a meaty smile that tightened Amarantha's throat for the second time that morning. "You be a sight for old eyes."

"Good day, sir. I have come to thank you."

"Seeing you hale be thanks enough. You gave me an' the wifie a powerful fright."

"I am sorry that I put you to the trouble of rescuing

me, and of paying the hospital to keep me." She reached into her pocket and pulled forth the coins that the nurses had given her.

"Keep your money, lass. The wifie's been fretting for weeks that we didna take you in ourselves and nurse you back to health. But our daughter was in childbed, an' Bess was needed in the country."

"Oh! Have you a grandchild now?"

"Aye, the eighth! Now, come inside for a dram o' tea. Bess just finished the baking an' she'll be glad to see you."

"Your wife is the baker in this village?"

"She's been baking for the dukes o' Loch Irvine since she were a wee one." With a glance at the field of ashes, he made a big exhalation through his nostrils like a horse. "Come. There be cakes just out o' the oven."

Inside, a fire blazed. A woman entered with a bakery tray.

"Lass!" she exclaimed, dropped the tray on a table, and enveloped Amarantha in an ample embrace. When she finally put her to arm's length, she gave Amarantha a long study. Gray haired, with light Scottish skin, she had a kind face. "'Tis a miracle! When we found you in the rain behind the shop, you were in such a fever Angus here could o' forged iron upon your brow!"

"I don't remember any of it. In truth, I don't even remember either of you. The nurses told me about you, and I have come to thank you."

"There be a fine lass, aye, Angus? But I knew it: apologizing to us for the trouble as you burned up in the wagon on the way to the infirmary. The manners o' an angel. Now, we'll have a cuppa an' you'll tell us all about what brought you to the village as poorly as you were that day." She drew her toward a chair at the table.

"What beautiful cakes," Amarantha exclaimed.

"Fit for a duke." The blacksmith spooned tea leaves into a pot.

"Have you customers here? Still?"

"No, lass," the baker said. "The duke's no' lived in the house for years, even afore the fire."

It was confirmation of the police's conclusions, despite what others believed.

"How Angus an' I miss the ol' days," Bess said with a cheerful sigh.

"Did you know him?"

"His Grace? Aye." She set a cake on Amarantha's plate. "We'd suspected you did too." She settled at the table. "After the fire, an' with you wishing to speak to him . . ."

"Did I say that to you?"

"Dinna you remember, lass?"

"No. I remember walking here from Leith and arriving in this village so tired I could barely stand. Then nothing after that. But in the hospital I had dreams—many dreams that felt like memories."

Angus and Bess exchanged a glance.

"What brought you here that day, lass?" Bess said.

Amarantha looked into the baker's broad, honest face. Then she told them the truth.

"Do you know of any reason that my friend Penny would seek out the duke?"

"I dinna, lass." Bess's brow creased. "But those rumors o' the devil be a pack o' nonsense."

"Aye, nonsense," Angus echoed.

"The lad I knew afore he went to sea could ne'er be what they claim."

"Will you tell me about him?" Amarantha said, her hands warm around her teacup. "When he was a boy."

The baker set another cake on Amarantha's plate. "The young master were all skin and bones. You'd ne'er seen such a homely lad."

"Really?"

"Aye, a wee monster he were, with that heavy brow, an' those fine coats hanging on him like he'd no flesh, only shadows between his big bones."

"I understand that he is quite handsome now," she said,

pleasure stealing through her that she no longer bothered to quell.

"He's a fine man now, lass." Bess clucked her tongue. "But too alone."

"He was not always so alone?"

"No. In those days, Her Grace took him about with her everywhere, to the parks an' museums an' to see all the great ships at Leith. An' to church, o' course. The old duke were oftentimes at his studies, you see. But when he weren't, there'd be parties like festivals, with music an' dancing an' all the grand ladies an' gentlemen in finery."

Like her parents' parties at Willows Hall.

She had always thought them so unalike: he a dangerous man of the world who had done violence and reveled in earthly pleasures; she an ignorant girl who had never studied and knew nothing about anything, even about the righteous missionary life into which she had thrown herself.

But she had never actually been that woman—not really.

"It all sounds marvelous," she said.

"You've ne'er seen the like, lass," Bess said.

By the hearth, the old blacksmith had folded his hands over his belly and his snores competed with the crackling flames. Amarantha took up the teapot and refilled the baker's cup.

"I adore hearing about parties," she said. "Do tell me every little detail."

As the sun fell, the couple invited her to take dinner with them and, later, to stay the night. The following morning, as Amarantha tied her hat ribbon, Angus appeared leading a horse. These days they had little use for the animal, he said, and she might put in a good word for them with the duke if she were so inclined. For, Bess added, it was clear that she was setting off for Kallin, and an honorable man like their master would never ignore the wishes of a lady.

August 1822
Central Highlands, Scotland

When Amarantha found the Allaways' farm, dusk was falling. As she tethered her horse, a pair of dogs rushed forward, barking. She offered her hands for them to smell and waited for their cavorting to cease, straining against her impatience.

From Edinburgh all the way to the mountains that bordered Loch Lomond, she had found traces of Penny's journey—consistently toward Kallin. But three days earlier she had lost Penny's trail. This morning her hosts told her that she might retrace the road to where a narrow path along a tributary creek led to a hidden farm. This farm.

Tucked into a crevice of a hill dipping toward the Fyne, and accompanied by two sturdy outbuildings, the stone and timber cottage with cheerful draperies peeking through the windows looked welcoming, exactly the sort of house Penny would find.

The door jerked open.

"Doctor—" The man's face was red and his farmer's shirt and trousers stained with drops of blood. "Did the doctor send you, lass?"

"No. I am seeking a traveler who might have come this way. But I have some medical skills. May I help until the doctor arrives?"

His eyes seemed to take her in now, her hair and her face. "Be you English?"

Her heart turned over. "Yes. Is my friend Penelope Baker here?"

He opened the door wide. "Come now, quickly, lass."

Inside, a fire crackled in the hearth and the place was clean. Through a doorway Amarantha could see a bed and a woman's prone form.

"Penny."

Penny's eyes twitched open. They were not the shimmering amber that had always danced with liveliness when Amarantha had needed levity most, but dull and shot across with red. Now they filled with tears.

Amarantha lowered herself to the chair and found Penny's hand on the coverlet. She grasped it, but no pressure returned hers; the usually strong, lithe fingers of a woman who had labored every day of her life were limp and cold. Her skin was not warm golden brown, but the color of dust, and lay listlessly over her features. There was blood on the quilt tucked up beneath her chin.

Amarantha had seen women like this before. In an instant she understood.

Gently cupping Penny's cheek, she swallowed back the sob clinging to her throat.

"You needn't fear. All will be well."

A tear crested Penny's eye and her lips cracked open. But she did not speak.

"Now, dear, strong friend," Amarantha said, "I must have one final confidence from you." Curling both of her hands around Penny's fingers, pain pressing at her ribs like nothing she had ever felt before, she said, "Give me his name."

AMARANTHA CLOSED THE bedchamber door. Mrs. Allaway sat in a rocking chair before the hearth. The cozy little room glowed with lamps and smelled of fresh bread.

"She is gone." The words sounded tinny to Amarantha's ears.

"May the angels take her into their care."

Amarantha finally allowed her gaze to dip to the bundle in the Scotswoman's arms. Tugging apart the clean swaddling, Mrs. Allaway revealed a tiny nose, miniature pink lips, two tightly closed eyes, and a fluff of silky hair.

"This be Luke, miss."

"Luke," Amarantha whispered.

"A fine, strong lad he already be. His mother suckled

him thrice before the bleeding stole her strength, but he took to it quick. I told her since my youngest went off the teat only Thursday, this lad's come just in time. Mother an' son had a nice long look into each other's eyes."

Penny's son came into her arms as so many infants had in five years—the children of patients at the hospital and of her husband's parishioners. And Amarantha's own tiny son, her perfect gift from heaven who had never suckled and whose eyes had never opened, whom she had held for a few precious minutes before he left her.

If Heaven did exist, Penny was there now, cradling Amarantha's son.

Tracing Luke's little features with her gaze, Amarantha spoke the promise that had given her friend the peace she needed to slip away.

"I will find your father, Luke. I will not rest until I do."

Chapter 12

The Dream

September 1822
Castle Kallin
Glen Irvine, Scotland

"I tried, Your Grace."

The girl standing before Gabriel was little more than a child. But the pleats across her pink brow beneath the lemon plaits of her hair and the crisp cap were those of a woman with far too many cares.

"I commend you on the attempt, Miss Finn."

"She attempted it four times, Your Grace," came a sharp voice at his side.

"Aye. As your letter helpfully informed me, Miss Pike."

"On the second attempt Cassandra swooned. But she tried it twice more."

He glanced at the woman standing by his elbow, the entire top of whose head of close-cropped hair he could see from above. Pike craned her neck, and serious brown eyes set in a pale brown face met his with impressive impassivity.

"Miss Finn showed fortitude," he said. "Fear o' heights is nothing to scorn."

Now Pike's brow knit too. "I would have completed the repair of the roof myself if—"

"If no' for the splint holding your leg together at present."

"Your Grace." She seemed to snip the words.

Gabriel drew in a slow breath.

"I'm no' chastising you for falling through the rotted floor o' the attic an' breaking your leg, Miss Pike," he said. "Indeed, as they're my attic an' my rotten floor, I beg your forgiveness for the incident."

"Maggie made an attempt as well," Cassandra said. "But she couldna grip the trellis ladder securely enough."

Good God.

"While you were inspecting the roof, Your Grace," Pike said, "a message arrived from the Solstice."

"What does Mrs. Tarry have to say?" he said.

"It was marked to you confidentially. I will fetch it now." Despite the splint, Pike departed silently, as all exemplary footmen did.

He returned his attention to the twenty-year-old Edinburgh lass who, a year earlier, had taken it upon herself to join the little colony that resided in his house.

Buried deep in a ten-mile-long glen with towering peaks on its northern end and easily defensible flats on its southern, Kallin was the ideal retreat for people desperate to hide from the world. He often mused that his rapscallion friend, Torquil Sterling, had chosen him for this project primarily because of Kallin's remote location and only secondarily because of Gabriel's ability to captain a ship across an ocean without anyone catching up to him.

"Now, Miss Finn," he said, moving to his desk. "Give me your report o' matters here."

She sat down across from him silently. The members of this household all had the uncanny ability to make no sound when they moved, which—he supposed—had been a useful skill for most of them before they had fled their previous residences.

"Feel free to omit any mention o' the roof." He removed the stopper from the inkpot and took up a pen. "I've heard as much as I care to about this damn roof—I beg your pardon, Miss Finn—about this blast roof." He dipped the pen into the pot.

"Aye, Your Grace," she said, folding her hands on her lap. "Aside from the roof—"

"Roof silence, Miss Finn." He upended the pot and knocked it on the ledger. Flakes of dried ink peppered the page. "What in the dev—where's the ink?" He dug in the desk drawers.

"Aside from the leaks in the roof, Your Grace—"

He forbore growling.

"—we've a shortage of basic supplies—"

"Such as writing ink?"

"—such as tea, coffee, sugar, polish, rope, firewood—"

"Firewood? There are woodlands up an' down the length of the glen."

"—laying hens, candles, lamp oil, lye, paint, glue, paper, an' writing ink. Molly also has a list o' needs from the distillery."

"Does she?" It was less question than sigh.

"Plum's been harvesting herbs and roots down at the village."

"Well, there's something."

"But we're short on salt. An' pickling spices. We also lack a suitable harness for the oxen."

"*Oxen*? When did you purchase oxen?"

"Molly traded five barrels of gin at Inveraray last month."

He narrowed his eyes. "Did she?"

"She didna tell you that last spring she an' Maggie were making gin, did she?"

"She neglected to share that wee bit o' information in the twenty-three—or perhaps 'twas an even two dozen letters the two o' you sent to me last March alone." He stood up as the study door opened. "Ah, Miss Poultney, I've just been hearing about the experiments with gut-rotting brew that you an' the mistress o' my distillery have been making there, despite my instructions to the contrary."

"Good day, Your Grace." The taking little brunette with skin as white as a porcelain teacup dropped a ridiculously deep curtsy for a woman mere days away from bringing a child into the world. "How be the roof?" She had the audacity to dimple up.

Inhaling slowly through his nostrils—a calming technique he had learned to do before battle—he turned again to Cassandra.

"Anything more, Miss Finn?"

"We're about to have a shortage o' linens."

"You wrote to me about a storage chest full o' bed linens that you discovered recently, aye?" *So many letters.* Their concern for apprising him of the use of his land and money was relentless.

"These be other sorts o' linens."

He tilted his head forward in question.

"Feminine undergarments, Your Grace." Her cheeks were now red, but her gaze did not waver. A better man he could not pay to do the work of land steward that Cassandra Finn did for no more than his promise that he would never, ever tell her father where she had gone.

"Hm," he said. "I suppose that is what I deserve for asking details."

Both girls were blushing now. Not for the first time he wondered whether any of Kallin's residents were aware of the man he had been until five years earlier. If so, they were remarkably discreet about it.

"We're also short o' nappies," Cassandra said.

He made the mistake of glancing at Maggie. Hands resting atop her belly, she was grinning.

"Dinna look to me!" She giggled. "Yet."

"Rebecca is helping at the Solstice three nights out o' seven, with her wee one, o' course," Cassandra explained. "She's been keeping linens both here an' there."

"I see." He moved around the desk. "Purchase whatever the house needs, Miss Finn."

She followed him toward the door. "Mr. Du Lac wrote that funds from the insurance on the Edinburgh house are finally at the bank in Inveraray."

Xavier had written directly to Cassandra? Interesting. Either she had become far more capable than even Gabriel knew, or his partner in Portsmouth wished to spare him further conversation about the pile of ashes in Edinburgh. Or both.

Good man. Good woman.

"I'll drive to Inveraray as soon as I have seen to the roof. Till then, buy the hens on credit, an' anything else needed."

"An' the firewood?"

"Woodlands," he said, gesturing toward the window. "Acres an' acres o' woodlands."

"Pike usually does the chopping, Your Grace."

Judas.

This girl—his land steward—was so young, so damnably young. So were all the others who kept this estate functioning. Yet they were still older than a girl he had once known, a girl who had thrown herself across an ocean and into a foreign land, and had not balked for even a moment when the world demanded of her what she had never given before.

A girl who still haunted his dreams.

"Are you telling me that we are shorthanded, Miss Finn?"

"Aye, Your Grace. With Plum gone to work for Mrs. Tarry in the village, an' Sophie sewing morning, noon, an' night to supply the shops begging for her gowns at Inveraray an' Oban, 'tis all Rebecca can do to cook an' clean an' assist Pike now that her leg—"

He held up his hand. "All right." He reached around Maggie and opened the door wide. "I will chop the wood."

Cassandra gasped. "You canna *chop wood*, Your Grace."

"I can. Now, go about your business—my business, that is." He offered her the scoundrel's grin that had once charmed females from Dover to Tobago.

With a rare ghost of a smile, she departed.

He returned his attention to the second of the two Scotswomen who had disappeared from Edinburgh and, in leaving her bloodied cloak behind, established his reputation as a monster.

"Miss Poultney," he said firmly.

"Your Grace," she said sweetly. "I—"

"Hush."

She bit her lips together.

"I understand that you an' my Master Blender, Miss Cromwell—on behalf o' whom I paid *gold* to apprentice for ten months with a Master Blender on no other isle than Islay where, Miss Poultney, the gods have blessed the distilleries with peat an' precious spring waters an' all sorts o' other magicks so that the sacred barrels may offer up malted ambrosia fit for kings—you an' she, I understand, are making *pig swill* on my land. In my distillery." The distillery he and Du Lac had constructed with their own hands. "Without my permission," he added.

Her grin widened. "Aye, Your Grace."

"Stow the dimples, Miss Poultney. I am furious with the two o' you, an' with Monsieur Du Lac for apparently approving it."

She blinked a few times. "You're keeping cool for being furious."

"I commanded a fifty-six-gun frigate for His Majesty King George, missy. I'm no' a man to fly off the handle." He attempted a slight loom. "That doesna mean I *canna*."

"Aye, sir."

"If you waste the barrels, which didna come cheaply, an' the labor, which is scarce, on fermenting bitter juniper berries for drunkards," he ground out, "there will *be* no malted ambrosia to sell to kings in several years an' make the fortune o' this estate, Miss Poultney."

"Gin be a quick cash crop, Your Grace."

"I understand the reasoning behind it." They were impatient for Kallin to bring in income. By the time he had left his family's estates at age thirteen his father's steward had taught him plenty about the patience required to husband the land. At sea those lessons in patience had served him well.

The problem was that his estate was in the hands of children. But he had been a child when he had achieved the rank of officer in His Majesty's Blue. And he'd been given the charge of much more than whiskey barrels and sheep.

Yet there was no denying that the women of Kallin were already performing miracles.

"Where is Miss Cromwell?"

"In the distillery, hiding behind the chemistry table."

He lifted a brow.

Maggie's dimples reappeared. "Pacing."

"Tell her I will speak with her when I've finished patching up the roof. Tomorrow."

"'Tis fixing to snow."

"Aye." He would have to make quick work of the repairs. Roofs and ice did not mix well, and these women did not need a man with a broken back laid up in this house all winter. Even when he was here briefly, as now, they barely tolerated him. "Now off with you, lass. An' no more climbing up trellis ladders, do you hear me? No' till after the wee one comes."

He should start searching for a medical man—a *female* medical man, if one could be found. As yet only three women had sought sanctuary at Kallin while with child. But more could come.

"Lass."

Maggie paused and turned curious eyes up at him.

"There are men aplenty in this countryside looking for work." Veterans, traveling laborers, boys who had watched their fathers march off to fight Napoleon who, now grown to manhood, had no war or other prospects. And Kallin needed workers.

Maggie said nothing, which for her was the wrong kind of miraculous occurrence.

"No?" he prodded.

"You'd best be asking Cassie, Your Grace."

"She would say no, wouldn't she?"

Maggie nodded.

"All right. Be gone."

Kallin's footman came forward propelling herself now with a shillelagh tucked beneath her arm.

Gabriel recognized the walking stick. Seamus Boyle, *Theia*'s surgeon during the three years Gabriel had commanded the frigate, had given him the shillelagh as a gift for his premature departure from the navy, a jest about his youth upon retirement.

Now, *there* was a medical man he wouldn't welcome within leagues of Kallin, an exceptional sawbones but a philanderer of the worst sort. Gabriel had gone to that hospital in Kingston the first few times simply to make certain Boyle was not propositioning the nurses and female patients.

No. That was a lie. One of the old lies he'd told himself for five years.

He had gone to that hospital for the girl. Again and again.

Pike proffered the promised message from Mary Tarry.

"'Tis a fine crutch, Pike."

"I found it in the attic."

"Before the floor caved in, I guess. Serendipitously."

Her lips remained a line.

"If you have any needs from Inveraray," he said, "add them to the shopping list Miss Finn is writing up—without, apparently, any ink."

"We make do," she said shortly.

"Aye. I know, lass," he said.

"If you don't like me using this stick, I'll find another in the woods."

"'Tis yours, Pike," he said, leaving off the title, as she had asked him when they had first met. He ignored the instruction whenever others were near. But in private he honored it, though he had no idea why she had made it. Every one of the residents of Kallin had secrets.

"Will that be all, Your Grace?"

He waved her away and snapped open the seal on the letter, glancing up to watch the girl's uneven progress toward the front of the house. These women were doing their best with the slimmest resources. He could only marvel at their tenacity and resilience.

Still, they would be the death of him.

In two years he had never so much longed for the cigar smoke-filled masculine retreat of the *Theia*'s wardroom, where his officers drank brandy and on occasion traded ribald stories. They had always halted those stories the moment he entered the room. A captain was master of his officers, never one of them.

His days on the *Fairway*, when he had still been one of the lads clamping his lips shut as his captain strolled into the wardroom, hiding laughter behind discipline, were some of his finest memories. His happiest.

He wondered if Pike smoked cigars, or whether the footman's breeches and coat she preferred were the limit of her tolerance for the male sex. Probably. Of all the residents of Kallin, Pike had come from the worst circumstance: abused daily, and at least two pregnancies ended by her rapacious master's fist to her belly. Small wonder she would rather break her own bones keeping the house habitable than allow a man near the place.

But she had survived. Through her own intelligence and ingenuity—and Torquil Sterling's network of accomplices in the West Indies, England, and Scotland—she had escaped and somehow reached Leith.

He ran his palm over his face and focused on Mary Tarry's writing. It was like the writer herself: firm, strong, competent. Wise and thoroughly no-nonsense, the daughter of Kallin's old butler and housekeeper had been Gabriel's first choice as keeper of the Solstice Inn. He had barely begun to explain what he needed when she accepted. Within six months she had restored the inn on the east-west road at the base of Glen Irvine, making it a welcome retreat for weary travelers and a moneymaker.

Every one of the women in Glen Village was loyal to her, and therefore to him.

Your Grace,

A young Englishwoman, Anne Foster, has come to the village—to stay, it seems. I've given her work at the tea shop. She sleeps at the Solstice. She has not asked for sanctuary, and seems content sitting in the corner of the kitchen writing in a notebook.

Perhaps this Anne Foster had extra ink. Or a pencil, for that matter.

She is asking questions about you—both of you and the Devil's Duke. I've told her you are not in residence. Still, she means to walk up the glen to have a glimpse of the house.

M.T.

He tossed the note atop the grate. If Mrs. Tarry had any idea how many people regularly poked about his properties, from Haiknayes to his ships berthed at Leith, she would not bother writing to him about one traveler's curiosity.

If this Anne Foster had not asked for sanctuary and was not wearing the Haiknayes star—the badge Tor had insisted would help identify women seeking sanctuary—she had no need of Kallin. He wasn't worried. The little community at Kallin and in Glen Village had managed to hide its purpose for more than two years already. One lone female would not unmask the Devil's Duke.

As he closed the ledger that Cassandra Finn carefully kept, the sun was dipping toward the hills across the river. He had time to *begin* the roof repairs.

Or chop wood.

Out in the cold he blew frosted air, bound his tartan more firmly around his neck, and hefted the axe. Logs from an ancient evergreen lay about the yard. From within the stable, the sound of an ox's snort came softly into the dusk. The river, gurgling on its way to the rapids farther downstream, was the only other sound. Even the dogs Pike kept to frighten away fox had retreated inside to warm themselves by the fire.

The stillness was sublime, like the mizzen watch on a winter night on the Sargasso—only without the creaking rigging and his bosun's snores emanating from belowdecks like a foghorn.

Nearby a rooster offered a pathetic crow.

"Poor bastard," he mumbled. "If you were a hen, they'd have use for you. But your days are numbered, laddie. Shame you canna chop wood an' repair a roof."

Now he was talking to chickens. Somewhere up there in the heavens, that rogue Torquil was splitting his sides laughing.

Smiling, Gabriel hauled a log onto the chopping block and brought the axe down.

SNOW CAME OVERNIGHT. After meeting with Kallin's Master Blender, Gabriel tugged a wide-brimmed hat over his brow, gathered tools, and climbed to the roof. Setting his boots firmly at the apex, he surveyed his domain.

The world glittered brilliantly: golden sun, azure sky, silver river, milky fields, and forests of the darkest fir stretching up the hills on either flank of the glen and tipped with snow. On the Irvine's opposite bank, a dozen deer stood out against the white, unworried about predators in this frozen paradise.

Days, weeks, months had passed in the past two years during which he had wished his father still alive, even his wretched brother, and himself standing beneath full sails on a cresting sea. But this—this heaven on earth—he could not be unhappy that this was his.

Kallin needed money. The insurance from the Edinburgh house inferno would help. The fine malt aging in the long shed would eventually secure the estate's prosperity. In the meantime, the women were indeed making do. In Portsmouth, Xavier was seeing to investments. All was well.

Gabriel drew a tunnel of frigid air into his lungs and released it slowly. For the first time since he had left the sea behind, he was content.

The temperature had risen since dawn and water ran in rivulets all down the myriad sloping roofs of the house. He pulled a tool from his belt and pried the offending tiles loose.

He was hammering a nail into a chipped tile when an uncomfortable tingle skittered up the back of his neck. *Damn wood chopping.* Setting the hammer down and reaching up to rub at the complaining muscles, he turned his head and saw her.

Everything—running water, crackling snow, his heartbeats—halted.

It was not every day that a man saw a dream materialize

before him. In Gabriel's experience, it had only happened on one other day in his life.

This time, like a faery out of ancient legend she stood on the hillside in snow up to her ankles, skirts whipping in the wind, hood thrown back to let loose wild tresses of mingled sunshine and fire.

He almost fell off the roof.

Grabbing the first thing that his hand hit, he gripped tight and dug his heels into broken slate.

Here she was. On his land. *She*. Not a trick of the light on gleaming snow. Not another woman of similar appearance to mistake for her at this distance, as he had done time and again in five years.

But she.

An English girl has come to the village . . . she is asking questions.

Anne Foster. Anne: her sister Emily's second name. Foster: her mother's family name.

A false name. Hiding in plain sight. *From him?* Who else could she possibly know in this remote corner of the world? This simply could not be an accidental trespassing.

Of all the curious spectators to his life, never in a thousand years had he expected to see Amarantha Vale here—or on any property he owned.

Below, Pike's dogs catapulted out of the house, vaulted over the fences, and flew across the field, barking madly and tearing up the hill straight for her.

He did not call off the dogs. Believed by Britons from Edinburgh to London to be a diabolical abductor of helpless maidens, and satisfied enough to be acknowledged as such, he considered the useful effects that a quartet of slavering, ebony whelps running breakneck across the slope would have on the delicate sensibilities of an Englishwoman. Also, of course, there would be the effects of the stories she would subsequently tell of this harrowing encounter, which were bound to be taken up by gossips and ensure his continued privacy and the privacy of the residents of Glen Irvine. It had been months since mention of the Devil's Duke had appeared in any paper. Fresh rumors would serve him well.

He failed, however, to consider the peculiarities of this particular Englishwoman: she was neither a maiden, which he had learned in the most painful manner possible, nor helpless, which he had learned without suffering any pain whatsoever—rather the opposite.

She remained still as the dogs greeted her like long-lost friends. Gathering about her with joyful leaps, sniffing her outstretched crimson mittens and wagging their tails, the turncoats showed themselves no more immune to her natural allure than Gabriel had been five years earlier.

At that time, however, he had not yet become the Devil's Duke. And the Devil had a reputation to uphold.

Lifting his fingers to his mouth, he let fly a whistle that could be heard above cannon roar; it pierced the wintery wind and reached the dogs' ears. As one, they broke from her and careened back across the snowy valley toward the house.

She shouted into the wind. He saw her throat stretch, her hand swipe the tresses from before her face, and her lips move—lips about which he had dreamed many frustrated dreams. But he heard nothing; the wind was far too strong.

This was idiocy, remaining here staring across the hillside, without moving. But concern for those in his protection and an equally powerful instinct for self-preservation prevented him from acknowledging her now. With the sun at his back, the brim of the hat shaded his face. She could have no idea that the master of Kallin, the duke himself, was playing handyman on the roof of his house.

She shouted again.

"Mary Tarry believes you are an urisk!" came to him over the frosty slope, barely audible and swiftly whisked away by the wind. Still it was her voice, the voice he had dreamed about like he had dreamed about her lips: vividly, repeatedly, for too many months before he had finally wiped the memory of her from his senses. *Unsuccessfully.* Invariably the memory of her returned whenever he was very tired, very drunk, or—damnably—very angry.

Now he did not reply. What could he reply? That if urisks had hearts that pounded like kettledrums, then certainly at this moment he might be one of those solitary, curmudgeonly creatures of legend.

Anyway, if he shouted the sound would not reach her; he was downwind. *Fortunate*, although not accidental. Centuries earlier the house had been situated with attention to the patterns of wind through the glen, to give its inhabitants ample warning of invaders approaching over the hills without giving the invaders the opposite courtesy. Thank God for his ancestors' strategic wisdom.

She remained with her hands at her sides, cloak billowing, and he thought—*he knew*—that this was simply another punishment for having misspent his youth so vilely. It seemed he would never be finished atoning.

Then she laughed.

Intoxicating laughter.

He must end this now. This was not, after all, a suitable time to make good on the agreement he had made aboard his ship in the midst of a storm: his pact with the devil.

That pact had seemed a wise choice in the moment. Seeing her now, here, however, it was eminently clear to Gabriel that the particular terms of that deal had been very poorly chosen.

Judas, his chest hurt.

Turning his back to the hillside, he took up the hammer, reaffixed the slate in its rightful spot, and drove a nail into the peg attachment. Another nail followed—unnecessarily—and yet another, until the thing was so well fixed in place that not even a tornado would wrest it free. Then he did the same with another tile. And another. And another.

For the next hour he did not so much as tilt his head to either side.

By the time he stuffed the tools back into his belt and finally allowed himself a quick glance at the hill, there was nothing there but snow and a lone black stream running from a crevice in the hill downward.

Excellent. Excellent.

He climbed down the ladder and into the dry warmth of the house and took the stairs to the ground floor two at a time. In the drawing room the dogs picked themselves up from before the hearth and circled him.

"Disloyal mongrels," he muttered.

An ancient chamber that had not been updated since his grandfather's time, it boasted comfortable furniture, thick tapestries, and a few paintings of former lairds of Kallin, each whiskered duke wrapped in tartan and bearing arms. Here and there were hints of the house's current residents: a book of poetry on a side table, a shawl draped over a chair, a sewing bag tucked into the corner of the sofa, and a cat lolling on a cushion.

He bent down and snapped open the door to the sideboard.

The cabinet was empty. Entirely empty. No brandy. No whiskey. Not even any gin.

"May I assist Your Grace?" Pike said from the doorway.

"No."

In the top cabinet his mother had kept vases. Desperate, he opened it anyway. Bottles gleamed within. He grabbed the cognac.

"Rebecca's little one, Clementine, has started to crawl," his footman said, apparently apropos of nothing.

"Did anyone call at the house while I was up on the roof?"

"A red-haired stranger stood on the south hill for a

bit. But she left without coming to the house. The gates around the pastures are always locked, as is the gate at the wall. Shall I inquire after her at the vill—"

"*No*. No stranger may come into this house or the yard or anywhere near. As per my usual order." He peered down at his toes and then at the empty bottom cabinet.

Rebecca's little one has started to crawl.

He swallowed the remainder of the spirits. He was colossally unfit to be the guardian of a group of young women and infants. He needed to return to Leith as soon as possible. Or London. Or Bristol. Dover. Anywhere but here. Find investors, potential partners. Let this odd little family trundle along with their overlord at a safe distance of eighty or two hundred miles away.

But first, he must get rid of a curious Englishwoman.

That old swell of infuriated pride was overtaking him, followed swiftly by the old familiar pain. He welcomed neither.

Mary Tarry seemed to have no idea that the new arrival was the daughter of a nobleman. Which meant that if he contacted her family and invited them to Kallin, she would have no choice but to reveal herself. But he could not invite anyone to Kallin without risking all, especially not the sort of gay socialites he understood the Earl and Countess of Vale to be.

Her elder sister, Emily, was another sort of woman altogether, a bluestocking who lived alone in London. How would she respond to the news that her sister was living under a false name in a Scottish village?

He would write to Emily Vale—anonymously—and bid her come fetch her sister.

Filling the glass anew, he threw back the dram. But no quantity of spirits could erase the images he conjured now—not of a pretty girl whose plentiful freckles and snapping eyes and unguarded tongue had entranced him. Rather, the image of the horror that his words had inspired the night he discovered she had married.

He could not see her again. Ever.

Best to leave the past in the past, where she belonged.

AMARANTHA SUPPOSED THAT could have gone worse. The dogs could have actually attacked her.

Walking alongside the river back toward the village, boots sodden and nose numb, she watched her breaths plume in little clouds and stuffed her hands more deeply into her pockets. Even bathed in brilliant sunlight this northern land was chilly—

This land of hills and rivers so glorious they stole the frigid air from her lungs and made her dizzy.

This land of people so kind that she, a lone woman, had found welcome in every place she had sought rest.

This land in which her motherless nephew was welcomed into another family's home as though he were one of their own.

This land of breathtaking beauty and generosity.

This land in which her quarry was impossible to run to ground.

She had *thought* it was he on the roof. His shoulders, the very manner in which he moved, even the way he raised the hammer—the man on the roof had seemed so *familiar*—as though he were the man she had watched so closely, so hungrily, in that other time and place far from this reality.

Apparently not.

Or the man on the roof was in fact the Duke of Loch Irvine, and he did not recognize her.

She did not know which prospect disconcerted her more: that she had traveled so far to find the duke, only to be told in the village he was not in residence at the castle and, when she made the two-mile walk in the snow anyway, to be met with locked gates and dogs; or that the man she had once been in love with did not remember her after only five years. Both were maddening.

The people of Glen Village must know something of

their overlord, even if they seemed reticent to speak of him. She would remain in the village and continue to ask questions until someone answered them. The Solstice Inn was wonderfully warm and comfortable, and the trade Mary Tarry had made with her was ideal: work at the tea shop for a cot at the top of the house and a corner of the kitchen when she was not working.

And she was weary. Weary of the journey. Weary of making friends only to swiftly lose them. Weary of being alone.

The river to her right, sparkling in the setting sun, rippled and bubbled comfortingly. Along the narrow road layered with snow, the stark trunks of birches and dark evergreen boughs and the tiny streams rushing down the hillside toward the river spoke to her of elves and faeries, of trolls and all the other creatures that had populated her childhood: her fondest friends besides Emily.

Now thanks to Mary Tarry she knew of another creature: the Scottish urisk.

Paul had told her that fantastical creatures had no place in a woman's imagination. *Imagination* had no place in a woman. Only virtue.

She wondered if the man on the roof believed in urisks, or if he had simply thought her a madwoman, standing on that hill, shouting into the wind.

Smiling, she tucked her hood more closely about her face and her steps were so light that her feet barely made marks in the snow.

Chapter 13

Luck & Strategy

To: Lady Emily Vale

London, England

My lady,

Your sister is in Scotland and in need of your help. At dawn on the morning of All Saints' Day, come to the south gate of Castle Kallin and you will be reunited with her.

—A Friend

1 November 1822
The Solstice Inn
Glen Village, Scotland

Emmie,

How good you are to have come for me!! How wonderful to embrace you yesterday!! I am sorry that my silence since sailing from Jamaica caused you distress! And I am deeply curious to know who sent to you that anonymous note, for I have told no one here my real name. That mystery, however, must wait. I must depart this place at once—before even you wake. I have more than a passing interest in the mystery of the Devil's Duke, and I have just learned that he rode from Kallin last evening to Edinburgh. Beloved sister, trust that I will be well, and that this time I will write to you!

—A.

10 November 1822
Allaway Farm

My lady,

The boy is healthy, happy, and growing. This is a fine family. They treat Luke as one of their own. They say the supplies you sent will make the winter like a festival. I will remain here with the infant. As promised, I will write to you regularly. I will know that you have held to your promise to me and have received this letter at the home of Lady Constance if you address your reply to me as: *Dear Patient and Wise Nathaniel.*

Your servant,
Nathaniel Hay

16 November 1822
Edinburgh, Scotland

Dear Patient, Wise (and Clever) Nathaniel,

Luck brought you and me to that posting house in Callander in the same hour on the same day.

*How grateful I am that you never ceased searching
for me! Here is proof that I have fulfilled the promise I made to you: a letter from the home of Lady
Constance and her husband in Edinburgh, where
I am staying in great comfort. Now, I beg of you:
more news of Luke!*

With gratitude,
A. Garland

17 November 1822
Willows Hall
Shropshire, England

My Precious Child!

How overjoyed I am to know finally that you are
safe and well!! Emily told us everything—how you
sailed to Scotland—to the Duke of Loch Irvine's
estate!—without a word to anyone—and we are
astonished!! (Your father, who is reading over my
shoulder, insists that he is not *astonished*, rather
positively *delighted* by your intrepidity.)

Now do come home. You have had your adventure in America, and in Scotland as well, and I am
certain that Lady Constance's cook does not make
pork medallions with gooseberries as well as Monsieur Ripon does at Willows Hall, although I have
no doubt her drawing room is luxurious.

Your return is expected daily by the suitors you
tossed aside when you preferred That Man. Mr.
Holt is the latest to profess himself smitten. His fortune is grand, but your father has no need of grand
fortunes, of course, and Mr. Holt is a mere Mister,
which you have already tried, to no good end. I
prefer Lord Mason and Lord Witherspoon, for they
are most handsome.

It is past time you remarry and provide your father with a grandson, whom he will take upon his knee and teach the method for tying a perfect Mathematical. Men do well with freckles, and your sisters have as yet produced only girls. For my part, I should like at least one granddaughter with your beautiful hair. How pretty your children will be! Hurry home, darling daughter.

Kisses,
Your Mother

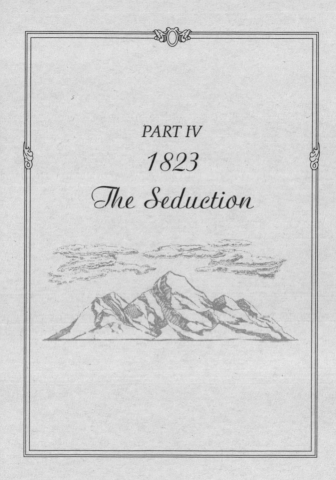

PART IV

1823

The Seduction

Chapter 14

A New Plan
(This Time Better)

18 January 1823
Port of Leith, Scotland

Dear Emmie,

I continue to await the Duke of Loch Irvine's arrival in Edinburgh. Some claim he has gone abroad, others that he hides at Haiknayes. My friend Sophie at Glen Village insists that he has not returned to Kallin since his abrupt departure the day you came for me. So I remain here. He cannot disappear forever.

Also, I cannot return home —possibly ever. Since you told Mama that I had gone to a duke's domain, her imagination has run away with her. She writes twice weekly extolling the virtues of this lord's new phaeton and that baronet's gold buttons. She *never approved of my first marriage, and I think she means to correct that history by throwing me at any lord who will accept me for my dowry. (I have long since suspected Paul married me to fund his mission, for he certainly did not choose me for my character.) I have written to Papa to tell him in no uncertain terms that the last thing I want is another husband (and that, since living in a society in which human beings are regularly traded for gold, I have no desire whatsoever for another dowry).*

To be closer to the docks where the duke berths his ships, I have moved from Constance and Saint's home in Edinburgh (where the newlyweds are deliriously happy) to the home of their dear friends Dr. Shaw and Libby in Leith. Here, as I await the duke, I have begun a modest writing project with a friend who has recently arrived from Jamaica. It is a memoir, but like few others . . .

March 1823
The Assembly Rooms
Port of Leith, Scotland

*A*marantha was not hiding.

Not any longer.

Not at least *monumentally* as Anne Foster, tea shop girl.

And not *precisely* hiding.

She just happened to be passing behind a potted palm when, from its other side, she heard her quarry's name uttered in an agitated hush. Not his actual name, the name that never failed to create a tickle of guilty pleasure in her stomach: Gabriel. Nor his family's name: Hume. Nor his title: Loch Irvine. Rather, the name everybody still seemed to prefer for him, despite the lack of disappearing maidens since the previous spring.

The assembly rooms were aglitter, chandeliers bathing all in a golden glow. Jewels twinkled, coy glances sparkled, and music spun temptingly through the night. She longed to dance; dancing had been one of her many joys that Paul had quashed.

But she had no time for frivolities now. Tonight she had come for gossip.

"The Devil's Duke, you say?" exclaimed the matron whose headdress sported a peacock feather that danced above the tips of the palm.

"The very one!" replied her companion, whose gown of pineapple pin-striped taffeta glared visibly through the fronds. "He has returned to Edinburgh, I tell you! I myself had a glimpse of him the other day on High Street. He rode a wild black stallion, huge and haughty for everybody to see."

"The man has no shame." The peacock feather quivered. "And with those two poor lasses still missing!"

"No doubt he's still got them chained up in his dungeons."

"And never saying a word to defend himself, as though he'd not a care that everybody thinks the worst of him!"

"They say he is still in need of a fortune to restore Haiknayes," Pineapple whispered ominously. "He will be looking for a bride again, mark my words."

This was news to Amarantha. She had thought Haiknayes was still locked up tight, as though the present duke cared nothing for his estate so close to Edinburgh.

"He'll not get his hands on *my* daughter!" Peacock said, aghast. "I shall lock her away myself before I will allow her within a mile of that devil."

For a moment Amarantha's thoughts were taken up with the memory of a young naval officer's hand, large and strong, *on her.*

"And that isn't all," said Pineapple in horrified accents. "They say he has hired a house here in Leith!"

Amarantha's heart did a turnabout. This was excellent news. If he were here, Dr. Shaw would certainly call on him.

While living with Constance and Saint in Edinburgh, at whose home Dr. John Shaw and his daughter, Elizabeth, were regular visitors, Amarantha had learned that during the previous spring the Duke of Loch Irvine had in fact spent more time in the company of young Libby and the doctor than he had courting Constance. It seemed he was as unusual as ever.

Now he was *in Leith*. The end of her long quest was in sight. She felt downright giddy.

"Don't tell me you are hiding, Mrs. Garland," came a pleasant voice at her shoulder. "I refuse to believe that you are shy."

She swiveled to meet the familiar crisp blue gaze of Thomas Bellarmine. Cousin to Amarantha and Libby's fondest acquaintances in Leith, he called regularly at the Shaw's house.

"Oh, I am not hiding, Mr. Bellarmine. I am eavesdropping." Honesty was her new life's plan: no more false identities, no more subterfuge, and no lies—not even little lies—not since she discovered Emily had been so desperately worried that she had traveled the length of England and half of Scotland to find her. That she had distressed Emily as thoroughly as Penny's disappearance had distressed *her* made her the worst sort of hypocrite.

Henceforth, even though the object of her pursuit lived in shadowy mystery, she would go forward openly and honestly.

"How shocking, madam." Mr. Bellarmine's conspiratorial grin made him handsome. "Have you heard anything of particular interest?"

"They," she said, gesturing toward the plant, "are discussing the return to town of the Duke of Loch Irvine."

"The Devil's Duke? Aha. Excellent fodder for gossip, of course."

"Do you believe the gossip?"

"It is a curious conundrum, in truth. One cannot deny that he is a mysterious character. But I once did business for my uncle with Loch Irvine's agent in Portsmouth, a Mr. Du Lac. Most unassuming fellow you would ever meet. French West Indian, I believe, which was a curiosity, to be sure. An honest man, though. I cannot imagine him working for a villain. Have the rumors intrigued *you*?"

"No." They made her more eager than ever to discover if anything remained in him of the young man she had known.

"I have heard ladies admire darkly dangerous men," Mr. Bellarmine said.

"I suppose some ladies might." If they were young, naïve, and impetuous. "The music is delightful tonight, isn't it?"

"Aha: a swift change in subject. I will gallantly reply, yes, positively delightful. It makes a man want to ask the loveliest woman in the place to dance. Will you do me the honor?"

"Thank you, sir. But I cannot—"

"I shan't take no for an answer, especially since as I approached you I noticed that your toe was tapping."

"Was it? How unguarded I am! I do want to dance—it's true." The good news was cause for celebration.

"Then dance you must, madam." He extended his arm. She accepted it.

As the patterns began, she looked over the ballgoers. To find an heiress bride, the duke might attend parties. High society in Leith was modest. But he must have reason to have hired a house here instead of in nearby Edinburgh. Invitations to parties arrived for her regularly now. She would meet him again, if not in Dr. Shaw's home then in some society matron's drawing room. It was as simple as that.

Her stomach spun with nerves. She wanted to laugh.

"—heard a word I've said just now," Mr. Bellarmine

said as the musicians played the final chords of the set. "How dispiriting to compose compliments and have them fall on deaf ears."

"Forgive me, sir. I am lost in thought tonight."

"I wonder what can you be thinking of. A gentleman, no doubt. Lucky bloke."

She blinked. "A gentleman?"

"I am not the only man here tonight to rejoice that you have put off your mourning black, Mrs. Garland. Who, I wonder, will have the honor of winning the fair lady's admiration?" His smile was friendly as he looked about the ballroom as though searching for the gentleman in question. "For correct me if I am mistaken, but you have come out this evening with suitors in mind, haven't you?"

"I have not."

His sandy brows rose.

"I am sorry to be obliged to correct you after all," she said. "Widowhood suits me."

"Madam, I admit myself astonished! You are—well, that is—you are so young. And lovely."

"Thank you, sir." She dipped a curtsy. "But I am happy in my present situation. I do not wish to change it." *Ever.* "Now, I have left Miss Shaw alone too long. Good evening," she said, probably too cheerfully, and made her way through ballgoers to the stairs.

Libby had retreated to the reading room upstairs almost as soon as they arrived. And Amarantha had learned what she had come to this ball to discover. They needn't remain longer, especially if nice young men would take from it the false idea that she wished to be courted.

She opened the reading room door into near darkness. It smelled of wood polish and the deep musty sweetness of books: the scent of her father's library at Willows Hall, and comforting.

A lamp on a table near the far end of the room lit the side of a tall wingback chair and, in that chair, a gentleman's shoulder, arm, and crossed legs. A book rested upon his knee, open. His hand glittered with a jewel as he turned the page.

In the rest of the dim room, no Libby stirred. But Amarantha had occasionally found the crowd-wary girl in unlit corners, on rooftops, and once hiding in a cabinet. She went forward.

"Libby? Are you here?"

The gentleman's hand paused with the page half turned.

Amarantha raised her voice. "I beg pardon for disturbing you, sir. I am searching for a friend. Have you seen a young lady in this room tonight?"

With hands that seemed incongruously strong around a mere book, he closed the volume and laid it on the table. Unfolding himself, he arose from the chair and faced her.

Amarantha's lungs seized up then plunged into her toes.

Across the shadows, the Duke of Loch Irvine rested his dark gaze upon her.

"Aye," he said. "I have now."

Chapter 15

Black Magic

*H*e was taller, perhaps, and thicker in the shoulders: the lean angles of youth had given way to the solid, muscular frame of a grown man. His black hair was shorter but still too long, and the strong features that had once almost startled a person with their intensity, now lit from below, seemed remote and fearsome. His coat was gorgeously tailored, his cravat elegantly tied, and the signet ring gleamed—a talisman of nobility. Yet he had the air of a great beast barely contained by the affectations of civilization.

"*You*," popped through her lips. As a finale to months of searching for him across the breadth of Scotland, the single syllable lacked all drama.

"Aye."

Practiced words, questioning words, and words of condemnation got stuck in her throat.

He walked toward her.

She commanded her feet to remain in place.

Then he was before her and she was looking up through shadows into the shadows of his eyes she had once found so enthralling. They were the richest brown—like chocolate truffles—and shone as though lit from a mysterious well of simmering desire and gentle amusement.

Still enthralling.

"You are seeking a friend, yet you have found me instead." His voice was low. "How whimsical o' fate to throw two strangers together in an isolated place . . . twice in a lifetime."

A blanket of heat was engulfing her body, a strange, wonderful familiarity woven with danger, as the darkness seemed to wrap around them. She had forgotten nothing about him—not his voice, deep and rough with brogue, nor the hollows of his cheeks, nor the ebony sheen of his hair—nothing except how the power of his presence had made her limbs weak.

Inconvenient lapse of memory, that.

At her sides, her hands made their way into fists. The strength in her fingers felt good.

"Fate has nothing to do with it, Urisk," she said.

"Urisk?"

"Solitary. Lives on a hill. Frightens away travelers."

"I know what an urisk is." A crease appeared at one side of his mouth.

Too familiar.

"I have been searching for you."

"You have," he said, not in surprise. "Because you imagine I have hidden the young lady you seek somewhere in this room. Or perhaps I have already secreted her away to my dungeons."

"Then you do have maidens locked in your dungeons?"

"'Tis what they say." A smile glimmered in his beautiful eyes. She wanted it to be a trick of her memory. She had fallen under the spell of that smile at one time.

Never again.

Pivoting, she strode to the door, seized the handle, and pushed it shut. Swiveling around, she put her back against it.

"I have been searching for you for months, in fact," she said. "At first indirectly and then with single purpose. But you are elusive. You know that, of course. You are intentionally elusive, I think. That ends now. For you see, Urisk, I shan't open this door until you have answered my questions. All of them."

He came toward her.

She had not anticipated quite such a speedy response, nor that he would not halt until he stood within a foot of her.

He reached around her hip for the door handle.

She turned the key in the lock and tossed it into her other palm a fraction of a moment before his hand encompassed hers about the handle. She gasped, jerked her other arm up, and dropped the key into her bodice.

"You're cold as ice." He sounded surprised. His hand was big and warm and firmly gripping hers, just as the first time he had touched her in that cellar years ago, and he was a wall of man, all broad chest and wide shoulders and height, and he smelled *delicious*—like sandalwood and sun and the wind and the sea. She breathed him into her nostrils and lungs. *Glorious*. It was the height of folly to touch him and smell him and have her eyes full of him all at once.

She had forgotten that a man could smell this good.

"Release my hand," she said a bit unsteadily.

He did, instantly, his heat and strength disappearing and leaving only the chilly door handle in her grasp. But he did not move away. And he did not speak. So she did.

"Your palm is callused. You are no longer a naval officer yet you still have the hands of a sailor, it seems. What have you been doing, I wonder, to make that so?"

"If you imagine the hiding place you've chosen for that key will prevent me from leaving this room, you'd best be reimagining, lass."

"I will happily give the key to you after you have answered my questions."

"I'll have no' need for you to give it if I've already taken it."

Tremors crawled from her belly into her throat.

"You do not frighten me." She snipped the syllables to hide the quaver.

His gaze that was black in the dim light scanned her face—her cheeks and hair and lips and chin.

"Then you are unique among women," he rumbled. "Now, open the door."

"Why won't you speak with me?" This was frankly terrifying. She had not anticipated this or planned for any scenario like this. She had imagined that when she finally cornered him he would act like a regular person and converse—unwisely, she realized belatedly. He had never been anything like a regular person, after all.

"Five and a half years, yet not even a little small talk?" she said. "Come now. Let us give it a try. I will start. I hear you have become a duke. And an abductor of innocent maidens. And possibly a practitioner of the dark arts. How do you find all of that?"

"Lass." The word was a warning shift of tectonic plates. "Open the door now or I'll be taking that key."

"You cannot deter me, Urisk." Now her words quivered quite obviously. "Either you will sit down here now and answer my questions until I have asked them all, or you will in fact be obliged to take the key from me."

In the darkness, the gleam in his eyes was like a knife's blade.

"As you wish," he said as though he whispered in her ear.

Her heart slammed into her lungs.

His hand surrounded her hip.

She gasped.

Large and strong, his five fingers and broad palm took complete possession of her flesh. He was not smiling.

"The key now," he said very deeply. His fingers moved on her buttocks. Not painfully. Rather, stroking, kneading as though she were bread dough.

She swallowed over the shock clogging her throat.

"No," she croaked.

He bent his head and in the murky silence in which the gay music of the ball was only a distant echo, she could hear his breathing, each inhale and exhale a perfectly controlled statement of composure.

"You are certain?" he said as calmly as though he were asking if she preferred tea to coffee.

"Yes."

His hand slid up her side and wrapped around her waist.

"What are you *doing*?" she rasped.

His thumb stroked along the ridge of her lowest rib and a horrible, wonderful cascade of pleasure descended inside her.

"Getting closer to that key," he said.

No air was reaching her lungs. Hot springs were erupting within her—from her throat to her belly—*everywhere*—and her head was dizzy and she simply *could not breathe*. She pressed her shoulder blades into the door, flattening her back against it. His grasp was at once light and complete, like the levity she had always felt from him, and the intensity.

"You wouldn't," she uttered.

"Aye," he said so close she could sense the movement of air between them. "I would." In one smooth movement he brought his hand beneath her arm. The base of his palm encompassed the curve of her breast, his thumb sliding over the soft muslin of her bodice.

Her throat was completely jammed. Her tongue would not function. For the first time in years her entire body was hot, fevered, *on fire*.

"You will actually do it?" she said without breath. "Reach down my gown?"

"You've given me no choice."

"What if I run away across the room now? Will you come after the key?"

"Go ahead." It was more animal snarl than human speech. "Run." His thumb traced a line up the side of her breast, and decadent pleasure curled through her. "'Tis what you always prefer."

The door handle jiggled. A firm knock jolted the panel.

Neither of them moved. If she shifted the slightest bit, her entire breast would be in his hand. Her stomach was a yarn basket of knots.

Another knock came. Another jiggle of the handle.

She could just make out his features, the sensual lips set in a hard line, the perfect slant of his cheekbones, the lock of satiny hair dipping toward his eyes, the drugging intensity of his gaze still on her.

He was no longer breathing with ease.

"Do you see, sir?" came Libby Shaw's voice from the other side of the door. "It is locked."

"Aye, Miss Shaw," a man said. "During a public ball it always be locked. Now, I'll just be finding the correct key." Keys jingled.

"Promise to meet me in a quarter of an hour," Amarantha whispered to the big, handsome, dark man whose hand was creating a hurricane inside her, "at the end of the block, by the green, and I will slip away and hide now. Then you will not be obliged to explain this circumstance. For I cannot imagine you wish to give everybody yet another reason to think the worst of you."

"Lass, if you imagine I care anything o' what anybody thinks o' me"—he bent his head closer and she felt the brush of that lock of hair against her brow—"you havena been reading the papers."

"Here!" the man exclaimed as his keys rattled again. "I've found it, miss."

"Invite me to your castle," Amarantha said quickly. "To Haiknayes."

"Haiknayes?" He was staring at her lips.

Brass clinked in the keyhole.

"'Tis a sticky lock, miss. I've to summon the locksmith here to see to a number o' doors."

"If you do not invite me to Haiknayes," Amarantha whispered, "I will go there anyway. I will gain entrance. I will scour the countryside around it. I will ask everyone every little question that occurs to me. I will learn what I must whether you wish it or not."

The door handle turned. She dodged to the side and the panel swung open. The duke seized it just before it slammed into her nose.

"Duke!" Libby said on the other side of it. "Were you speaking with someone else in here? I thought I heard a woman's voice."

"Good evening, Miss Shaw." His fingers slipped away from the edge of the door.

"I am glad to see that you have in fact come to town," Libby said. "Everybody downstairs is talking about it, of course. Silly gossips."

"Your Grace," the key man said. "Begging pardon for disturbing you and . . . ?"

"You havena disturbed me. I am alone here."

Another whorl of tingles flew up Amarantha's middle.

"You departed Edinburgh last summer without fulfilling your promise to me," Libby said.

"The house burned to the ground, lass, with all that was in it. What would you have had me do?" he said with a smile in his voice.

"I should like to see the collection at Haiknayes," Libby

said with the same familiarity with which she spoke to her father. "I have read that your father's collection of natural specimens at Haiknayes is in fact much larger and more diverse than the collection at your house in Edinburgh was anyway."

"Your Grace?" Dr. Shaw's words came from farther along the corridor. "What a welcome surprise to meet you here. How do you do?"

"Papa, the duke should fulfill his promise to allow me to study the old duke's collection. Shouldn't he?"

"Elizabeth, he has only just returned to town. No doubt he has plenty of obligations already."

"You have plenty of obligations, Papa, but you do good deeds for people every day. You even share your house with me and Amarantha, who occasionally require your attention, while the duke is a hermit. Duke, you did promise."

"That I did."

"Your Grace," Dr. Shaw said with a chuckle, "you mustn't inconvenience yourself."

"In fact it will be the opposite of an inconvenience, Papa. I mean to catalogue the old duke's collection. When I am finished, I will give a complete copy of the catalogue to you, Duke."

"Your Grace, I accede to my daughter's sense of fairness," Dr. Shaw said. "Now, Elizabeth, the president of the infirmary has agreed to meet you tonight."

"Has he?" she cried.

"But if we tarry here disturbing His Grace's peace you will certainly lose the opportunity below."

"Come along, then, Mr. Keymaster," Libby said. "I will tell you how to make an oil of graphite to loosen the locks in the building so that you needn't hire the locksmith. Don't forget, Duke!" she called back. "We will await your invitation. We will bring Amarantha with us, too. She is wonderfully sensible. And also very kind—far too kind, really. She has agreed to stay with us even though she has a family with magnificent houses in London and Shropshire and even Cumbria now." Her words began to fade down the corridor. "I'm certain you will like her."

"Forgive me, Your Grace," the doctor said, still close by. "As you are already aware, Elizabeth's excitement for a project occasionally overcomes her."

"'Tis my pleasure, Doctor."

A peculiar throbbing began beneath Amarantha's ribs. The Shaws and the Duke of Loch Irvine were obviously on even-fonder terms than she had thought. In three months of living with the Shaws, she had chosen not to reveal her quest to them. Perhaps if she had, if she had been *entirely* honest with her friends, she might have already fulfilled it.

"Elizabeth spoke just now of our friend Mrs. Garland," the doctor said. "She is intelligent and well traveled. I believe you will find much to admire in her."

"To be sure, I already do," came the duke's reply so close to the door that Amarantha felt the vibration of the words in her palms on the panel.

"She is downstairs now," the doctor said. "I would be happy to make the introduction. But perhaps you prefer a good book to dancing. Have you discovered anything worthwhile here?"

"More than I dreamed."

The door closed, sinking her into black silence disturbed only by the amber glow of the lamp at the other end of the room and her racketing heart.

He would not meet her tonight. And by the time she returned to the ballroom, he would already have departed. She knew this for certain.

But he could not evade her forever.

More than I dreamed.

Obviously he had not left off with the flirtatious teasing of his youth. That he could say such a thing to her now—*touch her so intimately* as though she were still a foolish girl . . .

But he had fooled everybody in Scotland, after all, for years.

Shaking herself free of the lingering sensation of his touch, she walked the length of the room to the chair in which he had been sitting. Taking up the book he had discarded, she opened it to the page in which the silken ribbon was lodged.

"'The magical properties of newts, frogs, and salamanders,'" she read aloud from the top of the page, "'and potions to be made when combined with the hair, fingernail clippings, or blood of virgins.'"

Snapping the book shut, she flipped it over. On the binding stamped in gold leaf was the title: *Black Magic: A Complete Compendium of Receipts.*

Setting down the book on the table, she walked to the door, returned the key to the lock, and left the room smiling.

THE MISS TATES were scandalized.

Rather, nineteen-year-old Jane Tate and seventeen-year-old Cynthia Tate were. Twelve-year-old Iris was sprawled on the bed with a kitten of indeterminate color.

"Amarantha, are you not . . . cold?" Jane's doe eyes widened. With lily skin upon which a modest blush always lingered and rosebud lips that never uttered a contrary word, Jane was precisely the sort of woman Paul had believed he was marrying until it was too late.

Still, Amarantha liked Jane. Her kindness was sincere.

"I am not cold." Her toes and nose were like ice. Yet inside, twelve hours since the Duke of Loch Irvine had held her, she was still hot as a brazier.

"This," declared Libby, "is the sternum." She tapped the tip of a wooden baton to the thin strip of linen stretched across Amarantha's chest. "Often referred to as the breast bone, it is not however beneath the subject's actual breasts."

"And what lovely breasts they are," Alice Campbell said, not raising her eyes from her work.

"*Miss Alice*," Jane whispered.

"False modesty never did anybody good, Jane." A confirmed spinster in her sixth decade, at whose house their little group of friends had taken to gathering, Alice was embroidering a stool cover and paying no attention to Libby's demonstration of the bones of the human skeleton using Amarantha as a model. "Amarantha's breasts are lovely," Alice said. "She may as well admit to it."

"Thank you," Amarantha said. "I hadn't anything to do with fashioning them, of course." She drew a slow breath, controlling the heated shiver that came with the memory of his thumb not far from the tip of Libby's baton now.

She had allowed it.

Five and a half years of tepidity, and in mere moments he had roused every dormant ember within her.

"If I'd had such breasts when I was your age," Alice said, "I would have been the toast of town."

"Who cares about breasts?" Iris flipped the kitten onto its back and ran a fingertip the length of its soft belly.

"Gentlemen care. They are wild about breasts, the poor creatures." Alice jabbed her needle through the square of linen that read "Enjoy life. You're a long time deid."

"Gentlemen don't care about them." Lounging before the dressing table, Cynthia watched herself in the mirror as she combed and recombed her own hair. "Common men do."

Alice snorted. "Cynthia Tate, you have a great deal to learn about men."

"Would you care to borrow my shawl, Amarantha?" Jane said.

"She is perfectly well," Libby said. "Aren't you, Amarantha? In the tropics you must have experienced considerably more discomfort than this, after all, not to mention marriage, in which one must be regularly undressed."

"Really?" Cynthia's eyes in the mirror were suddenly wide.

"If you're doing it right," Alice said.

"Thomas wishes to marry Amarantha, so he must want to see her undressed," Iris said, untangling the kitten from her hair.

"*Iris*," Jane gasped.

"Your cousin and I are fond friends, Iris. But I do not believe he wishes to marry me. And I do not wish to marry anyone."

"I don't understand that," Cynthia said, primping her hair. "I cannot wait for everybody to address me as *Missus*."

"This is the right clavicle," Libby said, running the pointer along Amarantha's exposed shoulder to her neck. "And this is the left clavicle." She slid the pointer along the other bone. "Their principal purpose is to allow the free movement of the arms away from the torso. They are connected to the true ribs"—she tapped Amarantha's breast where a man had put his hand the night before—"by the sternum, all of which function to protect the fragile organs of the chest cavity."

Fragile organ.

He had callously broken her heart, yet last night he had behaved as though he could tease her and she would fall breathlessly at his feet. Again.

Not again. No matter how weak her flesh.

The trouble was, he had actually taken her breaths. And for hours afterward her nipples had been deliciously sensitive.

Foolish flesh.

Famished flesh. In four years of marriage her husband had not touched her as intimately as a stranger had in a library.

He had called them *strangers*.

It would make her project of interviewing him easier. As soon as Libby finished the lesson, she would suggest they find Dr. Shaw and pay a call on the duke—the duke who as a young libertine had never touched her but who now apparently had no qualms about doing so.

"Is clavicle spelled with two *K*'s?" Iris had taken a slate upon her knee and the kitten set its tiny teeth to the chalk.

"Two *C*'s," Libby said. "The Scholastics did not use *K*'s. I wish Tabitha could hear this lesson too."

"She has gone to the shop for more paper," Amarantha said.

"The who?" Iris said.

"Scholastics were medieval scholars that wrote in Latin due to the Romans having conquered half of Britain," Libby said. "They did not conquer the unruly clans of the Highlands, of course. I will lend you a book about it."

"I should like to write a book like Amarantha and Tabitha's," Iris said.

"How intrepid you are, sister," Jane said. "I would not know a thing about writing a book."

"That is because you haven't had any adventures. Amarantha has."

"I am not writing, only scribing," Amarantha said. "Tabitha is dictating her story to me."

"Why isn't Tabitha writing it herself?" Iris said.

"She only learned how to write a few years ago," Jane said. "Amarantha writes more swiftly and fluently."

And some things were simply better done with a friend.

"Elizabeth dear," Alice said, "Amaratha's lips have turned blue."

"We have fifty-six bones still to review."

"Her phalanges are as pale as sheep's milk."

Libby set her fists on her hips. "Miss Alice, you *have* been listening."

"And her patellas are knocking together."

"*Pattelae.*"

"Won't you capture a chill, Amarantha?" Jane said.

"I am fine." *Burning up in sinful fire.*

She could still hear Paul's words on their wedding night: *Inordinate carnal desire is not love, my lady. It is lust. I will not put your pure soul in peril by tempting your flesh. I promise it will be quick.*

It had been. Very quick. And so painful that she had dreaded the next night. Yet that had not been the worst. The worst was when she eventually learned to bear the pain and finally ventured to touch him.

This immodest lust does not become you, Amarantha. Have no fear. I will teach you to control your impulses.

"You are very good to do this, Amarantha," Libby said. "Since women are not permitted to attend dissections at the university, I am entirely dependent on live volunteers. I wish Papa would allow me to purchase thieves' cadavers for study."

"I should like to see a dead body," Iris declared.

"No, you should not," Alice said. "They are not nearly as interesting as dear Elizabeth suggests."

A scratch sounded upon the door. "Miss Shaw." Alice's housekeeper proffered a letter. "This just arrived from the doctor."

"How unusual for Papa to send me a message when I am only here." Libby popped the wax seal. "Perhaps the president of the infirmary wishes to—" Her eyes widened. "Amarantha, dress quickly. We must return home immediately to pack."

"Pack for what, child?" Alice said.

"For the opportunity of a lifetime." Libby tossed tools and diagrams into her satchel.

"Good heavens, dear girl, explain this at once."

"The Duke of Loch Irvine has sent an invitation! Papa and Amarantha and I are going to Haiknayes Castle."

Chapter 16

The Devil's Keep

"What were you thinking, Gabriel?" Ziyaeddin said from the corner of the library where he lounged.

Standing at the library window, Gabriel studied the ribbon of muddy road that stretched to the closest tenant farm. Only a portion of the road was visible; trees had grown up and blocked the castle's view of much of the surrounding land. A late snow, melting now, cut a jagged path alongside the barrier that protected the north fields.

If he did not send men in there within the day, the earth would crumble and the entire valley would flood.

His predecessors must be scowling in their graves. He should have long since seen to such matters. The hope of Kallin and everybody there rested in these lands spread out before him, in these valleys that could be sown with wheat and barley, and in these rich hills that could pasture both cattle and sheep.

He had missed this land. And now he would make it right. In a month the lambing would commence. Then came the shearing. In the meantime the fields would be planted with grain, timber farming recommenced, and cattle purchased. Come harvest, Haiknayes would be making enough profit to send gold to Kallin. And wonderfully, all of it could be done with the labor of men.

Inviting eight town dwellers to the castle for an extended house party had not been in the plan.

Inviting *her* had been a colossal mistake.

What was he thinking, indeed?

"'Twas a business decision." Not *entirely* untrue. He and Calum Tate had been wrangling for weeks already, and now Tate's gout was ailing him. Inviting him to Haiknayes for a holiday seemed the easiest solution to softening up the savvy merchant.

But the real truth of it was that, standing in the darkness of that library, he had acted on impulse. With bright cheeks and defiant chin, she had blinked her lashes over those spectacular eyes he remembered like he remembered everything about her—*too well*—and he had wanted only one thing.

Again.

Only one thing.

The years had transformed the pretty girl into a beautiful woman.

"An' green eyes," he mumbled to the emerald vista that could not rival the brilliance of those eyes.

Moving to his desk, he took up a pen and wrote a message to Cassandra to accompany the sewing machine for Sophie in the village. Cassandra had made a fine case for the machine's potential to speed Sophie's productivity. Since dress shops were clamoring for her gowns, he could hardly reply that purchasing such a machine would deplete the ducal coffers yet again. As soon as his groom returned from Leith, he would send him off to Glen Village with the machine.

Apparently he could deny those women nothing, even if it meant destitution in the near future.

Nor, apparently, could he deny himself certain disaster.

Months ago at Kallin, sending her away had been wise. Reopening a wound was always foolhardy.

And yet.

He had touched her. And discovered that the reality was better than every dream. Soft and strong and warm and quivering with life, *she had accepted it*. With wide eyes, parted lips, and a quick pulse beating a rhythm in her throat, she had leaned in.

He needed more. He had always needed more of her. More and more and more.

So, after sixteen years he was finally home. And expecting guests.

One housekeeper and one manservant were insufficient servants to serve a party of eight.

"I've got to hire more servants."

"More servants?" Ziyaeddin's coat was of velvet, his lace cuffs languid, an affectation of calm belied by the intelligent gleam in his eyes. "For how many days do you intend to inflict these people on the peace and quiet of my house?"

"'Tis no' your house. An' you're welcome to join the party, if you care to."

"On my grave."

"Hermit."

"Barbarian. Who is she?"

"She?"

"The woman for whom you are now opening the doors of this castle for the first time since you took possession of it. You did not imagine I would guess it. Would you like me to paint her? In the regular fashion, of course. I would be delighted."

"Suggest it to her an' I'll toss you from the ramparts, cur."

"I am correct. There is a woman."

"There's always a woman."

One woman. Only ever one woman.

He went to the door. Within hours a fiery-haired Englishwoman would arrive and set to doing God knew what—searching for clues to condemn him, probably.

As soon as he had seen to hiring laborers to clear the trees and mend the trench and a few more servants for the house, he would discover her intent in seeking him out yet again. He would listen to her questions and he would give her the answers he must to subdue her curiosity.

Then, as before, he would send her away. This time permanently.

THE DUKE SENT a coach. Entirely black on the exterior, with no noble crest or decorative adornments, it was luxurious within.

A fortnight's sojourn, the invitation had read. *His Grace welcomes you and your daughter two days hence to Haiknayes, as well as your esteemed houseguest.*

In two days Libby had not ceased talking about the old duke's extensive collection of treasures gathered on his many journeys abroad: dried plants and mysterious rocks and the skeletons and pelts of exotic animals. The amateur naturalist's collection was a thing of legend. Part of it had burned along with the duke's house in Edinburgh, but the bulk of it had always been at Haiknayes.

When the coach rounded a copse and Haiknayes Castle appeared on the ridge before them, a string of nerves wiggled into Amarantha's throat.

It was nothing like Kallin.

Two massive towers, paired so closely that they were connected all the way up to the sturdy crenellations of the ramparts, reigned majestically over the valley. Surrounded by a wall taller than a man, with a gate of iron surmounted by pikes and a long, straight drive lined with ancient trees, Haiknayes was an imposing fortress. Windows pocked the sheer walls of the keep irregularly, and a giant crater marked one façade: the remnants of centuries-old cannon blast.

Yet in its power it was beautiful. Built of stone that was more luxuriously pink than gray, there was a lushness to both castle and walls. The hills brindled with snow and the dark pines rising along its eastern flank rendered it almost like the setting for a fairytale.

"Whose carriage is that?" Libby said, stepping down from the carriage and looking back through the gate toward the stable where a traveling coach stood unattended with its placid team.

"Perhaps the duke has other guests," Dr. Shaw said.

Amarantha moved toward the gatehouse. A wide, round structure, it commanded the corner of the wall that surrounded the keep. Stepping up onto the stone bench at the base of its stair, she poked her nose over the wall. On its other side was a tangle of winter forest dipping abruptly to a creek far below.

"'Tis a steep drop. If you're wanting to escape, lass, you'd best go by way o' the drive."

He stood at the top of the gatehouse stair, his eyes hooded.

"Is that an invitation, Urisk, or a threat?"

"Whichever you please."

"It is an impressive castle. Do you hide the maidens in the dungeons?"

"Aye." A one-sided smile transformed his lips.

Amarantha's fingers clung to the rock wall.

He descended the stairs to stand before the bench.

"Come inside an' I'll introduce you to the lot o' them." He offered his hand.

Amarantha suspected he must think her a fool in all sorts of ways. But she was not such a fool as to welcome the touch of his hand that had caressed her breast.

Gathering her skirts in all ten of her fingers, she climbed down from the bench.

He flexed his hand and dropped it to his side.

"Duke!" came a man's bellow from across the forecourt. "'Tis a fine thing you've done, opening your castle to us!"

From a gate on the far side of the forecourt, Mr. Tate, Mrs. Tate, and their three daughters appeared.

"Oh!" Libby said. "You have invited our friends too."

"Welcome to Haiknayes, Miss Shaw," the duke said. "Doctor."

"It is an honor to be here, Your Grace," Dr. Shaw said.

"An honor indeed!" Mr. Tate exclaimed. "Ha ha! Already chased my gout away! Loch Irvine, I might just have to capitulate to your demands about my ships after all." He had florid cheeks and a jovial air.

"Such a charming castle," Mrs. Tate drawled as though she owned one herself. The daughter of a minor English baronet, and full of her own consequence, she had married her noble blood to Calum Tate's Scottish mercantile fortune and constantly made certain everybody remembered it.

"Papa wished us to come," Jane said quietly to Amarantha. "He and the duke are doing business, and he said he could not bear to be even a day without us."

"Your Grace," Libby said. "May we see the collection without delay?"

"Without delay it'll be."

A narrow flight of exterior stairs led up into the fortress. From the entrance foyer they went into an enormous hall. Two stories high, with giant hearths at either end, it was of baronial dimensions and magnificent. An enormous table dominated the center of the room, tapestries covered the walls, and the sofa and chairs before the fireplace, along with the pelt of a great beast that decorated the floor, looked soft and inviting. Firelight glinted off two full suits of armor tucked in niches.

"This way, Miss Shaw," he said, gesturing to a door to a spiral stairwell. They all followed, climbing the tightly winding steps. At the top landing he pushed the door wide.

Libby passed by him and her gasp echoed.

From one side of the castle to the opposite was one large room, its ceiling a vaulted arch. Sunlight illumined dozens of glass cases bursting with bones, skulls, and rocks, jars of dried flowers and leaves, and bottles of murky liquid.

"Good gracious." Mrs. Tate lifted a kerchief to her nose.

"It is even better than you led me to believe," Libby exclaimed, and fell to her knees before a crate. "Do you see this? I believe it is the skeleton of a raccoon, an animal I have only seen in books. But it has no identifying label. There is work to be done here."

Iris drew a jar out of a case. "Look, Libby. An ear!"

Libby pulled her head out of a crate, objects clutched in each hand. "A fortnight will hardly suffice to catalogue everything in this room, even with Iris and Amarantha helping. Iris, take care. The wings of a desiccated bat can be extraordinarily fragile."

"Your Grace," Dr. Shaw said at the duke's side. "Thank you."

"'Tis my pleasure," he said, but his gaze came to Amarantha.

"JANE TATE IS not as empty-headed as she pretends to be," Libby said as Amarantha returned her writing materials to their case.

Morning sunshine glimmered through the thick fortress window frame of Amarantha's bedchamber. Everything about the castle seemed both harsh and gentle: vast halls and dark rooms built of cold stone covered with colorful tapestries; plain furniture adorned with rich draperies and soft linens; simple roasts served on gilded dishware; vast hearths blazing with warmth, and chilly stone nooks perfect for hiding; and the castle's master himself, dark and gruff and short of conversation yet gracious to all and unquestionably affectionate to Libby and Iris Tate.

"After dinner last night she spoke intelligently about Mr. Scott's latest novel," Libby continued. "I was surprised *you* remained so quiet on the subject. I heard you discussing that novel with Tabitha last week. I thought you liked it."

"Oh, after all of those hours in the carriage yesterday I was famished." Amarantha took up her shawl and went to the door. "My mouth was filled with cakes."

"*Ha ha*, as Mr. Tate would say. It is obvious that you and the duke have met before."

Amarantha's heartbeats skipped. "Is it?"

"I wish you would tell me why you did not speak all evening. I know you cannot possibly be frightened of him."

"There you are wrong. I am positively terrified."

"Not on my account. You don't believe that he abducts maidens, do you?"

"Absolutely not. It is clear to me that he has no intention of abducting you." Adopting her, perhaps, and possibly Iris Tate as well. He was not yet even thirty but the pleasure he seemed to take in them seemed so genuinely paternal.

"Good, for I would think you as silly as Cynthia Tate." She went into the stairwell. "He said that the library contains a volume of his father's illustrations. I should retrieve that before we begin working." She opened a door.

A veritable trove of bookshelves appeared before them, stacked with volumes.

"Magnificent!" Libby exclaimed.

"Yet I haven't even spoken a word," came a man's voice

from across the room. "But my nurse always did tell me I had remarkably good bone structure."

He lounged in a chair by the hearth. He was handsome, young, and neither English nor Scottish: his tongue, skin, and features marked him quite obviously a foreigner.

"Oh! Who are you?" Libby said.

He lifted black brows. "I might ask you the same."

"Then ask it."

"Alas, I cannot. For every mote of my attention is engaged in enjoying the vision of you beneath that monstrous sculpture of Saint George hanging above the door. Like an angel at the feet of the triumphant Lucifer. Light and dark. Beauty and grotesque. It is positively Caravaggesque."

"*Caravaggesque* is not a word, at least not in English," Libby said. "You might, however, say *Caravaggio-like*. And Lucifer was not, of course, triumphant."

"He won a kingdom of his own in the end. I should think that counts as a triumph."

Libby crossed the threshold and craned her neck to peer up at the stone carving over the lintel. "Saint George did not fight an angel, rather a dragon."

"I stand corrected," he murmured.

"I hope we are not disturbing you, sir," Amarantha said. "We have come in search of a single book."

"Be my guest." His gaze followed Libby across the room.

"Here it is," Libby said, plucking forth a volume. "Precisely where the duke said it would be."

"I should like to draw you," the man said.

"Draw *me*?" Libby said.

He nodded.

"A caricature?"

"I do not draw caricatures."

"You cannot possibly wish to draw a portrait of me. I have no remarkable features or distinguishing physical characteristics to make a portrait interesting," she said, opening the volume. "Unless you are an uninteresting person, I suppose, who prefers regular features to unusual features." She glanced up at him again. "Are you?"

"I believe I am now becoming one."

"Why did you not stand when we entered the room? Your English is excellent and your clothing is fine. In English society, gentlemen are required to stand when ladies enter a room. I am not a lady, of course. Amarantha is the daughter of an earl, although she doesn't remind people of it, unlike Mrs. Tate, who reminds everybody who will listen that she is the daughter of a baronet. You must know you should have."

"I believe a question lurked somewhere in there." A smile played about his lips.

"I am asking if men in your homeland are not required to stand when ladies enter a room."

"In my home, never. Would you like me to stand?"

"No," Libby said as though surprised. "I am merely curious that you did not."

He set his book aside. Taking up a walking stick with a silver handle and clutching the chair arm with his other hand, slowly he stood. He was lean and very elegantly dressed, and his hand was tight about the cane: the straining knuckles whitened his dark skin. "You may now cast away your curiosity and be at ease," he said.

"Oh," she said. "I beg your pardon."

"Do not. Contrition is entirely inappropriate on the face of an angel."

"You are teasing me, aren't you?"

"I might be," he said.

Snapping the book shut, Libby left the room.

"Good day, sir," Amarantha said, and followed her friend.

She found Libby in the room at the top of the castle.

"A Luna Moth! Extraordinary!" Libby said. "Where is Iris? I asked her to come up directly after breakfast."

"Here I am! Papa and Dr. Shaw have ridden out with the duke to hunt birds for dinner. Dr. Shaw said Papa should not ride, but Papa said his foot feels capital and anyway it's much more pleasant to talk about business in the saddle than indoors. I cannot understand why, when I should think business is prodigiously dull no matter where one talks about it."

"Men are generally odd creatures," Libby said with a furrow in her brow. "Except Papa and the duke. Here, Iris. This crate first."

When the streams of sunlight across the floor shortened, Amarantha rose from her knees and dusted off her skirt.

"Can you spare me, Libby? I would like to stretch my legs." And find him.

"Take care that Mrs. Tate does not see you go, or she will tease you again about your liking for exercise in order to bring to everybody's attention Jane's delicate constitution."

"Jane is so dull spirited," Iris said. "She doesn't even care that we are living in a haunted castle."

"There really are no such things as haunted castles," Libby said.

"Then why does everybody call the duke a demon?"

"Because everybody is silly. Do pass me that skull."

In the foyer, Amarantha gathered her cloak. There were few servants about, and no one else around either as she pulled the hood over her hair, tucked her hands into her pockets, and walked to the gate in the forecourt wall.

In the keystone of the arch, a star had been carefully carved. With six points and a crossbar at the base of the top triangle, its lower points touched three other symbols: a trio of wavy lines, a triangle, and a vertical almond.

To see it in situ now, when six months earlier she had seen it all over Edinburgh—on gateposts and the corners of buildings—gave her the oddest sensation of possession. Which was ridiculous.

Continuing through the gate, she passed beneath the tree branches. To one side, another wall separated the drive and a church.

On the hill opposite, a horseman appeared on the road, the hooves of his enormous mount churning up the slushy mud. Two dogs ran alongside, large and shaggy. The Duke of Loch Irvine had returned.

Amarantha awaited him. He was alone, and she had come here for precisely this moment—her twirling nerves be damned.

The master of Haiknayes and Kallin rode a massive black beast and wore a black coat. He was altogether intimidating, and when he reined in the horse before her the sight of his splendid shoulders and powerful thighs did nothing to lessen the effect.

He removed his hat.

"Good day, my lady."

"Good day, Urisk."

Gabriel allowed himself the smile he had been resisting for days. He knew he was every sort of fool. *He didn't care.*

But he caught himself at a half smile. No need to be an utter fool when a partial fool would do.

"So it's to be Urisk now?" he said.

"It suits the location. And you are no longer a sailor." The sunshine illumining her face picked out every shade of cream and gold and pink, and made her eyes like gems. The roundness of girlhood had gone from her features, leaving the sleek, soft beauty of a woman. "Do you ride a black horse and wear black clothing to convince everybody that you are in fact the devil, or simply because you like the color?"

"If it's the former?" he said.

"Then I should be terrified of you."

"Are you?"

"I haven't decided. But I have not yet seen the dungeons."

As he dismounted she watched him. To feel her watching him—again—after years—was like waking from an opium dream. He felt it beneath his skin.

"If you intend these as guard dogs, they are not very good at it," she said, bending to run her fingertips through the fur between a hound's ears. Dappled sunlight from between the branches of trees only just beginning to bud dotted her skin, mingling with the riot of freckles across her nose and cheeks. "Do they usually help to keep away curious people?"

"No' this time, obviously."

"They are kittens. What are their names?"

"Lucifer an' Diablo."

She laughed. As though she had touched him, he felt it in his bollocks.

"Really?" she said.

"Aye."

"And your horse's name?"

"Beelzebub."

A smile lingered on her lips.

"The dogs at Kallin were also ridiculously friendly," she said. "The locked gates of the grounds, however, were not." She lifted her gaze to him. "Last autumn I went there. I stayed at the Solstice Inn at the village. Not as a guest. I worked for the innkeeper, Mrs. Tarry. It was she who suggested to me that you are an urisk."

"Aye," he said.

Her fingers stilled in the hound's fur.

"I went to *Kallin*," she enunciated very clearly.

"Aye."

"You are not surprised."

"You have come here," he said.

"Twenty miles from Edinburgh. By invitation. Kallin is eighty miles of mountainous roads away."

She had intended to surprise him. He should now pretend to be surprised.

"I knew you were there," he said unwisely. But he could not lie to her. Let the entire world believe fantastical stories about him. To this woman alone he would never tell untruths.

"You knew I was there. You knew it then. Last autumn?"

"Aye."

For a stretched moment she simply stared at him.

She walked away.

He followed, leading his mount along the road toward the church. He reached her side and she did not break stride.

"It was you," she said. "On the roof."

"Aye."

"I thought it was you," she said to the road ahead. "I assumed you had forgotten me."

"No."

"I see."

Probably not. *Certainly not.*

"I walked up to the castle a number of times. Thrice weekly, in fact," she said.

"'Tis a distance from the village."

"Since speaking to you was my purpose in traveling to Kallin, that distance was immaterial. I was never admitted to the castle grounds. The place was thoroughly locked up. Yet you were apparently in residence the entire time?"

"Aye."

"How exceptionally taciturn you have become." She tucked her hands into her sleeves and moved with even, steady steps, just as she had when he had walked miles through cane fields and down dirt roads simply to remain at her side.

"Have I?" he said.

"I have been loath to believe the rumors of your

reclusiveness," she said. "But perhaps all of this isolation has had a deleterious effect on your ability to converse. Or perhaps you are simply reveling in solitude after sharing cramped ship's quarters for years with so many others."

"Could be." He bridled his smile yet again.

"Yet now you have invited all of these people here. For a party, no less."

"You required it."

She halted. "*I* required it?"

"Aye."

"You are the most—the most unusual man." She shook her head and the sunlight danced in the fiery locks that peeked from beneath her hood. "Do not attempt to convince me that if not for what I said the other night in that reading room you would have not invited Mr. Tate here to discuss business or Libby to study your father's collection. I won't believe it."

"Then I'll no' attempt to convince you. 'Tis the truth, though."

She breathed very markedly for several inhalations, the clasp on her cloak glittering with the abrupt rise and fall of the most beautiful breasts in creation. Unlike five years ago, now he knew what it was to have that in his hand. *Her.*

"I see," she finally said, moving toward the church again. "Apparently you do in fact still enjoy teasing. I can only hope that you will be more forthcoming in answering my questions."

"Questions o' the devil?"

"I will ask the questions, Urisk. You will answer them."

"You've no respect for my consequence. I'm a duke now, you know."

"Yes, I had heard that somewhere."

"You'll find no answers," he made himself say.

"Let us see if that is true." Halting again, she faced him and for the first time in five and a half years Gabriel wished the entire world away—everything but this woman. He had forgotten this pleasure, the acute pleasure of walking beside her, feeling her near, his senses filled with her voice and colors and the cadence of her movements. That simply trading words with another human being could forge a well of joy in his stomach seemed a miracle. He had forgotten this. He had made himself forget.

"Last winter," she said, "my friend Penny Baker left Kingston unexpectedly and alone. She took passage on a ship bound for Scotland. There was nothing left for me in Kingston, so I—"

"Nothing?"

"I am a widow. When my husband died, his mission passed to another man."

"Aye."

"We have returned to single syllables, it seems."

"I know you are a widow."

"You do?"

He took a step closer and Amarantha willed herself to remain in place.

"Do you imagine I would touch a married woman as I touched you?" His head bent a bit and an ebony lock dipped over one dark eye. She wanted to swoop it back with her fingers then explore—to touch him as he had once touched her. He was temptation and mystery at once.

"I have no idea what you would or would not do."

"You went to Kallin to see me," he said. "You came here to see me. You canna stay away from me."

"It is clear at least that your arrogance is as vigorous as ever."

"My appreciation for the obvious is as well, lass."

"I came here to learn what part you played in my friend's death."

The amusement disappeared from his features.

"When I disembarked in Leith, I searched for Penny. Her trail led toward Kallin. I found her in a farm cottage by the River Fyne. She was very ill. Shortly after my arrival, she was gone."

"Gone?"

"Passed away."

As though a shade had fallen over his eyes, she could not read the expression in them now.

"You believe I'd something to do with it?" he said.

"Why else would she have tried to travel to Kallin, despite the danger?"

"The danger?"

"Penny was not a planter's daughter or a missionary. She was a freedwoman and half-sister to my husband. Yet she traveled without escort across a land considerably more vast than the island upon which she had always lived. But when I found her I discovered that she had not journeyed across the ocean entirely alone."

"Was there a man?"

"In the cottage in which I found her, the day before I arrived Penny had brought another being into the world. A son. I found her minutes before she breathed her last. And the only words she spoke to me were your name."

Chapter 17

Prayer, of a Sort

For a moment he only stared at her. Then he turned away and scraped his hand over his face.

"She sailed to Leith?" he said, his voice muffled against his palm. "Directly from Kingston?"

"Yes. I questioned every sailor in port until I found evidence of the direction she had taken. Then I went after her. I did not come here to accuse you of evildoing."

"You'd no' be the first."

"I came here to try to understand why, without friends or companions, and without telling anyone—without telling even me or her mother or sisters that she was with child—she traveled across an ocean to you."

Wind through the belfry high above made a hollow whistle.

"Where is the child?" he finally said.

This she had not expected. She supposed she should have.

"He is with the farmer and his wife. The woman had

only just weaned her own babe from the breast and took Penny's child to nurse. When I told her I found this astonishing, she said that her father had helped found the abolitionist society in Glasgow, and that all of God's children are brothers and sisters. She and her husband are good people. Penny's son is safe." She folded her hands.

"He's no' mine."

"I did not suggest that he was, did I?"

"I didna know her. I know nothing o' her except what you've told me now."

"Fine."

"You believe it?"

"I have no other word on the matter than yours, do I?"

It was as though no time had passed, not a year, not a month, not a day. His gaze upon her was fixed, waiting, as though he knew she withheld her thoughts. It gave her the oddest, most unsettling sensation of wanting and wariness at once. Years ago, there had only been the wanting. And pleasure. And guilt.

Now she had no guilt. Now she had purpose.

"In fact, the child is fair," she admitted. "He is like my husband and my husband's father. Penny was not fair. And of course you are not."

"Babes are sometimes born fair, then turn dark later." He crossed his arms over his chest. "Perhaps my mother was fair," he said, his eyes hooded. "Or my father."

"I know they were not." She could not seem to look away from the thick muscle defined by the fabric of his coat sleeves tight over his arms. *Foolish, heedless flesh.* "Nor your grandparents."

"Aye?"

"It was, of course, the first inquiry I made of you after Penny's death."

"You've known it—"

"Since last autumn. Moreover, I know you were not in

Kingston last winter. I have, you see, done quite a lot of research."

His arms fell to his sides.

"Then do you think, lass, you might've told me all o' this the other night?"

"At the assembly rooms?"

"Aye."

"You did not give me the opportunity. And, admittedly, I was nervous. I was not expecting to see you. Not at that moment, anyway. It took me off guard." As had his hand on her hip, then her buttocks, then her breast. But she needn't admit that.

"You're no' nervous now?"

"A bit. You are obviously a little mad. Allowing everybody to believe you are some sort of depraved warlock is not the behavior of a sane man." Her sweet lips were tight, as though repressing a smile. "Rather, encouraging people to believe it. I saw the book you were reading in the library that night."

"Aye, I'm probably mad." Where this woman was concerned, definitely. And by God if it didn't feel fantastically good to know she did not believe the rumors about him. "But no more mad than a woman who secretly searches for a missing friend for more than a year when she might ask any o' her own friends to help, a woman who pretends to be a peasant in a tiny village in the middle o' Scotland when she is the daughter o' an earl. No?"

"Do not presume to understand me," she said, the pleasure gone from her eyes. "When I went to Jamaica I left behind everything that was dear to me. I was alone. Penny threw open her home and embraced me as a sister. She gave me another family. I have absolutely no interest in how you have spent the past five and a half years. I have long since put that curiosity behind me. I came here now to learn what Penny sought from you at Kallin, which I hoped would lead me to her son's father, whom she was obviously searching for in Scotland. For that reason only."

I was alone.

Judas, he'd been a fool.

Then and now. A reckless fool.

She had changed. The sincerity in her voice was the same as the girl that had driven him so mad—so irrevocably, desperately mad that it had altered the course of his life. That she was here now, standing before him, could not be real.

But the light of deviltry in the cloverleaves was gone, the spontaneous flare of joy in her smile absent. Now emotions passed across her features coolly, cleanly. He could read those emotions as though they were drawn with a fine pencil tip upon paper.

"Lass, I am sorry for your loss. Deeply sorry."

Her lips parted.

He waited for her to speak.

She pivoted and walked into the church.

Of sober gray stone and all simplicity without, within it was carved and mellowed and ancient, almost foreign. He had not entered it since he had been a boy, not since he and his cousin had shaken the dirt of Scotland from their boots and set off to sea, to war—and other horrors of their own making.

A lamp burned before the sanctuary. In a side chapel votive candles flickered in the blue and red light filtering in through a window. He watched her walk toward the chapel, step into the colors cascading from the sky, and rest her fingertips upon the stone railing.

Tying his horse, he hesitated in the doorway. The likelihood of erupting into flames if he crossed this threshold seemed fairly high. But, by God, *she was here*. Whatever the reason she had come, his damn heartbeats would not slow.

He passed within. Sacred stillness coated him, bathing

his ears with silence and curling into his nostrils. He walked toward her.

She dropped to her knees on the floor, folded her hands neatly before her, and closed her eyes. Splashed with the rich rainbow, her skin was not comfortably creamy, but gold and crimson and blue. He took in the drape of her gown on the bare stone floor and the heels of her boots and the hint of ankle revealed, thirsty for these details of her after the desert of years.

"Lass, there be kneeler cushions in the—"

"Hush, Urisk. I am praying."

There was nothing for it but to go to his knees as well. *"Judas—"*

"He is listening." She glanced upward.

"This floor is bloody cold an' hard."

"Not unlike its overlord, I daresay." She did not turn to him or open her eyes. He took his time studying her.

"How do you endure it?" he said.

"The cold, hard heart of its overlord? With patience and good manners."

"Praying on your knees, on the stone."

"Oh. This is nothing. I was married to a missionary for five years."

"Aye." In his own ears the syllable sounded surly. "You were an unlikely candidate for that post."

Her face snapped toward his. The emeralds glittered with fire.

"You're no' married now," he said.

She rose to her feet and left the church. Gabriel went after her. She was striding up the drive toward the castle, between the rows of trees with their nearly bare branches. But when she reached the gate she halted.

Sweeping off her hood, she looked upward.

He did not follow her gaze. Her face held him rapt. She had a pert nose upon which no powder obscured the plentiful freckles, a chin that was slightly pointed, arched brows, and lashes the length of a man's fantasies. His fantasies. He had fantasized about her so many times, so acutely, that awaking from the musings he'd often found himself disoriented. When he did so while standing at the helm, he finally made himself halt that imbecility.

Mostly.

"What is the significance of this symbol?" she said.

"'Tis a secret."

"Oh, please."

"I'm no' inventing this." He laughed. "It *is* a secret."

"A secret you will now share with me, Urisk."

"Are you familiar with the Order o' the Rosy Cross?"

Her brow crinkled. "The Rosy Cross?"

"The Masons."

"There is a Freemasons lodge in Kingston. Some of Kingston's most influential men are members, but also much less exalted men. So the lairds of Haiknayes belong to a cult?"

"A brotherhood."

"Are you a Mason?"

"My father an' brother were. Have I satisfied your questions?"

"Not yet. And I wish you would not call me *lass*. I am no longer a girl."

"What would you have me call you?"

"Mrs. Garland."

"No."

"Why not?"

"I'll no' call you by another man's name."

Above her right brow was a tiny scar, years old, barely pink, that he had never seen before. Her cheeks were glowing. He wanted to lay his lips on those pink peaches, one at a time, and taste their dusky heat. And on the little scar.

"What caused that scar?"

"A scratch that healed poorly. No one else has ever asked me about it."

"I've no manners to speak o'."

"When you are speaking to me, at least. With your other guests I have noticed you are remarkably gracious."

"I want to taste it," he said.

"It?"

"That scar. I want to taste your every imperfection."

The glow upon her skin became a thorough flush.

"You never used to speak this way to me."

He smiled. "I was an idiot then."

"Do you speak to all women like this? Wait—no—I don't want to know."

"Aye, you do. An' no, I dinna. Only to you, Amarantha Vale."

"You are impertinent," she said with a twitch of her lips that softened the chastisement.

"From the mouth o' the most impertinent woman I have ever known."

"I think you are trying to frighten me away."

"Does a man's desire frighten you?"

She drew a slow breath and visibly set her shoulders back.

"If it did, men being what they are, I would be cowering in corners daily."

"You are wrong," he murmured, smiling.

"About the general lustfulness of the male sex?"

"About yourself. You are still that girl."

"I should think I would know that best. Now, do return your attention to this symbol, Urisk. The other parts of it, attached to the Freemasons' star—What are they?"

"The flame, the mountain, the wave," he said, unable to look away from her face.

"A tongue of fire. A mountain peak. A wave, as of an ocean. They are not diabolical symbols." The clover-leaves were thoughtful. She had seen a world that most young English noblewomen never did. She had worked with her own hands as no other woman of privilege he had known.

He wanted to tell her the truth. The entire truth. Not even the villagers near Kallin knew all.

"Fire, earth, and water," she said. "They are the ancient elements—three of the four—lacking only air."

"I am familiar with the feeling."

"You must cease this flirting, Urisk. It is not having the effect you wish."

Slowly he drew air into his lungs, but they would not fill. Apparently having his heart trounced five and a half years earlier had done nothing to make him less of a thorough ass.

"The crossbar on the top point," he said. "It is the symbol for air."

"I see. But what does it mean?"

"Nothing."

"I don't understand." She turned her beautiful eyes to him and for a moment he was without speech.

"It means nothing now," he finally said. It was merely a convenient symbol Torquil had chosen to help communicate the secret of safety without words. And somehow it had sufficed.

"Why haven't you told anyone the truth about this?"

"No one has asked."

"*No* one? The Hounds of Hell must be much more effective than they led me to believe."

"When a ship's come into bad luck an' run through its stores o' fresh water," he heard himself saying, "the crew depends upon barrels to capture rain."

"A ship?"

"The officers have first claim on that rainwater."

"You have just changed the subject so abruptly even Iris Tate would remark on it."

"'Tis their privilege."

"I suppose I must play along." She tilted her head. "As an officer, you never acted on that privilege, did you?"

"A commander who hordes what his men need to survive has no honor," he said as though it were the most obvious thing in the world. "But, lass, when he finally takes a cup into his hands an' tastes that water . . ."

"I have no idea what you are trying to say to me."

"Amarantha Vale—"

"Garland."

"'Tis unconscionably good to see you again."

"If you had not barred me from Kallin last autumn, you might have seen me again much sooner."

"Aye."

"You will not seduce me this time, you know."

A slow, one-sided smile curved his lips. "Is that my intention?"

"I don't know. Perhaps not. Perhaps you simply invited me here from curiosity. Whatever the case, I have not come here for you."

"'Tis a disappointment, to be sure."

"One, however, that you must accept."

"No other woman has ever spoken to me as you do."

"They are all probably terrified of your dungeons."

"Except you."

"Except me." Real dungeons were not always built of iron and stone.

"Will you leave," he said, "now that you know I've no answers about your friend?"

"I promised Libby that I would assist with her project. You won't throw me out, will you?"

"Never."

"And I have not finished interrogating you."

"What more will you ask?"

"Isn't it obvious? I want to know if the secret you are concealing has anything to do with Penny's child."

"You believe I am the devil, after all?"

"I will discover why you keep Kallin locked up tighter than a pirate's treasure chest. And I will learn why, when Glen Village sits on a well-traveled byway, its only residents are women. Not a single man. Isn't that intriguing?"

"It might be."

"So tell me, Urisk, what exactly are you hiding?"

Chapter 18

The Knight

Amarantha looked up into his face made of stark angles and shadows and wondered how anybody could mistake him for a diabolical doer of evil deeds. He had the most beautiful eyes, full of laughter and heat. She could fall into them, *into him*.

After so long, she had not planned for this.

"If I tell you the truth now," he said, "will you leave?"

"Yes, if Libby does not need me."

"What if I need you?"

"I have already said that I am not on the table."

"Good Lord, lass, you've just put an image into my head that'll fuel my dreams for weeks—months," he said with the roguish grin she had missed.

She had *missed* his smile. She had missed *him*. Coming here had obviously been a very bad idea.

"Are you hiding Cassandra Finn and Maggie Poultney at Kallin?"

"Aye. Locked up tight in the mountains I've a castle full o' females. Now will you go?"

"You seem eager for me to do so."

"I've an estate here to put to rights. A trench to mend, a road to rebuild, fields to plow, any number o' tasks to attend to."

"Then you should probably go about doing those tasks."

"I should." His gaze dropped to her lips. "Truth is, I'm having the devil o' a time remembering you've no' come here to be seduced. My mind's preoccupied now with how to accomplish it."

"I am not seventeen any longer."

"Thank the Almighty."

"More importantly, I am not the naïve girl I was then."

"You've said that. Still, 'tis a relief to hear it."

"Why? Because this time I shan't make a cake of myself over you?"

"Because this time I can be sure that when I ride away now to hire hands to dig out that trench, you'll no' be marrying another spineless preacher before I can return."

Hoofbeats startled her from astonished paralysis and the dogs bolted toward a rider approaching along the drive.

"Good day!" Thomas Bellarmine called as he neared. The chill of the morning gave color to his skin. "Mrs. Garland, how glad I am to find you."

"Good day, Mr. Bellarmine." Her voice wobbled. The man beside her apparently thought nothing of teasing her mercilessly now, again. He had no heart.

Clearing her throat, she went toward the unexpected arrival.

"Have you been searching for me?" she said.

"Yesterday I called at Dr. Shaw's residence." He dismounted. "When I found the knocker up I called on Miss Campbell. She informed me of your journey." He looked at the duke. "Your Grace?"

"Aye."

"Thomas Bellarmine, at your service." He bowed

deeply, but was back up in an instant and proffering to her a letter. "Miss Campbell requested that I convey this to you. It is the reason I came. I don't mean to intrude on your party, Your Grace."

"You havena." His eyes were keen on the other man.

"Miss Campbell was excessively eager for you to have that letter," Mr. Bellarmine said to her.

"I shall read it without delay. Will you return to Leith now?"

"You've had a long ride, Bellarmine," the duke said. "Come inside an' take a draught."

"I am honored, Your Grace."

"See that, lass? He has respect for my consequence. You could take a lesson. Bellarmine, I dinna suppose you're a preacher?"

"No, sir. I am in Law. At present, actually, I work for my uncle who is a merchant of tea and other goods. I once finalized a contract for him with your agent in London, Mr. Du Lac. Capital fellow."

"Stay the night, Bellarmine. As many nights as you like." He drew his horse toward the stable block, the dogs rambling after him. "You'll have to care for your own animal. My groom's away an' there's only Tate's man to see to the lot."

"Of course. Thank you, Your Grace!"

The duke disappeared inside the stable.

"He is as unusual as everybody says, isn't he?" Mr. Bellarmine said, chuckling.

"I suppose so." Gabriel Hume was in fact exactly the man she had known: confident, unashamed, and an outrageous flirt. Only the shadows in his eyes were deeper now.

"I am especially grateful for his hospitality, for it gives me opportunity to spend more time with you."

"And your cousins," she said, stepping away quickly. "For they are here too."

"Mrs. Garland, I beg of you, forgive me for my

impertinence at the ball. The truth is that you are the finest woman I have the pleasure to be acquainted with. That is to say, I admire you enormously and I do hope we will be friends, as you have befriended my cousins."

"Thank you, sir. I should like to be friends."

"Capital." He glanced again toward the stable. "Your other *friend* will not mind it?"

"Hm. This prying is a poor start to our friendship, I think."

"Do forgive me, madam." Amusement ruined his contrition.

"Thank you for bringing this letter. I will leave you to see to your horse."

Inside, the hall was deserted. Amarantha went to the hearth in which a great fire crackled, settled into the comfortable sofa before it, and opened Alice's letter.

Dear Girl,

I write with alarming news. Tabitha went out to the market and returned as pale as a specter, then retired to her bedchamber for the night without dinner. This morning she came to breakfast equally ashen, and requested that I accompany her on the walk to school. I insisted that she tell me immediately what had occurred, reminding her that honesty is the only virtue required for residence in this house. But she remained close-lipped. When I said that I would write to you and insist that you return at once she relented, but she would only give me a message for you. Here is the entirety of it: "He is here." Whoever "he" is, it is clear that she fears him.

I hope you fare better in the demon's lair.

Yours,
Alice Campbell

Amarantha shoved the letter into her pocket and ran to the stairwell. She collided with the duke. His hands caught her.

For a moment his grasp tightened, holding her close, and his gaze scanned her face swiftly.

He released her.

"What has happened?" he said.

"I must find Dr. Shaw."

"Are you ill?"

"No. There is news in the letter Mr. Bellarmine brought. My friend in Leith is in danger. I must help her. I will return there at once."

"What danger?"

She tried to move around him. "It does not concern you."

He moved into her path. *"What danger?"*

"There is a man there who seeks to harm her. She is terrified. I must go."

"Can she leave Leith?"

"Leave? Her only friends are there." Modest tradesmen and women, all of them, like Dr. Shaw and Alice Campbell, members of the fledgling abolitionist society. "She has no other place to go. But she cannot remain there. I must take her to England, to my family's home. She will be safe—"

"'Tis too far. She must come here. Write a letter to her. It willna require but ten minutes to harness a carriage." He started across the hall.

"You will send your stable hand to Leith now? Night will come on before he reaches the city. And you said he was away already."

"I will go. Quickly now, lass. Write the letter."

"Wait, no. What are you—Stop! You will drive to Leith as it grows dark, to fetch her here?"

He crossed the room again and came so close that she had to tilt her head back to look into his face.

"You have said your friend is in danger. You are distressed. What else do you imagine I could do?"

"Six months ago you locked the gates of your estate against me. Three nights ago in Leith you refused to speak to me. Now you wish to *help* me?"

"Aye."

"I do not understand you!"

"There's nothing to understand." He touched her chin, abruptly, without warning, and a shock of pleasure darted through her so deep she had to capture her gasp between her teeth.

"I am merely off to assist a princess in need," he said with a half smile.

She shifted her face away from his touch.

"Do not tease about that time. I have only bad feelings about it."

A moment passed. "I see."

"But that hardly matters at present. You cannot leave here now. You have a house full of guests."

"The only guest I have an interest in has just told me she intends to leave," he said quite soberly. "This solution suits me better."

"Are you doing this to . . . to . . ."

"To?"

"To secure entrance to my bed?"

She could feel the heat climbing into her cheeks as his smile returned.

"Secure entrance?" he repeated. "Is there a lock on that bed, then? I'll no' be hesitant to search for that key too."

"Will you be serious for even a moment?"

"I am. Now I'm off to Leith. Will you give me leave to depart?"

She shook her head. "You truly are unbalanced, just as they say."

"Amarantha Vale, you'll no' escape me so easily this time." He moved away again. "That's no' a threat, by the by," he tossed over his shoulder.

"Of course it isn't. For it is nonsense."

"'Tis a promise."

Then he was gone and with appalling clarity she understood: he had no idea that he had broken her heart. And now, just as he had done then as a dashingly blithe tease with the reputation of a scoundrel, he was playing with her.

But she was no longer the naïve girl from that time. Both he and her husband had seen to that. Now she knew how to protect her heart. This time she would not fall.

Chapter 19

The Dungeon

*G*abriel's guests were gathered in the hall when Alice Campbell entered ahead of him and declared, "We are here! What have we missed?"

"Alice? How good it is to see you!" Amarantha crossed the hall, but her worried gaze was upon him. "Where is Mrs. Aiken?"

He gestured toward the foyer behind him. She passed him swiftly and went through the door. In silhouette from the pale afternoon sunshine, without words both women reached out their arms. Pale hands met dark, clasping tightly, and green eyes and brown both shone with relief.

"Thank you, my friend," Mrs. Aiken said.

"We must direct our thanks to our host," Amarantha said, turning toward him.

"'Tisna necessary." The words were all he could manage. His tongue was failing him again. Blast it, but pretty women would be the death of him. One pretty woman in particular. His heart, which was lodged firmly between his tight throat and other tight parts, was beating to quarters. Seeing her again, after only a day, was like finding wind on a dead sea.

"What an affecting reunion," Mrs. Tate said with a curl of her lip.

"Mrs. Aiken," Amarantha said, "may I introduce you to Mrs. Tate? You already know her daughters, of course."

Mrs. Aiken curtsied. "How do you do, ma'am?"

Tate's wife nodded.

"And this is Mr. Bellarmine, who is cousin to Jane, Cynthia, and Iris."

He bowed.

"I will help you settle in," Amarantha said, drawing her friend toward the door to the kitchen. "Come, we will find the housekeeper." They went out.

"Mrs. Garland did not mention that the girl was a negress," Mrs. Tate said. "How extraordinary that she sent you to fetch her, Your Grace."

"I volunteered."

"What a generous host you are, to be sure. Naturally Mrs. Aiken will lodge in the servants' quarters."

"She is not a servant," Miss Shaw said. "She had a seamstress shop in Kingston, Jamaica."

"How quaint colonials are," Mrs. Tate said with pinched lips.

"Miss Campbell, we did not expect to see you," Dr. Shaw said. "It is a happy surprise."

"I couldn't very well allow the devil to ride off from my house with the young woman under my protection, now could I?" she declared, eyes twinkling. "Iris Tate, here is your kitten." She pulled forth the animal from her big bag. "Delightful creature. Tore up the draperies in the parlor only yesterday. I am happy to have this excuse to put it into your hands. Your Grace, I don't care if you've got three dozen maidens locked up in the cellar of this castle, and if you lock up the rest of us there too. I am grateful for the rescue!"

"Your servant, ma'am." He bowed.

She cracked a laugh. "Now, Elizabeth, have you found the bones that you were looking for?"

"I have," she replied.

Behind Gabriel, Mrs. Tate whispered to her husband, "You cannot approve of this—this *invasion* of polite company."

"Keep your counsel, woman."

"I shall not. This is unacceptable." She moved to Gabriel's side. "Your Grace, your generosity to a—a *person* in need is all that is admirable. However, while I understand that in Miss Campbell's *unusual* household my daughters have taken tea with Mrs. Aiken, you can see how deleterious it would be for them to be obliged to consort with her on equal social terms here. I am certain you understand."

"If it distresses you to share a castle with any o' my guests, ma'am, you are welcome to leave. I can have the coach readied for you within minutes."

Tate cleared his throat and strode into the center of the hall. "Now, now, 'tis a merry party we are, with no' a care in the world!"

Gabriel's housekeeper appeared. "Your Grace."

He went to her.

"We've run outta beds. We've no more bedchambers either."

"Mrs. Hook, this castle once housed fifty men at arms."

"They'd have been sleeping on the floor o' this hall."

"Mm. I suppose they would have. I will move to the gatehouse. It will solve the shortage."

"You mustn't," Amarantha said behind him.

Her voice. Her actual voice. In his house. It could not be real. Yet here she stood, close enough to touch, with thorough charity in her eyes—for him.

Judas. He'd best tear one of those suits of armor off the wall and don it.

"I mustna what?" he said.

"Your guests need you here," she said. "Mrs. Aiken and I will go to the gatehouse."

"'Tain't fitting for your ladyship to double up while the gentleman there has his own bedchamber." Mrs. Hook glowered toward Bellarmine. He stood alone by the sideboard, staring into a cup of tea.

"It is fine, of course," Amarantha said. "I have spent the night in much worse straits and survived it." With a quick smile, she disappeared into the stairwell.

I have spent the night in much worse straits.

Would that he had survived that night. Would that after it he had forgotten about the girl with the cloverleaf eyes who had held his hand and given him purpose that night. But then he would not now feel this lunatic elation, this sensation pressing at him that after five and a half years his life had finally begun again.

He took his coat from the peg. "I'm off to the village to hire a footman," he said to his housekeeper, "an' a lad for the stable."

"From the village?" She crossed her arms. "I'll no' be giving orders to a peasant."

"Unless you prefer that I dress up in livery an' wait on table—"

"Your Grace!"

"—you will do as I wish. We have a full house, Mrs. Hook. Let us acquit ourselves as gracious hosts."

By God, he felt good. A sennight earlier the world had seemed grim: insufficient funds to support Kallin; unproductive farms at Haiknayes; and a miserly merchant whose cooperation he depended on now hinting that his interests would forthwith require more commitment on Gabriel's part.

Now nothing seemed insurmountable. For the first time in years, he felt like he could conquer the world.

"You saw him enter the bank." Amarantha repeated Tabitha's words as she set her pen, inkwell, and blotter on the dresser and closed her traveling case. With a comfortable cluster of furniture beside the hearth, the gatehouse was an ideal writers' retreat. "But you are certain he did not see you?"

"Almost certain." Tabitha drew a needle through a length of linen on her lap.

"You always sew when you are anxious."

Her friend's hands stilled. "How can I have come this far, Amarantha, done what I have done, and yet remain so afraid?"

"You are one of the least afraid women I have ever known, Tabitha. That you are willing, nay eager to tell the world your story proves it." Amarantha sat down beside her. "Will you now tell me the man's name?"

Tabitha's fingers curled around hers. "I cannot."

"You are safe here. Free."

"And Penny? Was she safe here?"

Amarantha drew her hands into her own lap. "Women can be bound in many ways. You know that as well as I."

"But not men?"

Amarantha could not resist smiling. "I suppose I don't really care if men are."

"I know that is not true."

"You are mistaken."

"Amarantha." Tabitha's dark gaze was uncompromising. "Not all men lie."

"Only the men I mistakenly choose to love." She took up her cloak. "I must go see how Libby's work progresses. And find a rock with which to quash myself over the head for ever confiding anything private to you."

"He would not have brought me here if he did not admire you."

"I cannot, Tabitha."

"Cannot like a duke?"

"Cannot trust a duke. That duke, rather. Libby says that her project should require at least a fortnight. You and I will have ample time to write, if you are able," she added.

"I am."

"Your memoir will be a fantastic success. Tomorrow we will begin writing again. I will send Mrs. Hook here with tea. Now rest until dinner."

The afternoon had lengthened and wind swept through the forecourt as Amarantha crossed it. Thomas Bellarmine stepped away from the shadows at the wall of the fortress and came toward her.

"Are you hiding, Mr. Bellarmine?"

"Not at all. There is already a man of mystery in the house. And what an extraordinary person the Duke of Loch Irvine is. I overheard my aunt saying that he had gone voluntarily to collect Mrs. Aiken and Miss Campbell from Leith."

"He did." And she still did not entirely understand why, except that he was a little mad.

"Mrs. Aiken . . . She is a friend of yours from the colonies?"

"She was a member of my husband's church and attended the mission school. We grew very fond."

"I see."

The sour flavor on Amarantha's tongue was familiar. In Jamaica plenty of people disapproved of friendship between whites and blacks. But in Leith Amarantha's acquaintances were few and most were members of the abolitionist society.

"I am off now to assist Libby," she said. "Good afternoon, sir."

"I wish you would call me Thomas."

"Thank you, but, our nascent friendship notwithstanding, we are not well enough acquainted."

"I fear I am beginning to make a habit of unsuitable behavior," he said a bit oddly, and looked at the ground.

"Will you join me inside?" she said.

"I—I will walk for a bit. In the garden, I think. It's a tangle of weeds. No gardener, I guess. But I don't suppose I'll notice."

"Mr. Bellarmine, something troubles you."

"Mrs. Garland, how perceptive you are. Or perhaps I am merely a poor dissembler. I should beg Loch Irvine for lessons in adopting a mysterious façade. The ladies certainly seem to admire that sort of thing."

"I don't think he adopts any façade. I do think he enjoys teasing."

"Teasing? Madam, it seems we know two different dukes." He attempted a chuckle.

Amarantha went to his side. "Thomas, I should very much like a stroll in the garden now as well."

He peered at her skeptically. "You are shivering."

"Then we must walk swiftly to encourage warmth." She tucked her hand into his arm. "Lead the way, sir."

He squeezed her hand upon his arm. "What a fortunate man Reverend Garland was."

SHE WAS NOT in the hall. She was not in the upper chamber with Miss Shaw and Iris Tate. She was not in the library or in the south parlor. He went to the kitchen. She was not there either. *Blast it*, he'd swear the woman was intentionally eluding him.

Perhaps she had gone for another solitary walk. To the church? He would pray for an hour on the cold stone floor. Two hours. However many she required.

"Mrs. Hook, have you seen—" He could not bring himself to say the name.

"The lady with the fiery hair, Your Grace?"

He scratched his chin. "That transparent, am I?"

"Mr. Ziyaeddin afforded me a hint o' the direction o' the wind."

"How helpful." The late-afternoon sun was slanting through the kitchen door, which was thrown open to allow the breeze to cool the room. The place smelled of meat and spices. *Pie*. The scents of cooking here were like a welcoming embrace. In this kitchen his mother had instructed him in the manners he must possess to sit at great lords' tables. When he had announced that he would never eat at table with great lords because he intended to be a sailor, she had smiled and said that after he grew weary of sailing the seven seas and returned to land again he would be glad to know how to comport himself among men of power.

He wondered if the household at Kallin had enough supplies to bake pie. He would send a ham. Rather, three. And a sack of flour. And a dairy cow. If he could afford to purchase them.

He had hired all the hands in the village for the trench. He would hire local men for the lambing. More for the shearing. Then to market with the wool. And the deal he was planning with Tate to share cargo space would net thousands.

Yes, indeed, things seemed rosier all the time.

With practiced ease and a massive knife his housekeeper chopped onions. She was a wretched baker, but a fully competent cook. Still, he should hire an actual cook—and release her again when he left?

He wanted to stay.

And he wanted *her* to stay: the lady with the fiery hair who turned him inside out even now, after everything.

"Mrs. Garland be in the cellar, Your Grace," his housekeeper said. "No' an hour since when she came in with that upstart I gave her the key to the cellar an' she's no' returned it yet."

"Upstart?"

"Aye, an' him all cow's eyes at her."

Bellarmine.

"Odd she's not come back up yet," Mrs. Hook said. "But she dinna seem the sort o' lady to forget returning a key."

He thought of the brass key in the reading room, buried between her breasts.

Snatching up a candle, he swung open the cellar door and descended the narrow stairs. Beyond a shelf of wine bottles, he found her standing before the iron bars of a cell. Only the light of late afternoon that poked through a window illumined her face.

"No maidens," she said.

"Disappointed?"

"Vastly. Why haven't you converted these cells into storage spaces?"

"You've a particular fondness for storage cellars? I wonder why."

"I am asking why you still keep a jail in your house."

"I've no' lived at Haiknayes since I was a lad. But if you wish, I'll order the place renovated immediately. Once I've a bit o' ready cash." He could not manage to stanch his smile.

"No ready cash?"

"None to speak of."

"So you are in need of funds at present?"

"Aye."

"I see."

"What do you see with those cloverleaf eyes, lass?"

"Cloverleaf'? Don't be absurd."

"I was being poetical."

"I think I prefer your taciturn prose." A hint of pink stained her cheeks. "Thank you for bringing my friends here. I am grateful."

"In fact you are relieved. Who is Mrs. Aiken?"

"A friend from Kingston."

"Why is she in Scotland?"

"She sailed here."

"By God, you'll make me pull teeth, willna you?"

"Her business is none of yours." The blush beneath the freckles darkened.

For five and a half years he had dreamed of this, her flushed skin, its soft, radiant beauty. Now here she was, within reach.

He should resist.

Greater men than he had fallen to much lesser temptations.

Lifting his hand, he touched her—barely—stroking the line of her delicate jaw with one knuckle. Her lashes twitched.

Judas, she still felt like beauty, perfect beauty. Five years ago she had been hot, damp, the tropical heat and her arousal radiating from her. Yet now her skin was cool.

Still, he was halfway to an erection.

Upon a little breath, her lips parted, offering a glimpse of her pink tongue.

Three-quarters of the way.

"Lass," he said none too steadily. "You can trust me."

"I really cannot fathom how you imagine that I would."

"She is safe here. But she would be safer if you told me her troubles."

"Why are you touching me again?"

"I've a list o' reasons, beginning with you're so damn touchable."

"I wish you would not," she said, turning away from him and putting her back to the cell.

"Tell me Mrs. Aiken's trouble," he said.

"Why do you wish to know?"

"I want to help you."

She looked at him. In the cloverleaves were defiance and anger he had never seen there.

"When after a considerable struggle Tabitha was able to purchase her own freedom," she said, "she married a freedman. A year later, he was murdered. His murderers said they did so at the behest of a man who wished to have her as his mistress. They said that if she did not obey, that man would wrest her to another island where no one knew of her freedom, and keep her there. She escaped onto the first ship that would conceal her, and she sailed here. She saw this man at Leith two days ago and fears that he has come to Scotland in search of her, and that he will find her."

"I willna allow it."

"You have no authority over her."

"Lass, I'm a duke."

"And she is a free person. What's more, I don't believe your business partner's wife would be particularly pleased over your championship of a former enslaved woman."

"Mrs. Tate can go to the devil."

"Cynthia Tate certainly thinks they all already have." A glimmer entered her eyes. "And possibly Jane too."

"Children will fear the dark," he murmured.

"I think you revel in people believing you are a demon."

"'Tis what it must be."

"Why? To accomplish what?"

"Let me help Mrs. Aiken."

"It is not your trouble to solve."

"Allow it to be." He took a step toward her.

"What do you hope to gain from—" She threw up a palm. "Don't—What are you doing?"

"Trying to get closer to those lips."

"*Those* lips?"

"I have had so many fantasies about those lips."

"Fantasies?" she said as though she were swallowing the word.

"Aye, fantasies. Your lips on mine, an' elsewhere. On me. They entrance me."

She leaped backward, putting a yard between them. "How can you *be* this way?"

"Entranced by your lips? It requires no effort whatsoever."

"*Stop.* I am grateful to you for going to Leith and bringing Tabitha here. And your kindness to Libby is commendable. But I do not understand your interest in the particulars of my friend's situation. Given all, it would be witless of me not to believe that you are doing all of this in order to wrest something from me."

"Something?"

She pinned her lips tightly together. Then she muttered, "I am no longer a downy girl."

"I believe you have insisted on that three or four times already. Perhaps five."

"Have you not listened to anything I've said? Have you not heard my words about Penny, searching for a man who obviously abandoned her? Or Tabitha, who fears a man so greatly that she has fled the only home she ever knew?"

"You believe your fate will be the same?"

"Of course not. My skin gives me protection that theirs does not. But I am not naïve. No longer. In this world, women are prey if they do not protect themselves when they are able."

"All right." He leaned his shoulder into the iron bar beside him and crossed his arms. "We'll pretend that I am a scoundrel intent on taking advantage o' a woman." He nodded toward her. "You."

Her nostrils flared. "You make sport of my words?"

"Wait. I've no' finished. Now, let us pretend that you are a widow without any other entanglement. You havena another entanglement, have you?"

"Entanglement?"

"Bellarmine's been sniffing around you." He seemed abruptly forbidding standing so casually in his own dungeon.

"Crudely stated," she said.

"Aye. But accurately?"

"Perhaps."

Unfolding his arms he came toward her.

"Perhaps, how?" he said in a decided growl.

Her pulse was reckless. "Perhaps I am madly in love with him."

"I'll change your mind."

"I am not madly in love with him."

His lips curved into a devil's smile. "'Tis good to hear."

"I don't know why I am speaking to you like this."

"Whatever the reason, I approve."

"You . . ." She could not seem to detach her gaze from his mouth. "You make me feel things I have not felt in years," she said upon a rush of breath.

"What things?"

She pressed her back against the cell bars. "You must know."

"Tell me anyway." He wrapped his hand around the bar by her head. "I want to hear the words pass through those lips."

"Is this what men like you do with women?"

"There are no men like me. An' I only do this with you, here, now. What do you feel?"

"I feel . . . *weak*."

"No' exactly what I hoped to hear."

"With longing," she whispered.

He swallowed hard. "All right. That's better."

"Not better for me."

"Aye. Better for both o' us."

"I will not succumb to you."

"Why not?" Taking up a lock of her hair, he spun it around one finger then leaned in and seemed to draw a long inhale. "You're no' a girl, an' I'm no' a foolish lad. This seems the ideal time to succumb."

"I am wiser," she forced through her lips. "I know the longing is false."

"It feels plenty real to me." The backs of his knuckles touched her cheek again, the softest caress that made her shudder. This time she did not flinch away.

"But I have regretted one thing," she said.

He bent his head and his next words came so close that she could feel his heat upon her skin.

"What one thing have you regretted, lass?"

"That I did not make you kiss me the morning the *Theia* sailed. I wished you had kissed me. Then."

He drew back.

Then he stepped back.

"You believe you could have made me kiss you that morning?"

"Yes. I was not so naïve that I could not see you wanted to."

His features seemed carved from stone. "'Tis the *one* thing you have regretted?"

"Yes. I—"

Beyond the cell window, a woman screamed in the forecourt.

He pivoted and took the steps three at a time. Amarantha went after him. Following him through the kitchen, she burst out of the building into the cold and a scene of confusion.

Wails emanated from a window above. The housekeeper, the kitchen maid, the footman, Tabitha, and Mr. Bellarmine all seemed to be rushing from different directions toward a single spot. And on the flank of the castle, Mrs. Tate was sprawled immobile on the ground.

Chapter 20

Candles

"I didn't, Papa!" Cynthia Tate cried. She and her father had retreated to a separate chamber, but everyone who was gathered in the great hall could hear them. "Forgive me, I beg of you!"

Dr. Shaw entered the hall.

"Doctor, tell us at once how she fares," Alice demanded.

"The ankle is broken. But it is a clean break and Elizabeth has set it expertly. Otherwise, Mrs. Tate has suffered a number of uncomfortable bruises. I have given her a draught, which should allow her to sleep."

"We are so grateful, Doctor," Jane said. "Your Grace, on behalf of my family, I apologize for this disturbance."

"Accidents happen." His eyes were hooded.

"But *how* did it happen?" Alice said.

"Mrs. Tate indicated that she tripped over the kitten," Dr. Shaw said.

"Out the window? Who would believe that?"

"Not I," Libby said, entering the room. "Given the

distance of the window from the floor, the width of the wall, and Mrs. Tate's height, it is impossible."

"Are you suggesting, Elizabeth, that Cynthia pushed her mother out the window?" Alice said.

"Of course not," Dr. Shaw said. "Come, Elizabeth. You will wish to change before dinner."

They went from the hall.

"Bellarmine," the duke said, taking up a carafe. "Will you take a dram?"

Thomas looked up from his study of the floor. "Don't mind if I do."

"I should like to drink whiskey, too," Iris declared.

"When you're older," the duke said, and for the first time in hours he smiled. He carried a glass to Jane. "Drink it, lass. 'Twill help."

Wide-eyed, Jane sipped, and coughed.

"Take it slowly," he said. "Anybody else care for whiskey?" His gaze came to Amarantha, unsmiling now. "Or rum?"

"Aha, the exotic brew of the Indies," Thomas said. "Although I suppose not so exotic to some members of our party."

"If you are suggesting, sir," Tabitha said, "that Mrs. Garland and I were wont to drink spirits in Jamaica, you are mistaken. We are good Christian women."

"I—I—" A flush crept over his cheeks. "Not at all, Mrs.—ma'am. I beg your pardon for—that is—for—" He bowed. "I do beg your pardon."

"Mr. Bellarmine," Amarantha said. "Mrs. Aiken is teasing you."

His brow pleated.

"My husband owned a sugar mill," Tabitha said. "His customers paid him with molasses which he used to distill rum."

"Raw rum is only suitable for hollowing out a man's insides," Alice stated.

"No' if a man adds sugar to the glass," the duke said. He was watching Amarantha, not with pleasure, she thought, and she was a tangle of contradictory emotions.

How on earth could honesty feel so utterly confusing?

"Well now." Mr. Tate strode in. "Mrs. Tate is fast asleep an' the girl's gone to bed."

Jane moved toward him. "Papa—"

"'Tis no' a punishment, Janie. She wishes it." He clapped his hands over his waistcoat. "Now, Duke, where's that roast we've been smelling all day? Nothing like country air to give a man a hearty appetite."

IT WAS A merry feast. Without Mrs. Tate to insist on appropriate seating arrangements, everybody sat wherever they wished. Leading Tabitha to the place at the right of the head, the duke bent her ear throughout dinner. Occasionally he spoke to Iris at his left, who was mostly occupied with the kitten in her lap. He did not once look at Amarantha.

"His Grace asked many questions about Jonathan's distillery," Tabitha said after tea as they walked across the forecourt to the gatehouse. "He is well-informed. Has he a distillery of his own?"

"I don't know." She entered their quarters. "I know little about him. Once I thought I did. But he is a stranger now." A stranger who still made her weak with longing. She turned to close the door and a young man was mounting the steps. Lean and pale-skinned, with a shock of short brown hair, he had the resting energy of a creature just on the cusp of manhood.

"Milady, His Grace wishes to see you at church at once."

"Now? It must be nearly midnight."

"At church?" Tabitha turned a meaningful look to Amarantha.

"I cannot. Tell him—"

"Begging your pardon, milady, but he said if you dinna come now, he'll come an' collect you. An' he said to remind you that he be a duke."

Amarantha laughed, then snapped her mouth shut.

"Mrs. Garland will come in a moment." Tabitha closed the door on the youth. "You must go."

"For what purpose? No. I should not—"

"Amarantha, he looks at you the way my Jonathan used to look at me."

Her breaths stole from between her lips in hopeless little wisps.

"That cannot be."

"You lecture me not to run away from my fears, yet here you are doing so yourself." Tabitha fastened the cloak clasp beneath Amarantha's chin. "If you have not returned here in thirty minutes, I will send Dr. Shaw after you."

"Ten minutes."

"Twenty-five."

"Have you a clock?"

Tabitha pushed her toward the door.

Frigid wind swept across the forecourt. The young man held forth a coat.

"'Tis a frightful night, milady. His Grace bade me bring this."

It was heavy, the black wool draping to the ground. *His* coat. Dragging courage into her lungs with the cold air, she said, "I am ready."

The youth halted at the door of the church.

"You are not coming in?" she said.

"I was only to fetch you." He bowed and disappeared into the darkness.

Lit with pillar candles the length of the nave, with more candles in the side chapel in which she had knelt the day before, the church glowed warmly despite the chilly air. The Duke of Loch Irvine stood at the far end, before the chancel. When the door creaked closed, he turned to face her.

"Have you summoned me for a diabolical midnight ritual?" Her question echoed in the high stone vaults.

"You came."

"I obeyed under threat."

"You came," he said again.

"If you are planning to sacrifice me to a horrid demon, you should not have used such cheerful candles. Black would have suited the occasion better."

He walked toward her and Amarantha could not make her feet or legs function. He was all angles and shadows and wide shoulders and sure stride and he did look like a devil.

Then he was no more than a yard away and it seemed that he would not halt. She backed up and banged into the door. He stopped barely a foot from her.

"You came," he said in a quiet, deep voice—nothing like a devil—rather like a prayer.

"If the white candles are meant to symbolize purity," she said, pushing off her hood, "I think it is probably important for you to know that you have chosen the wrong victim. I would not want the ritual spilling of a virgin's blood to be in vain."

"Dinna insult my candles." His gaze moved over her hair. "They cost the worth of an honest man's day's wages an' wanted a quarter hour to light."

"The young man that led me here to my doom did not light them?"

The slightest crease teased one side of his mouth. "A devil's got to see to his own candles if he's to do the thing correctly."

"I see. They are very nice candles. Thank you for the loan of your coat." She tugged it off and gave it to him.

He tossed it on the ground.

"Now," he said.

"Now you will produce some sort of ritual dagger, I assume?"

"If by dagger you mean my pointed charm, aye." In the fire-lit darkness his eyes seemed peculiarly bright.

"What is this about?"

"By God, now that you're here, I'm having trouble re-calling it."

"Church," she prompted. "Candles. Diabolical ritual. Uncompromising order to obey."

"Amarantha Vale—"

"Garland."

"—allow me to be clear now." He moved forward and the space between them became mere inches. His shad-owed gaze raked her face. Lifting a hand, he placed his palm on the door beside her and bent his head. She tilted her chin upward. If he wanted her lips closer, she would satisfy him in that. She wanted it too. She wanted him and she was frightened. Dressed up in candlelight and gentle humor, there was danger here.

"Clear," she barely managed to mouth, "about what?"

"If I were a dishonorable man"—his words came as soft heat across her lips—"I would have kissed you that morning."

"Oh?" It sounded like a sigh.

"An' I would kiss you now."

"But you won't?"

"God knows, I want to."

"You—"

"I willna."

The air was entirely still around them, all silent save for the wind singing against the church walls without. They were entirely alone and she was cold and hot, and trembling fiercely.

"What if I want you to kiss me now?" She nearly choked over her courage.

"I've no' asked you here to make love to you."

"You did not ask." She could not stop staring at his lips. They were beautiful: lush and dusky and carved by a divine sculptor like his cheekbones and heavy brows and fine flaring nose. The longing to feel him pressed out from beneath her skin. She wanted her fingertips on his face, to touch every feature. "You demanded."

"I have a piece to say."

"Why didn't you say it in the dungeon?"

"You're a churchy woman."

At present she felt far from churchy. Her entire body was alive as it had not been in years, her breasts prickling and belly tight. She needed more than her fingertips on his face. She needed her lips on his. *Finally.*

Damn her fear. Damn her certain knowledge that this would end—*must end*—poorly. She wanted him.

"If you only intend to speak to me, you needn't stand quite so close," she said. "Or close at all, really. You are trying to tease me."

"No."

"Then what are you doing?"

"I'm making a show o' heroic self-restraint." He seemed to draw a deep breath. "Now listen, woman—"

"*Woman*? I think I prefer that to *lass.*"

"Aye?"

"It sounds thrillingly savage. Highlanders, you know."

"I was born an' raised here in Midlothian."

"You have an estate in the Highlands. That must count for something."

"I'm no' a beast."

"This really is not the best circumstance in which to try to convince me of that."

"You already know I am no beast. Amarantha . . ."

"Gabriel," she whispered, tasting his name on her tongue for the first time. It was sweet and rich and sacred all at once.

She saw the hard constriction of his throat.

"In a church now," he said, "I have a promise to make to you."

"A promise?"

"I will never lie to you. An' I ask you to trust me."

"Why should I?"

"I'm a wee bit desperate, you see."

"Desperate, how?"

"Desperate to have you."

"How is that intended to make me trust you?"

"If you willna trust me," he said, "I'll have to resort to a ritual."

She could reach up, grab his taut jaw between her hands, and draw his mouth to hers. "What sort of ritual?"

"Mysterious gestures. Muttered incantations. The usual sort."

"And the ritual sacrifice would be . . . ?"

"Me, o' course." He seemed to inhale close to her temple. "I'll even give you the knife to perform it."

"The knife?"

"You've always held it anyway." His hand fell away from the door. "Now," he said. "Go."

"Go?"

"Go."

"Go?"

"Aye. I'm taking up the gauntlet you've thrown down."

"What gauntlet?"

"I'll no' touch you."

"You won't?" she said upon what sounded a bit like a groan.

"No' until you trust me again. Now, go."

She could not move; her limbs were frozen. She blinked.

"Blast it, woman. Go."

"You know, I don't care for being ordered about by a man."

"O' course you dinna. *Go.*"

Dragging open the door, she slipped out. The wind battered her the length of the drive. Torches had been set at intervals all the way to the keep. *For her.* She knew it was all for her. He had said the entire house party was for her.

But how could she believe it? In four and a half years of marriage *her own husband* had done nothing for her.

She mounted the steps to the gatehouse on peculiarly light feet.

"You have just missed Jane Tate," Tabitha said as Amarantha removed her cloak.

"She came here? This late?"

"Yes. What happened at the church?" Tabitha's eyes were worried.

"That can wait." She wanted to hold it to herself, to savor it privately for a time. "Has Mrs. Tate's condition worsened? Or is it Cynthia?"

"No. Jane is distressed about another matter, Amarantha. Her parents have betrothed her to a man without her consent."

"Oh, good heavens. That is unfortunate indeed."

"She is afraid of him and came to seek counsel of you, who have been married."

"But I consented to my marriage." She hung her cloak on the peg. "Who is this bridegroom she fears?"

She turned to meet Tabitha's silence.

"He is the Duke of Loch Irvinc."

Chapter 21

The Seventh Sin

When Gabriel entered the stable, the new stable hand was attaching the final leather to the gig.

Ziyaeddin stood beside it.

"Mrs. Hook tells me you are leaving," Gabriel said.

Ziya gestured for the lad to go and took up the horse's lead to draw it and the carriage from the building. "With the moving of furniture and the invasion of my library—"

"*My* library."

"—and the screaming women being tossed from windows, peace has gone from this place."

"The house in Leith is too small for your canvases."

"The chimneys function and the butcher delivers weekly. In comparison to a skiff in the middle of the sea, it is a palace."

They passed into the sunshine. Ziyaeddin climbed into the gig, set his cane beside him, and took up the reins.

"You, I suspect, will remain here as long as she will. You are a fool, Scot."

"Possibly." He smiled. "Probably." But she wanted him. Of that he was now certain. "Godspeed."

"Peace be with you, my friend. If at all possible in present circumstances," Ziya added, and flicked the reins.

"Mick," Gabriel said to the lad emerging from the stable. "Bring me the saddle you've just polished. An' my horse's blanket."

"Off to the trenches, Captain?"

"I am." He took Beelzebub's bridle from a hook. "Am I to understand by this obsolete title that you've an interest in the navy?"

"Aye, sir. I dream o' it. Spent my younger days on the sea with my uncle. He was a fisherman. I miss it fiercely, Captain."

"How old are you, Mick?"

"Nineteen next month, sir."

The night before, the lad had done Gabriel's bidding with good humor and without question. He was young and strong, and not unintelligent. Ziya could use a man like this at the house at Leith, and the lad would be close to the docks.

"Just the laird I've been looking for!" Tate's voice boomed through the stable.

"Good morning, Mr. Tate. Miss Cynthia." Gabriel bowed.

The girl dipped him a swift curtsy, her gaze shifting swiftly to the youth hefting the saddle.

Glancing up, Mick's eyes widened.

"Mick, be about your business now," Gabriel said, taking the saddle.

"Aye, Captain." Darting another glance at the girl, he went.

"Papa," she said, "May I go see Mama now?"

"Go along."

She hurried away.

"How does Mrs. Tate do this morning?" Gabriel said.

"Perfectly well! Ankle's swollen up. But the doctor's dosed her with laudanum."

Gabriel buckled the girth. "An' Miss Cynthia?"

"As you've seen, the poor lass be all nerves." Tate shook his head. "Now, my Janie, she's a jewel. Never frets nor pesters nor says a contrary word to a man. An exemplary female."

Gabriel repressed a yawn.

"An' she's a sight for the eyes," Tate said.

If a man liked conventional, somewhat listless beauty.

Gabriel drew his horse from the stall. On the drive, he mounted.

"My Janie would make a fine duchess."

And there it was: the offer Gabriel had anticipated since the moment the Tate family had arrived at Haiknayes. Neither parent had been subtle.

"What do you say to that, Your Grace? Tate an' Hume Mercantile!" he said, making an arc with his arm as though spelling it out in the sky. "Your friends in the navy an' my gold. Men in ports from Leith to Bridgetown'll envy the partnership."

"You've sufficient influence at many o' those ports already, Tate. You hardly need a partner. Nor does the Royal Navy require that British merchants be former commanders in order to have reason to protect their ships."

"O' course," Tate blustered, waving his hand again. "But a man's wise to shore up every advantage he can. 'Tain't lad's play, this business."

"I'm certain you canna be suggesting, sir, that I am a lad," Gabriel said. "Or that I consider a ship a plaything."

"No, no!" He made a jovial scowl. "Come now, Loch Irvine," he said with an abruptly forthright air. "She's a little beauty, an' docile as a tulip. 'Twould ease our negotiations to be family."

The man was clever—much cleverer than Gabriel had

understood before. This was not an offer. It was a condition.

"Mr. Tate, I'm no' searching for a wife at present."

"Ha ha! What vigorous young man is? I'm no' insisting you rush to the altar, lad. Sew your wild oats before we finalize matters. After that . . . a man's private concerns are his own." He offered a confiding poke of his forefinger. "I wouldna be eager to do business with you if I didna trust in your discretion."

"I am honored by your trust, sir. But I dinna care for ultimatums, nor for men who neglect their wives—whatever the justification."

Tate's smile looked painted on. "You're a savvy negotiator, Duke. I expected as much from a man o' your experience."

Now the blackguard was trying to sweeten him up.

"I've matters to see to. I look forward to continuing our conversation about cargo, shares, an' fees after lunch." He gave Beelzebub the rein.

IN KEEPING WITH her new vow to be at all times forthright and honest—however wretchedly confusing it was—when early morning became late morning and still the duke had not appeared in the company of his guests, Amarantha donned cloak and bonnet and left the fortress in search of him.

She was only halfway along the drive when he appeared at its end, riding his great big black horse toward the castle.

He wore no intimidating black coat today, instead a duster of unremarkable hue and breeches and boots suitable to the countryside. Yet even the manner in which he sat astride the creature and held the reins as though he barely needed to touch the magnificent animal for it to do his bidding seemed to proclaim his dominance of everything about.

"Off to church again, lass?" he said, touching the brim of his hat. "Memories o' your last visit there so fine you canna stay away, no doubt."

"Not at all," she said, tucking her hands into her pockets. Best to keep them far from where they might grab him. "But I suspect it would do your blotched soul good to revisit church this morning."

"Blotched, hm?" The smile hitched sideways.

He dismounted with great control yet an entire lack of concern for ducal elegance. He was a strong, virile man-beast, not remotely like the English noblemen that filled her mother's letters. He removed his gloves and laid them atop the saddle, then took his hat into his hand.

"I dinna recall committing any sins o' late."

"Oh, you have."

"I also dinna recall you being quite so concerned with the state o' a man's soul."

"I knew very little about religion then."

"You've had your catechism since?"

"And then some."

He fixed the reins firmly at the base of the animal's mane and patted the great, muscular stallion on the haunch. It started forward, and then trotted directly into the stable.

"There is a diabolical talent, to be sure," she said. "Does every creature on this estate do its master's bidding, without even a spoken word?"

He came forward and stood before her.

"No' every creature," he said rather low. "But I am working on it."

He smelled like heaven, like the wind and the coming spring and some subtle hint of cologne.

"You are not my master," she said.

"True. An' I would never want you to do anything without words anyway," he said with an almost-smile. "No' for me. Or even to me. I am particularly fond o' your voice. As well as other bits o' you." His gaze dipped to her breasts. "A weary horse that sees home will always go toward it eagerly."

"You should lift your eyes now."

"An' an enchanted man that sees the woman who has enchanted him will take a long look just as eagerly."

"I have no enchantments. You, recall, are the dark lord who reads books on magic potions."

"I would like to have a potion now that would wipe the care from those pretty eyes. What is amiss, lass?"

"How swiftly he forgets."

"Never," he said emphatically.

"Your blotched soul is amiss."

He seemed to rest back on his heels, comfortable in his big, powerful manner.

"All right, this mystery ought to be easy enough to solve by running through the usual sins. Let us see . . . I've no' committed gluttony lately."

She allowed herself to peruse his shoulders, chest and legs. If he could ogle her, it seemed only just.

"You do seem fit," she said.

He was watching her ogling him. "'Tis all the climbing on roofs an' chopping wood."

"Chopping wood? Are you so short of funds that you cannot afford to hire a man to chop wood?"

"Well . . . 'tis a wee bit complicated."

"Which I know you will not explain. So, perhaps we should return to your sins."

"Rather, lack thereo'."

"I will be the judge of that, Urisk."

"Call me Gabriel again."

"I do not believe I shall. Avarice?"

"No. In fact, no' three hours ago I proved my resistance to avarice quite impressively."

"You did?"

He placed a palm over his heart. "On my honor."

"I am not certain that is firm enough grounds to convince me of anything. But we can return to avarice later. Envy?"

He laughed. "What reason have I to envy another man?"

She shook her head. "You truly are astonishing."

"My point exactly."

"Which brings us to vanity."

He smiled beautifully. "I suppose you will now add pride to that."

"I am on the fence about pride, actually. It is clear that you care about your estates."

"Thus the roof repairing," he said, "which serves to strike sloth off the list too."

"But I do not think you are proud of them."

Abruptly he sobered. "No' at present. But I will be."

"And just there, behind those words, is the concealment. Your sin of choice, Urisk, seems to be dishonesty."

He said nothing for a moment, only looked steadily into her eyes that he had ridiculously—*wonderfully*—called cloverleaves. Finally he spoke.

"How did lust fall off the list?"

She blinked. "Lust?"

"You made it through six o' the Seven Deadly Sins, then skipped lust an' went straight to the Ten Commandments. Due to your gauntlet, I canna put lust into action at present. But I was looking forward to at least discussing it with you."

"You are impossible."

"Aye. Impossibly happy that you're standing here on my land, Amarantha Vale." He smiled the lovely smile, the gentle, contented smile she had once believed he reserved only for her.

"Dishonesty, Urisk, is an unkindness to those to whom you lie."

"Concealment isna dishonesty, lass. But it is, on occasion, necessary."

"Perhaps there is a gray area." In which she had lived for five and a half years. "I suppose you consider it necessary to conceal your betrothal to Miss Jane Tate?"

He frowned. "I'm no' betrothed to Miss Tate."

"Last night, when you were in the church trying to seduce me, she told Mrs. Aiken that she is betrothed to you, and, incidentally, that she is terrified of the prospect."

"Well," he said upon a great exhale. "'Tis remarkable how many insults a woman can pack into a single sentence."

"I beg your pardon?"

"An' well you should beg it." Moving away he lifted his hand to pass it up and over his face, and into his hair. Finally he dropped his arm and turned again to her. "Firstly, I am no' betrothed to Miss Jane Tate. I'm no' betrothed to anybody."

"But, why would—"

"Forgive me for interrupting, lass. But I am about to engage in a bit o' grand speechifying in my defense. I prefer to make the speech in one go, if you dinna mind?"

She shook her head.

"Much obliged." He nodded. "Now, where was I?"

"You are not betrothed to anybody."

"Aye. Secondly, to protect the guilty I'll no' supply names an' dates as proof, but I can say with great certainty that 'tisna entirely unknown for lasses to misrepresent the truth o' such matters. But even had I no personal experience with this, I would surely know if I were betrothed at this time."

He paused as though expecting her to comment. Amarantha pulled her lips between her teeth.

"Excellent," he said. "Now, thirdly, at the risk o' displeasing you with ungentlemanly frankness, I will admit that whether a timorous mouse is terrified o' me or no', I couldna care less. I've already told you how little I care o' the opinion anybody has about me—present company excepted. An' fourthly . . ." He walked toward her until he was very close. "Last night in the church I didna try to seduce you. I didna even touch you—though that was, admittedly, a challenge. An' I dinna intend to touch you again, no' until matters in that pretty an' damnably complicated head o' yours take a turn. What do you have to say to that?"

"I may speak now?"

"Aye, but my speech includes a fifthly, so make it brief."

"I concede your fourth point," she said. "My susceptibility is surely at fault. Candles notwithstanding, I realize that the ease with which you succeed in seducing me does not mean that you intend it. So I suppose that in some ways I have changed very little in five and a half years."

His eyes arrested. "Your suscepti—succeed—Clarify those words now."

"I thought you had a fifthly."

He looked up at the branches of the trees above and she heard him pull in a breath. His gaze met hers again.

"I intend you no harm, Amarantha," he said cleanly. "I thought I made that completely clear last night."

Her foot fell back, enlarging the space between them. "Yet I remain unconvinced."

His jaw muscles flexed rather dramatically.

Then he started toward the stable.

She followed. "Is that all?"

"What else would you have me say? You've no right to be angry with me."

"I am not angry with you about the betrothal—rather, the not-betrothal. I was not even angry before the first three points of your speech."

He halted at the door. "No?"

"No. Generally I believe anger springs from hurt—"

"That sounds about right," he growled.

"—and I am not hurt. That is, I was not. I was not even surprised when I heard the news."

"You werena surprised?"

She shook her head.

"No' even after last night?"

"No."

His brow cut downward. "Go."

"Go? Again?"

"Aye."

"From the yard here?"

"From my house. From my land."

Treacly heat rushed through her. "You are throwing me out?"

"It seems I am."

"After you said that you are *happy* I am here?"

"No' under these circumstances. An' you want to go. You are eager to go."

"I am?"

"Aye. An' as you have made your purpose here clear, but I have no further concealed matters to reveal to you, you may as well. Mick!" he called through the open stable door.

The young stable hand appeared.

"Aye, Captain?"

"This lady intends to depart Haiknayes shortly. Make any animal or vehicle available to her as she requires, to go anywhere she wishes. She will give you instructions."

With an abrupt bow reminiscent of the young naval officer he had been, the duke said, "Godspeed, ma'am." He strode past her toward the castle.

In her pockets, she made her hands into fists.

"I am not leaving Haiknayes, Mick." Not until she had got what she came for. "But I would enjoy a ride now. A saddle horse, if you please."

HE WOULD WRING Tate's neck. Then he would wring his own, for good measure.

He had thrown her out.

By God, he'd been feeling astonishingly good before that moment there on the driveway. Better than he had in months. Years.

He had thrown her out.

When would he cease being a coward—sending away the woman he wanted *for the second time*—because he was afraid of what? Having his heart crushed again?

"Pour a dram of that for me, too, Your Grace." In the corner of the sofa before the hearth, cocooned in shawls, Miss Alice Campbell looked like a little bird tucked into a winter's nest. He carried a glass of whiskey to her.

"You're fond o' spirits, Miss Campbell?"

"And equally fond of requiring young, handsome gentlemen to wait on me. Once I was occupied with doing so day and night, but now of course I have little occasion to." She accepted the glass. "To your prosperity, Your Grace."

"An' to yours, ma'am." He took a long swallow.

"It is frankly unbelievable that Mrs. Tate tripped out of that window," she said.

"Aye?"

"But Cynthia Tate is several inches shorter and considerably slighter than her mother. However lacking in character I feel the girl to be, I do not believe she was physically capable of pushing Mrs. Tate over that sill."

"Your conclusion, Miss Campbell?"

"That you worked your black magic to be rid of Mrs. Tate so that you might have free rein of her maidenly progeny."

He bowed.

"You do not deny it?"

"I can neither deny nor confirm, ma'am."

"Cannot or will not?"

"Six o' one . . ."

"Your Grace," his footman said from the doorway. Gabriel turned away from Miss Campbell's merry eyes and looked upon the face of a ghost.

"Greetings, cousin," Jonah said. A familiar grin lurked about his mouth. "Have you missed me?"

Chapter 22

A Rooftop

"Libby, who drew this?" Amarantha ran her fingertip along the edge of the portrait of Libby's face and shoulders, drawn in pencil on a thick sheet of paper. "It is perfect. Is it Jane's work?"

"That man in the library did it." Libby tugged a gown over her head then smoothed it out. "See the other side?"

Amarantha flipped over the sheet. In firm, curling script it read *To the Angel of Regular Features*, and below that, *The Dragon*.

"It is an extraordinary likeness. Did you sit for him after all?"

"No. I haven't seen him except that once with you. The picture just appeared here this morning."

"What a talent he has, to render your face so well after only seeing you once— and so briefly."

"Iris said he left this morning. Do button me up. I am eager to discover if the duke's new guest is a man of science and intelligence."

"New guest?"

"He arrived just after lunch."

Iris popped into the room. "Amarantha! Tabitha said to tell you that she cannot tear herself away from writing and will not come to dinner. It must be a very exciting book."

"I would not describe it as exciting." Rather, harrowing. "But I believe it does her heart good to write it."

Libby led the way down the winding stairwell to the great hall, where the long table was set for dinner. Everyone else save Mrs. Tate was already present, and Amarantha forced herself to meet the duke's gaze.

"Mrs. Aiken begs you to forgive her absence from dinner this evening," she said. "She is engaged in a writing project which needs her entire attention."

"I say, cousin, what an odd duck you have become," came a gentleman's drawl. "You spent the afternoon filling my ears with tales of canals and spring crops, and entirely failed to mention that you have yet more beauties hiding under your roof." Mr. Jonah Brock stood across the room, a glass of wine dangling from his fingers. "And here I had already thought I was a lucky fellow, with the Miss Tates to please my eyes," he added with a handsome smile.

The duke moved away from the sideboard. "Allow me to—"

"Mrs. Garland and I are already acquainted," his cousin interrupted. "Reverend Garland and I were particular friends before his unfortunate passing. Madam, it is a great pleasure to see you again." He bowed deeply.

In appearance he was entirely unlike his cousin. With gold hair that curled in appealing ringlets over his brow, laughing blue eyes, and a flare for fashion that suited his slender frame, he presented a picture of manly grace and gentility.

"Sir." She did not curtsy. "How unexpected to see you in Scotland."

"I would say the same, except of course that we know my cousin likes to surround himself with beautiful women."

Ignoring that comment, the duke introduced him to Libby and Iris.

"Are you a man of science, Mr. Brock?" Libby said.

"Not strictly speaking, Miss Shaw. I was steward for five years of an extensive property in the Indies. Such a position requires a man to understand the properties of nature to a certain extent—the chemistry of soil content, the vicissitudes of climate, and the like. I am afraid, however, that science is not of especial interest to me."

"And yet you held the position for half a decade."

"Of necessity," he said with a winning smile. "Not all of us can be dukes, of course."

"I should think to manage a plantation successfully for five years would be a great achievement," Jane said softly.

Mr. Brock offered her a taking smile. "You are generous, Miss Tate."

Throughout dinner, Mr. Brock was charming toward all. To Dr. Shaw, Mr. Tate, and Thomas he spoke with intelligence that showed him to be a man of sense and information. To Alice and the young women he offered light flattery mingled with solicitous attention to their interests. When he mentioned that he and his cousin had served together in the navy, he was easily convinced to share stories of their many adventures.

Only their host said nothing to him throughout dinner, and only Amarantha knew that a snake had entered their midst.

It did not distress her for her own sake; she had long since come to terms with the unfortunate influence of Mr. Brock's friendship on her husband. But for Jane she grew concerned. The eldest Miss Tate was all pretty blushes for the newcomer.

At tea afterward, Libby announced that a meteor

shower had happened the previous night and was likely to be happening again now.

"I am far too old to stand out in the yard with my neck craned, Elizabeth," Alice said.

"I seem to recall that the best place for star-watching in this castle is the roof," Mr. Brock said and, as they climbed the steps to the roof, continued to chat with the others as prettily as a town beau.

By the time they reached the top of the stairs, Amarantha was all over hot with anger and cold with memory. For all his winning manners, she wanted no part of Jonah Brock.

"I will turn in now," she said as the others wandered out across the rooftop.

"Won't you stay to catch a glimpse of a shooting star, Mrs. Garland?" he said. "I understand that a wish made upon one has an excellent chance of coming true." He smiled, and then his gaze shifted to their host.

"I will see you to the gatehouse," the duke said.

She moved away swiftly. "No, thank you. I am fine on my own."

GABRIEL CROSSED THE hall, took up two glasses, and filled them. Setting one before his cousin, who lounged in a chair, he set the other atop the mantel.

"What brings you here, Jonah?"

"Why of course this warm welcome, cousin. I feel entirely at home again."

Gabriel stared at the man who had been more of a brother to him than his actual brother.

"You have not written," Jonah finally said. "It has been five and a half years."

"Aye."

"You have condemned me to exile."

"You go where you like without my interference or approval. As you always have."

"Come now, cousin." His mumble was subdued. "Did

not those stories of our past exploits warm your memories for our friendship?"

"They reminded me o' the reckless fools we once were."

"Ah. The duke speaks." His fingers played with the edge of his glass. "I imagined you here—as this." He waved his glass at the darkened hall. "Do you remember? I wished it for you, for my brother-from-another-mother to become lord of the manor, master of Haiknayes and Kallin, host to all the most interesting people in Scotland. And now here you are, welcoming to Haiknayes blustery merchants, stalwart physicians, risqué spinsters . . . even a lovely widow." He allowed the word to linger. "What an excellent host you have turned out to be. And the improvements on the estate here are worthy of you as well. Thank you for the tour today, by the by. I was impressed."

"Were you?" he said without parting his teeth.

"Yes." He looked down into his whiskey. "I am not the villain you wish me to be, Gabe," he said without a trace of raillery. "Oh, it's true: once upon a time I tried to teach you to be heedless. Truly reckless. But it never took, did it? Even in the midst of our fun, you always wanted responsibility. You craved authority. It is in your blood, I suppose. You deserved the *Theia*, you know. I never resented you for winning that command instead of me."

"I am glad to hear you approved o' the admiralty's choice. Now, enough with the soliloquy, Jonah. What do you want?"

"Isn't it obvious? I want your friendship again."

"You'll no' have it."

His face went slack. "So swiftly you decide?"

"'Twas you who decided it that night in Montego Bay." The night that had changed Gabriel's life forever.

Jonah stood up abruptly and pivoted away.

"One mistake and you wipe our friendship, our past, entirely clean? Am I never to be forgiven, Gabe?"

"Murder is no' a mistake, Jonah."

"It was an accident. I was drunk. We were always drunk. *You* were drunk that night too."

"Aye. But I recall having good reason to be. An' I didna kill a man."

Facing away, his cousin was silent a long moment.

"I would not have done it," Jonah finally said, the quiet words nearly swallowed by the crackle of flames, "if you had not said what you did. Do you remember your words to me that night, Gabriel?"

He remembered everything about that night: the night he had got leave from his superiors to return to Jamaica for a single purpose, only to learn that the girl who had promised to wait for him *had not*.

"Dinna blame me, cur."

"Ah, there's the old Gabe, snarling like a feral dog." Jonah looked at him over his shoulder. "Do you know . . . Charlotte came to care for me. Eventually." His eyes were unnaturally dull. "Perhaps I am not such a thorough villain after all. Or perhaps it was merely her goodness. Imagine, a woman with a heart so pure that she could grow to love the man who killed her brother."

"She didna love you."

Jonah turned to him sharply. "You don't know that."

"Aye, I do. She was Gregory's property. You were Gregory's steward. She had no choice but to submit to you. There can be no love where there is no liberty."

His cousin looked away. "It is the way of the world, Gabriel. You know that as well as I."

"The world is what we make it, Jonah."

"It is, if you happen to be a captain of a naval frigate. Or a duke."

"Your Grace," Dr. Shaw said from the doorway. "Oh, I beg your pardon, gentlemen."

Gabriel went forward. "Doctor?"

"Mrs. Tate has had a difficult day and I anticipate more discomfort to come. I have advised her not to travel."

"She's welcome to remain as long as necessary, Doctor."

"Will you share a nightcap with me, Dr. Shaw?" Jonah said. "My cousin will not drink to my health. But a medical man cannot refuse that toast, can he?"

Gabriel left them to the whiskey. Tonight he did not crave spirits or authority or anything other than a woman with eyes that spoke her thoughts even beneath the light of falling stars.

She had not left Haiknayes. She had remained, despite him. She had questions she wanted answered, so he supposed she had good reason to remain.

He took the steps to the gatehouse three at a time and nearly collided with her as she came through the door.

"Oh!" she said. "What are you doing here?"

"Where are you going?"

"Tabitha went to the kitchen for a snack. I was going to keep her company. Perhaps as busy as you were with all that glowering at your cousin you forgot that my friend did not dine with the rest of—"

"There's no one inside?"

"No."

He grasped her hand and drew her within, then shut the door behind them. She tugged away.

"What are you doing?" Her words sounded thin. She held her hand close to her stomach.

"You didna leave."

"Obviously not. I did go riding, though. What beautiful countryside this is, so different from Kallin, less dramatic yet equally stunning. Are you here to throw me out now? In the middle of the night?"

"No. Never leave. Never."

Her eyes widened. "What has happened?"

"Nothing except that I retract my order. You canna leave."

"Now you are demanding that I *stay*?"

"Aye." He smiled.

Amarantha's knotted stomach became a flight of swallows.

"You know," she said, "today on my ride I gave this— this back-and-forth between us—some thought. And I am convinced that it would be best to—"

"When will you let me touch you again?" His gaze was on her mouth.

"That is what I was about to speak to." He was so close, entirely filling the space and her sight and every sense, a big shadowy wall of perfect lips and intoxicating scent and sculpted jaw and hair that she could sink her fingers into. "This vow to honor the supposed gauntlet I threw down . . . Are you playing a game? Give, take, give. That sort of game?"

"When you look at me," he said, each word slow and clear, "'tis as though I am seeing that girl, the way you looked at me then."

A ripple of fear and pleasure went through her. "Nothing remains of that girl."

"It does. You rode for four hours today, alone."

"How do you know that?"

"My house. My horse. I pay the stable hand."

"If I had known that I would be so closely monitored—"

"You would still have ridden for four hours alone. I've never known a woman so eager to run free o' the bridle."

"*Bridle*? Have you just compared me to a—"

"You're a wild one, Amarantha Vale." The rough wave of syllables over his tongue was a caress.

"You have interrupted me four times now. You have never interrupted me before in our acquaintance. I think Mr. Brock's visit has distressed you."

"Acquaintance? Our *acquaintance*?"

Her heartbeats were so loud she could hear them in her ears. "I rode because I needed to . . . go."

"Yet you are here now. With me."

Her palms were pressed to the wall behind her.

"I am," she said.

"I am now going to kiss you. Finally. How are you with that?"

Nerves raced straight up her throat. "What about all your talk of trust?"

"To hell with trust. I'd rather return to lust. Much more satisfying in the short run. The long run can take care o' itself."

"It would be a mistake. A greater mistake than I have already made."

"Then or now?"

"Then and now. Twice. Since. *Always*," she whispered.

"My God." His voice was ragged. "Amarantha—"

She slipped out from between him and the wall.

"I should go," she said, pulling the door open.

"To where? 'Tis fixing to freeze."

"I won't feel it."

"Stay here in the warmth," he said. "I'll leave. It'll be hell, but I'll leave."

"I would like to walk."

"You rode for four hours today."

"A brief walk. I am somewhat overheated."

She went. The gate was locked. There was no way out. Pivoting and running along the wall that bordered the courtyard, she reached the garden gate. It was locked too. No escape.

Bridle.

His words—the locked gate—the castle itself seemed to be mocking her.

Recrossing the courtyard in the flickering light of the torch that was dimmed by the brilliance of the stars, she hurried up the gatehouse steps.

The chamber was empty. She had told him to go, and he had done as she wished. Smoothing her hands over her disordered hair and gown, she felt acutely the sensations of her own palms and fingers upon her body. Desire spun in her. Five and a half years of denying it had not destroyed it.

She went down the steps, into the courtyard, and to the keep.

No one stirred within, every room empty and dark. She climbed to the roof. As she walked onto the parapets the cold wrapped around her. The stars were brilliant, each tumbling onto another like little sheep running over a nighttime hill. Staring into them, she waited for a star to fall until her eyes blurred.

A footfall sounded on the roof.

She swung around.

He stood at the open door to the stairwell, moonlight illumining the living vision of her fantasy man.

"All the gates are locked," she said.

"If you wish it, Amarantha Vale, I will give to you every key in the place."

"So that I can escape?"

"So that you willna need to."

"I don't want to escape. Not at this moment."

Across the roof he walked toward her. Her heel hit the crenellation, and then he was upon her, so close she could see the fever shining in his eyes.

"Now," he said, his voice very low.

"Yes. Yes. Y—"

He brought their mouths together.

Hands surrounding her face, fingers sinking into her hair, he offered her the most beautiful gift: his lips on hers for a long, long perfect moment. His mouth. Real and perfect. Gentle, controlled strength.

Drawing away only far enough to look into her eyes, he said, "Worth the wait."

"Yes," she whispered. "Yes."

With his hands he tilted her face upward a bit, and then bent his head again. This time he gave her more than beautiful stillness. He kissed her softly, cupping her face and taking one taste at a time. Tingles in her lips became falling stars inside her, sizzling downward.

"Mm," he murmured. "Better than both whiskey an' rum."

"Much better," she whispered, lifted her hands, and laid them on his chest. He was so hard, an alien male landscape for her hunger. Fanning her hands out, she pressed her fingertips into him, needing to put her hands all over him and feel him everywhere. He was breathing roughly, his mouth a tantalizing inch away, his eyes closed.

"What are you doing?" His utterance was tight.

"I want you." She whispered the forbidden words. "I have always wanted you."

With a groan, he captured her mouth beneath his. Her lips were open yet he did not recoil.

"This mouth," he whispered, and that was all before he kissed her again, his caresses urging her lips to part wider. She wanted to kiss him back, to move her lips against his and to feel all the heat of his mouth.

So she did.

A rumble of pleasure came against her palms. He kissed her deeper now, his hand sinking into her hair and holding her mouth to his, closer, a decadent, hot, wet meeting of lips. It was wholly new and free. His lips were soft and demanding, his tongue skimming hers, caressing, making her want more so swiftly.

She broke away from his mouth, but both of his hands held her close.

"You make this feel so good," she said upon a little pant.

"'Tis the fun o' kissing, wild one. An' touching."

"Touching?" She was not at all certain of his meaning.

"Aye," he murmured. "Touching." From the curve of her throat his fingertips traced the sinew in her neck as though it were precious and desirable. Such a spring of happiness bubbled up in her.

"*Yes.*"

"'Tis an unspecific word. Yes, you are enjoying this?" So softly, he stroked along her shoulder. "Or, yes, you would like more."

"Yes." She laughed.

He set his lips upon her throat.

Heaven—tickling, hot, delectable heaven curled into her breasts and made her nipples ache.

Slowly, delectably, he allowed his knuckles to slip around the side of her breast, and then his hand. He brought their mouths together again and the caress of his tongue made her need to feel him. Awake with need, she was shaking.

Then his hands were moving, scooping around her shoulders, down her back, drawing her closer, drawing her to him. Her thighs came against his, her hips, her breasts against his chest. His arousal was obvious, and hard, but he did not put her away, as though he wanted her to feel how he desired her. She was flushed and hot and did not know what to do with her hands. She *yearned* to touch him. He held her with only one hand spread across the small of her back, and as he bent to kiss her throat his hand surrounded her breast.

Soft whimpers from her throat scored the midnight silence. It was like nothing she had felt, nothing in the world—his hand holding her entirely, intentionally. His fingers stroked, touching her nipple through the gown.

"Beautiful woman," he murmured against her throat, his voice unsteady.

Touching her was affecting *him*.

"Speak again," she whispered.

He brought his lips to hers and his thumb passed across her nipple again, then circled it, playing, taunting. It seemed he knew precisely where to touch her to make her need more.

"What would you have me say?" he said, his lips brushing the corner of hers, then her throat.

"Anything. I want—" She caught her confession between her teeth.

"What do you want, wild one? Give me your order. You have but to utter it an' thy will be done."

"I want to hear in your voice how touching me moves you."

"Moves me?" He drew a shuddering breath. "*Undoes* me." Upon the words, his hand slipped around her buttocks, cupping it completely, and he fit her to him. "Do you feel what you do to me, wild one?"

"More," she heard herself say.

He gave her more, urging her to him with the power of his hand until she was seeking him without any urging. Allowing him to press her knees apart, she welcomed the hardness of his body against hers. Sweet, tight heat was rising in her, tangling her inside and making her need even more. With nothing but clothing between them he was making her make love to him, and she wanted it.

Fingers sunk in her hair and mouth commanding hers, he let her bear up against him. She was wild for it—for the friction of their bodies pressed so intimately together, scandalously, beautifully. Hunger licked like flames between her legs, hot and raw and needing him there.

Pleasure fell open within her, her cry of surprise becoming a moan of ecstasy as the convulsions swept up her body. She gulped air and more tumbling whimpers sought to escape against his lips. She swallowed them back. From cheeks to toes her skin felt afire with shock and shame—and *triumph*. Hands gripping his hard arms, she felt his kiss on her tender lips with her whole body, as though he kissed her everywhere now.

"Gabriel." The word was barely audible, and shaking.

"*Judas*, woman." His hands were tight about her waist. "You are—your lips, your voice—"

Sliding her palm up his chest, she did what she had always wanted to do: she touched him as he had touched her that morning in the empty shop, with her fingertips, meeting the firm flesh and bone of his jaw and stroking, discovering the day's growth of whiskers that made the hot contractions echo deep within her again, and then allowing her fingertips to stray across his lips.

"I dreamed of touching you like this." She struggled to draw full breaths, caressing the man she had craved since before she even understood what feminine craving was. Naïve and innocent, too ignorant to imagine anything more and too in love to imagine anything better, she had fantasized this.

He remained still, his eyes dark shadows watching her, his breathing reckless.

Drawing out of his grasp, she stepped back and sliced her palm across his cheek.

He blinked hard and shifted his jaw.

"That," he said, "was no' quite what I expected to happen next."

"*That* was for making me have wrongful thoughts about a man who was not my betrothed when you *knew* that I was too naïve to understand how you were affecting me."

For a moment he said nothing. "You said you'd put it behind you."

"I did. I thought I had." She took a big breath. "Obviously I haven't."

"All right."

"*All right*? Is that the sum total of your reaction? I have never struck another person in my life, yet you stand there as though being struck by a woman is a daily occurrence for you. Perhaps it is. Of course it is. Oh, dear God, have I learned nothing? *Nothing*?" she said, jerking her face upward.

"Being struck by a woman—by anyone—is no' a daily occurrence for me, fortunately," he said with beautiful control in his voice. "For, unsurprisingly, it smarts."

She stared at her stinging hand, then at him.

"Good Lord, what have I done? You make me forget myself entirely. Forgive me."

"Have you been wanting to slap me for five an' a half years?"

"No. You have just inspired my memory."

"I'd like to inspire it more. But only the part before the slap, if we can arrange that."

Biting both lips between her teeth, she walked swiftly toward the battlements.

"Please go. I don't want"—this weakness, this desperate desire to be near him and to have more of him and to laugh with him—"I don't want you."

"You do. You know you do."

"Yes, I do. But please go now anyway."

"What wrongful thoughts?"

"Have so few women admired you lately that you must reach back into ancient history to find comfort in the virginal fantasies of a girl?"

"Every word that falls from those lips drives me a wee bit madder. Have pity, lass."

"I really believe that your madness needs no assistance from me."

"If I have ever been mad, woman, 'tis entirely because o' you."

"No." She faced him across the nighttime glittering with frost and starlight. "I think you truly are mad. You must be to continue this mysterious concealment."

His brow knit.

"More silence," she said. "You continue to refuse to share your grand secret with me. Then perhaps you will answer specific questions. Why do the women of Glen Village hold you in such awe that they conceal your secret too? Why do the Edinburgh police allow the symbol of the so-called Devil's Duke to decorate gateposts and alleyways all over the city? Why does no one remove those marks—marks I think have nothing to do with the

Freemasons but are there to guide young women eager to find the Devil's Duke? And why do Bess and Angus Allen still admire you—*trust you* despite your blackened reputation and the mysterious fire that nearly destroyed their livelihoods? Deny me answers to those questions, if you will."

His breaths made stark plumes of starlit cold.

"How do you know Bess and Angus?"

"I went there. Months ago I went to the place that everyone said the missing girls had last been seen. I looked for you there and when I did not find you I sought information about you."

"Months ago?" he said almost too quietly.

"I could find little trace of Penny, but I had reason to believe she was searching for you. You could not be found in Edinburgh. No one seemed to know where you were."

"I was in London, at Westminster. The prime minister an' the king knew where I was."

"I did not actually wish an audience with you, specifically. I believed that if I found Cassandra Finn and Maggie Poultney I might find my friend. I went to your house that day of the fire. Inside it."

His eyes widened. "You were in my house? *My* house?"

"I was ill at the time, in a terrible fever. I don't actually recall any of it, but in the hospital I had vivid dreams of the inside of a house I had never seen before."

"Hospital?"

"It was weeks before I was able to think clearly again, and many more weeks before I was well enough to leave hospital and return there. It was then that I spoke with Bess and Angus."

"*Weeks*? My God, Amarantha." He shifted partially away and ran a hand over his face. The gesture was so familiar—*so him*—she ached despite her shaking. "I dinna know which is strongest now: anger that you didna share this with me when you first told me o' your search for your friend, or terror for what you might have suffered if you actually were in the house when the fire—" He broke off and took a hard breath. "But the strongest feeling I'm having now, I'll admit, is pleasure an' pride for the brave, enterprising woman you are. Why didna you contact me, write to me, *find* me so that I could help you find her?"

"I tried! I went all the way to Kallin."

"You used a false name. You didna trust that I would help you."

"Why should I have trusted you?" she cried. "You, of all men?"

"I never gave you reason to think me a dishonorable man, Amarantha. Ever. Despite what I wanted o' you. Despite what I could have taken from you, had I chosen to."

He had only taken her heart.

"I have never known what to think of you," she said. "But in truth it is my own feelings that I do not trust, my feelings for you that are tangled up with the past."

"So 'tis easier to believe me a villain?"

"I did not want you to be the devil! Every piece of evidence was pointing toward you, and I wanted to hate you because of my own guilt for what I had done then. I had allowed it to happen between us, despite the promises I had made to others. I wanted the fault to be yours. I had to know for myself if you were truly what they were saying of you."

Gabriel's gut was churning with the most painful sensations. Anger and incredulity. *Despair.*

"You actually believed that I could be abducting an' murdering young women."

"No. *No.* How can you not understand? I was betrothed to another man yet I could not stop thinking about you, longing to be with you, even months after—I needn't tell you this. You *knew* how I felt."

Months?

"I thought I did," he said, less certain now.

"I made such a horrible mistake marrying as I did, misunderstanding a man's character so thoroughly, trusting him so blindly that despite what I *knew*, I believed his lies. When I came to Scotland and heard the rumors about you, I had to know the truth. I could not bear that the man who had made me laugh and fall in love with each moment of every day—that he could truly be a monster. A seducer of innocence, yes. I had long since known you to be that. But not what they said you were. It was simply not possible. I had to prove to myself that at least once my heart had not been entirely blind."

Her heart.

Her eyes were glittering.

"If you have nothing to hide," she said, "tell me the truth about Cassandra Finn and Maggie Poultney now. Where are they?"

"Kallin."

The cold wind twisted about the battlements.

She brushed past him and through the door, and her footsteps receded swiftly down the stairs.

Chapter 23

A Prelude to a Kiss

What she had allowed him to do to her . . .

What *she* had done.

What she had *said*.

She had never imagined a man would want to touch her without putting himself inside her.

She had allowed it, shown him her hunger, and he had not been disgusted. He had *welcomed* it.

Wild one.

He called her wild one, as though the girl she had been years ago was more truly she than the woman she had become.

No lamp burned in the gatehouse window as Amarantha hurried across the forecourt. Tabitha must have finally closed their manuscript for the night. The writing of it exhausted her friend, but they both knew it was the right thing to do. Tabitha's story—and other stories like hers—must be told. People in England and Scotland and Wales, so far from Britain's western colonies but who enjoyed the fruits of those islands—the sugar in their tea and confections, the cotton and indigo that was so popular in seamstress shops, and the coffee and chocolate on breakfast tables—people must learn the horrors of the lives of the people who lived as chattel to produce those luxuries. Once they did, they would not allow it to continue.

Opening the door to the gatehouse quietly, she rubbed her palms over her frozen cheeks. On the rooftop she had not felt the cold. He had not allowed it.

"Amarantha?" Tabitha said from the darkness.

"Forgive me for waking you."

Tabitha came into the moonlight. She wore her cloak, gloves, and boots, and she clutched her traveling bag in one hand.

"Why are you dressed for travel?"

"The courtyard gate is locked, so I knew you were not at the church. I did not know where you had gone, but I could not search for you in the castle. I have waited only for your return."

"For my return? What are you doing?"

"I must climb out that window," she said, gesturing, "and down to the stream bed. But I require assistance. There is nothing sturdy enough to tie the rope I have fashioned in place. The drop to the stream bed is steep."

"*No.* Of course I will not assist you in running away in the middle of the night, into the cold and darkness, alone. Have you gone mad?"

"I cannot remain here."

"Has someone given you insult? Mrs. Tate is horrid, I know. Or was it one of the men? Has Mr. Bellarmine—"

"No. He is kind and respectful, as are Dr. Shaw and the duke."

"Then the servants? Have any of them—"

"No, Amarantha." Her eyes were fraught. "You do not understand. You *cannot* understand, no matter how sympathetic and compassionate you are. You will never have this fear."

"But you are angry, too. I can see it. Let me at least try to help you, if I can. Tell me what you fear here."

"I wished never to speak his name, never to reveal him for fear of his retribution, on both myself and you."

"Him?" Sickness crawled up her throat. "The man who caused Jonathan to be murdered?" The man who wished to replace Tabitha's freedom with shackles again.

"Amarantha, I saw him here tonight. He is Jonah Brock."

MORNING SUNLIGHT SLANTED through the kitchen windows.

"Mrs. Hook, where is—" Gabriel still could not say the name. Not even now. "Where is she?"

"Mrs. Garland's gone with the others."

"Gone riding?" She was indefatigable. She needed more than cards and tea and passive pursuits to slake her thirsts. She needed him.

"To Kallin, Your Grace, as you gave Mickey instruction yesterday."

"To *Kallin*? No."

"Now there," she said with a shake of the rolling pin, "I canna say I've the hearing o' a girl, but I'm no' deaf yet. The lad said Kallin."

"Did she go alone?"

"Mrs. Aiken an' Mr. Bellarmine went along."

Judas, he was a fool. She had filled his head with a fantasy and he had played right into her hands.

No. He could not believe that. She had spoken sincerely, honestly. And he had been a fool anyway.

He found Mick polishing tack.

"Yesterday you said I was to give her any vehicle or mount she pleased, Captain," he said earnestly. "She ordered up the light carriage an' said she an' Mrs. Aiken and Mr. Bellarmine were to leave before sunup, by your orders."

"My orders?" As though that woman would do anything he ordered.

"Aye, Captain. The gentleman drove, o' course, ladies being weak as they are."

Not those ladies.

But it was some comfort. In the company of two others, she could not travel swiftly. He would ride, and either catch them on the road or bypass them. Then he and the intrepid girl who had become a woman of passion would have a good long talk.

Right after he kissed her again.

PART V

1823

The Duke

Chapter 24

The Secret

Glen Irvine, Scotland

After two days in a light carriage journeying over roads pocked with late-winter's displeasure, it was too much to expect Tabitha to remain calm, but she made a valiant effort.

Arriving finally at Kallin, the greeting they received was not, however, what Amarantha hoped.

"His Grace is no' in residence," the young woman at the outermost gate said firmly. She had yellow hair plaited tightly beneath a straw hat, and she wore a long coat, heavy boots, and lines of worry across her pale brow.

"Yes, indeed, for he is currently at Haiknayes," Thomas said cheerfully. "He has sent us here with instructions to await his arrival."

It was the story Amarantha and Tabitha had told him. Though he was clearly suspicious of it, he had assisted them without question.

"Fret not," Amarantha said when they had turned back

toward Glen Village. "They will give us warm welcome at the Solstice Inn."

Mary Tarry, the keeper of the Solstice Inn, showed no surprise at Amarantha's elegant gown, costly bonnet, or fine kid gloves. Instead she received their party with the same forthright welcome she had given Anne Foster months earlier.

"Welcome back, Mrs. F—"

"Garland," Amarantha supplied.

"Mrs. Garland it is," she said with a wise eye. "I'll have refreshments in the parlor for ye an' yer companions immediately."

Amarantha glanced at her friends. Thomas was directing Plum in the distribution of luggage to their bedchambers.

"That would be lovely, Mrs. Tarry," she said quietly. "But I would prefer a spot in the corner of your kitchen."

Mary Tarry smiled reluctantly. "I've no doubt, lass."

IT WAS CLEARLY a rare occurrence: the local laird striding into the inn's kitchen and spearing every person there with the dark fire in his eyes. Everybody—from the cook plucking chickens, to the maid stirring a pot, to the inn's fiddler plucking a tune, to Sophie sharing news with Amarantha as she sewed an exquisite undergown—everybody halted their activities and stared.

Kilted about the hips in dark blue tartan, he stood with muscular legs firmly braced as though on the deck of a ship. The sight of his half naked calves sent Amarantha's pulse into an aggressive canter.

"Where is she?" he snarled.

"I am here, Urisk," she said, setting beside the inkpot her pen with which she was writing a letter to Kallin's steward. She did not stand; her wobbly knees might not support her, and she was through with cowering from any man's displeasure.

He came forward and towered menacingly over the table. Then, as though only now noticing the stillness of all but the stew noisily bubbling in a pot over the hearth, he waved his hand.

"Be about your business," he said less harshly.

When the others had renewed their fiddling and chatting and stirring, Amarantha spoke quietly.

"Why have you come here? Your guests at Haiknayes—"

"The devil take the lot o' them."

"That is what people are saying, of course."

There was laughter behind the disquiet in his eyes.

"If you intend to read me a particularly long lecture," she said, "it would probably be best done elsewhere. Everybody here was happy until just a moment ago."

He rounded the table, took a seat backward on the bench beside her, and looked down at her letter.

"There's a mistake," he said.

"What—where?" She pulled her hands away from the page. "No there is not. My penmanship is excellent."

Under the table, he caught her hand in his. His thumb brushed over her palm. Pleasure scurried straight up her center.

"'Tis in the salutation," he said, stroking again.

"Oh?" It was difficult to make sound without air, and even more difficult to lift her attention from where the plaid dipped between his thighs. She dragged her eyes upward.

"Aye." Resting his gaze upon her lips, he traced the tip of his thumb up the inside of her forefinger. The fluttering reply between her legs shot her eyes wide. Slowly, one edge of his lips curved upward. It was the roguish grin of years earlier, but tempered now. There was no teasing in it, only pleasure.

Another of her fingers was thoroughly caressed beneath the table.

"What is the mistake in the salutation?" She could

barely whisper as his thumb trailed up the tender inner skin of her third finger.

"It shouldna be *dear sir*," he said, holding her hand with only his fingertips against her palm and the pad of his thumb over the base of her ring finger where, five years earlier, she had worn her betrothal ring.

"Shouldn't it?" she said.

"It should be *dear Miss Finn*."

Cassandra Finn was *steward* of Kallin?

He released her hand and rested his upon his thigh.

"When did you arrive?" she said.

"Night before last. They didna tell me o' your arrival till this morning."

"So His Grace was actually in residence when we sought entrance yesterday?"

"Aye. Hard asleep after a night spent in the lambing barn."

"The Laird of Kallin and master of Haiknayes not only repairs roofs and chops wood, he also brings lambs into the world?"

"'Tis my understanding the ewes do most o' that work."

"I daresay," she said.

"In truth, I know little o' sheep. The farmers lambed. I carried an' repaired. After swabbing decks an' hauling cargo, barn work seems a holiday," he said with an almost-smile. She wanted to reach up and caress it. And then she wanted to put her lips on it. "The estate's a wee bit shorthanded."

"And you supply labor, yourself, wherever needed?"

"Aye." His gaze scanned her face. "When I'm no' otherwise occupied with a beautiful woman on a rooftop."

"From ship captain to duke to devil to farmhand. What will you attempt next, I wonder."

"In fact these past few days I have been considering a new venture."

"Have you? Mercantile, no doubt. This must mean you have finalized your business partnership with Mr. Tate."

"The venture I have in mind requires a different sort o' partner altogether." He bent his head. "Why did you leave Haiknayes without word?"

"Mrs. Aiken's pursuer," she said, curling her fingers around the lingering sweetness he had produced there, "is your cousin."

His brow dipped. Then he took up her letter and tucked it into his coat pocket.

"Come, lass," he said, standing. "'Tis time you had a tour o' Kallin."

HE COMMANDED A light carriage from the Solstice's stable and drove her and Tabitha into the glen and up the narrow road along the river. Unlike in October, the birches were now entirely bare of leaves, no snow blanketed the valley, and the rusty red and emerald of the hills rising to either side were stark. Yet it was the same untamed, peaceful beauty through which Amarantha had walked a dozen times, seeking answers.

Seeking him.

Not a rigid, contained fortress like Haiknayes, Kallin was a collection of parts spreading from a central tower, a fortified manor house of stone resting comfortably amidst grazing pastures and paddocks, flanked by outbuildings and nearby woodland.

As the carriage approached, the door opened and a footman appeared, small and slender and garbed in neat breeches and coat that approximated modest livery.

Tabitha touched the top of Amarantha's hand. The footman was brown skinned. And a woman.

"Your Grace," the footman greeted him stiffly.

Another young woman emerged from the stable and went to the horses' heads. With a pale face liberally coated in brown freckles, she wore men's clothing too: trousers, shirt, waistcoat, and cap.

"Miss Pike," the duke said to the footman, offering Tabitha his hand to descend. "Where is Miss Finn?"

"She is doing inventory with Molly in the distillery. Shall I fetch her to the house?"

"No. Leave her be. I'll find her there."

The foyer was broad and high, laid with a wooden floor that shone with polish, and appointed simply with a finely carved bench and a brass candelabrum on a table by the doorway.

Sophie entered behind them.

"Good day, Your Grace," she said with a quick curtsy.

"What brings you from the village, Miss Crowne?"

"Last night I told Mrs. Aiken about the sewing machine. When you left the Solstice just now with Anne— that is, *Mrs. Garland*"—she grinned at Amarantha—"I saw that Mrs. Aiken went with you, so I rode up behind the carriage. Mrs. Aiken is an accomplished seamstress." She turned to Tabitha. "Would you care to see the machine?"

"Very much."

With a bright smile, Sophie led Tabitha away.

He took the step that brought him close to her.

"Alone, at last," he said.

"The promised tour, Urisk?"

AMARANTHA STOOD AT a window in the highest story of the central tower. The glorious glen spread out in every direction: the glistening river; the mountains rising far to the north; and the fields that stretched along the flanks of the river to the south, salted now with sheep.

"Do the residents of Glen Village come and go as they please, as Sophie just did?"

"Some." He stood in the doorway, one shoulder leaning into the doorjamb.

They were in a parlor, sparsely furnished but lovingly, just as the handful of other rooms in the manor that he had showed her. This one included a rocking cradle near the hearth and a collection of wooden alphabet blocks. She had not yet seen an actual person.

"Do those belong to Rebecca and her little one?"

"Aye," he said.

"But Clementine is too big now for the cradle."

"'Tis for Miss Poultney's wee one."

Amarantha's stomach felt abruptly very empty and odd. "Maggie Poultney has an infant?"

"Aye," he said. "Nearly six months old now."

"Who is the child's father?"

"The lout her father had promised her to," he said in a low rumble.

"She did not care for her fiancé?"

"She didna care for the beatings he gave her."

"I see. And Cassandra Finn?"

"A pious lass devoted to doing the work o' God," he said, moving toward her. "Like another lass I once knew."

"Doing the work of God—here?"

Coming to stand before her, he crossed his arms comfortably. "She believes it to be."

He seemed so settled, so entirely at ease, his gaze upon her as peaceful as the house was in its beautiful valley.

"Why are they here? And Miss Pike? And your groom, who seems to be Irish by her speech? And Sophie? And all the women at Glen Village who are loyal to you too?"

A glimmer of deviltry shone in his dark eyes.

"'Tis no' a harem, if that's what you're thinking."

"I probably should be thinking that, shouldn't I?"

He smiled. "How is it, Amarantha Vale, that you know what a harem is?"

"How is it, Urisk, that you would even mention such a thing to a lady?"

"A lady who journeyed thousands o' miles alone in

search o' a friend, then hundreds more in search o' a scoundrel?"

"You are admitting now that you are a scoundrel?"

"I was referring to wee Luke's father, o' course."

"Why . . . all of this?"

"Come," he said. "I've one place more to show you."

They left the house, the dogs trotting along with them and occasionally dashing off to investigate scents.

"How many women live here?"

He opened a gate to a footpath.

"Eight. Two have rooms at the Solstice as well. Two who once lived here stay now only in the village. The three other women who have care o' the sheep live in the farm a half mile along the valley."

"There is no one else here? No men?"

"None. By their request."

"Except you."

He chuckled. "If they could send me away forever, they would."

To one side of the footpath a trail rose steeply beneath tree cover. "This way." He offered his hand.

"Thank you." She picked up her skirts with both hands. "I can manage."

For a moment his gaze upon her was thoughtful. Then he went ahead of her up through the trees.

"I don't suppose you are taking me to a private hideaway in order to have your wicked way with me, are you?" she said half-hopefully.

"With such a skittish filly? What would be the fun in that?"

"Skittish filly? Are you saying that I must be broken to . . . to . . ."

"To ride?" He laughed. Then in an entirely altered voice: "No. Never." He lifted a low-hanging branch and waited for her to pass beneath. As she did, he said, "I would die before I would see you tamed, wild one."

Swiveling her neck, she met his gaze.

On the battlements in the dark it had been so easy to fall into him. Now she hardly knew how to be with him, whether she should touch him. She wanted him, as she had years ago, with that same powerful ache. But her feet would not move forward, and her hands that needed to be on his solid, muscular strength would not obey; they were buried in her pockets.

With a deep breath, he gestured to a place beyond her shoulder.

"We have arrived," he said.

They had come to a crumbling line of stones, the sort of old fence that wended all across Scotland, this one overtaken by woods years ago. Set against the remains of the wall was a large stone. Carved in bold capitals in the center of the stone was Sanctuary, and carved around the word were names.

"Molly," she read, "Margaret, Pike, Cassandra, Rebecca, Zion . . . Did you make this?"

"They did, to honor my former partner's death. I didna know it was here till my visit last fall when Miss Finn showed it to me. Her powerful sense o' duty to me required it, I imagine," he added, the lines deepening about his mouth. "They're no' all trusting. With good reason."

"Who was your partner?"

"Torquil Sterling."

Her fine cinnamon lashes fanned.

"Torquil Sterling? The rakehell merchant? The Torquil Sterling who lived in Kingston and Montego Bay and anywhere else on Jamaica that he could find gambling and spirits, and women unafraid to be seen enjoying both with him? The care-for-nothing man who engaged in fisticuffs with planters and tradesmen and sailors indiscriminately, for the amusement of it?"

Gabriel scratched his jaw, recalling the occasions on

which Tor's fist had collided with it for no particular reason other than the drunken foolery of young men.

"Much o' the year, aye. When he wasna traveling."

Her face was like an intricate map, its legend so familiar to him that he could navigate it in starlight, sunlight, and, he suspected, no light at all.

She shook her head. "They said that he ran African captives illegally under cover of sugar and indigo, that he paid custom house officials exorbitant bribes to turn a blind eye."

"Who said it?"

Watching the thoughts pass behind her eyes, he waited for her voice that was to him like the music of the river and wind in the boughs and every church bell he had ever heard.

"Plenty of res—respectable people," she finished, and her gaze swept him up and down.

"You'd best no' be doing that, lass, or I'll be stealing you to a hideaway now after all."

She pressed her lips together and Gabriel wanted to bite them. All of her. But she was holding herself distant today again. Her words from the ramparts had seared themselves upon him like a brand: *I made such a horrible mistake marrying as I did.*

He must wait for the wild creature to come to him. Even if the waiting was testing every fiber of his self-restraint.

"Explain, please," she said, pinning her attention to the stone.

"'Twas the appearance Torquil kept as a cover for what he said to me was his calling."

"A religious calling?" she said with obvious disbelief.

"No. But a calling, nonetheless: assisting women to safety."

"The opposite of his reputation, then."

"Aye."

"And you—" She stole a glance at him. "You were his partner in this?"

"One o' them. He had others, a dozen or more, but all o' them men an' women o' actual character."

"Unlike you," she said with a small smile. Sunlight falling between the trees struck her skin like petals of gold.

"Some in the Indies. A tradeswoman in Plymouth. A merchant in Bristol. An' in Nantes, the man who became my partner after Torquil's death. Good people, still busily doing what they're able now."

"How did you become involved?"

He leaned back against the trunk of a tree and folded his arms.

"Years ago, when I was still sailing, I had a bad night."

"I understood you had those occasionally." Her eyes were following a rivulet of silver water rushing haphazardly along a gully between the trees to the Irvine below.

"This night was exceptionally bad." The worst of his life. "My cousin, Jonah, killed an innocent man."

Her gaze snapped up to him.

"He was never tried for it," he said. "Never punished."

"But—You knew about it?"

"Aye, after Jonah came to tell me. He was insensible with distress. It was an accident. They fought, an' the man fell. Hit his head."

"Yet you did *nothing*?"

"The man was a cane worker, brought on ship before the law changed."

"An enslaved man?"

"He had bought his freedom. But my cousin's employer was a rich planter. Even had I accused Jonah publicly, he wouldna suffered for it."

"Perhaps not, but to remain *silent*—You should not have."

"Jonah was a brother to me. More than a brother. He

had saved my life when we were lads. An' . . . there was more to it."

"What more?"

"Earlier that night I had spoken words that had nothing to do with him. Angry words. Jonah misunderstood them. Afterward, he told me that those words had given him justification to fight the man."

"What were the words you spoke?" she said.

No one should come between a man an' the woman he wants.

"Words unfit for a man o' honor." So he had sought out the only friend who would hear his confession without judgment, a rakehell with whom he drank and gamed, but whom he had not truly known until that night. "Sterling offered me a penance for the wrong I had done. He said that in helping him I could atone, an' he made me an invitation. I accepted it."

"He said, 'Lieutenant Hume, help me illegally wrest abused women from their captors and hide them where they will not be found,' and you said, 'Of course'? Just like that?"

"Just like that, lass."

Except he had been *Captain* Hume.

She backed away several steps, then pivoted about. The bracken crunched with her swift descent between the trees.

He caught up with her on the footpath. She walked quickly despite the bumpy trail, her cheeks and the tip of her nose rosy from the cold.

"I have had a thought just now," she said as though she weren't running away from him.

"What thought?"

"That I have occasionally been wrong."

"You have just had that thought? For the first time?"

She halted abruptly and stared at him for an extended moment.

"For years you have done this, kept these women's secrets, given them a safe haven away from those who wish to harm them, and all while the world has believed you to be a villain?"

"I am a villain. I've the dungeons to prove it."

Her lips were tight between her teeth, her eyes aglitter.

"Come," he said, moving away from her because if he remained he would surely do something unwise. "There's a fine pair o' oxen an' a dozen new lambs in the barn on the other side o' those pastures."

"You imagine I wish to see these animals because . . . ?"

"No' the animals. 'Tis the northernmost we can walk an' still return to the house by lunchtime."

"Why do you wish to walk north?" she said, following him, her beautiful voice light now, the nearest sound to heaven he knew.

"'Tis no' for me, lass. 'Tis for you."

"Then why do *I* wish to walk north?"

"To run as far as you can go, I imagine. Today, that is. Now, if we'd another fortnight or two, we could ride up to Inverness, then hail a boat to Orkney. You canna go farther in these islands. Though I'm no' certain you would want to go quite that far, in truth —no' in this season. 'Tis a punishing long boat ride, they say, an' I hear 'tis blistering cold the entire—"

Her hand slipped around his elbow, resting so lightly upon his coat he could barely feel it. But there it was. She had taken his arm. Finally.

"Journey," he finished with a choked throat.

Miracles were falling from the heavens like snowdrops, and it had only required a short story about the night his life had turned inside out.

"We will save Orkney for another day, then," she said. "For now, the oxen and sheep are an excellent plan." Her eyes were on the road ahead, her smile oddly shy.

He did not remark on it, or on the unprecedented touch

of her hand. They spoke of the glen and the furnishings in the house and the dogs following at their heels and the clouds and all inconsequential matters—nothing of import, just as they had years ago when he had burned to take her hand, to hold her, to make her his, but had not allowed himself even a taste of her. Yet it felt like paradise. The spring crackled about them and the day was fine and warm as they walked as though fantasies were indeed real.

At their destination, the oxen were appreciated, the lambs cuddled, and the return walk executed with no woman's hand tucked on his arm, instead dangling at her side, close to his. It was temptation and satisfaction at once, and insanity above all. He'd had her pleasure in his hands at Haiknayes, and now this distance again.

She was silent for some time before she spoke suddenly.

"Penny could not have come here for sanctuary."

"No?"

"She had a large, affectionate family and many friends. She had been free since infancy, and had good work at which she made a decent income. Why would she have left Jamaica to make a lengthy, arduous, uncertain journey across a foreign land where she had no friends, if she had no need?"

"You did."

"I was looking for her. And my family has friends in Edinburgh. At any time I might have—" Her eyes widened anew. "Good heavens, Torquil Sterling was brother to the man Constance Read wed. Before she wed him, you *courted* her."

"Aye."

"Because of her acquaintance with Torquil's brother?"

"No. To my knowledge, he had no idea o' Tor's activities."

"Oh. Then was it for Constance's wealth or her beauty?"

"Her wealth would have been useful here." He made a nod to the house they were approaching. "But no."

"She is extraordinarily beautiful."

He nodded. "'Tis what they say."

"You will be gentlemanly oblique now. I guess that is appropriate when one breaks off a betrothal."

"There was no betrothal. Only conversation. I never intended to wed her."

"How odd that you courted her, then. But I suppose that is the way of exalted lairds and such." She waved her hand as though at all the exalted lairds strewn across the pasture. "Courting this woman and that without concern for the outcome."

"Is that what exalted lairds do, then?" he said, feeling acutely the peculiarity of speaking of this with the only woman whom he had actually intended to wed.

"She was looking for you."

"Constance Read? No. She was no more intending to—"

"Penny. She said your name. Not Kallin. Nothing else. Only your name." Her eyes were overly bright. "Why?"

"Your Grace!" Pike was riding toward them from the house. "Your guests have arrived in the village. Zion rode up immediately to inform you. They're all at luncheon now, but Mrs. Tarry says they intend to continue on here after they rest."

"I've invited no guests to Kallin."

"Other than me and Mrs. Aiken," Amarantha said.

He looked down at her and was wholly bemused. She was not a guest. She had never been a guest.

"Who are they, Miss Pike?" Amarantha said.

"His Grace's guests from Haiknayes."

"The party at Haiknayes has come *here*?"

"Miss Pike," he said, "instruct Zion to return to the village swiftly and bid Mrs. Tarry to delay the party as long as possible. I will ride down myself immediately."

She nodded, turned her mount about, and rode off.

"What will you tell them?" Amarantha said.

"That the house is in poor repair and they will be more comfortable at the Solstice."

"But they will certainly wish to come up to see the house. Will you lock the gates and doors and pretend it is uninhabited? What about the sheep, and the well-used paths and driveway? They will know that you are not telling the truth."

"I never expected this." He raked his fingers through his hair. "Kallin's a bit out o' the way for house parties from town, lass."

"And Thomas will be perplexed that Tabitha and I have come here but others may not. Your cousin will find Tabitha and—It is my fault. I came here, and you followed. I did not expect it, but you came, of course, to protect the secret you have protected so carefully for years. If not for me, they would not be here. They would not have even been at Haiknayes. I have—"

"No." He grasped her hands. "You are no' to blame. I am, for imagining I could keep this secret."

"I will not allow it to be ruined. Not because of me." She pulled her hands from his and started quickly for the house. "We will simply arrange everything so it seems to be a typical house. So that they will not wish to stay long, we will make it slightly uncomfortable, dampen the bed linens and serve the food cool and be mysteriously short on things like sugar and teacups—"

"That last will be easy to pretend," he said with a smile that tangled the nerves in Amarantha's stomach. Even in the midst of fear and anxiety, he had always given her pleasure.

"We will hide the Sanctuary in plain sight. And in a few days they will leave here none the wiser. Once they have returned to Edinburgh and tell the story, it will even serve to prove to all that there is nothing interesting here. But there is one thing we should probably do that the residents of this house might dislike."

"What is it?"

"I think it would be best if we found some men."

Chapter 25

A Revelation

The women of Kallin gathered in the drawing room to confer. After some debate, with arguments on all sides carefully weighed, it was decided that the remote estate of a bachelor staffed entirely by women—especially a bachelor with the Devil's Duke's reputation—was simply too ripe for misconstruing.

Zion set off with two fast horses to the Allaways' farm to fetch Nathaniel.

Molly Cromwell, the chief of Kallin's distillery, suggested another male addition: the vicar of the tiny hermitage several miles up the glen. Reverend Clacher had thrice come to Kallin at the behest of the women: on the first occasion to do a Christian burial of a babe—whose babe, no one specified—and later to baptize Rebecca's and Maggie's newborns. On those occasions the hermit had made it clear he had no judgment on the laird, the house, or its residents.

"He's a true man of God," Molly said. An enslaved

woman on Barbados where she had labored in a rum distillery her entire life, she had been among the first women to arrive at Kallin. "And he has a discerning palate for fine spirits," she added with a wink.

It was agreed that the Scotswomen Maggie and Cassandra, and Hannah the Irishwoman, would act as house servants, while Molly would go no farther than the kitchen, with Claire, also West Indian, who had arrived recently and was already cook. Sophie, Rebecca, and Clementine would remain in the village until the guests departed.

With the whirlwind of preparations completed, the women gathered again.

"None o' you will go anywhere alone while the party is here."

Everybody's attention went to the duke, who had remained silent throughout the earlier discussion.

"Won't that be noticed?" Pike said.

"Perhaps. But I will have your word on it now. All o' you."

The women gave it, one after another.

"An' Miss Finn an' Miss Poultney will go by aliases," he added.

The barking of the dogs in the yard, and then hoofbeats, announced the arrival of riders making a swift approach to the house. Cassandra opened the door.

"Good day, miss," Nathaniel said, removing his hat. "I'm Nathaniel Hay, come to play one-armed butler for a time."

Amarantha went forward and onto her toes to kiss him on each weathered cheek.

"You've found the devil, have you, my lady?"

"I will tell you nothing until you have told me all news of Luke since your last letter reached me in Leith. But first"—she glanced at his mud-speckled trousers and coat—"you cannot greet the guests wearing that."

Coming beside her, the duke extended his hand to Nathaniel.

"Thank you for arriving so swiftly, Corporal Hay."

Nathaniel gaped at the duke's hand. Without taking it, he bowed.

"Your Grace. It's my honor to have your trust."

Amarantha laughed. "Nathaniel, you must swiftly become accustomed to the singular ways of this household, and of Kallin's laird too."

"After this past year at your service, my lady, I've experience tolerating singular ways."

A gig drew up to the house, with Molly at the reins and a small, elderly man tucked under blankets beside her.

"No funerals? 'Tis a holiday! An' I dinna mind a wee bit o' subterfuge for a righteous cause," Reverend Clacher said with a hearty chuckle as Cassandra fit him in one of Pike's waistcoats, which would not button over his belly.

"I see you've been eating the stores of brandied cherries I brought you in the fall, Reverend," Molly said.

"Aye, Miss Cromwell." He patted his belly. "What else is an old man to do when the winter blows through the cracks o' his house?"

"I'm off to fetch our guests," the duke said, casting a glance about the foyer where the household had gathered again. "Extraordinary women. Each o' you."

"We know," Maggie said with a brilliant grin.

Smiling, his gaze came to Amarantha. She had the most ridiculous urge to go to him, take his hand, and carry it to her lips, as she had once wanted to do when she was a naïve girl whose heart controlled her.

DINNER WAS A fine affair, with rustic country meats and cheeses and sweets, including a tart that Thomas and Miss Alice both declared as fine as anything they had tasted in Edinburgh or London. Tabitha had remained in her room, pleading a headache, and every word that Jonah Brock spoke made Amarantha marvel at his pretense.

Now, replete and comfortable in the drawing room, the travelers lingered in conversation.

"Interesting what you've done with the place, Gabe," Mr. Brock said, glancing about as he accepted a cup of tea from a little old potbellied footman with rosy cheeks. The room had been prepared with windows cracked open at strategic locations and the chimney partially blocked so the chamber was both drafty and a bit smoky. "But I haven't been here since we were children, of course, when the duchess still presided. Your father did not like Kallin much, as I recall. Imagine that, a recluse who preferred living close to town rather than in this remote place. But I understand that my uncle bequeathed that preference to his second son, didn't he?"

The duke lifted a glass of port to his mouth and said nothing.

"Ha ha! Dinna listen to those rumors, Mr. Brock," Mr. Tate chortled. "The Devil's Duke 'tis no' but a story invented by upstarts to frighten ignorant folk. Aye, Janie?"

Jane cast her gaze down to her cup of tea.

"I think it would be capital if you were a devil, Duke," Iris said. "For then you could do away with my sisters."

Cynthia sat by a window, an odd, agitated brightness in her face.

"Miss Iris," Mr. Brock said, "I find your sisters' company entirely pleasing."

"Thank you, sir," Jane replied with sweet fervency. They were the first words she had spoken since emerging from the carriage.

Finally, as the guests bid their host good-night, Amarantha went to Jonah Brock.

"Mr. Brock, do remain and indulge me in a brief tête-à-tête."

"How refreshingly direct you are, ma'am," he said,

watching the others depart. "I wondered how long it would be before you—"

"I have no interest in rebuking you for the unsavory influence you had on my husband during the months before his death. If a man can be so easily swayed from his convictions, his friends should not be blamed for his sin. Rather, his own weak character should."

"Yet still I deserve your rebuke." He tapped his fingers against the back of the chair beside which he stood.

"How did you know that Mrs. Aiken was among my party at Haiknayes?"

"I beg your pardon?"

"How did you discover that she had come to Scotland?"

"Mrs. Garland, I am not acquainted with this—this Mrs. Aiken."

"I know you are. But you must know that here in Scotland you have no power to harm her. When the letter of proof of her freedom arrives from her former master, Dr. Shaw will petition the courts to establish this incontrovertibly while she resides in Scotland, and England and Wales as well."

"Madam, I am happy that she has such loyal friends in you and the doctor. I assure you, I wish her well too, whoever she is."

"Will you claim that you have not threatened her?"

"I could hardly threaten a woman I don't know, could I?"

"Yet you have before," Tabitha said behind Amarantha. She stood in the doorway, the duke behind her.

"I cannot allow you to fight my fights, Amarantha," she said. "And I don't wish to run for the rest of my life. Mr. Brock, eighteen months ago in Kingston my husband's murderers claimed that they killed him in his mill at your behest. They said that if I did not do as you wished, you would seek to end my freedom."

"Madam," he said tightly, "I have never seen you before. Why would I wish you harm?"

"Are you claiming that those men lied?"

"They most certainly must have, for I have never sent any man to do such a deed, for any reason, no matter what the rumors of me claim. Cousin, will you stand as character witness for me against this accusation?"

The duke remained silent.

"Mr. Brock," Amarantha said, "will you swear now that you did not know Mr. Aiken?"

"I cannot, for I did know a miller by the name of Jonathan Aiken. He was a hardworking man, and fair. Mrs. Aiken, I am sorry for your loss. To lose one's beloved—" He seemed to flinch. "You have my sympathy. And I wish you success in your freedom. I have no doubt it was well earned."

"I did not earn my freedom," Tabitha said. "I claimed it as my human right."

"Ah." His gaze slewed to the duke. "You've revolutionaries under your roof, Gabe. Hold tightly on to your title and estates." Bowing, he departed.

Amarantha went to her friend. "Tabitha, do you believe him?"

"How am I not to? He does not know me and I know of him only by sight and reputation."

"Mrs. Aiken," the duke said, "could my cousin have served as a convenient excuse for those men to threaten you into leaving your mill?"

"Given his reputation, his past . . . yes." She nodded but her eyes were empty. "I believed them. I fled. I have lost my husband's mill—my mill—through my own fear."

"It is rightfully yours and will be in your possession again," Amarantha said. "Come now. We will celebrate this news with well-deserved sleep."

Amarantha made herself leave the room and go to her bedchamber and undress and climb beneath the cozy covers, and tell herself not to dream of him, of his touch—both innocent and scandalous—and of how well he seemed to understand her.

AGAIN, IT SEEMED, she did not wish to be found. But he did find her eventually in the little greenhouse which, years ago, his mother had built onto Kallin's southernmost flank. Late-morning sunshine filtered through the glass and made a crisp, bright halo about her.

"What are you doing?" he said, stepping up behind her and looking over her shoulder.

"Good morning, Urisk. I am beginning to think that immediate interrogation is the way of devils and dukes." She did not lift her head, but continued with the pot and dirt on the table before her. "But I admit myself ignorant of such things, having circulated mostly in humble circles since my debut, you see."

"You are in fine spirits, it seems. Good."

She turned her face up to him and a smile danced in her eyes. "I am relieved at the outcome of last night's conversation with your cousin. You are staring at my lips."

"Give me permission to do more than stare."

Swiftly she returned her attention to the pot. "I am all dirt, you see."

"If dirt suits you, it suits me," he said, and inhaled her fragrance of winter fir. "You were well acquainted with my cousin on Jamaica, it seems."

"Does it?" Her fingers tucked around the base of a plant, scooped it tenderly from its pot, and placed it into a larger pot.

"Last night I overheard you speaking with him o' personal matters."

"Oh? Were you lurking outside the parlor?"

"Lurking is one thing a man o' my height canna do."

"I was not well acquainted with your cousin. My husband and he spent considerable time together in the months before Paul's death."

"Did they?" He didn't care. "You'd no joy in that?"

"They were an unlikely pair. People remarked on it. But Paul enjoyed the friendship."

He leaned back against a table and gripped the sides of it with his hands, lest he leave them free and available to take hold of her. *Only when she invited it.* And she would.

"Will you make me court you for nine weeks again, lass, or can we snip a few weeks off that total. Perhaps seven or eight?"

"Your teasing fails to rouse me, Urisk." Her fingers were moving more swiftly now, patting the soil in place and brushing bits of it from the leaves.

"Then what can I do to rouse you—again?"

"My husband always wondered why, when we would pass your cousin in town, Mr. Brock would offer me such elaborate bows."

Gabriel rubbed a palm over his face. "I said *rouse*. Not *douse*."

"He became obsessed with it." She set the pot on a tray and reached for another plant. "He spoke to me of nothing else for weeks. When his obsession became wearisome, I told him that you and I had been well acquainted."

He paused in the act of crossing his arms.

She glanced at him.

"You needn't be astonished," she said. "I omitted the part at the end, those last two conversations we had. I daresay you don't remember those conversations anyway."

Abruptly, Gabriel's heart was beating very swiftly. "I do."

Her fingers stilled. "Do you?"

"O' course I do."

She began arranging dirt again.

"In any event, the details did not matter to Paul. He was not interested in Mr. Brock's deep bows for my sake, it turned out, but for the sake of your cousin's soul. He decided that his ministry had neglected planters in favor of enslaved people, but that it needn't any longer, for both were needy of salvation. He chose to make your cousin his first project."

"Project?"

"For reform. He believed that given your cousin's many sins, he was ripe for a thorough conversion."

"He wasna?"

"Within a month my husband was playing cards with him twice a week. For money. I think Paul even drank spirits with Mr. Brock, which he never did otherwise, not even wine."

"What o' the conversion?"

"Oh, it went in the opposite direction. Your cousin has always been persuasive, of course. There, I have finished. I have no idea what these plants are but Claire seems to believe that someday their fruit will be delicious." Wiping her hands on a towel, she reached behind her to untie her apron.

Gabriel caught her hands. He bent his head. Wisps of her fiery tresses escaping her kerchief tickled his cheek.

"Those deep bows he gave to you on the street," he said close to her ear. "I never introduced you to him. If you tell me that scoundrel was having sport with a lady—with *you*—I will find him an' give him a taste o' my displeasure."

She swiveled, breaking his loose hold on her hands and bringing her body within inches of his.

"He and I were never formally introduced. But he had brought me the news, of course, so, yes, I was acquainted with him." The sunlight made merry with her eyes, but the green was sober.

"The news?"

"The news of your death. The false news, that is." She shifted to take up a pot on the table and the brush of her hip and arm were like the caress of a specter to his fogged thoughts.

"My death?" He hardly heard himself.

"You needn't deny it. Though it was more than five years ago, it seems like a lifetime really. I was gullible then, as we have already established, so I cannot fault two young men of your habits for having a bit of fun at my ex—"

He grasped her arm and turned her to face him. "He told you I was *dead*?"

She tugged to free herself. "Of course."

He released her. "I knew nothing o' the lie."

"Please." Stepping to the side, she moved around the table. "I told you, it is ancient history."

"Amarantha, I will willingly admit that I was every kind o' fool then—more than a fool. But I had no idea he told you that lie."

"Your Grace?" Maggie said behind him.

"I am occupied, Miss Poultney."

"Reverend Clacher has been nipping at the rum. He's fallen asleep on the foyer chair an' is fixing to slide off it."

He looked over his shoulder. "Then prop him up, lass."

"Miss Iris an' Miss Alice are placing bets on which direction he'll tumble."

"Well, place your bet too, then grab him before he lands on the floor," he said impatiently.

"But there be the dog—"

"I am *occupied*, la—"

Amarantha swished past him, went around Maggie, and out the door.

Maggie dimpled. "No' now, Your Grace."

He scraped his hand over his jaw.

"Now that I've your attention," Maggie said, "after propping up the reverend, would you be telling Cassie where she's to do the ledgers an' receipts in privacy, so no one discovers her about it?"

He frowned, but it only made her grin.

"An' do you know when they'll all be leaving, by chance?" she said.

AMARANTHA FOUND JONAH BROCK alone in the drawing room.

"Eschewing the grand tour of the distillery today in favor of mucking about in the dirt, Mrs. Garland?" His gaze slid over her stained apron. "I'd no idea you had a green thumb. But you are variously talented, I have learned." His eyes were cold. He might have been drinking already; a wine bottle sat open nearby.

It made no difference to Amarantha.

"Yes, I am," she said, whipping off the apron and balling it up. "You are upset with me that I believed the villainy those men claimed about you—regarding Mrs. Aiken. Aren't you?"

"I am," he purred like a sleek golden lion. "Although, admittedly, *upset* seems such a mild term for what I am feeling at present."

"You have no right."

"Yesterday I knew you could not be speaking the truth. You do blame me for your husband's inability to hold his liquor, don't you? Off of a ladder, our elevated man of God—of all ironies. Wretched way to go, though. Oh, I know you told everyone that he went from fever. But I—" His voice stumbled. "I heard the truth. And you have come now to demand that I find a ladder to climb, so that I might also fall to my oblivion."

"You are horrible."

His gaze slid away. "You will no doubt disbelieve me when I vow now that his death was an unpleasant shock to me. I had come to actually enjoy his friendship, you know."

"I am not here now to speak with you about him."

He floated a hand languidly in the air. "Enlighten me, madam."

"After the *Theia* sailed—"

His gaze came to her abruptly and very clear.

"You told me he was dead," she said. "It was a lie. You knew he was well. You lied to me intentionally. Cruelly. Without his knowledge."

"I did."

Chill crawled through her. But it mattered nothing now, really. The world had changed. She had. There was nothing left in her of the girl who had twice thrown her heart into love—first in passion with a man who made her world spin off-kilter, and then in hope with another man she had misunderstood until it was too late.

"Have you discovered only now that my cousin was unaware of that little mistruth?" he said. "How timely."

"Timely?"

"Tate means for Gabriel to wed his daughter."

"The one has nothing to do with the other." She went to the door.

"If it is any consolation," he said, "I am being punished for it now."

"Unless you anticipate a bolt of lightning to shortly strike you down, I really don't see how you imagine I could be consoled by that."

"I had imagined a preacher's wife would be forgiving," he murmured.

"If in your intimate friendship with my husband you did not learn that I was a thorough failure as a preacher's wife, then you knew him very little after all."

A smile slowly curved his lips. "You hid it so well. For years, I imagine. But you truly are all the spark and fire my cousin said you were. Until my ears bled. It was nauseating. It still is."

She frowned.

"My cousin is as smitten with you now, Mrs. Garland, as he was then. If you cannot see that then you deserve your fate."

"Fate does not rule me, Mr. Brock. No one rules me any longer."

She left him. Bypassing Reverend Clacher, who napped contentedly on his footman's chair in the foyer, she took up her cloak and went out.

The day was cold, the sky brilliant blue quilted in snowy white and every shade and shape of gray. The hills beckoned.

Wind greeted her on the slope. She strained as she climbed, her skirts tangling about her legs and her chest tight with the effort. Reaching the crown of the hill, she stared out across the valley speckled with sheep and thick woodlands and the wide ribbon of the Irvine.

The heavy beats of a horse's hooves came to her. She pivoted to face him, hating that he understood her so well that he had known to find her here.

She tore the hair from before her mouth. "I believed you dead!"

He slowed his mount.

"No' lately, lass."

"The *Theia* had barely been gone a fortnight. He told me it was ambushed and you and your crew were killed. I *believed* him. I don't know why I believed him. But perhaps I did so—so willingly, without question—because I had believed what you said to me before you left. I was naïve and impetuous. But you knew that. Indeed, you depended on that."

Astride his great fearsome warhorse he said nothing.

"After he told me of your death, he claimed that it was secret information, that I was not meant to know it, that he could be jailed if I revealed it to anyone. Jailed! Of course I believed him. I had no reason not to—not then. I was acquainted with few men, and all of them men of honor. But I could not bear knowing so little about what had happened to you. I went to the naval bureau and asked for news of your ship, but they had none. So I returned the following day, and the day after that. Every day for a month they said they had no news of your ship."

Gabriel could not doubt this. By then the *Theia* had been hundreds of leagues away, on his first glorious assignment as its commander. They would not have shared that information with a curious girl. And no one on the island except Jonah and an obliging vicar had known what that girl meant to him.

"Weeks later I finally learned that you were alive," she said, "that the *Theia* had not been ambushed. Then I understood."

"What did you understand?"

"About the letter."

The letter.

She took his silence as lack of understanding.

"The letter that your cousin wrote, in which you supposedly declared your intention of marrying me immediately, and told me to wait for you."

He remembered every word of it: three lines it had taken him days to compose, days without drink, without sleep, without enough time to prepare his green crew and patched-together ship for an assignment he had never anticipated—the assignment that would establish his career, the orders directly from London. Among all its vessels in every sea, the Admiralty had chosen *Theia*. Yet even in the heady cloud of pride and the press of preparations, he could not cease thinking of a girl in whose presence he had never felt more right in his own skin and right with the entire world. A girl who drove him mad with need.

"I wrote it," he said.

"Make as many claims of honesty as you wish. Despite knowing better by now, I do find them alluring. But they will not convince me that a man who has lied to everyone in Scotland for years cannot still lie to me."

"I wrote the letter."

"You did not. You had promised that you would not write to me."

"I never promised that."

"I had asked you not to write to me. I *insisted*."

"I wasna your lapdog to order about, lass." He'd been

a daft cub with a heart full of arrogance and a head fixed on having everything he wished, and damn the consequences.

Her brow was troubled, the cloverleaves clouded. "It hardly matters who wrote it."

"It matters to me."

"Eventually I understood it all, clearly," she said as though he had not spoken. "Gossip, however wicked, can be enlightening. They said you had taken up with a woman in Montego Bay. Who was she?"

"Annabelle Lesson."

Her eyes widened a bit. "You admit to it?"

"No' to taking up with her." She had been Torquil's lover, the couple with whom he had spent his single day ashore before sailing east, the day he had thought would be his wedding day. "But she was a friend."

"So, I had imagined, were we friends," she said, subdued.

"An' I."

"I wanted to disbelieve the rumor. I wrote to you. I needed to know the truth. I never sent that letter, of course. By then I was married. In my thoughts I had betrayed my vows to my husband but I could not do so in deed. In any case, soon I came to believe the gossip. I had no reason to disbelieve it."

"Except my word."

"And your cousin's, your dearest companion's. Do you know what I wanted most then?"

"To forget we had met?" As he had that first night, the night that changed the course of his life.

"For you to be dead."

"Given what you believed, I suppose your wish to hold a pistol to my head wasna unreasonable."

"No, you misunderstand. I had no wish to do violence to you myself. I wanted the story your cousin told me—about the bandits—to be true. I wanted you to have died.

I believed at the time that I could endure that grief, even as painful it was. But I did not believe that I could endure the heartbreak I had so impulsively brought upon myself. And"—she stared at the ground before his horse—"I think I did not want to ruin the memory. I knew fully that what I had done, meeting you privately, being with you when I felt as I did, that it was wrong. And I wanted you to be dead so that I would not hate you for playing me for a fool."

"You're mad," he said.

"Probably. Then, at least."

He dismounted, released the reins, and went to her. Her hair spun about in the wind and moisture sat upon each rosy cheek.

"Did you want me to be a scoundrel who had abandoned you, lass, or at the bottom o' the ocean? You've got to choose one."

"Why not both?"

With the pad of his thumb he stroked a teardrop from her cheek. But she did not lean into his touch as she had those years ago.

He withdrew his hand.

"Would you have wed him if you hadna believed me dead?"

"Yes."

It was the final proof he needed. Despite the teardrop, and despite the passion of her kiss on the ramparts, she was cold, immobile, an alabaster statue of a woman who had discarded her heart. His hopes could not make it otherwise.

With thickness in his throat that he could not speak through, and a furious emptiness gathering in his chest, he turned away from her and moved toward his horse.

"Why did you write to my sister last autumn?" she said. "You did, didn't you?"

He turned to her.

"She told me of the anonymous note claiming that I was here and in danger, bidding her come to Kallin and fetch me to England. You played on everyone's fear of the Devil's Duke, hoping she would respond immediately. And she did. You wrote that note."

"Aye."

"Why?"

"I wanted you gone."

"Gone?"

"Off my land. Away from Kallin. Out o' Scotland, if I could make it so."

Her lips fell open. "Why didn't you simply come to the village and tell me that?"

"I didna want to see you."

"You—? Not even for a brief conversation?"

"No."

"But—"

"Never."

She backed away. "You really are the worst sort of beast."

"*I* am?" he exclaimed. "You wanted me *dead*."

"No. I wanted *you*." Her cheeks were two spots of crimson on cinnamon-dusted ivory, the cloverleaves brilliant. "I wanted you with all of the unguarded passion of a girl who did not know how to separate lies from truth. And when I believed that you died I wanted to die too. Do you wish to know the real reason I married four days after I learned of your death? Here it is: to restrain myself from swimming out to sea to die with you. *That* is what an idealistically naïve and ridiculously histrionic girl I was. That is how susceptible I was to the game that a cavalier young man played with me. I married not because I wanted a husband, but because I wanted a *child*. Because I needed a reason to want to live."

Her words fell into the wind and were snatched away.

"Yes," she said to his stunned silence. "I was that drunk on a fantasy I had invented myself. So you see—"

He took a step forward and pulled her into his arms and covered her mouth with his.

She responded without hesitation, her lips opening to meet his kiss, her fingers clutching his shoulders, her breaths mingling with his until the air was gone and there was only the heat of their mouths and the frigid wind swirling about them. His hand came around her jaw, surrounding her, drawing her into him, and he kissed her beautifully. His lips left hers to trail over her cheek and then her jaw, to her throat. She gripped him hard and struggled to breathe.

"You're set to break my heart again," he uttered. "I willna allow it." He held her with both hands and pressed his lips into her hair, his teeth against her bone. "I willna fall again, witch."

"Then why are you kissing me?"

"'Tis the only thing I've a will to do." Taking her face between his hands, he captured her lips again. They were soft and sweet and blessedly eager, rising to him, seeking him. He tasted them, tasted her with his tongue, and she let him inside. His fingertips sank into her hair, and the heat of her mouth, the grip of her hands, the caress of her tongue went through his entire body. He shuddered.

"Perhaps more than kiss," he said against her lips.

Then she was wrapping her arms about his neck, and he was drawing her body to his and feeling her entirely. Her hands were tight around his shoulders and she was having him, taking *him*, hungrily, pressing her breasts and thighs against him, and then her hips. She was small and strong and willingly, eagerly climbing up him. *Finally.*

Some shred of self-preservation that yet remained in him, some mote of reason learned before he had sold his soul to the devil, made him spread his palms and fingers across her back and pin them there. He wanted his hands on her round behind, pulling her tighter against him. She rocked to him and her sigh of pleasure mingled between their lips with his strangled moan.

He dragged her off him and backed to arm's length. Her eyes were unfocused, her hair thoroughly tousled from his hands, and her lips ripe red and glistening.

In desperation, he cast his eyes upward.

"Yes," she said breathlessly. "Yes, good idea." She pulled away from him entirely and smoothed her palms over her hair. "Best not to do *that* again. Especially not in full view of the house and sheep farm—and *me*. Good heavens, you do have a knack for making me forget my scruples."

"Damn the house, damn the farm, an' damn your eternally stupid scruples, woman. We will do that again, an' much more, I assure you, as soon as can be."

Her eyes flared with surprise. Then with anger.

Gabriel's chest filled with the most unwisely heady optimism.

"Those"—he pointed to the clouds rolling over the hills—"are carrying a mighty ice storm. I have no intention o' making love to you for the first time with you fearing for your life."

"I am not afraid of storms," she said, turning her face toward the clouds. In profile, her nose was too pert, her chin too pointed, her brow too high. She was the most beautiful creature he had ever seen.

"I have not feared a storm since the hurricane," she said. "You did that to me. You changed me—obviously in other ways too," she added with an absent gesture of her hand. "But for quite literally teaching me calm in the midst of storm, I should have thanked you years ago. So I will finally. Thank you, Urisk."

"I could eat you whole."

"That was not the response I expected. But I suppose by now I should be accustomed to that—"

"I am mad for you."

"—and to my body's betraying reactions to at least half of the things you say to me." A pink flush had overtaken her cheeks and neck. Her gaze scanned him, jaw to knees, lingering meaningfully about his hips, and finally resting upon his mouth. "What is the actual likelihood of rain or snow falling here soon?" she said with glorious unsteadiness. "And if it did rain or snow, how wet and cold do you think we would become?"

He could hardly breathe. "Very wet."

"You are not referring to the rain, I think."

"An' no' in the least bit cold."

"I daresay," she said upon a thick inhale.

"Go."

"Go?"

"How is it that you canna understand the word *go*, woman?"

"I can! It is only that you say it to me at the most inconvenient and frankly unlikely moments. It is really no wonder I don't always anticipate what you will say. You are contradictory."

"Get off this hill an' away from me. Now."

"Do you see? Contradictory," she said, backing away. "Am I to go away from *you* or the storm?"

"'Tis one an' the same at present."

"I see," she said, beginning to turn toward her descent. "But I may not offer you this opportunity again."

"You will."

"Contradictory and overly confident. Are you coming?"

Not quite, but he was perilously close.

She took the hillside in long, indecorous steps. Five and a half years ago the girl straining to be free of her restraints had captivated him. This woman, entirely free of shackles, filled every part of him with truly insane euphoria. He watched her body move, her arms swinging, the wind wrapping her skirts about her legs and buttocks, and her hair flying every which way. His cock was as hard as a yardarm. He needed her riding it. He needed her coming while she rode it. Twice. Thrice. Four times, each time deeper, her shouts louder, her hands—

"*Are* you coming?" she called over her shoulder.

"I'm waiting till you're far enough away that I'll no' be able to catch up with you."

"I am a quick runner," she shouted back.

"I will take that under advisement."

Her laughter caught on the wind and tripped up the hill, wrapping around him. Judas, if he stared any longer at her perfect behind, at her thighs—

Her back was straight, proud, yet she was a little thing—a little thing he had dreamed of taking like this, on a lush hillside in the wind, grasping those shoulders with his hands, urging her knees apart, spreading those thighs—

He scraped his hand over his face. He must wrest control of the damn fool green lad clearly still in command o' his bollocks. And his brain.

When she was far enough away to assure safety, he called to his horse and followed.

THE SNOW FELL wet and thick. Entering the house, he enquired of his false butler where to find her ladyship.

"She's in Maggie's bedchamber with the little one," Hay whispered then cleared his throat. "Your guests have gathered in the drawing room to play a game of charades, Your Grace," he said at full volume.

Damn his own rule never to enter any of the residents' bedchambers at Kallin, for any reason. And if she were with the nursing mother she wished to be away from him, clearly. She was wiser than he, most certainly.

He wanted her in his arms again. And then in his bed.

She had given a moment's consideration to making love to him on a hillside in the freezing rain. He was dying.

Glancing at the falling snow and considering walking out into it to cool off, he went instead to the drawing room.

Bellarmine, Miss Campbell, and Iris Tate were enacting a farce for the elder Miss Tates, their father, and Mrs. Aiken. They all greeted him and returned swiftly to the game. Jonah sat removed from the others, his hooded eyes on Jane Tate. Gabriel took the seat beside him and curled his fists around the chair arm ends.

"Charades, cousin," Jonah drawled beneath his breath during a burst of laughter from the play actors. "Shoot me now."

"I'll gladly level a pistol barrel at you, but no' for your sake."

"Aha," Jonah said. "You and the fair English widow have spoken about my little lie, I see. She inquired about that earlier."

"You read my letter."

"Of course I read it, you dolt. You were raving mad about the girl, beyond what I had ever seen. You sent her a secret letter, for God's sake. What true friend would not have read it?"

"Why did you lie to her?"

"I believed you were being too precipitate. I wanted her to marry the parson so that you could head off to naval glory."

"You wanted me to die at sea so you could move one place closer to the title."

"*Not* true."

"I would kill you, Jonah, an' toss you in the river if I thought nobody would find the body."

"Go ahead," he said dully. "I've nothing to lose now."

Across the room, Jane Tate cast Jonah a shy glance then dropped her lashes.

"You have something to live for there, it seems," Gabriel said.

"Ah, yes," Jonah said, subdued. "The maiden whose father intends her to be the next Duchess of Loch Irvine."

Gabriel's hands relaxed about the chair arms. "No' if I've a say in the matter. Which, fortunately, I do."

"I used to dream of coming into the title," Jonah said, his eyes still on Jane Tate. "Not of you dying. I never wished that. But of being your brother, instead of that lout enjoying that honor."

"Why did you come here now, Jonah?"

"There was nothing left for me on Jamaica. Would you like to hear my confession, Gabriel?"

"No. I am having a good day." Exceptionally good. If Amarantha did not appear in the drawing room soon, he would go looking for her. He could borrow Pike's shillelagh and knock on Maggie's door from a distance.

"When Charlotte died," his cousin said, "I was devastated. For months. I had no will to do anything, not work, not even drink. Sometime in the midst of it I realized that what I was feeling—the unspeakable grief—was what your little English girl must have felt when I gave her that lie." His fingers played absently with a frayed fringe of the drapery beside his hand. "And so I did an odd thing, cousin."

"Did you?"

"I courted her husband."

Gabriel turned his eyes to Jonah. "Beg your pardon?"

"I sought the reverend's friendship. I made a deal with him. I told him that if he occasionally indulged with me in the pastimes of regular men, a drink, a game of cards, that I would attend his church."

"You're daft."

"Did you ever meet him?"

"Aye," he said, and felt his teeth grind.

"He was so starched and righteous and tight," Jonah said. "She was miserable. She wore a fine façade. Nobody knew it." The animation slipped from his features. "*Few* knew it," he amended upon a shaking breath. "I wanted to fix him. Change him. Because of what I had done—the lie. I wanted to make him more like you."

"Fool."

"That is the thanks I get?"

"Aye."

"My plan was not, unfortunately, a success. He was not wise enough to know what he had. But he was not all bad, Gabe. In fact, I came to quite like him. He had good intentions, if little imagination. And he was enormously well-read. We had some fine debates—"

"I dinna care."

After a moment Jonah said, "She was mystery to him. An alien creature."

A renewed round of laughter arose from the game players.

"Duke!" Iris Tate called, bouncing in her chair. "You must come play, even if Mr. Brock cannot due to his twisted ankle."

Gabriel offered Jonah a skeptical brow. "Twisted ankle?"

"Will you come play, Duke?" Iris shouted.

"Aye, Miss Iris," he said, standing up. "But I'll no' be donning ridiculous hats an' false moustaches. It doesna suit my consequence to playact."

Chapter 26

The Unexpected

20 March 1823
Castle Kallin
Central Highlands, Scotland

Dear Emmie,

It rains and snows at once today, and all here have eschewed the outdoors. I have spent the afternoon with Tabitha, writing her story as she dictates. As we near the end I am more persuaded than ever that her tale must be told. To force a woman to live in containment is to destroy her spirit. To make her live in fear as well is to destroy her will . . .

*B*y closeting herself with her writing partner for the entire snowy afternoon, Amarantha managed to stave off the urgent need to satisfy her desire for the Duke of Loch Irvine's lips and body against hers again.

After dinner, as the ladies arose from the table to retire to the drawing room, the duke announced that he had no interest in port, thus forcing the other gentlemen to accede to their host's whim. As they all went from the dining room, Amarantha felt her skirt snagged, and halted to detach herself.

The heel of the duke's boot was hard upon her hem.

Then his hand was wrapping around hers and he was dragging her out of the light and beneath the stairs into darkness.

"This is most unusual, Urisk," she whispered.

"This dress," he said, putting her firmly between himself and the wall, and his fingertips just barely touching her forearms. "You wore it to drive me mad."

"This is an unexceptional gown."

"Must be the exceptional woman wearing it, then."

"And you are already mad." She rested her hand on his arm, and the madness filled her too in fine tendrils of pleasure. "You admitted it yourself just today. And I think at other times. I don't remember. I am having trouble remembering anything at this moment."

"Except how irresistible you find me."

"I needn't remember that. I *experience* that with no effort whatsoever."

Without any preamble, any permission asked or granted he kissed her. His breath upon her lips was soft, his touch gentle, at first tentative, as though they had not tried to consume each other on a mountainside earlier that day. One of his hands circled her waist, warm and big and holding her lightly.

A sigh began in the depths of her chest and escaped her throat.

His lips moved to the corner of her mouth, then to her cheek and ear where he set tender, beautiful kisses everywhere until she was sighing again and again, and smiling.

"This is, admittedly, a much better end to today than I had anticipated upon waking."

"The day's no' finished yet, my beauty."

She pulled back from his caresses. "Please do not call me that."

"Beauty?"

"Yours."

"I will make a deal with you, lass."

"What sort of deal?"

"I will call you whatever you wish if you'll put your hands on me again. Now."

She obliged. A sound of thorough contentment rumbled beneath her palms.

"I'll be howling at the moon tonight," he uttered.

"This was your idea."

"I enjoy howling," he said, and bent to her cheek, where he laid one soft kiss after another. Then her neck. "You hid from me this afternoon."

"I was with Tabitha, writing. She is well. Relieved. And she is eager to return to Edinburgh. She hopes to depart as soon as the snow abates."

"A fine plan. Now, where were we?"

"You were preparing to howl at the moon." Both of his hands were on her body now, easing her toward him until her hips met his. Her eyelids dipped. "I will be returning to Edinburgh with her."

His hands halted their descent down her back. "No."

"No?"

"You'll no' leave here so soon."

"You cannot order me to stay."

"I can try to convince you." His fingers threaded through her hair and he kissed her, this time longer, then *more*, taking her upper lip then the bottom lip one at a time, then her whole mouth. "Open for me, ambrosia woman," he murmured, and she did so and tasted his desire upon her lips and in the caress of their tongues.

There was such heat opening in her body, and need. She lifted her hands to his shoulders and felt it, felt *him*.

"You make me . . ." she whispered between kisses. "*Want*," she breathed. "Want you."

"'Tis good news."

"But I will not be convinced to remain here with love-making."

"Then I will ask," he said, stroking his thumb over her lower lip. "Will you stay here at Kallin long enough for me to memorize every shape an' texture o' your lips, Amarantha?"

"The mystery of Luke's father is not here."

He drew back.

"Yesterday I spoke with everyone here," she said. "None of them have ever heard of Penny. I don't believe I will find the answers I seek here. I must return to her family and to those who knew her."

"No."

"No?"

"You'll no' sail to another continent in search o' anyone, especially no' a phantom man. For pity's sake, woman," he said, tilting her face up to his. "When will you leave off living your life for everyone but yourself?"

"I promised Penny that I would find her son's father."

"Then we will hire an investigator."

"How could a stranger discover intimate details of my friend's life that I cannot?"

"He makes his living at it, so he must. An' while he is busy at that, you will stay here an' continue to kiss me."

She pushed against his chest and he released her.

"You will stay here voluntarily," he amended.

"Just as the residents of this house must stay? You cannot contain women, Urisk."

"The locks on the gates are no' to keep them in, but to keep others out."

"What if the men who are the legal masters of these

women—Maggie's betrothed, Cassandra's father, the man who bought Molly off the auction block, the father of Rebecca's child who would have the right to seize Clementine— What if any of those men hunt until they find this sanctuary?"

"We must hope they willna."

"Even if they do not, even if no one ever comes looking for them, this is not a complete life, hiding away from the world. Don't you see that?"

"Aye, I understand no' living a complete life," he said soberly. "What do you wish, lass?"

"Freedom for the women here to go and come as they please." Her voice was soft steel, her eyes overbright. "To live and—and to love as they wish."

"Then they'll have it."

"What will they have?"

"Autonomy."

"The women of Kallin?"

"Aye. 'Tis a brilliant idea, in fact. No more endless letters filled with minutiae. Why didna I think o' it myself?"

"Because women have the best solutions to everything," she said. "Women should also have noble titles in their own rights, by the way."

"Some Scots do." His hand curved around her waist again, drawing her close.

"Clearly Scots are more civilized than all others."

He laughed. "A civilized beast, am I?"

"Women should captain ships too."

He stroked his knuckles gently over her cheek.

"You can captain my ship anytime you please, lass."

"By ship do you actually mean . . . ship?"

He laughed. "I did." Then his hands spread over her lower back and he drew her snugly against him. "But if you would rather—"

"Wait."

He groaned. "Have mercy on a starving man."

"Will you truly do it?"

"Aye. I will turn over the governing o' Kallin entirely. They can make whatever sort of constitution they please: monarchy, democracy, tyranny in the case o' Pike—"

She laughed.

His hands tightened. "Your laughter," he said against her hair.

"My laughter?"

"Intoxicates me." He kissed her brow and she felt the movement of his chest as he breathed, his life and strength and vitality.

In the darkness she found his face with her hands, and went onto her toes to find his mouth with hers.

"An' these lips," he said. "These lips taste as sweet an' salty an' rich as I always imagined they would. Finer. Like ambrosia. Trite simile, I know. But we've already concluded that I am no poet. An' kissing you, I feel like a god. So, there you have it: ambrosia."

"You imagined the flavor of my lips?"

"An' the silk o' your skin here. The flutter o' your heartbeat here." He touched her neck where her pulse was reckless.

"My heartbeat does not flutter."

"It does now." He took her mouth with his, and then with the most natural ease he pressed her gently into the wall with his body. Thigh to thigh, hips to hips, chest to chest, she felt every bit of his muscle and his arousal.

"Flutter," she whispered. "Yes, yes, flutter, I see now."

"The arc o' your neck here," he said, following his words with his touch. "Your soft, strong shoulder. I fantasized sinking my teeth into this shoulder."

"Your teeth?" She shuddered, wanting his teeth in her shoulder quite acutely. "And you say you are not a beast."

"I never said that." He kissed her jaw, tilting her head up to stroke the tender curve of her throat with his lips, then with his tongue. She was all trembling and aching.

"Where else?" she whispered, wrapping her hands around his arms that were thick with muscle.

"The beauty here," he said, and she felt the lightest caress upon the side of her breast, barely a touch.

"Only there?"

"An' here." Both of his hands rounded her ribs beneath her breasts. "This strong cage that contains the least containable heart I've ever known."

"I cannot breathe. Your diabolical touch is drawing out the air through my skin and clothing."

"You'll need to take a good full breath now, lass."

She did so. Upon her exhale his thumbs swept up and over the curves of her breasts and across the tender peaks.

"Oh." She gripped his arms. "Gabriel."

"When you say my name," he said against her throat, caressing her arousal through the layers of her clothing, "I want to have all o' you at once."

"Yes," fell over her tongue.

"Yes?"

"On the hill—earlier today—if the weather had not come." Her breaths were fast. "I want you. Now. I want you."

In the darkness, she felt the shifting, the change in the air that surrounded his body.

"Now?"

"Now. This morning. Yesterday. Five and a half years ago. On the ramparts at Haiknayes. Always."

"Here?" he said.

"Perhaps we could—that is—later—after the others have—*oh.*"

He caressed her breasts again, and need pulsed in the taut tips and between her legs. He did it again, sending perfect pleasure down her center. Then he moved his hips into hers.

She moaned, and he captured the moan with his mouth. The kiss was deep, complete, his tongue taking hers.

"Here?" Then he was tugging down the bodice of the gown she had not worn to entice him but she loved that it had because she wanted this. The fabric gave way and his hands were on her skin, his palms surrounding her breasts and fingertips closing around her nipples and stroking.

Her sighs were lost as she closed her eyes and allowed it, whispered, "Yes, *yes*," until she was arching her back, strung with pleasure.

In the darkness, his mouth closed over her nipple.

She groaned, shocked and filled with pleasure. It was hot, wet, his tongue playing, caressing, and her body was responding, throbbing, readying so swiftly.

He murmured so she felt the words vibrate against her breast, "Here, where we could be discovered?"

"Yes. You make me need as I have never—You make me an abandoned woman, Gabriel," she said upon hopeless laughter.

"You have always been this, wild one. I've just opened the gate." His hands swept down her sides and over her hips, and she felt her skirts rise.

"Really?" She was panting, her fingertips digging into his chest, her heartbeats furiously fast. "Here? Now?"

"Trust me," he said against her lips and his hands gathered the fabric.

She nodded swiftly. "Only *don't stop*."

He went to his knees as his hands trapped her skirts upon her hip bones, and she was entirely exposed and shaking.

"What are you—"

The heat of his skin scraped her inner thighs. He licked her.

"Oh—" She gasped, felt his tongue, the caress that sent her to her toes and made her spread her knees.

"What are you doing? How are you—" Moans spilled from her one after another as she made herself accept his mouth on her, made herself accept his hands giving her no quarter. It was nothing she had imagined, nothing she had felt before, soft and firm at once, and gloriously wet and hot. He took her into his mouth as though he were tasting her, savoring her. Her legs were weak, her palms pressed the wall, the darkness swallowing her whimpers as she allowed herself to feel the pleasure. She had not known a man could do this, could *be* this.

With tender force he opened her, touched her, stroked her, and made her rock her hips forward seeking more, as she tightened within. The pleasure came. Hot and lush and explosive, it happened against his tongue, to her cries of astonishment that she swallowed one after another as he was consuming her. They were beautiful, the tumbling contractions that came one after another, spreading. Her flesh was ready to take his. She needed it now—needed to be taken. She did not even care that there would be pain and discomfort. She would have this memory of his tongue on her and that would be enough.

She was trembling all over, her legs shaking. Yet he did not draw away swiftly, rather, slowly, his thumbs stroking over the ridges of her pelvis, his mouth ascending to the base of her stays.

With a heavy inhalation that lifted his wide shoulders, he pressed his brow to her ribs and his hands wrapped tightly about her hips.

"Judas, woman," he uttered low, "how you command me—my every breath an' thought and wish."

Loosening her hand from the wall, she threaded her fingers through his hair and stroked him.

His great, powerful body shuddered.

"Come kiss me," she whispered. "If you have any kisses remaining."

He rose, her skirts falling as he took her face between both of his hands and lifted her chin.

"Infinite for you," he said. His lips were warm and

tasted of both his mouth and her scent, a strange and heady mixture. "Have you had what you need?" he said.

She allowed her hands to slide down his chest. "Not entirely." Her fingertips found the top of his trousers.

With a harsh breath, he grabbed her wrists.

"You'll no' have that, lass."

She blinked but the darkness was nearly complete. Suddenly she could hear voices from the drawing room: laughing and animated conversation, the sounds of another raucous game.

"No?" she said.

"Aye, there's a 'no' you canna demand that I retract."

"I can admit surprise. You once had something of a reputation, of course. Don't you want to? With me?"

"I have wanted little else for—well, since a stormy night in a storage cellar." He bent and kissed her mouth so softly, so perfectly that as he drew back she went onto her toes to follow him. He lifted her hands and brought them together to his lips. "But I have changed," he whispered against her palms. "You changed me."

"*I* did?"

"Aye. Irrevocably."

He released her and moved away.

"I don't know that I approve of this particular change," she said.

He barked a laugh. As he moved into the lamplight in the foyer she could see the spark in his eyes.

"Come, lass. We'll have been missed."

Amarantha smoothed her hands over her hair and discovered it a passionate tangle.

"I will be along in a moment," she mumbled.

He chuckled. Then his footsteps moved into the foyer and the conversation from the drawing room got louder as he opened the door to enter. Amarantha stood in the darkness, waiting for her cheeks to cool and wondering that she felt no shame. Only happiness.

"Milady."

Something tugged at the coverlet tucked up around her chin, plucking her from dreams of Gabriel's hands on her.

"Mm?" she groaned.

"Milady, you *must* come now. 'Tis urgent."

Amarantha started up. Maggie Poultney stood beside her.

Before she had tumbled into bed, the moon had sat high behind the parting clouds. Now through the windows she could see that it kissed the mountaintop. The hour was much later.

"Swiftly now." Maggie held forward a gown.

"What has happened?" Her bare feet hit the frigid floor and she pulled the gown over her head. "Is Mrs. Aiken—"

"I'll take you there." The Scotswoman buttoned Amarantha's gown swiftly. "But we must be quiet or we'll wake the others."

Dragging a shawl from her traveling trunk she slid her feet into slippers and hurried after Maggie. Through a twisting labyrinth of corridors she had not yet mastered, they went in silence, and shortly Amarantha was thoroughly lost.

Through a partially opened door, golden light flooded the corridor.

"God be with you, milady," Maggie said, and disappeared up the stairs.

Amarantha drew the door open.

It was a small chapel, lit dimly with a handful of candles. Vaulted in the medieval fashion, with great stained glass windows that were dark now, it boasted neat rows of chairs near the east end which rose two steps to the rounded chancel.

Reverend Clacher stood at the center of those steps. He wore a stole about his neck and held a book in his palms. At the base of the stair were Tabitha and Nathaniel. And in the middle of the aisle was the man of every one of her fantasies.

He strode toward her, his gaze on her intent. He did not halt a proper distance away from her but came close, as he had from the beginning when she had thought him a great hulking creature.

"For a man who does not attend services," she said, "you do seem to enjoy spending time in church in the middle of the night."

"Only with you, lass," he said as his gaze slipped down to where the ribbons of her nightgown poked out from her hastily donned gown at the bodice.

She glanced again at the two by the vicar.

"Is the Reverend to do a service?" she said. "Now?"

"Aye. A special service at my request."

"Do you know, Shark Bait," she said, blinking away the sleep that still clung to her. "You are the most unusual nobleman—really the most unusual *man* that I have ever known. But if you wish to have a service in the middle of the night, I will attend."

"You just called me Shark Bait."

"Maggie awoke me from dreams of a young naval captain."

"You dreamed about me." The pleasure in his smile dashed away all remaining thoughts of sleep.

"I have always dreamed about you, even when I should not have," she said. "Now, shall we commence this? It must be midnight and—What are you—Oh, *oh*."

He was on his knee before her and taking her hand and her heartbeats were careening and she could not breathe.

"'Tis a beast o' a man, I am. But war breeds no other sort, an' when a thing's got to be done, I see no cause for delay." The rumble of rough syllables pressed through her shock. He held her gaze as he had held her body earlier, with the virile strength of the beast he admitted to being that had always awoken the thrill in her, and the longing.

"Amarantha Garland, will you be my wife?"

Chapter 27

Temptation

*P*erfect astonishment on her face was as taking as joy and amusement and anger and consternation and every emotion Gabriel had ever seen shape those features made of clay and faery dust. It was not the ideal emotion at present. But it was stunning.

"Will I—" she began, blinked, and the cloverleaf gaze snapped past his shoulder to the other end of the chapel. She snatched her hand from his. "You have *not* waked me in the middle of the night to—for this. I will not believe it. What sort of game are you playing now? More charades?"

"No game." His heart was beating harder, faster, hotter than his ribs could contain. "Never games. Marry me, Amarantha."

For a brittle interval of torturous silence, she only stared at him. Then understanding lit her eyes.

"Has my—has my father written to you?"

"Your father?"

"My mother told me—That is, nothing. Nothing. I— *Nothing.* Oh, do stand up. Please."

"No' until you give me an answer."

She shook her head once.

He climbed to his feet. Then he took her hand and led her toward the door to the corridor.

"Your Grace?" Reverend Clacher called.

"A minute, vicar," he said, pushed the door open and drew Amarantha into the corridor. Her eyes were chased with sleep, her hair escaping its thick braid, and a line ran across one cheek where the bed linen had impressed its edge into her skin. "You wear no cap when you sleep."

"What an interesting observation, Urisk. No, I do not wear a cap when summoned abruptly from sleep in the middle of the night to go I know not where. But the moment you adopt an ear trumpet, I promise to start wearing a cap twenty-four hours a day. Will that suit you, old man?"

"Judas, you're a delight."

"You do not want to marry me."

"I do." Desire pressed at him powerfully: the ache he had felt for her since he had first seen her, first heard her, first witnessed her courage. Knowing her now, that ache had become actual pain, in his chest and in his damn breeches. He lifted his hand and allowed his fingertips to rest upon the delicate bone of her jaw.

"Amarantha, I willna take you to bed unless you are my wife."

Distress rippled over her throat.

"I appreciate the respect you are showing me," she said. "But, even were I to hold myself to that standard, given your many assets I imagine it would not be difficult to find another woman—multiple other women—to relieve that particular need without resorting to marrying any of them. Or me."

He smiled.

"Which of those words amuses you?" she said.

"You are the only woman that can satisfy the need."

The pleasure left her eyes.

"No lies," she whispered. "Please."

"Amarantha, I want you in my bed. I need you there."

"I am sorry, truly. But that does not suffice to alter my conviction on this matter."

Conviction.

The alabaster statue had returned.

"Hm." He made as though he were studying the floor in thought. "Well, you will have this estate, though o' course I promised just tonight to give it over entirely to the maidens in the dungeons. It would be a shabby thing to recant so soon."

"Or ever, really," she said thinly.

"There is Haiknayes. Impressive castle, that one. The cellar leaks, but the ramparts are especially fine on a starry night, they say."

"They do?"

"Aye. So there's an advantage: the run o' Haiknayes. In fact, you will have everything o' mine, my title, my name, my gold—"

"All of that excess gold you have lying about."

"—an' my lands. All in return for a few quick words spoken before that altar in there. 'Tis a bargain, really."

"Your lands are handsome." Her eyes seemed to soften, and her gaze dipped to his lips, then lower. Lifting one hand, she laid her palm upon his chest and trailed her fingertips downward. "Exceedingly appealing, really."

He snatched her hand from where it was creating havoc in at least two separate regions of his body.

"None o' that, lass, till you promise your troth to me."

"Pity." Her breasts were rising on quick little breaths, swelling against her gown.

Good God. Could a man take a woman against a wall outside of a church? Yes. Yes, he could.

"Did I mention, you will be a duchess?"

"I have never wished for a title."

"O' course you havena. Neither did I at one time. But I discovered it comes with all sorts o' privileges. They let you walk into dining rooms before everybody else, an' theaters an' the like. An' there's a coronet. 'Tis a wee bit elaborate for my taste: a horde o' gold strawberry leaves. But your beauty will improve it. Come now. Do this."

"Do this?" she repeated blankly. "Between the two of us, truly you take the prize for madness."

He wrapped both of his hands around her face and the lust in him felt fierce and especially urgent. He captured her open mouth beneath his. She tasted of warmth and surprise, and then desire. Her hands grabbed his arms and she did not push him off. She gripped hard, so tight that each fingertip was a nail driven into his flesh.

She drew away slowly. Her lips were red, her eyes fevered.

"I will make love to you," she said. "I should like that very much. Very . . . much. But I cannot marry you." Touching her fingertips to his lips, she whispered, "But thank you for asking."

Then she was gone, into the darkness without candle or lamp, with only his heart.

SHE LAY AWAKE, her eyes open to the final remnants of moonlight. She could not sleep. She suspected she might never sleep again.

He did not knock but entered without warning or permission. Closing the door and turning the key in the lock, he walked toward her removing his coat and then his waistcoat, and left them where they dropped.

"I have decided to give you a taste o' what you will be missing," he said with a gorgeously husky quality to his voice, and untied his cravat.

"Y-you have?"

His neck was all sinew and strength and she was staring.

"Aye." He was lifting his shirt and her eyes widened. Muscle. *Beautiful muscle*, in his chest and arms and waist, and taut skin to which the candlelight clung in undulating shadows, and black hair tapering in a line that disappeared beneath his breeches. He was male beauty she had never imagined.

"A taste?" she said.

"A meal, in truth. But only one," he said, unbuttoning the fall of his breeches. "Do you understand?"

Her throat was closed. She nodded.

He paused in his task. Every nerve of pleasure and fear and anticipation gathered in Amarantha's stomach.

With the fall of his breeches only half unfastened, he came forward and stood before her, bare feet planted so firmly on the floor that he could not possibly feel the cold. But with the magnificent expanse of his naked torso and arms before her, she no longer could either. She was afire already, remembering what his mouth could do to her, and his hands.

"The cap," he said with simple pleasure.

She nearly sobbed.

As she sat very still, he removed the pins and set the ruffled linen cap aside. His fingertips came beneath her chin and gently he urged her to lift her face. A crease marred the brow she had always thought so sober, even when he smiled, so suited to his natural authority.

"Does what you see displease you?" she said.

"No' enough light." Taking up a candle he went to the hearth and lit it from the glowing embers. Then he put more wood on the grate and brought the candle to the table by the bed, where he lit the lamp.

"Now I can see the beauty o' which I have dreamed every day for five an' a half years."

"You needn't flatter me. I require no seduction now."

"No flattery. No seduction. Nothing but the truth. I will never lie to you, Amarantha. I have said it. Many times. I have promised. When will you believe it?"

She stood up and reached for his face. He grabbed her hand and pressed his lips to her palm.

"If you please," he said, "remove that ridiculously chaste garment, an'—"

"Remove it?"

"Aye."

"But if I remove it, I will be wearing nothing."

"Aye. Nothing but me."

Heat leaped from her belly into her cheeks and her nipples prickled. She reached for the skirt of her gown.

"Allow me," he said.

She stared fixedly at his collarbone as he took her nightgown in each hand and began gathering it up. By the time it was skimming her thighs, his big hands were full of the fabric.

"Ready?" he said.

"Y-yes." Her voice wobbled.

He dropped the fabric and it fell to her ankles again. Curving his palms around her shoulders he kissed her softly.

"Your lips," he murmured, "your fingers, your hair, your eyes, your chin, your throat, your lashes—"

"What are you—"

"—your palms, the occasional glimpse o' your ankle, your ears: each o' these alone suffices to make me want you beyond endurance."

"My ears? Really?"

"Aye. You needn't reveal any bit o' skin more, if you dinna wish."

"But I do wish it. May I . . . that is . . ."

"Lass?"

"May I touch you?"

His throat jerked. "Aye."

"I may?"

"If it will give you pleasure."

"Will it give you pleasure?" she said.

"Me?"

"If I touch you."

"Amarantha." He spoke above the clamor of his heart-beats. "I have been dreaming o' your hands on me since the night we met. If you dinna touch me, I'm likely to perish here on the spot."

Her eyes shone with the oddest light. *Relief.* An improvement over uncertainty and confusion, to be sure.

She touched him, tentatively, so softly he barely felt it. And then with growing confidence she stroked her fingers over his chest and to the base of his throat then along his arms.

"This—touching you—fills me with such longing," she whispered, trailing her fingertips downward, over his nipples. "I wonder if it is a sin to believe that I am in heaven now."

He closed his eyes and swallowed his groan. Wrapping his hands around her waist, he drew her to him, against him, and he made her feel his need.

"If so," he said, bending to kiss her just beneath her perfect ear, "then I will have plenty for which to ask forgiveness."

"Not to me," she said, her hands sliding up either side of his neck and into his hair. "Undress me now."

He swept the garment over her head and discarded it, and she stood naked before him.

"I cannot—cannot seem to cease tre-trembling," she said bumpily, her eyes very wide.

The wild creature had returned, curious and hungry but uncertain.

He pulled her to him, wrapped his arms about her, and she pressed her cheek and palms to his chest. Every bit of her skin felt like fire against his.

"I have never done this," she said. "Undressed. As God intended it." She lifted her face and her smile was brilliant. "It is positively *delicious*."

"Wild one," he uttered.

He swept her up into his arms to her tumble of laughter and deposited her on the bed.

He did not tell her how beautiful she was, not her breasts or hips or legs or buttocks or any other divine part of her revealed by the removal of the nightgown. Instead he treated each just as he had treated each of her fingers in the Solstice's kitchen: with devoted attention. Her skin was caressed, her buttocks adored, her legs lavished with attention until she was breathless with sighs, and her hips and abdomen kissed with exquisite care. Her breasts were worshipped, their fullness enjoyed by his hands and his lips, and her nipples sucked so thoroughly that she was lifting her back from the bed and parting her thighs much sooner than planned.

So he gave her his hand there, where she longed to be touched, and his fingers, which made touches into torment and then into sublime satisfaction. She came like that, suddenly, surprise in her cries as she moved against him.

Without asking now, she touched him everywhere she could find skin to touch, his arms that were thick with muscle and his chest and waist, his shoulders. The taut dampness of her body again became an empty ache that she needed filled. Unfastening the remainder of the buttons on his trousers, she thought he would take her then— wanted it even knowing that it would bring the end too soon.

He did not. Drawing away, he left the bed and refastened the buttons.

"What are you doing?" she said.

He took up his shirt and coat.

"The meal is over. I hope you enjoyed it." He moved toward the door and reached for the key.

"But that was not an entire meal!"

He scanned her body with his shadowy gaze. "No?"

"The soup, perhaps. And entrée, at best."

"Still unsatisfied?" The partial smile played about his gorgeously talented lips.

"You neglected to serve the principal remove." The words quavered between outrage and hilarity.

"Principal remove, hm?"

"Yes, of course. But perhaps, being a beast, you do not know all the courses of a civilized meal."

He dropped the shirt and coat. "I'll give you civilized, wild one."

She sprang off the bed and flew across the cold floor and into his arms. Their mouths met, hands assisting, famished, as though they had not just kissed or touched, as though they would find in each other's mouths and hands what they sought most desperately.

"Principal remove," he growled upon laughter, and lifted her entirely off the ground.

The bed now seemed miles away and far too civilized after all, and they had already waited for years. They took each other there, at the door, against the wall. He groaned upon entering her and became very still, and she choked back her sobs of happiness and kissed his jaw and neck and shoulders and every part of him she could reach. For a wonderfully extended interval, they remained like that, Amarantha disbelieving that this kind of love could be real and Gabriel simply making a valiant effort not to end it all prematurely.

Then his mouth found hers, and she learned the great joy of being adored as she was being pleasured. It was a revelation to her. She had never been touched as he touched her now, with reverence and care and hunger all at once, as though to love like this were to both take and give. He gave, and gave, until she was moaning again and neither of them could wait another moment.

Eventually he carried her back to the bed.

She lay on her side looking at him, hands beneath her cheek and delectable weariness in every limb. She stretched her legs to tuck her toes beneath his calf.

"'Tis ice you give me now?" But he did not move, only his mouth stretching into a smile.

"My toes are always cold here."

He sat up and took her feet into his hands. His palms were warm.

"Will you continue that all night?" she said sleepily.

"Aye, if you wish." His thumb stroked the sole of her foot and she sighed. "Anything you wish."

"I wish for there to be no need for women to run away from men who intend harm to them, from men who do not treat them with . . ."

She closed her eyes as his fingers stroked, his heat once again awakening her desire, this time languid and safe.

"With?" he said.

Love.

"Respect," she said. "Can you do that, Urisk? With this haven you have created, can you make all other men cease harming women?"

"I canna, lass."

"The world is full of messiness," she said.

"Aye."

She fell asleep to the rhythm of his caress.

HE AWOKE WHEN he felt the loss of her warmth, of her silken hair spread over his chest, of her soft skin against him. He forced his eyes open to find mere embers illumining the chamber. As any sailor on a sightless sea, he searched with his hearing.

Sobs rose in the darkness.

He found her sitting on the floor, her back to the bed, arms strapped around herself. Her knees were pulled up tight to her breasts. She shook with great convulsions. He grabbed a blanket and went to the floor and wrapped it around her. She made no protest, only swiped at the trails of tears on her face.

He settled beside her and swallowed a yelp. The floor was ice. But she had been down here for longer. Women were remarkable.

"I know, princess," he said softly. "I dinna care for heights either. If you wish, we can remain down here on the ground for the rest o' the night."

She lifted a face stained with tears. Her lips wobbled into a smile.

"You," she whispered, "made me laugh through a hurricane."

He ached so fiercely he wanted to shout to the entire world.

Reaching one hand out of the cocoon of blankets, she stroked his cheek. The caress went through him like hot oil.

"What is amiss, my lady?"

"You will now say, 'Allow me to help,'" she said, her fingertips slipping down his neck to his chest, and then curling up inside his hand, just as she had done that night in the cellar.

"Will you allow it?" he somehow managed to say, though hoarsely.

"You cannot. They were dreams. Bad dreams. Memories," she said. "I had a son." The words fell into the silence. "His name was Edward. I named him after my father. He lived for only six minutes." Fresh tears welled in her eyes. She scrubbed her hand beneath her nose and sniffed. "I don't know why I dreamed it, or why I am weeping like this now. Or why I have just told you."

"I knew it already." And grieved, elated that she had survived, suffering with her loss, and furious that the pompous Reverend had had the privilege of being there to hold her as she wept—not he. The day the tender ship brought the letter that had told him of it, he ordered his quartermaster to break open a barrel of rum and serve a cup to every man aboard. Astonished, they had welcomed the celebration, and he had raised a cup with them beneath the blue Mediterranean sky. Then he had gone to his quarters, locked the door, and gotten drunk. It was the first and last time he ever did so aboard his own ship.

"How did you know?"

"Jonah occasionally wrote to me with news." Monthly in the first two years. Gabriel never replied, and eventually the letters ceased.

"After I lost my son," she said, "my husband never again touched me with desire."

Gabriel's stomach turned over.

"The blood had alarmed him," she said. "There was so much more than there should have been. I did not understand that then, not until later, after I had attended other women at births." She spoke now without emotion, telling the story as though someone else had lived it. She donned the alabaster statue as she required it. "He did not know that at first."

"You told him."

"Yes. He did not wish to hear it."

"He was a coward, Amarantha."

For a stretched moment she said nothing. "He was not a cruel man. He gave me a home, ample food and clothing, and some time to pursue my interests—Mr. and Mrs. Meriwether's hospital as well as my friendships beyond the mission. He did not approve of them, but he allowed it."

Food, clothing, and disapproval: the stuff of her marriage.

"After a time, he ceased touching me entirely. He was afraid that another pregnancy would kill me. He told me he treasured me too greatly to bring me harm." She ducked her head and her next words were muffled against the blanket. "Months before the accident that took his life,

I found him with one of the Englishwomen who worked at the mission, a married woman. He said she had offered him consolation after the death of our son, and that since he had been afraid of making me ill again, he had continued to go to her. He told me this as though he meant it to comfort me. Or perhaps to exonerate himself." Her nostrils flared. "I had suspected it. But every time I spoke of it to him he denied it, furious with me for accusing him. It was not until I actually saw them together that he could no longer lie."

She turned her face away.

"But the worst of it was my own fault," she continued. "I had trusted him. I had given my faith and affection to him, and I tried to please him, only to learn that I had misjudged a man again—so thoroughly." Her eyes gleamed as she looked at him. "I will never give myself into a man's power again. Do you understand? You must understand."

"When you trusted in his fidelity," Gabriel said, "you didna misjudge a man again. You misjudged a man for the first time."

Allowing the blankets to fall away from her, she climbed into his lap, wrapped her arms about his neck, and brought her mouth against his. He kissed her and ran his hands over her soft back and buttocks. Then he rose with her in his arms and laid her on the bed.

He made love to her slowly. This time, however, he spoke to her of her beauty as he touched it: the freckles that made her face unique and the pointy chin that made it imperfect; the long cinnamon lashes that were very fine except when they shrouded the cloverleaves; the lips that had uttered impertinences to an officer in the King's Navy and still spoke outrageously to a duke, and that he would never be able to taste enough; the slender hands that one of his could swallow and that he wanted all over him; the feet that were indefatigable, sometimes inconveniently so;

the soft belly that would surely again know the heartbeat of a little one.

Upon this last she began to weep anew, but she smiled as tears dribbled into her hair. He kissed her damp eyes and hair and lips, and she wrapped her arms about his neck and pulled him to her and made him give her what she needed.

Afterward, she lay awake, watching the rhythm of his breathing, the gentle rise and fall of his chest, and his face at rest: the noble jaw, sensuous mouth, the flare of his nostrils, the arc of his nose, and the tumble of too-long locks over his brow.

"After you departed Kingston," she said, and saw his lashes twitch, then his chest fill on a deep waking breath. Slowly he turned his face to her.

"Several days after you departed Kingston," she said, "a maid with whom I was friendly at the hotel told me she pitied me."

His eyes were like onyx.

"Did she?" he murmured.

"She said it was a shame for me that Mrs. Jennings was such a fine watchdog of my virtue, for you had extraordinary stamina."

"Every man at twenty-three has stamina."

"Does he?"

He pushed himself up onto his elbow. "If he has properly bridled himself, aye."

"She was trying to embarrass me. I only realized that much later. At the time I was too naïve to understand her meaning. You knew that I was naïve."

"Aye."

"What did you want of me?"

His features lost all thoughtfulness, all pleasure. He said nothing.

"Tell me," she said. "What did you want of me then? It matters nothing now, of course. I will never be that girl again. In truth, I feel not five and a half but five and a half thousand years older and am entirely changed. Still, I find it curious, the ways in which—"

In a single movement he closed the space between them, scooped his arm around her, and claimed her mouth. Then they were chest to chest and he was kissing her again as he had at first, drinking from her lips, from her mouth. Twining her hands through his hair, she welcomed his weight atop her, the heat of his skin, the brush of whiskers against her cheeks and chin.

"Amarantha." His voice was deep, his arousal taut against hers. "Marry me."

"No."

He rocked to her and she moaned.

"Marry me, wild one," he murmured against her neck, "an' my exceptional stamina will be at your service whenever you wish."

"I suspect—" She gasped, gripped his arms, and let him pleasure her. "I suspect your stamina will be at my service whenever I wish anyway."

"So be it." His tongue was tracing little arcs of heaven upon her throat.

"So be it?"

He lifted his head. She could see every lash that cast shade on his dark eyes, and every tiny crease on his skin put there by the ocean sun. He was beautiful, strong and powerful and gentle and good, and she loved him.

"Dinna marry me if you canna," he said. "Only stay with me."

"Stay with you?"

"Aye. Run when you must." Tenderly his fingertips stroked back a lock of hair across her brow. "But always return to me."

Amarantha's heart beat so furiously, she knew he must feel it against his chest pressed to hers.

"Without marriage?" she said.

"As you will. However you will. Only let it be forever." His smiled a half smile. "Make a dishonest man o' me, lass."

"Gabriel," she whispered. "I need you now."

He obliged. He filled her again and they were, for a time, one.

Chapter 28

Kisses First

The sky was brilliant blue, the earth silvery white. Not wanting to brave the frigid morning before the sun burned away the ice, Amarantha went to the place in the house she felt the happiest: the greenhouse.

Her body ached in the manner it did after a vigorous walk, except more specifically, and she had slept little. But she could not remain abed. If he woke while she was lying there staring at him, he would take her into his arms and make her believe in a fantasy again.

She was trimming spent leaves when Jane opened the door.

"Amarantha? I am so glad to find you here." Her voice was unusually high.

"Good morning, Jane." She set down the shears. "Is something amiss?"

"Cynthia is *gone*."

"Gone? Gone, how?"

"She did not sleep in her bed last night. I thought she

did. I saw her go to the bedchamber she shares with Iris. But when Iris woke this morning she found—"

"Pillows!" Iris exclaimed as she burst past her eldest sister. "She's so surly when I wake her, when she didn't rise and dress before breakfast I never realized she wasn't being her usual miserable self."

"We only discovered it when she did not come down to breakfast."

"She disguised her absence with pillows?" Amarantha said. In her childhood she had done the same to escape onto the estate undiscovered.

"She has gone off with the stable hand," Iris pronounced.

"With Miss Pike?" Amarantha untied her apron.

"The stable hand from *Haiknayes*," Jane said, twisting her hands before her. "A young man!"

"I don't understand. He did not come with you here, did he?"

"No. Only our old coachman. But Iris believes that our sister and Mick contrived for him to follow us here and wait until she could find opportunity to steal away. Amarantha, she is *eloping* with him!"

"Romantically?" Young Mick was hardly the portrait of a romantic hero. But she herself had made a similar mistake at Cynthia's age.

"After Papa was so displeased with her for Mama's fall from the window," Jane said, "Cynthia spoke passionately about how she wished a dashing hero would come along and rescue her."

"Then in the next breath," Iris said, "as though we don't have a jot of sense—like *her*—she started to go on and on and on about wonderful and handsome and clever Mick." Iris rolled her eyes. "She's positively silly for him."

"And from this you concluded that he followed you here and has stolen her away?"

"We believe she went with him willingly," Jane said. "Two of her gowns are missing, and some underclothes."

"Have you told your father?"

"No. I fear he will be furious."

"Perhaps." Undoubtedly. "But our first concern must be for your sister's safety. Iris, go now and find your father."

Iris screwed up her nose. "Must we go after her? Couldn't we simply let her run away? We'd all be much happier."

"*Iris*," Jane said. "Our sister could be in terrible danger."

"If she went willingly," Amarantha said, "I doubt her life is in danger. Iris, please go find your father."

With a nod, the girl darted away.

"Jane, you must inform His Grace."

The maiden's lashes fanned. "Oh, Amarantha . . . must I?"

"Of course. At once. He will surely know where to search for them in this country."

Jane's fingers plucked agitatedly at the ribbons hanging from her bodice.

"Would you come with me to tell him?"

"No. I must go to the stable and ask Miss Pike to prepare—"

Jane grasped Amarantha's arm. Her face was nearly as white as her gown.

"It is going forward," she said in a hushed rush.

"What is?"

"My betrothal. To . . . His Grace. Papa showed me the betrothal contract. And it is signed." Jane's composure disintegrated. "It is *signed*, Amarantha! Papa says it is a legal document, which is binding on both sides. He says that even if I wished to break it off with the duke I could not. But I do wish to, Amarantha. I wish it with all my heart!" Tears made pretty streaks down her porcelain cheeks. "I know that my sister's disappearance must be my first concern, and I feel wretchedly guilty for giving even a thought to this. I should be grateful that my father thinks so highly of me that he should wish such an honor for me. But—but—Oh, Amarantha, what shall I *do*? What *can* I do?"

She could not think. This was unexpected and frankly unbelievable.

"Are you so terrified of him, then?"

"No. Not—well, not as I was before. I think he must be—that is, Elizabeth and Dr. Shaw like him. And *you* like him. I must trust in the opinion of others, for mine is unimportant. But—but, Amarantha . . ."

"Jane, are you in love with Mr. Brock?"

"I find him infinitely wonderful! So gentlemanly and solicitous and amusing. A woman could always feel safe with him. Yes, oh, *yes*, I *do* love him."

"I am certain there must be a solution to this." And to the confusion in her heart. "We will find it. But first your sister must be found. Come. I will go with you to tell the duke." And see the man who had stolen her heart so thoroughly that—again—even in the face of incontrovertible evidence, she wanted to believe the best of him.

WHEN SHE ACCEPTED him, he would hang a bell around her neck so that he could find her at any time. And he had no doubt that if any man tried such a thing, she would remove the bell and clock him over the head with it.

"Whistling, Your Grace?"

Maggie and Pike were coming toward him. Gabriel bowed very deeply.

"You see what I told you, Maggie?" Pike said. "There will be no living with him now."

"There will be no living with me ever again, in fact, Miss Pike. I hope that prospect affords you great joy. Call a meeting, ladies."

"But won't your guests—"

"The devil take my guests, Miss Pike." Except one of

them. He would do all the taking in that case. "Eleven o'clock. In the chapel. An' dinna fret. You will like the outcome, Miss Pike. You too, Miss Poultney."

Amarantha was brilliant to advise him to turn the whole running of Kallin over to its residents—as wise as she was beautiful and as clever as she was bighearted. He would say that to her as soon as he found her. After he kissed her. Kisses came first.

"Lasses, be off with you now. A man's got work to do. Canna stand about gabbing all day."

"He has fallen off his rocker," Pike mumbled.

"How was the chapel last night, Your Grace?" Maggie said with lifted brows.

"No' quite what I hoped, Miss Poultney. But all is not lost." He went out onto the drive. Molly was picking her way along the slushy path from the distillery building toward the house.

"Miss Cromwell," he said. "Canna stay away from the place, can you?"

"No, Your Grace. There's so much to be done."

"An' you love it. 'Tis no use denying it, lass. 'Twas the same for me with the sea. There's no keeping a man, or woman, from that which calls most powerfully."

"But you've a fondness for land now."

"That I do." It was true—trenches and sheep and farmers and attic floors. He was fond of it all. More than fond. As his mother had, he loved it, every last acre and roof tile and person in his care. "Now, have you by chance seen Mrs. Garland come by here, take out a horse, stroll to the river perhaps?" Or run up a hill and subsequently declare her enduring passion for him.

"She took breakfast early, but I haven't seen her since."

"All right, then. I've called a meeting in the chapel at eleven o'clock at which I intend to give Kallin over entirely into your an' Miss Finn's care. Now, dinna rush matters. There are details to be decided, an' Du Lac to consult. In the meantime, carry on, lass." He bowed.

Her eyes were round.

He laughed. "I said, carry on, Miss Cromwell. For another hour yet I'm master o' the place. As such I expect to be obeyed."

"Yes, Your Grace." With a glance back at him, she continued toward the house.

He went to the stable. Before he turned Kallin over to its mistresses, Mary Tarry must be told. She was as much to credit for the success of this refuge as anyone. A quick ride to the village and back, and then he would see about removing his unwelcome guests from the place.

Perhaps he could claim the well had gone dry. Except that fifty yards away from the house flowed a river of fresh water straight off the mountains.

He grabbed Beelzebub's bridle from a peg.

He could claim there was trouble with mice overrunning the place, due to the late snow. Except Maggie's cats had cleared the house of mice months ago.

A *ghost*. That was it. He would invent a wicked ghost to frighten them all back to Edinburgh. Except that they hadn't been afraid of a murderous abductor.

Or he could tell them all that he had simply had enough of their company and they must all swiftly be on their merry way so he could continue making love to a fiery-haired Englishwoman. Honesty was always best.

"Loch Irvine!" Tate's voice echoed through the building.

"Good day, Tate," Gabriel said

"Off on farm business? You men o' property be always haring about the countryside," he added with a chuckle.

"Never a dull day." Or night. Not any longer. Gabriel draped the saddlecloth over the stallion's back.

"I'm gratified you've come to your senses about my Janie. She'll be a stellar duchess."

Gabriel looked over his shoulder. "Explain yourself, sir."

"The betrothal contract that you signed with the other

contracts we completed yesterday." Tate's voice was genial, but his eyes were hard. "The moment I saw it I told my Janie the news. She's thrilled, o' course."

"I've no' signed a marriage contract. I've no' even seen one."

"Now, now, lad. You canna be going back on signed legal documents."

"Show me the contract."

Inside the house, Tate laid the pages before him. It was as he said: detailed and dated and signed.

"'Tis a forgery," Gabriel said.

The merchant gave him stare for stare.

Gabriel went to the hearth and tossed the contract in.

"You'll wed my Janie," Tate said, "or I'll be informing the police an' newspapers o' your little seraglio here."

"Seraglio?"

"Ha ha! Play innocent, but I know the truth now. I'd only to see the devil's lair for myself afore I understood matters." He leaned back and rocked on his heels. "For some time now I've heard rumors at the docks o' your fondness for females o' all stripes." He nodded sagely. "Colorful little aviary you've collected here, duke. Now, dinna hear me wrong! I've no complaint with a man taking his pleasures how he chooses. No doubt in your travels you learned a thing or two o' the pleasure to be had in enjoying a number o' women at once. Had myself a bit o' fun o' that sort years back. Nothing to be ashamed o'."

"Have you lost your mind, man?"

"I've no' concern for my Janie," he said, waving it away. "Keep her at Haiknayes or take a house in town, if you care to. She'll no' have any idea what be passin' here. An' no one else will either. 'Tis my promise to you, lad." His eyes narrowed. "If you sign a contract today."

"I have no intention o' marrying your daughter."

The merchant shook his head, his bushy brows coming

together. "Be you certain, lad? It'd be a shame to have to tell the police an' newspapers about it."

Blackmail.

"You've plenty o' gold, Tate, an' she's a pretty girl. Any other man—"

"Mrs. Tate's set on nobles for all three girls."

"So you have invented a story about my household?"

"No need to invent it when the public eye's been on you for years already. I only need to fan the sparks."

"You canna blackmail me, Tate, if I've done no wrong."

"I can, Your Grace, if you care to keep this"—he offered a broad sweep of his arm—"secret."

"Get out o' my house. Now. Or I will set the dogs on you."

Tate flinched. But he recovered swiftly.

"Ha ha! To be the man who brings the Devil's Duke to his knees! I'll be the hero o' Edinburgh, revealing to the world the sins o' the devil."

"Now you're accusing me o' a *crime*?"

"Aye. The Lord Advocate'll throw me a parade. Men from Glasgow to London will be clamoring to do business with me. Might even wrest an English title for my Janie out o' it. Much better than a Scottish laird. Her mother'll be pleased."

"You've no proof to condemn me o' any crime."

"Dinna I?" Upon a hard smile, he bowed. "Looking forward to seeing your neck in a noose, Your Grace."

HIS BACK TO the drawing room doorway, the Duke of Loch Irvine stood with his face raised toward a painting of a grizzled Scotsman in tartan and wielding a sword. On the table below the painting was an open bottle and a glass. His shoulders were rigid, his stance wide and solid.

Whiskey before noon.

Amarantha cleared her throat.

He pivoted, and his eyes came immediately to her.

"Ladies." He did not bow and he did not look at Jane. And he did not come forward.

Amarantha urged Jane into the room. The girl took half a step then halted.

"Your Grace." She offered a low curtsy.

He watched her with sober eyes.

"Tell him, Jane," Amarantha said.

"Your Grace," Jane began again, her fingers twisting in her ribbons. "My sister, Cynthia, has . . . has . . ."

His gaze upon her seemed to grow keener.

Jane's fingers twisted the ribbons tighter.

"Lass, dinna fear," he said with calm that belied the intensity of his eyes. "Speak your piece."

"My sister has eloped with your stable hand from Haiknayes," Jane said in a whispered rush. "They departed last night while we were all abed. Cynthia left no note, but she had been speaking for days of how much she wanted to be free of—of—of Papa's displeasure, and how fond she was of Mick, how she believed he admired her and—"

He started toward them and Jane made a tiny leap backward.

"Does Tate know?" he said to Amarantha.

"I sent Iris to find him."

Moving swiftly past Jane, he touched Amarantha's arm as he went around her and through the door.

"Mr. Hay!" he called into the foyer. "To the stable, swiftly. Bid Miss Pike come here at once." He returned. "Where might your sister have asked him to convey her?" he said to Jane.

"I—I don't know. Cynthia has never before done such a thing! Do you believe he intends ill to her?"

"We must hope not. Tell me every word she said to you."

Haltingly, Jane repeated Cynthia's rhapsodizing about the boy.

"Where could they have gone?" Her voice had become a squeak.

Miss Pike appeared in the doorway. "I'm here, Your Grace."

"Has Tate already called for his chaise?"

"No. But not a quarter hour ago he saddled Mr. Bellarmine's horse and rode off as though he'd someplace to be. I assumed he was going to the village."

"Bellarmine's horse? Blast it. Return to the stable an' make Beelzebub ready."

"Yessir."

"Your Grace?" Nathaniel said. "May I help?"

He glanced at the veteran's stump of a shoulder. "Can you ride swiftly?"

"As quick as you need."

"Good man. Ready a horse an' provisions for the road."

"Amarantha!" Iris hopped into the room. "I cannot find Papa anywhere! Miss Alice says that she saw him stuffing shirts and whatnot into a traveling bag."

"Perhaps he knows of Cynthia and Mick's flight," Amarantha said. "Perhaps he has already gone in pursuit of them."

"Possibly." His eyes were oddly distant. Evasive. "Miss Tate, 'twould be best for you, Miss Iris, an' Mr. Bellarmine to return to Haiknayes. 'Tis likely Mick has gone in that direction, an' your mother will need to know."

"Yes. Of course. Thank you, Your Grace. Come, Iris." With a worried face, she grasped Iris's hand and led her away.

"Perhaps Alice should accompany them," Amarantha said as he turned to her.

He captured both of her hands and lifted them to his lips.

"My lady, good day." His voice caressed the formal words. Then, turning her hands over and placing kisses upon each palm he added less smoothly, "Judas, you're beautiful."

"Why did you ask Nathaniel to accompany you, not your cousin?" she said, drawing her hands away.

"Jonah knows Scots. I'll send him to Inveraray. 'Tis the closest port, an' Mick's got a hankering to sail."

"While you search in the direction of Haiknayes. Yes, that is wise." She moved toward the door. "We should—"

His arm came around her waist and he pulled her against his chest.

"First things first." He bent to her and kissed her. It was no quick caress but tender, and then lasting, as though he had all the leisure in the world to stand in his drawing room in the midst of a crisis and make love to her.

When he separated their mouths, his gaze went from one feature of her face to the next, slowly.

She said, "I am not a thing." And smiled.

"No. You're no' a thing. You are the only thing," he said soberly. "An' for robbing me o' five and a half years o' you, I plan to give my cousin the bruising o' his life." He kissed her again, pressing his lips to hers, his arms tightening momentarily. Then he released her and went to the door.

There he paused and turned only partially toward her. He bent his head. "You will be here when I return?"

There was a quality to his voice, a raw vulnerability that burrowed into her memory.

"Gabriel?" she whispered.

Dropping his hand from the door frame, he came to her in swift strides, took her face between his palms, and brought their mouths together. He kissed her deeply, fiercely. Like a goodbye.

As he pulled away, her fingertips slipped over his coat, needing to stretch the contact, to hold him. Then he was gone, and she was alone again.

Chapter 29

A (Desperately Conceived) Plan

From the uppermost story, she watched him and Nathaniel ride along the river until they entered the woods and were no longer visible. Then she found Thomas in the carriage house, lashing luggage onto the Tates' traveling chaise.

"Where has your uncle gone, Thomas?"

For an instant he seemed surprised. Then his features crumpled.

"Loch Irvine has told you, hasn't he?"

"No."

"You needn't deny you are in his confidence. I saw how the two of you were last evening, when you came into the drawing room after dinner."

"He has told me nothing. Now you must. Your uncle hasn't gone after Cynthia, has he? Where then did he go in such haste this morning?"

"I don't know."

"*Thomas*."

"I tell you, I don't *know*." His hands came up around his head. "But even if I did know, it would change nothing. You care about him—Loch Irvine—don't you? You mustn't, Amarantha. Steal your affections back from him as swiftly as you can now. As your friend, I say protect yourself for what is to come."

"Thomas, *tell me* what is happening."

"I believe he has sent Cynthia away," he said. "*Done* away with her, even."

"Done away with her? The duke?"

"My uncle! I have reason to believe he paid that servant, the stable boy, to seduce my cousin and carry her off to God knows where to—Good *Lord*. She could be already—She is lost to us already," he said harshly. "All because of my cowardice."

"Your uncle was displeased with Cynthia for your aunt's accident. But she is his daughter. How could he—"

"So that he can blame it on Loch Irvine! Uncle told me he might blackmail the duke."

"Blackmail? Sacrifice his own daughter? For *money*?"

"I tried to dissuade him from it. But I have no weight with him. I am entirely at his mercy, Amarantha, through a mistake I made years ago."

"What mistake?"

"I cannot tell you. I am unable to halt him now."

"But why would he wish to blackmail the duke? Doesn't he wish Jane to marry him?"

"Loch Irvine declined. Weeks ago, long before we all met at Haiknayes, my uncle told me that if he could not force the duke to wed Jane he would take him for everything he's worth. I thought it was all bluster. I never imagined he would see it through. Then last night he spoke of the duke's *harem* here and how he would expose it, and then I knew my uncle had lost all reason. Harem!"

he exclaimed. "Why, I've never seen an estate run so smoothly with so few servants. If that is the result of hiring mostly women, then I say everyone should do it!"

"Your uncle intends to make these accusations without proof?"

"He has proof. Just now, when Jane and Iris were packing their belongings, they brought to me garments Cynthia had left behind." His throat worked. "Stained in blood. *Blood.* I've no doubt my uncle put the blood on them. Even after so few days in Loch Irvine's company I can see that the rumors about him are balderdash. He is a much finer man than Calum Tate, certainly! Can you see now what my uncle intends? If he cannot have the Loch Irvine title and lands for Jane, he will see the duke hanged, simply for defying his wishes."

"That seems . . . extreme. To say the least."

"Men have done far worse in pursuit of their desires." Jonah Brock's voice came behind her. "And the people of Edinburgh still seek justice in the mystery of the two missing girls."

"But those girls—" She halted her words.

"Surely came to harm in some other manner?" Mr. Brock said. "Undoubtedly. Yet my cousin has done nothing to dissuade everyone from the conviction that he is at fault."

"Do you believe he has gone searching for Cynthia, as he said?"

"Do I believe he has gone off to rescue the damsel instead of pursuing the man bent on his destruction?" A grim smile lifted one corner of his mouth. "Of course he has, Mrs. Garland. My cousin is a hero. An actual hero. And heroes never think of themselves first." The smile faded. "But you already know that."

She did not understand his meaning, but there was no time to decipher it. Cold panic sluiced through her.

"We must *do* something," she said.

Mr. Brock entered the carriage house and went to the gig.

"How much time do you require to pack, my lady?" He looked over his shoulder at her.

The panic disintegrated. Purpose filled its place.

"Thomas," she said, "I need your help."

"Whatever you require. I should never have given my uncle reason to come here, but I—when you asked—and Mrs. Aiken was in such obvious distress—I thought only of myself. I must now make it right. Give me instruction."

"Be quick about your journey to Haiknayes, Thomas. I will meet you in Leith in two days. Mr. Brock, a quarter hour."

For the first time since she had known him, his smile seemed genuine.

THEY HALTED ON the journey only to change horses. The road was rough and the gig as unsuited to it as it had been a sennight earlier in the opposite direction. By the hour she stumbled from the carriage and rang the bell until Dr. Shaw's manservant woke and opened the door, Amarantha was frozen and sore and muddled with weariness.

Moving toward the stairs, she passed the foyer table and in the candlelight caught a glimpse of her mother's hand on the face of a letter. She took it up and went to her bed.

EXHAUSTED FROM TOO many hours in the saddle—and pushed beyond even a patient man's endurance by the theatricals to which he had been treated when he found Cynthia Tate and Mick huddled in an abandoned hut, theatricals that had ceased abruptly as soon as he told the pair their fate—Gabriel entered his house to find Cassandra and Pike waiting for him with news of every one of his guests' departures and a note.

A note. *From her.*

Three lines on a sheet of paper folded and sealed to deter prying eyes.

Unnecessarily so. Anybody could read the message and have no idea that she was anything more to him than a casual acquaintance.

Scraping a hand over his face, he squeezed his eyes shut.

She had gone. With Jonah.

That history was refashioning itself, albeit with a cruel twist, did not especially bother him. That she trusted his blast cur of a cousin—*despite all*—did.

"Miss Finn!" he bellowed. "Miss Pike!"

"We are standing right behind you, Your Grace," Pike said.

The hour was after midnight. Yet here they were, awaiting his orders in the light of a single candle.

"Is everyone well?" he said. "None the worse for the upheaval?"

"Aye," Cassandra said somberly. "We're all well."

"Good. Excellent. As soon as my horse has rested, I'll be off."

"To Haiknayes?"

"To Edinburgh." To deal with Tate. "Beginning at this moment, we will proceed as I informed you an' Miss Cromwell this morning."

She nodded.

"Go to bed now," he said. "I'll be out o' your hair before you wake, as you've long wished," he added with a forced grin at Pike.

He turned toward the fire.

"You are welcome to visit any time, Your Grace," his footman said. "We might even give you the best guest bedchamber."

A smile cracked his lips.

When he turned around, they were gone.

AMARANTHA SLEPT FITFULLY, and upon waking had one certain plan: she must finally call on Emily's influential friends in Edinburgh.

As she gulped down a cup of tea, she opened her mother's letter.

15 March 1823
Willows Hall

Darling Daughter Amarantha,

Your father is at wit's end. (In truth, I am, but he tells me I may write that he is as well.) We cannot endure another moment of your absence from the bosom of your family. Nearly six years are too many to never see our precious child!

And now your sister, Emily, has told us an Extraordinary Tale (which she should have told us immediately but did not! Oh, disloyal progeny!!) that last autumn you made your journey to the Duke of Loch Irvine's castle alone, without escort, without even a single servant—across the breadth of Scotland!! My heart gives me horrid palpitations when I think of it—the travails you must have endured on the road—the wretched food—and of course all of those dreadful Scots everywhere! I fear, darling, precious daughter, that the Tropical Sun baked your brain and you no longer recognize Civilized society. I am persuaded, however, that if you come home now you can be encouraged to recall it.

To entice you, (on your elder sister's strong recommendation) I am withdrawing my insistence that you marry—immediately, at least. By year's end will do. And I will button my lips as to your choice of husband: you may marry entirely as you wish (although, since the Unfortunate Incident of the amphorae which was found filled with an Un-mentionable Substance, I much *prefer Sir Elliott to Lord Brill). Your father promises to settle upon you a dowry of whatever amount you wish, and only insists that it must be grander than your first dowry. (My lord has been investing in the dreadful 'Change again, and is dancing about the house tossing guineas left and right, when he is not weeping and moaning the continued absence of his second-eldest daughter). All we ask is that whomever you choose, he intends to give you a home on* this *island and none other.*

Do come home now. Let us see your face again and hold you to our bosoms. We miss you, we love you, and we wish only for your happiness.

With love,
Your Fond Mother & Father

Amarantha blinked away tears and went to summon a hackney coach.

The home of Constance and Saint Sterling was in the heart of Edinburgh's New Town, austerely elegant on the outside and beautifully warm and comfortable within. Its mistress was three or four years Amarantha's senior, tall and luxuriously gorgeous, with tumbling golden hair and eyes as vivid as the Caribbean Sea. Even a trio of thin scars across one cheek did not mar her beauty, and her gigantically distended belly made her even more striking yet. A duke's daughter and substantial heiress, she knew everyone in high society from London to Edinburgh.

As she crossed the parlor to Amarantha without any evidence of discomfort in her ninth month of pregnancy, she extended both hands.

"Amarantha!" she said, her voice as voluptuous as her figure. "How happy I am to see you again. Why have you remained away so long? You only moved to Leith, not to the Orient!" She chuckled and drew her to a sofa. "How are Libby and the doctor? You must tell me every little detail about you these past three months."

"Libby and Dr. Shaw are at Haiknayes."

Constance's golden lashes fanned. "Haiknayes Castle? Well, I suppose they have been fond friends of Haiknayes's master. I did not know he had returned from—from wherever he had gone," she said with a chuckle. "If they have left you entirely alone in the house, you must come stay here until their return."

"I was at Haiknayes as well."

"Oh, delightful! How do you like the duke? Isn't he a great big dark wonder of a man?"

"I believe he is being blackmailed."

"Blackmailed? Good heavens."

"My own family is too far away, but I must try to help him. I understand that you and he parted on good terms."

"Despite my scandalous behavior that precipitated the end of his courtship? We did. He is a forgiving man. And a man of honor." She tilted her head. "But perhaps you are already aware of that? Amarantha, has he—"

"He is in danger. Constance, will you help me?"

Vibrant eyes subdued, she nodded.

Amarantha told her only what was needed—no more than she had told Thomas and Mr. Brock. Constance vowed her assistance, and her husband Saint's as well, and promised to send a rider to her father at Castle Read immediately.

"In the meantime, I will send a note to the wife of the Lord Advocate this afternoon. She is always eager to come and share a good gossip. I cannot easily go out now—rather, Saint does not like me to stray too far from the house," she said, linking her arm cozily with Amarantha's as they walked to the door. "He imagines the moment I am out of his sight the baby will arrive. You must come stay with us until the Shaws return home. We will be able to plot more easily. It might even distract Saint from nagging me." She smiled then squeezed Amarantha's hand. "When you are ready, my carriage will gather you. We will foil Mr. Tate's plan, whatever it is."

Amarantha's nascent hope flew away when she returned to the Shaws' house to find Thomas on the stoop, his face drawn.

"It has already begun," he said as rain pattered on the pavement around them. "When I arrived in town an hour ago I went directly to my uncle's house. He had gone out, but his personal servant said he had been up half the night writing letters to the chief inspector of the police and the *Caledonian Mercury.*"

"We must go there now and await him."

Hesitant admiration showed on his features. "It seems that your courage eclipses even your generosity."

"You are wrong on both accounts," she said as he handed her up into a hackney coach. "For I am literally shaking with fear and I am doing this entirely for myself. How did you make such excellent time here?"

"I took one of Loch Irvine's horses and rode directly here."

"You left your cousins alone on the journey?"

"Miss Alice and Mrs. Aiken went with my cousins, and Loch Irvine's stable hand, Miss Byrne, rode on the box with my uncle's coachman and a pair of pistols in her lap. My cousins were remarkably well protected!"

The Tates' house was large and prominent on the street. Amarantha was unsurprised by the display of wealth within, from hand-painted wallpaper to gilded lamps.

In his study, Mr. Tate was pacing along the length of the room. An enormous marble-topped desk dominated the space and portraits of noble estates decorated the walls.

"Nephew! Mrs. Garland? Has the party at Kallin broken up? Ha ha! Didna know myself to be the glue that stuck the thing together," he said with a chortle.

"You left without my cousins," Thomas said. "Without even word to any of us."

"True, true! I told the duke I'd business matters o' a pressing nature to see to here." He slapped his palms over his waistcoat. "Where are they now? Upstairs unpacking, I daresay?"

"Jane and Iris are at Haiknayes with my aunt. I came straight here to speak with you. Uncle, Cynthia ran away from Kallin the night before last."

"Ran away? Naughty puss."

"She eloped with the duke's stable boy. Loch Irvine has gone searching for them, of course. I wished to search as well but I thought it best to bring Jane and Iris to my aunt, and then come inform you. We can leave for Kallin immediately if you wish."

"Now, now," Tate said, tucking his thumbs into his waistcoat. "No need to go rushing around the country-side, lad. Troublesome lass. 'Twill serve her right to have a little upset."

"Mr. Tate," Amarantha said, "your daughter's reputation will be ruined."

"Aye." He patted his belly. "But 'tis too late to do a thing about it now. Must do my best for my Janie instead."

"That is why we have come here." Thomas stepped forward. "We believe that you intend to expose the Duke of Loch Irvine to the police on invented crimes unless he agrees to marry Jane. Is this true?"

Tate's eyes narrowed, "Why would I do such a thing, lad?"

"I don't know. You have never seemed to me the sort of man to seek vengeance. Can you assure me then, that this is not your plan?"

"Nephew, you're a fool." Tate shook his head. "Did you no' *read* the contract you wrote?"

"The shipping contract?" Thomas's face paled. "Did Loch Irvine sign it? As I drafted it?"

"Aye." Tate's mouth slid into a slim twist.

"Oh, God." He turned to her. "Amarantha, there is a clause in the contract that gives the partners full possession of cargo and vessels in their shared venture upon the accidental or sudden death of either. It is meant to cover contingencies that might arise before the ship reaches its destination."

"Is that legal?" Amarantha said.

"It could be contested. But my uncle required that I include it, and I had no qualms at the time. I might have with an older man, perhaps one who indulged heavily in drink. But the duke is young and healthy. And frankly I assumed he would strike that clause from the contract." He swung back to the merchant. "You intend to swiftly sell the proceeds and invest the money in a higher stakes venture with a quick return, don't you? My God, Uncle, you would cause an innocent man to be hanged so that you needn't go to debtors' prison?"

"Debtors' prison?" Amarantha exclaimed.

Thomas's shoulders heaved. "We are broke, Amarantha. Tate Mercantile hasn't a shilling in the bank."

"No' for long," Mr. Tate said.

"Loch Irvine will find Cynthia and—"

"He'll no' find her," Tate said with certainty. "An' I've proof already to see him hanged."

"Mr. Tate, you must not do this," Amarantha said.

"Mustn't I?" He seemed to study her for a lengthy moment. "What's your interest in it, then, lass?"

"Seeing that an innocent man is not condemned."

He lifted a single brow. "What solution do you suggest instead?"

Her heartbeats were too quick. "How much money do you require to settle your debts?"

His bushy brows rose. "'Tis a substantial sum."

"My father will pay it."

"Amarantha, no," Thomas said. "Even if your father

agrees to it, my uncle will never cease demanding payments. It is the damnable insurance of blackmailers."

"True enough, lad." Mr. Tate stroked his whiskers. "Luckily a better solution has occurred to me. Mrs. Garland, I'd be pleased to call your family mine. What say you to this handsome young man as a husband?" He gestured to his nephew.

"Uncle!" Thomas jerked forward. "What are you—I won't! That is, Mrs. Garland is a fine person and any man would be fortunate to have her. But I will not marry simply in order to settle your debts."

"You'll do as I wish, nephew, or I'll crush you. You know I can."

"Uncle—"

"What say you, Mrs. Garland? Take my nephew to wed an' I'll forget all about your duke's sins, hm?" His smile widened. "Aye, there's a wise lass," he said, nodding. "Experienced enough to know a fine deal when you hear it, but young enough to bend to the will o' true love. Ha ha!" He clapped his nephew on the shoulder. "Thomas, lad, your children'll have noble blood."

"This is madness!" Thomas said.

"No, lad. 'Tis good business. An' this lass knows it."

"Amarantha, you mustn't—"

"I will do it. Thomas, are you amenable?"

"O' course he is." Tate chuckled. "He has no other choice."

"Mr. Tate," she said, "you must first give me a written statement attesting to the Duke of Loch Irvine's innocence in the matter of your daughter's disappearance and a promise that you will not publicly impugn his character or any person associated with him."

"That's impossible, Amarantha," Thomas said.

"Not for such a clever man. As soon as you do, Mr. Tate, I will write to my father and—"

"Ha ha, lass. Do you mistake me for a neophyte? You'll no' escape our deal so easily."

"I have no intention of escaping. But my father must see to publishing the banns before Thomas and I can wed."

"No' in Scotland. You'll be at the altar beside my nephew tomorrow morning or our bargain's off."

"Furnish me with your assurance by the end of today, Mr. Tate, and I will see you in the morning at church." She extended her hand. Mr. Tate shook it.

Chapter 30

Dissembling

22 March 1823
Edinburgh, Scotland

Dear Emmie,

How is it that I have done so much, seen so much, changed so much from the girl I once was, yet my entire worth again now resides in my value as a man's possession? You will not like my new Plan. For I don't even like it. But I can see no other way. And when you come here and I can tell you in person, in confidence, my reason for this program, you will agree that it is the only solution . . .

"*T*his is the worst plan I have ever heard," Constance said across the parlor from where Amarantha sat at a little writing desk. "And I have been involved in some *very* poorly conceived plans."

"That is true," her husband murmured. Saint Sterling reclined in a plain wooden chair as comfortably as though it were a satin bench. Lean and muscular and sharply attractive, he had an air of sublime sangfroid so utterly unlike Gabriel's aura of virile power that Amarantha could not fathom how Constance had welcomed the courtship of two such different men.

"It must be done." Scratching her name at the bottom of her letter to Emily, she took up the sealing wax.

"Won't you allow us to do something?" Constance said. "Immediately, that is?"

"I cannot. Not yet. And I could never put you in danger at this crucial time—any of the three of you." She gestured to Constance's belly. "Anyway, if you became involved now Mr. Tate would realize that you also know information about the duke that must be concealed, and he would blackmail you too."

"But we *don't* know any information." Constance slid Saint a glance that suggested there was more to her words. But Amarantha hadn't time for their secrets. She had enough of her own to conceal.

"That is for the best," she said.

"Tate could not blackmail anybody if Saint were to stick him through with a sword," Constance said. "Miserable little mushroom of a merchant."

"There now," the master swordsman said. "My brother was a merchant, albeit a scurrilous one. So in that, I suppose, Torquil was quite like Tate."

The knots in Amarantha's stomach tightened.

So many secrets to conceal.

Thomas had begged her to tell him the truth about the duke. She had said that if he did not believe they would suit, she would withdraw. He had insisted that he would do anything to protect others from his uncle's villainy in which he had played a part, but that he could not wed a woman obviously in love with another man. He begged her to wait until she had spoken with the duke before they bowed to his uncle's wishes.

But Mr. Tate could at any moment publicly reveal the community at Kallin. And, frankly, she feared her resolve would dissolve if she saw Gabriel before the deed was done.

"With your clever mind wrapped around this too," she said to Constance, "and with Emily's and our fathers' help when they arrive, we will devise a long-term solution to silencing Mr. Tate. For now, this short-term plan must suit."

"Amarantha, you simply must not go through with this false marriage."

"Temporary marriage."

"To petition for annulment, Mr. Bellarmine will be obliged to accuse you of adultery. Does he know that?"

"He has agreed to it."

"Your reputation will be destroyed."

"It hardly matters. I have no intention of marrying again."

"Then here is a thought: what if once Tate is bested, Mr. Bellarmine decides that he is happy with you as his wife and will not grant you an annulment after all? What if *Parliament* will not grant it?"

"Then I will be married." She stood up. "Now, I must—"

"This is no minor subterfuge you intend to engage in."

"You should know," Saint said with a lifted brow.

"I do!" Constance agreed. "And I know your family will be horrified, Amarantha. Emily would—"

"Stop, I beg of you, Constance. I am grateful for your help. Indeed, I depend on it to ruin Mr. Tate's plans. But this—in fact this is tearing me apart and I cannot—You do not understand all that is at stake. Believe that I am doing what I must to ensure the safety of many more people than he alone."

The azure eyes popped wide. "More people than the duke?"

"Please."

After a moment's hesitation, Constance nodded.

Amarantha took up the letters to her sister and father. "I must go to post these."

"It will be dark within the hour. I will send a footman—"

"I would rather go myself." If she had to sit any longer enduring her friends' compassionate disapproval while she waited for the morrow she would go mad.

"I will call a carriage for you." Constance moved toward the bell.

"I will walk." She had walked across this city before, anonymous—she understood now—so that she could find him without again letting him into her world—without again losing her heart to him.

That, obviously, had not gone according to plan.

The afternoon was cool, clouds of mingled white and gray clustering about the blue and casting the cobbled streets, austere façades, and bare tree branches into dappled brilliance.

She posted the letters and turned away from Constance and Saint's house. Exhausting herself seemed the only solution to the anxious misery wound so tightly in her chest, as it had once been the solution to her restless discontent in her parents' home—her antidote to uselessness. She had run and run and run across fields and over hills simply to find a purpose that had some meaning to it. She understood this now, finally.

When the sun fell and she passed a lamplighter going about his task, she turned back.

Dinner.

Tea.

Sleep if possible.

She was always best when she had a plan.

As she neared Constance and Saint's residence, she

entered an arched alleyway and checked her stride when a mounted rider passed into the shadows at its opposite end. With a muted clicking of hooves, the horse halted and the rider dismounted.

His wide shoulders silhouetted by the lamplight beyond the mouth of the alley, even the manner in which he set his hat atop the saddle, filled her at once with peaceful pleasure and the most horrid agitation.

"I will make it clear," he said, walking in purposeful strides toward her. "I'll no' allow this happenstance meeting in the dark to have the same ultimate outcome it did five an' a half years ago."

"What? What are you—"

Then he was upon her.

"I've no intention o' sailing away on a ship tomorrow, an' I'll no' be convinced o' *anything* by you, especially if it has to do with another man or letters or propriety or reputations or—"

"You are *insane*."

"Always when you are involved. Why did you leave Kallin?"

"You must have found Cynthia Tate and brought her here, or you would not have come."

"No."

"*Oh*. No. But perhaps they are already settled somewhere safe. But you must go and find them."

"Why did you leave Kallin?"

"Didn't Cassandra give you my note? I wrote to you that I—"

"That you'd pressing matters to attend to elsewhere. Aye. I read the note. All thirty-six words o' brevity. Meriwether wrote longer prescriptions for the chemist."

"I don't know what you mean."

"Amarantha." He bent his head and scraped his hand over his jaw. When he raised his eyes to hers again his features looked harder. "Tell me what is amiss. Just tell me. I've no' the heart for foolish misunderstandings this time."

Hot emotion was flooding her chest.

"I do have matters—a matter—to attend to here. Gabriel—"

"Gabriel?" He frowned. "'Tis about to be serious."

"Yes. It is." She stepped back from the lure of his body. "But now it is late, I am tired, and I would like to return to Constance and Saint's house. Perhaps, if you wish, you might call tomorrow afternoon."

"I dinna wish it. I've just been there searching for you, woman. An' we'll speak here. Now."

"Here? In this alley? In the dark?"

"With no more delay. Now say what you've to say an' then I'll tell you why you are wrong."

"I am sorry that I misled you."

He tilted his head. "Misled?"

"I fear that I led you to—that is, I *know* that with my actions the last few days at Kallin I led you to believe that I . . . that I—"

"That you want me. You didna lead me to believe that. 'Tis simply the truth."

"Of course there is quite a lot more to being with a man than wanting him." She forced out her confession. "I am marrying Thomas."

His features transformed. "Marrying? *Bellarmine?*"

"Yes."

"No."

"Yes. Tomorrow, in fact."

"No." He came toward her. "Never."

"Don't. Please, don't." Throwing up her palm, she backed away and let the prepared words fall out. "He is a good man. Intelligent. Kind. Decent. Hardworking. Not at all indolent like the men my mother has suggested I wed. And he is charming and mild tempered. I have grown ever so fond of him over the last few months, you see. Before

I went to Haiknayes—" Her throat caught. If she spoke only truths perhaps she would come through this. "That very night in the Assembly Rooms, before I saw you, he spoke to me of his feelings. Seeing you again, that is, re-membering the past so vividly confused me a bit, and I admit that I got somewhat carried away—"

"Carried away? Is that what you call it?"

A shiver of perfect cold slid up through her. She pulled her hood tighter around her face.

"I am not that girl any longer. I tried to tell you that, but you have not listened to me."

"I have listened to every word. I have memorized every syllable. I know you now as I knew you then."

"A fortnight does not suffice to gain a thorough under-standing of another person."

"You said that you dinna wish to marry. You *said* it. *Three days ago.*"

"I don't. I did not, that is. But my parents wish it. They have grown adamant, in fact, and I find that I can no longer deny them."

"Then marry me."

"I . . . I cannot."

"You love me." His jaw was taut, his shoulders rigid, yet the heat in his eyes wrapped her in intimacy.

"I cannot deny that there was once something be-tween us."

"There will always be something between us, prin-cess."

"You mustn't speak like that. It only serves to remind me of the pain of the past."

"'Twasn't all painful."

"Perhaps not for you, sailing about the world on heroic missions. But I have told you what my marriage was, how in the thrall of emotion I made a terrible mistake."

"I wasna your mistake, Amarantha."

"I don't trust you!"

He remained silent, a wall of man a mile away.

"I wanted to," she said, the false words tasting peculiarly honest. "I thought perhaps I could. But when Jane told me of the marriage contract, the signed contract, I—"

"A fabrication, designed by Tate to force my hand."

"I believed it. Only for a moment. But a moment was sufficient to show me my mind."

"Your *mind*?"

"I have poor judgment in men. I have proven it. So this time I am allowing my parents to make the decision for me."

"You are lying."

Desperation filled her. She could only shake her head.

He came forward. "What are you doing, lass?" he said quietly.

"Planning my future."

"With another man you dinna love."

"Thomas is a very different sort of man than Paul was."

"Neither o' them are me. An' you want me. You have always wanted me."

She moved away from him. "I must go."

"You've learned o' Tate's villainy," he said. "How?"

She pivoted to him. "How, exactly. For you did not see fit to tell me. You wonder that I do not trust you? There is your answer."

"Is Bellarmine"—his voice was gravel—"forcing you somehow?"

"No. Thomas is above reproach."

"I willna pretend to understand how you believe this will hinder Tate. But you are doing it for me. For Kallin. You must be."

"I am doing it for *me*. This is what *I* want."

He seized her waist in his hands, pulled her against him, and covered her mouth with his.

He did not allow her to resist and she did not wish to. Sliding her hands over his shoulders and to his neck, she tasted him a final time and touched him. She could kiss him forever, allow him full ownership of her mouth and body and heart, and never have her fill of the glorious strength and tenderness of him. Then he was wrapping her in his arms and she was clinging to him, her fingertips burrowing beneath his coat, impressing the sensation of him upon her skin and senses.

"Marry him," he said harshly, his hands holding her tightly to him. "Marry anyone you like. But then allow me to be the man your fears fashioned, no' a maiden's chivalrous fantasy, but a man who takes what he desires when an' where he likes, who cares only for pleasure. I'll have no trouble being that man, Amarantha Vale. Before I met you, I had plenty o' practice at it."

Lit with black anger, his eyes raked her face and to where her breasts pressed against his chest. Dragging her hood down with one hand he lifted her face, his gaze hungry on her lips. Then, ducking his head, he brought his mouth against her throat.

His kiss was hot, urgent, a thorough, consuming possession and swiftly descending, his hands pulling her body up to him, making her back arch. Bending, he opened his mouth over her breast. Her gown was no protection: it gave way to his fingers, then his lips. Banding her arms about his neck, she let him have her, groaning when his tongue took her nipple, then his *teeth*. She felt it like a shock between her legs. Her cry echoed along the archway.

Lifting her, he set her back against the stone and his command came against her neck: "Your skirts."

"My—?"

"I burn for you, woman. I have always burned for you. Now *lift your skirts*."

She obeyed, pulling up the fabric and letting him push her knees apart and trap her against the wall.

Reaching between them, swiftly she unfastened the

fall of his breeches with shaking fingers. His eyes shone darkly. Then he was grabbing her up, hitching her thigh over his hip, and making her take him.

She moaned, pulling him in until he was seated so deep she could feel him in her belly.

"This," he said thickly against her cheek, his voice rough. With a hard thrust, he drove deep. "No fences. No walls." And again, harder. "No barriers." His hands moved her on him, the heat and friction of him filling her. "You need this."

She sank her hands into his hair.

"I have dreamed this," she whispered.

For a moment there was no movement. Then he bent his head and took her mouth beneath his. When he drew away from her lips, holding her tight, commanding her body with his hands and arms, he did not take her as he had warned. He gave. He made love to her. In an alleyway. In the semidarkness of mingled moonlight and lamplight, as though he had hours to please her—as though no one could see or was likely to see—as though if anyone passed by he would merely say, "Move along, nothing of note here" and continue to make her strain to him. She came in sharp, sudden contractions. They seized her entirely as his muscles beneath her hands hardened. She reached between them and touched him, as she had not even had courage to do at Kallin. His shout of release filled the archway with a man's pleasure.

She kissed his lips, his cheeks, the whiskers on his jaw, his eyes and abrupt brow and the bridge of his nose, and then his mouth again. The ache inside her was so powerful, she could draw no words from the darkness. Within she was all fire and light and broken desperation. For the first time in years she felt like that girl again, the girl who had fallen in love with him so thoroughly, without fear.

"Dinna allow yourself to be caged, wild one," he said

roughly, his brow against hers. "No' for me. No' for any reason."

Turning her face away she pressed her palms against his chest.

He released her, drawing away and fastening his breeches as casually as though it were the most usual thing in the world to make love to a woman in an alleyway. As she smoothed her skirts and tugged her hood over her hair, he watched her.

There was, of course, nothing more to be said.

She started off.

He grasped her hand.

"Amarantha, I—"

"Allow me to do this. For, God help me, I cannot grieve your death again." She tugged free and hurried past his horse and away.

When she returned to the house, Constance told her that word had come from Castle Read: her father, the Duke of Read, was in London, but she had already sent a swift rider there. He should arrive within days.

At dinner her hosts asked no more questions, and afterward Amarantha went to her bedchamber, washed her body of the remnants of her adventure in the dark with a beast who was nothing of the sort, and pretended to herself that she felt nothing. She had plenty of experience doing that, after all.

Chapter 31

For Love

Amarantha was packing her traveling trunk yet again when Libby Shaw came into her bedchamber.

"You must not marry Thomas Bellarmine."

"Libby! I thought you still at Haiknayes."

"When everybody arrived there, and Papa and I heard the news of foolish Cynthia's ridiculous elopement, we thought it would be best to take ourselves out of the way before Mrs. Tate began screaming. Again. You were good to leave a message for me and Papa at the house in Leith so that we would know you had come here, but now Mr. Brock is downstairs and he has told me of your plan to marry Mr. Bellarmine and I cannot fathom it. Amarantha, the duke quite obviously admires you—a *lot*—and you like him too. Even I can see that, and I usually don't notice such things, at least that is what Cynthia always says. Anyway, I hope you will reconsider."

"Mr. Brock is here? In this house now?"

"He came in after me. He is talking with Saint. It

seems he was acquainted with Saint's brother in Jamaica. Constance is strolling down the block with the Lord Advocate's wife."

With an hour yet till she was required to be at the church, Amarantha still wore the plain gown in which she had walked through the park at dawn in another futile attempt to walk away her misery. But she went swiftly down the stairs.

"Mrs. Garland," Jonah said, moving across the foyer as she descended. "I must speak with you. In private."

She went into the drawing room.

He closed the door and said, "He has done the unthinkable." He blinked hard several times. "I still cannot—I cannot *believe* what he has done."

"Mr. Tate?"

"My cousin. Gabriel has deeded Haiknayes to me, the entire estate. And the property here in Edinburgh as well."

"But—Why would he do such a thing?"

"Tate said—"

"Tate? You have spoken with him today?"

"I went over there hoping to make him see reason. I have in the past consorted with unscrupulous scoundrels, Mrs. Garland. I intended to warn him against attempting blackmail. I had little real hope of changing his course but I could not allow you and Bellarmine to take him on alone. But I found him in high good humor. Mrs. Garland, my cousin has made a vow to Tate that he will not defend himself against any accusations of villainy, concerning Cynthia or any other girl. And to prove this vow, he has given Haiknayes to me with the promise to Tate that I—" He seemed to recoil a bit. "That *I* will marry Miss Jane Tate."

Amarantha's knees were unsteady. She lowered herself onto a chair.

"I do not understand my cousin's mind," he said. "He is a far finer man than I. But I do know that Tate will not be satisfied with this. If I were to wed Jane Tate, the moment it was done Tate would renege on his word and publicly accuse Gabriel of villainy."

"Then you must return to Kallin. You must *find* Cynthia Tate and bring her here immediately. And I will go to Mr. Tate now and extract a promise of his good faith."

"How? What promise will suffice from a man of no moral character?"

A lifelong familial connection to an English earl, and her father's obliging purse.

"It will buy us time until the Duke of Read arrives and can offer his aid. And influence."

Jonah nodded, but his face was still drawn and he made no move to leave.

"Why do you hesitate?" she said. "You must depart for Kallin at once."

"My hesitation—My hesitation is not in that. It is that I am not worthy of Haiknayes. I am unfit to be its master. For nearly five years I barely managed to hold Gregory's plantation together, and it was a far smaller estate. More importantly, my cousin loves that land and that damn fortress more than even he knows. I cannot take it from him."

"It seems to me that you haven't any choice."

"But that isn't all," he said, his fingers crushing his hat brim. "Mrs. Garland—*Amarantha*—I cannot marry Jane Tate. It would not be fair to her, nor to—" His throat worked.

"To whom?"

"However lovely I find Miss Tate, and however gratified I am by her admiration, I am not yet healed of—of the heart broken by—by another woman's death." His voice scraped over the words. "A woman I loved more than I imagined I could ever love anyone."

"Your mistress, Charlotte?"

He shook his head. "No, though God knows I deserve every misery now for having used her as I did."

"Then who?"

His face was stark. "My wife."

"You were married?"

"For three short months before she sent me away."

"Sent you away?"

"She was ashamed of me, Amarantha. Ashamed of the man I had been and even more ashamed, I think, of her attachment to me."

"I am sorry, Mr. Brock, for your loss and for your unhappiness now."

He made a sound of hard, hopeless laughter. "You offer your condolences to the thief who stole your happiness years ago?"

"Years ago. While your grief is obviously still fresh. When did your wife perish?"

"Last summer," he said, his blue eyes empty now. "But I only learned of it at Kallin. Until then, I had thought her well and still in Jamaica."

"At Kallin?"

"I overheard you speaking of it."

Understanding came swiftly.

"*Penny*," she gasped.

"Yes."

The single syllable abruptly made everything clear.

"You and—*Penny*. You became acquainted with her through my husband, didn't you?"

"He cared nothing for her. But she cared for him. When she learned that a man of my stained reputation was meeting him, she came to me to tell me to leave him be. After that"—he looked down at the floor—"she came only for me. Despite herself."

"You *married* her? But she was—"

"Remarkable. Beautiful. Extraordinary. And strong willed. She would not have me without the vows."

Amarantha's heartbeats came painfully.

No' until you are no other man's.

Tears caught in her throat.

"Yet she parted from you," she said.

"I took passage eastward until my funds ran dry. I did not know what my destination would be. I barely even recall where I went or what I did. I'd no idea she had left Jamaica. When I discovered you at Haiknayes, I longed to ask you about her."

"She came to Scotland looking for you."

"For *me*?"

"I believe that when she could find no trace of you here, she attempted to find your cousin."

"She sent me away. I never imagined she might come after me." He clamped his eyes shut. "And if he weren't so elusive, she might have found him."

"Mr. Brock, Penny had good reason to search for you. You have a son."

All the pride and self-derision slipped away from his features. "A son?" he said very quietly.

"He is on a farm not far from Kallin, with the family who took Penny in and where I found her after months of searching for her. She had left Kingston without warning or explanation, and I feared for her safety. When I discovered her, I discovered him too. Your son is safe and well."

"Amarantha." Tears slid down his handsome face. "Thank you."

"Do not thank me. I did not do it for you. I think perhaps that I did not even do it for Penny. Mr. Brock, we must hurry now and do whatever necessary to save the most obstinately generous man in the world. For he is about to make a sacrifice of himself for all of us."

"THE LADING PAPERS, Tate. Accurate to an ounce." Gabriel put the stamped documents into the merchant's outstretched hand. "You'll have no trouble with the customs house in Bridgetown. An' if by chance you do, give them the assurance that I stand behind it. They willna know yet that I'm gone, o' course," he said more acidly than he intended. But a man was bound to let slip a snarl or two when he was agreeing to his own exile.

"Ha ha! If the cargos o' these vessels net what they should, lad, you might escape the noose yet." He had the gall to chuckle.

"Aye. Now, as you dinna own *this* ship, I'll be asking you to disembark so I can make ready to sail."

Tate tucked the documents into his coat. Patting them to his chest in satisfaction, he glanced about the state-room. The night before, Gabriel had dismissed the ship-master. He'd no money to pay the man, and he could sail the damn brig to perdition himself.

"Do you know what convinced me to let you keep this little beauty?" Tate said. "Brock's promise to hand over to me half the annual income o' Haiknayes."

"He'll no' inherit, Tate, till the powers that be see my corpse."

"No need to hurry that along, lad. No' unless Mr. Brock gives me trouble." He strode to the door, chuckling. "Aye, 'twill be a banner year for Tate Mercantile." He mounted the causeway to the main deck.

"Uncle!" Thomas Bellarmine came running from the quay. "There you are! I went to the customs office and the fellow there told me—Loch Irvine?" He skidded to a halt and sketched an awkward bow. "How do you?"

"No need for pretty manners, nephew. His Grace is my man now."

"Your—?" Bellarmine looked between them. "I don't understand. What has happened?"

"Bellarmine," Gabriel said, "I'm on a tight schedule. The harbormaster's given me a three o'clock departure an' I've a crew to collect from the pubs before then, and provisions to take on, so I'm a busy man at present. That, an' I've had enough o' your uncle for—well—for the remainder o' my life, however brief 'tis likely to be. Get him off my ship."

"There he is!" Iris Tate scampered up the gangway. "Duke! We've looked all over town for you! But Libby and the doctor don't know your address here and Mr. Brock said nobody at the Mariner's Club had seen you in weeks and—" She stumbled to a halt, frowned, and crossed her arms tight. "*Papa*," she spat. Then she swiveled around and ran back to the rail. "He's here! They're both here!"

A moment later Amarantha was ascending the ramp and boarding his ship and Gabriel felt the oddest sensation of history ending and beginning again at once.

She had never come aboard the *Theia*. He had invited her to tour his ship many times. She had always declined, holding firmly to the separation of their realities beyond the hospital.

Now she came to him and stood not two feet away and lifted her beautiful eyes to him. Her hair, tied in a ribbon, was in disarray, her cheeks were pink beneath the damp gray sky, and her gown was plain and creased. She was a heaven of haphazard beauty and it required every ounce of his self-restraint not to grab her and kiss her.

"Lass," he said with a ridiculously thick tongue. "I imagined you on the way to the altar by now. What are you doing here?"

"Obviously not going through with our plan to rescue you from the noose, which you have made obsolete."

Relief was so thorough he made a sound—a sigh, a grunt. He was a beast in truth.

"'Twas a poorly conceived plan," he finally managed. "Truly."

Spots of crimson leaped onto her cheeks. "Yes, well, desperate times . . ."

"You've come to kiss me goodbye, an' I'll no' refuse that." He grinned his scoundrel's grin. "But first, I've a word to say to you." He moved close to her and his head got full of her scent and her eyes were bright and *by God* he wouldn't leave without touching her again. He clasped her hand and heard her little intake of air. Her fingers were cold and trembling. He spoke quietly. "I've sent word to Du Lac that if anyone is in trouble beyond which Mary Tarry can assist, they're to contact you."

Her face jerked up. Her lips were within easy kissing distance now.

"Forgive me," he said. "I'd rather no' have put you in the way o' the blackguard's notice"—he cast a glance toward Tate—"but you are the only person I trust, an' you've family to protect you if—"

"*No.* You needn't do this, because you are not going anywhere."

He entwined their fingers and brought them against his chest.

"Lass, I knew this would happen someday. I've expected it. 'Tis true I'd wished to delay it as long as possible. An' I'd hoped to have assurance that you would be—" His damn throat closed. Best that way, though. If he told her about the pact, she'd think him madder than she already did.

"No," she repeated. "You are not leaving."

He breathed in deeply, simply to smell her and the sea at once.

"Now," he said, lifting her hand. "For that goodbye kiss." Bending his head he touched his lips to her knuckles.

She snatched her hand away. "You will *not* kiss me goodbye."

Abruptly he was aware of a cluster of people, none of them sailors, gathering on his deck: Iris Tate, Alice Campbell, Libby Shaw, the doctor, Mrs. Aiken, and Jane Tate.

Jonah came forward through the crowd.

"Gabriel, you mustn't agree to any of Tate's demands," he said. "If he goes to the police with false tales, Dr. Shaw and I will stand as character witnesses for you, and I'm certain Bellarmine will as well."

"Of course!" Bellarmine said.

"I'll send you straight to jail, nephew," Tate said.

"Not without implicating yourself," Bellarmine retorted. "I'll do it, too, if you continue this wicked crusade against him. It's the honorable thing to do." Thomas glanced at the others, his gaze resting for a moment on Mrs. Aiken.

"The Duke of Read is en route from London," Jonah said, "as well as the Earl of Vale and his son-in-law, Lord Egremoor."

"Ha ha!" Tate laughed as he strolled toward the rail. "'Twill be a festival o' nobles. The more the merrier, I say, to hear the proof I've gotten o' the Duke o' Loch Irvine's diabolical deeds!" He spoke at booming volume. On the quay, a pair of passersby paused to listen.

"Lass," Gabriel said softly, bending his head to her again. "Only you know the reason Jonah mustna do this, so only you can halt it."

"We will find another way."

His eyes were beautiful, dark and confident.

"I dinna need protecting. A man like me never does. They do." He turned from her. "Now, everybody, I'll be setting the sails shortly. So unless you've business in the East Indies, you'd best disembark. Miss Shaw, thank you for your work on my father's collection. Jonah, you've an estate to see to. Bellarmine, mind your own business. Tate, I'll see you in Hell." He bowed. "Good day, all."

With a smile to her that carved a hollow in Amarantha's insides, he strode toward the gangplank and down to the quay.

A hackney coach clattered to a halt beside the ship. Cynthia Tate hurled herself out of it and fell against the duke's chest.

"I am here!" she cried, righting herself with the assistance of his big hands and shaking out skirts of fluffy yellow tulle. "I am here!" she shouted again, twirling in a circle and shouting yet again to the passersby, "See, I am here! I am well! I haven't even a scratch on me!"

Gabriel ran his palm over his face.

"Lass," he said. "I told you to—"

"To remain at the inn, I know!" she said. "And Mickey *did* try to convince me to obey." She giggled and extended her hand to the young man climbing out of the coach. He wore white breeches, a white waistcoat, and the blue coat and black hat of a naval officer. "But I'm afraid that we *married* women are simply too headstrong and determined to heed instructions when other people's lives are at stake. Especially if those other people are our own personal hero." She smiled up at the duke. "Isn't that right, Mickey?"

"Aye." With a shy smile he glanced at the people on deck.

"Cynthia Tate," Alice exclaimed. "Is that a *smile*, child?"

"It is Cynthia *Pyle* now," she said, pulling Mick up the gangway. "And I am not a child. I am a Mrs.!" She extended her hand to display a pretty gold ring then turned another brilliant smile toward the duke, who was mounting the deck. "Thanks to His Grace."

"What is the meaning of this?" Mr. Tate demanded. "Loch Irvine, what sort o' man hoists a poor girl he's abducted onto his servant when he's through with her?"

"No one abducted me!" Cynthia cried for the crowd gathering on the dock below. "In fact, after Mickey and I eloped, His Grace very kindly found us where we had got lost on the road. Then he hired an exceedingly comfortable carriage for our return to Kallin, and then he saw to our wedding. It was ever so cozy! Dear Jane, darling Iris, I was *devastated* that you could not be there to hear my Mickey say his vows to me, and Reverend Clacher pronounce us man and wife. It was *exquisitely* romantic."

Iris rolled her eyes.

Jane kissed Cynthia on the cheek.

"I am happy for you." She smiled at Mick. "For both of you."

"Tate," Mr. Brock said, "here is proof that your accusations against my cousin are false. Are you prepared to withdraw your threats now?"

Mr. Tate's jowls flared with a heavy exhale. "I've still a fine story to tell the newspapers about the duke's little nest o' birds in the mountains."

"Uncle, you've gone mad!"

"Now, now," Mr. Tate blustered. "There's no telling what a man o' his low character'll do next. Daughter, come home this instant an' I'll forget all about this misbehavior."

"I shan't go home." Cynthia clung to Mick's arm. "Ever again."

Her father's face turned crimson.

"I am safer by far with my Mickey and the duke than I am at home," Cynthia said. "And so would you be, Jane. And Iris. You know it's true. At Haiknayes, Papa pushed Mama out the window!"

"I knew it!" Alice said.

"Papa," Jane whispered. "You didn't."

"He did," Cynthia stated. "I saw it happen but afterward they both told me not to tell a soul. Papa *threatened* me! He said he would lock me in a chamber for a *month* if I said a word to anybody. They were so worried about whether the duke wanted to marry *you* while *I* was walking around terrified of my father!"

"Mr. Tate," Dr. Shaw said, "did you do as your daughter has said?"

"Tripped on her own hem," Mr. Tate said.

"Mama was not wearing a long hem that day," Cynthia cried. "He did it intentionally because she disapproved of Mrs. Aiken as a guest in the castle. Papa was trying to frighten her into not offending the duke with her criticisms."

"Tate," Gabriel said, "did you attempt to murder your wife? In my house?"

"I'll no' hear another word o' slander," Mr. Tate said. "'Tis the final straw, Loch Irvine. If you'll no' return my daughter to the bosom o' her family, then I say good riddance to the both o' you. Jane, Iris, come."

The duke shook his head once. "Jonah, remove the documents from his coat pocket."

After a brief scuffle, Mr. Brock succeeded in wresting a handful of papers from Mr. Tate.

"Burn those," the duke said.

"Gladly, cousin."

"Miss Tate." Gabriel turned to Jane, took her hand, and bowed over it. "Forgive me. I should have said this to you days ago: you are refreshingly kind, an' as lovely as any man could wish o' the woman with whom he will enjoy dinner every night, an' breakfast every morning," he added with a wink at Mick. "But my heart is already given to another. Has been for years. An' forgive me for what I must now do."

The doe eyes were watery. "Now?"

"Miss Campbell," the duke said, "Cover the child's ears."

Alice attached her palms to the sides of Iris's head.

"Ow!" Iris exclaimed.

"Tate," the duke said, "you are a vile bastard. I will meet you at dawn tomorrow on my property in the city. Name your weapon. I will cut you down with whichever you choose. Bellarmine or Shaw will have to serve as your second, for I'll no' be allowing you out o' sight o' a man I trust till I've put you in your grave. Forgive me, gentlemen," he said to Dr. Shaw and Thomas. "Whichever o' you agrees to it, my cousin will make the arrangements with you."

"Papa, you *mustn't*," Jane said. "Dueling is illegal."

"Not to mention, the duke will most certainly kill him," Libby noted. "He was a decorated naval officer."

"Dr. Shaw," Jane pleaded, "I beg of you—tell my father he must not accept this challenge."

"Now, now, Janie," Mr. Tate said. "A man's got to defend his pride."

The duke crossed his arms. "You are only defending your insatiable greed, Tate."

Amarantha moved forward.

"Mr. Tate," she said in her most elevated voice, "do decline His Grace's invitation to shoot you dead tomorrow morning. At once. And know that, if in the future he should hear even a rumor that you have spoken poorly of him, he will be thrilled to immediately renew his promise to cut you down." She smiled at his eldest daughter. "Jane, I should very much like to introduce you to my friend, Lady Constance Sterling. She has a marvelously luxurious house in which you and Iris will be delightfully comfortable until your mother returns to town. Her husband, you know, is a renowned swordsman," she said, with a glance at Mr. Tate.

Cheeks crimson, he faced the duke. "Loch Irvine," he said shortly, "I accept your withdrawal from our business arrangement."

"Get off my ship."

With a glower at his nephew, Mr. Tate hurried down the gangway.

"Come, Jane, Iris," Alice said when he was gone. "His Grace has had enough of the Tate family now for one day. Cynthia, bring your young man. We will toast to your nuptials. Any excuse for champagne, I say."

Jane took Iris's hand, offered a watery smile to Jonah, then went.

"If the duke isn't sailing off to America or China or wherever after all," Iris said to Libby descending behind her, "may we still play with the bones at Haiknayes?"

"I am not playing with them, Iris," Libby said. "I am studying them. Tabitha"—she linked arms with her—"when you and Amarantha have finished your memoir, I really do think you will find the old duke's collection fascinating."

Tabitha cast Amarantha a laughing smile and went with the others.

Thomas moved to Amarantha.

"I know what you were willing to sacrifice for others," he said quietly. "You showed me how to be courageous too."

"Thank you, Thomas."

"Honestly, I haven't felt this good in years." He bowed to the duke. "Your Grace." With a nod to Mr. Brock, he followed Dr. Shaw from the ship.

"I am abruptly de trop here," Mr. Brock said with a smile. "Mrs. Garland, I request the pleasure of your company—"

"No' at this moment."

"Of course not. Good God, I'm not such a bumblehead as all that, Gabe."

"Aye, you are. Now be off with you before I decide you're to have Haiknayes after all."

His cousin's eyes went wide. "You knew I didn't want it?"

"Aye, you idiot. After ten minutes riding the land I knew. An' I'd no intention o' you actually running the place."

"Damn it, coz, I've been terrified for the past several hours, and not only because I thought I would never see you again. Why didn't you tell me—" His lips snapped shut. His eyes slewed to Amarantha. "I see," he said shortly. Then he laughed and bowed deeply. "Mrs. Garland, I hope to speak with you tomorrow." He departed the ship with a light stride.

"Tomorrow?" Gabriel turned his beautiful gaze to her and a tunnel of sweet nerves ran straight up her center.

"When you look at me, I feel breathless," she said. "Even now."

His lips slipped into a half smile. He walked to her and took her hand.

"Answer the question," he said in a low voice and his thumb stroked over her palm.

"Your cousin is the father of Penny's child."

"I'll kill him."

She smiled. "They were married."

"I'll still kill him. 'Twill feel good after all these years."

"Come now," she said, allowing him to draw her close. "You have had your little revenge on him finally."

"Too little. Next time I'll have to think o' something more painful."

"You needn't. On the drive here from Edinburgh, he told me that he has never forgiven himself for killing Charlotte's brother. His conscience is deeply troubled."

"It should be."

"You will not forgive him?"

"He kept a woman against her will, Amarantha. For that, I canna forgive him."

"Your mother taught you to respect women, didn't she? Or perhaps both your parents demonstrated that respect."

"An' you," he said.

"And I?"

"You showed me."

"You were already a man when we met."

"I was a lad full o' pride an' arrogance. 'Twas a wonder you could bear me."

"It seems I have extraordinary inner resources."

"You were extraordinary. You still are. You frightened the drawers off o' Tate."

"Not at all. It is your murderous skill that he fears."

"Why didna I think to call him out sooner?"

"Because," she said, smoothing her palm over his

waistcoat, "you are not in the habit of making demonstrations of your power."

"I've no idea what that means," he said. "But I do like to see those lips smile."

"Why didn't you bring Cynthia here as proof of your innocence?"

"When I found them, she wouldna agree to return to Kallin unless I vowed to no' inform her father."

She smiled. "She could not resist playing the heroine, I suppose. I hope her father remains cowed."

"You an' Lady Constance put your clever heads together an' find Jane Tate a noble title to marry. Tate'll forget he's ever been to Kallin."

"I cannot."

"You would rather I shoot him at dawn?"

"Jane is already in love. I cannot encourage her to wed to suit the wishes of others." She lifted her eyes to him. "A woman should be with the one that her heart cries out for."

"Amarantha," he said. "Marry me."

Her lips closed tightly. He bent his head and touched his lips softly to her temple. Then to her cheek. Then to the side of her mouth, and then her throat.

"You are everything to me, woman. Always. Eternally."

"No. Not always."

He lifted his head.

"You wanted the navy more than me," she said, "which was perfectly reasonable, I realize now. It was your life."

"No," he said. "You were my life. In nine weeks you became that."

"No. Not *always*. Not *everything*."

"Lass—"

She backed away from him. "You sent me away."

He shook his head.

"I came to you last autumn"—her voice broke—"to

Kallin. I sailed hundreds of miles, rode and walked dozens more, to find you."

"No, wild one. You went to Kallin because it was a destination, an excuse to be free o' your confines. Where will you run to next, Amarantha? What adventure will you invent to give you reason to run?"

"I was not running. I was looking for you!"

"Yet you used a stranger's name. Why?"

"I was cautious. I was *frightened*."

"You were misguided. For hear this, woman—if I were buried in a box underground an' you walked along the street above I would know you were near. If I were at the bottom o' the sea an' you sailed overhead, I would know it was your shadow passing across the sun. For five an' a half years I've thought only o' you. When you wed him, you broke my heart. When you went to Kallin in secret, you broke it again. An' I deserved it both times. For I never deserved you. I've known since the day we met that all the medals o' honor I could collect would mean nothing to you. An' in every hour since then I've done all that I could to ensure that if I would ever be given the chance to win you, I might." He drew a hard breath. "Then you hurled yourself back into my life like a madwoman, even more wild an' beautiful than—"

"You have done all that you could?"

"Aye."

The man she had known in Kingston had not been a recluse, rather a pleasure lover, with acquaintances and friends across the island. She had never believed the gossip about the diabolical hermit; it was simply too absurd. The obvious pleasure he took in the people of Haiknayes and Kallin only proved it.

Which meant that he had become a recluse by design.

I would give it all up to have you.

"The secrets you have kept," she said, "the accusations you failed to deny, the gossip you weathered by shutting yourself off from the world, all to keep safe those in your protection—You told me you did it to *atone*."

"Atone. Court you." The corner of his mouth tilted up, a rueful, humble affirmation. "Six o' one, lass."

"But I was *married*."

"Aye." The laughter left his eyes. "The day I learned it was the day this all began." He moved to her and stood before her. "I knew there would be no other woman for me, Amarantha. I returned for you. But I was too late. An' after I lost you, there was nothing else I could do. I couldna be with you. I needed at least to be a man you would admire if ever we met again."

"You waited?" she whispered. "All of these years. You waited for me to come find you, just as you promised you would?"

"For however long you are on this earth, whether mine or no', I will wait for you." He tilted his head. "Extraordinary stamina, recall." He lifted her hand and pressed his lips to her wrist. "What'll you have me do now, lass? Take to the sea an' follow you about the world? I'll do it. For now that I have you, wherever you run, I will also go. Seems to me best no' to allow you out o' my sight."

Tears sparkled in her eyes. "I do not want to run anymore."

"Aye, you do."

"I believe that I know my mind better than you, Urisk."

"'Tis no' in your mind, lass," he said quite seriously. "'Tis in your heart."

A tear dropped onto her cheek. "You are in my heart."

"I've been hoping you would notice that."

She tightened her hold on his fingers, but her hands shook. "You are my adventure, Gabriel."

"I'm—" His voice caught. "I'm glad to hear it." Then with her hand snugly in his, he went to his knee before her. "Now, for pity's sake, lass, put a man outta an eternity o' misery an' say you'll have him finally."

"I wonder how our lives would have altered had you gone to one knee and proposed to me on the dock that morning."

"I considered it, actually."

"Did you? Why didn't you do it?"

"The whites, o' course." He lifted a brow. "'Tis a chore bleaching the stains out, lass."

"I see. Then I must be glad you spared the knees of your breeches." She offered him a little smile. "If not both of our hearts."

He pulled her down onto his knee, wrapped his strong arms about her, and kissed her quite thoroughly.

"Have me, love, an' I'll spend the rest o' our lives showing you it was worth the wait."

She sank her hands into his hair, held him close, and whispered the words he had so long wished to hear.

HOURS LATER, in darkness lit by a single candle, with the only sounds the soft slap of water against the quay and her lover's hard breathing, Amarantha collapsed onto his chest and buried her face in the cave of his shoulder. Laughter tumbled from her lips and across his damp skin.

"If you are laughing at my performance," he murmured, his hands circling her behind, "I will simply have to go one better the next time."

"Better?" She sighed, and kissed his shoulder, then the hard bone that ran to the base of his throat, then his chest. "I really don't see how that could be possible."

"Allow me five minutes." His palms smoothed along her thighs. "Then I'll show you."

She tucked her face against his neck. "Am I dreaming? Or can this truly be real?"

"I have had so many dreams o' this, I know 'tis real this time."

She lifted her head and set her palms on the mattress to

either side of him, and her hair draped down like rippling fire. With one hand he smoothed it behind her ear. It fell forward again.

She smiled. "You cannot tame even my hair."

"I will never wish to tame anything about you." His throat moved in an awkward jerk. "You are here," he whispered. "Still here."

"Where else would I go when I only want to be with you? And when I am on a ship in the middle of the night?"

"The morning I left Kallin, I believed I would never see you again."

She sat back, and then slid off him and tucked her legs beneath her.

"Why did you believe that? Had you already formed your plan to sail away to the east?"

"No." He pushed up onto his elbow.

Her gaze went to his arm. A flush of pink began on her cheeks then trailed down her neck to her chest where, beneath his gaze, her nipples were stirring to peaks. She breathed deeply, swallowed, and her eyes shifted back to his.

"I—" she said, and drew another thick breath. "What were we talking about?"

He wanted to laugh. Instead he said, "Tell me what you desire."

A dart wrinkled the bridge of her nose and she lowered her gaze.

"I am—I am not accustomed to speaking my desires in the bedchamber," she said quick and quietly, and then firmer: "Anywhere. I am not accustomed to speaking my desires *anywhere*. Too often I have been told they are wrong. Misguided. Ill-conceived. Improper. Unchaste." She lifted her eyes and defiant fire sparked in the clover-leaves. "I think perhaps that I run because I do not wish to be told that I may not."

"You want me," he said. "Tell me how."

"What if you do not want what I want?"

"There is nothing you could want o' me that I dinna want. Trust me."

"Trust you," she whispered as though tasting the words. "That," she said abruptly, looking down. "I want that."

"My arm?"

"That muscle. There. The one you use to chop wood." Her lips were quivering.

"It requires more than the use o' one muscle to chop wood."

"That one is . . ." In the candlelight the dark flush was a shadow across her face and breasts. "It is *beautiful*." She met his gaze and her shoulders rose and fell on swift, hard breaths. "I want to bite it. And lick it."

"My God, woman, what are you waiting for?"

She laughed and the joy in the music of it made him mad to touch her. He turned her onto her back and kissed her mouth, then her throat, then the luscious curve of her breast. Slipping his hand between her legs, he stroked her. She sighed, and then moaned, and rose to him.

"What—" She gasped. "What of my request to bite and lick—*oh-ohh*—that muscle?"

"You needna request, lass. Just do."

Springing up, she did, grabbing hold of his arm and pinning her beautiful lips to his skin. Then her hands were on his chest, pressing him back as she lavished him with her teeth and he felt it in his hardening cock.

Mouth on his arm, she straddled his waist, spread her thighs, and pleasured herself on him. It was stunning, the passion of her body, her fluid eagerness, the hunger in her mouth. When she began whimpering, he surrounded her buttocks with his hands and pressed his finger inside her.

She gasped and cried out, crying again as she accepted him deeper, and then letting him ease her against the shaft of his cock. Then the tremors rose in her, and she sobbed, the sound breaking from her throat as she bore down on him, her body entirely open, shuddering, *his*.

"Now," she said. "Make another of my dreams come true."

She let him take her, rocking herself onto him, bucking when he touched her and matched his caresses to his thrusts. She called his name and he told her he loved her, twice, and then a third time because she asked him to.

She was wrapped in his arms with her back against his chest and their legs tangled, and she had finally caught her breaths when he said, "I made a pact with the devil."

She turned her head and her cheek brushed across his whiskers.

"I beg your pardon?"

"'Tis I who should beg yours."

She swiveled around in his arms and placed her palms on his chest.

"Perhaps you should explain."

"Seven months after I left Kingston, *Theia* came into a fierce storm. She was breaking apart. I'd eighty-four men aboard. I made a pact with the devil."

"I see."

"You're no' shocked."

"I have read a lot of scripture." Her lips were beautiful. "What was the pact?"

"I told him that if he brought all my men through the storm alive, I'd give him what I wanted most in the world."

"Let me guess: a golden ship. Or, no—a chest full of gold. Or—" She gasped. "You did not promise Haiknayes!"

"No. Something I wanted much more than Haiknayes," he said. "Someone."

She blinked. "Me?"

"I promised him that if I ever had you for a single night, an entire night, he could take me away after that an' I'd no' resist."

She did not speak for a full minute.

"Only the one *night*?" she finally said.

"Aye."

"Not the day too?"

He screwed his brow up. "Well, at the time I was still plenty angry with you."

Laughter cracked from her. Smiling, he drew her tight against him.

"Did all of your men live?" she said quite soberly.

"Aye."

"Yet here we are."

"For now."

"This is not our first entire night together."

"At Kallin—"

"I left after dawn," she said. "*That* was our first night."

He ducked his head to look into her eyes. "Sailors are a superstitious breed, lass."

"Apparently." She traced a fingertip along his jaw.

"That night, in the chapel," he said, "I needed you to marry me."

"Needed?"

"So that if you had me that night, as beneath the stairs you'd said you wanted, I would know that if the devil took me afterward, everything I had would be yours."

Her eyes filled with tears.

"You needn't have feared," she whispered, as he kissed her brow and cheeks and the tip of her nose. "For it was not the devil who saw you through that storm."

"No?"

"I prayed for you. Every day."

His lips stilled on her hair.

"For your safety at sea," she said. "Every day for months and months, even though you had abandoned me. I could not cease loving you." She reached up and drew his mouth to hers. "So you see, Devil's Duke, all of this time you have been misnamed."

"It seems so," he said, and smiled through her kisses. "What name will you invent for me now that all the others no longer suit?"

She tasted his mouth again, then again, and pressed her nose to his skin and breathed him in.

"A name that I think has suited you all along."

"Aye, lass? What's that?"

She whispered, "Mine."

Epilogue

Home

26 May 1823

HMS Patriarch
Lat. 41, Long. −35

Dear Gabe,

Who knew sailors could be so tetchy when woken in the middle of the night by the wails of a colicky child? I have instructed Luke's nurse to bring him to me when this occurs, for—astonishingly—I have a calming effect on him.

He will soon be in the arms of his aunts and grandmother, and I will be on my knees begging their forgiveness so they might award me the continued care of him—if I am not imprisoned. A fine is more likely—gold for a man's life—which will never, however, remove the stains from my soul. I fear, cousin, that, years from now when the time comes for us to depart this earth, our paths will finally diverge forever: mine downward, yours in the opposite direction.

Until then, your duchess has requested regular news of her nephew, which I shall gladly supply.

J. S. B.

9 June 1823
Haiknayes Castle

Dear Emmie,

Have you ever shorn a sheep? It is fantastically difficult! I made a hash of it, with tufts of wool flying all over the place. I laughed until I actually fell on the ground. Gabriel had to pick me up and carry me home.

I am thrilled by the news that Brittle & Sons will print a second edition of Tabitha's memoir so soon! She writes to me that Thomas is already scheduling more of her public lectures throughout England—they are drawing enormous crowds. With the profits she wishes to establish a modiste shop in Edinburgh. She often speaks of returning to Jamaica for her sisters, whom she misses dreadfully, and freeing them if she is able. Thomas intends to accompany her. The depth of their love has surprised them both, I think.

My best to Colin, and Gabriel's to both of you too. (He sits beside me now, paging through the shipping report. Once a sailor, always a sailor—which suits me perfectly.)

With love,
Amy

October 1823
Haiknayes Castle
Midlothian, Scotland

"They will come!" Amarantha entered the library waving a letter.

Lifting his attention from the pages strewn before him, Gabriel smiled. She came to him, slid onto his lap, and took his face between her hands. He encircled her waist with his arms and she kissed him.

"Who will come?" he murmured when she finally released his lips.

"The Duke of Loch Irvine's most accomplished baker and her husband, Bess and Angus Allen. We will have the most delectable cakes in all the land."

"You invited them here? To stay?"

"There is no blacksmith for miles around, which is ridiculous, and Nathaniel declined to come since Mary Tarry invited him to live at the Solstice. Now *there* is a romance of which we can be proud."

"Aye." His hands moved lower.

"And I cannot eat one more of Mrs. Hook's terrible biscuits. Thus, my invitation." She swiveled on his lap to peer at the papers and felt the bulge of his desire pressing into her behind. Closing her eyes she shifted against it. "How is it that you can be doing dull correspondence, yet *this*."

"I have but to see you." His palm surrounded her breast and he drew aside her hair and kissed the nape of her neck. Amarantha leaned into it.

"What is the dull correspondence?"

"A letter to the architect we will engage for the property in Edinburgh," he said muffled against her skin. "So it seems we are at cross purposes with Bess and Angus."

"Absolutely not," she said on a little sigh. His fingers were doing what she liked best on her breast. "We will be fabulously eccentric and convey our baker and blacksmith around with us like ancient kings did."

"Practical." His mouth was hot and deliciously good on her throat.

"Isn't it? Mm. But—*architect*? We cannot afford an architect. We cannot afford a new house!"

"We've come into a bit o' money."

With a twist of her body, she forced him to meet her gaze. "From where?"

"Your father."

"*My* father? How? When?"

"Last November, in fact."

Her eyes widened. "Did he—oh, no—my mother— good heavens—did he—did my father make you an offer for me? *Last year*?"

"He did."

"Yet you did not tell me?" She leaped off his lap. "I cannot believe it."

"You are justified in your disbelief, love." He smiled and proffered a letter. "I read it for the first time just now."

She snatched it and read.

"It seems your sister told him that you went to Kallin before even returning to Shropshire."

"Yes, of course." She glanced up from the letter.

"Because you couldna stay away from me," he said with a one-sided smile of pure masculine confidence. "Because you loved me even then."

"It was luck that took me there," she said, drawing both of her lips tightly between her teeth.

"'Twas strategy," he replied.

Her eyes twinkled. She looked again at the letter. "Why did you read it only now?"

"It went missing in a pile o' correspondence while I was traveling. I've only just found it."

"It is a lot of money."

"Still opposed to dowries?"

"The exchanging of money for women? Yes." A

mischievous smile graced her lips. "Perhaps we could call it a wedding gift."

"Aye," he said.

"We could lay the new fences on the southern hill," she said.

"Aye."

"And repair the—"

"Aye."

"And rebuild the—"

"Aye."

"And still have—"

"More than half left to send to Kallin."

She climbed back onto his lap and encircled his shoulders with her arms.

"How kind of my father to give us such a substantial wedding gift."

"You dinna mind it?"

"If it will make you happy, I am happy."

"Woman, you are all I need to be happy."

She let him draw her close. Eyes closed, she felt the even cadence of his breathing and the hard beating of his heart, the solid muscle and bone of him, and his arms so strong around her. Joy pressed outward beneath every inch of her skin.

"Am I glowing?" she whispered.

"Glowing?"

"I have swallowed the sun."

His arms tightened.

"Now," he said into her hair, "I've a gift for you."

She leaned back. "For what occasion?"

"Our anniversary."

"Married five and a half months does not an anniversary make," she said skeptically.

"Come." Lacing his fingers through hers, he led her from the room and down the narrow winding stairs, then out of the keep and onto the hill.

They walked hand in hand through the grass and the

cool, sunny brilliance of the day was all about them, golden and red leaves drifting from the trees, the hillside emerald, the music of autumn in the wind that curled her skirts about her legs and carried the birds' songs.

Months earlier in the summer, on the apex of the highest hill within sight of the castle, he had strung a carved wooden swing from a branch of a big old tree. Here, he said, she could pause in her travels about the estate, and from the castle he would be able to see her.

To this tree and swing they now came. On the seat was a small box of very fine wood. She opened it.

"A backgammon set! It *is* our anniversary," she exclaimed, and looked up into his eyes full of shadows that she adored.

"I love you, Captain."

"An' I you, wild one." Bending his head, he laid the softest of kisses on her lips. Then another kiss, somewhat more ardent. And another. Then they were in each other's arms and entirely oblivious to the breeze and the sunshine and everything but the pleasure of each other.

Decidedly breathless, she took his hand and, intertwining their fingers, drew him down to sit on the grass.

"Now," she said without releasing him, "concerning the question of luck versus strategy, I have come to believe that a combination of both is often the best approach . . ."

Historical Inspiration & Thank-Yous

A few decades ago sweeping historical romances were all the rage. As of the writing of this novel, however, "Regency" historical romances that include dozens of characters, span many years, and take place in multiple unfamiliar locations are far less common. But I was weaned on Dorothy Dunnett and John Jakes, as well as Tolkien and McCaffrey, and occasionally I adore writing big novels as much as I enjoy reading them. So when Amarantha and Gabriel and the women of Kallin explained the story they wished me to write for them, (despite not inconsiderable anxiety) I bowed to the request.

To my readers who love my books, whether big or small or somewhere in between, I am so happy you found me and honored that you stay with me. And to my editor, Lucia Macro, who not only does not counsel me against writing books like this, but improves them immeasurably, as well as to everyone at HarperCollins who brings them so beautifully to bookshelves—especially my publisher Liate Stehlik, and Carolyn Coons, Shawn Nicholls, Caroline Perny, and everyone in the Production and Art Departments, among others—I offer thanks upon thanks.

The history of the Caribbean in the early nineteenth century is incredibly complex. The actions of individuals, communities, and entire nations during this period are equally as horrifying and heartbreaking as they are fascinating and inspiring. Indeed I found in real history every inspiration for Gabriel's project at Kallin and for Amarantha's twisty, turny path toward understanding the wide world and her own heart.

The story of the women of Kallin first took root in my imagination when I read *The History of Mary Prince: A West Indian Slave*, a short memoir by a former enslaved woman, in which she describes decades of abuse and suffering at the hands of her captors, as well as her religious conversion and marriage in the West Indies, and her escape during a journey to England. Olaudah Equiano's earlier and much longer memoir, *The Interesting Narrative of the Life of Olaudah Equiano*, was wildly popular in England (eight editions were published between 1789 and 1797, while Equiano traveled throughout England giving lectures that were attended by hundreds), and helped inspire Parliament to pass The Slave Trade Act of 1807, which criminalized the trade from Africa. Both memoirs inspired in my imagination the idea for Torquil Sterling's project—and Gabriel's secret—as well as Tabitha's story.

Mary Prince's narrative begins with a preface by Thomas Pringle, a Scotsman who offered her a paying job after she escaped her captors, and who saw to publishing her memoir as part of his petition to ensure her legal freedom wherever she might travel in Britain, including back to the West Indies. Pringle notes: "The narrative was taken down by Mary's own lips by a lady who happened to be at the time residing in my family as a visitor." This became the model for Tabitha and Amarantha's writing project, which begins while Amarantha is living with the Shaws. Edinburgh bubbled with abolitionist fervor in the 1820s: the Edinburgh Abolition Society, established in 1823 by well-to-do merchants and professional men is the real historical social world in which I imagined John Shaw and Alice Campbell active.

Most of the history one reads when studying abolitionism is not, however, positively inspiring. Paul's disgusted words about how planters equated enslaved men and women to livestock is historical. A particularly relevant example: After the devastating hurricane of 1780, the governor of Barbados wrote, "The depopulation of the negroes and the cattle, especially the horned kind, is very great, which must . . . be a cause of great distress to the planters," but that "fortunately few people of consequence were amongst" the thousands dead (quoted in Schwartz, *Sea of Storms*, p. 94–5). Likewise, when Paul tells Amarantha that enslaved people on Barbados demanded emancipation, he isn't speaking of a new phenomenon. For decades already, enslaved people had been demanding their freedom in both small and large rebellions across the Caribbean. Plantation owners retaliated swiftly and brutally. The only successful slave revolt ever, however, began on the French colony Saint-Domingue in 1791. Upon wresting independence from France in 1804 that island nation became Haiti, the homeland of Gabriel's partner, Xavier Du Lac.

Likewise, Paul's position that a missionary's project should be to convert enslaved people to Christianity to ensure the salvation of their eternal souls, but not to fight for abolition, was common in the British West Indies during these decades in particular. After Parliament criminalized the slave trade in 1807 and rumors began circulating that full abolition was coming soon, the wealthy planter class grew increasingly mistrustful of politicians in London, claiming they didn't understand matters in the islands. During these years, missionaries on the islands were more acutely aware than ever that they walked a fragile line. They were more likely to caution their flocks against demanding freedom and instead encourage them to focus on improving the state of their souls for the afterlife. The work of abolitionists throughout Britain—in England, Scotland, the West Indies, and the east as well—finally did result in the Slavery Abolition Act of 1833, which made Britain the first colonial empire to illegalize slavery.

For the sake of this story, I represented one matter disproportionate to historical reality: Tabitha, her husband, and Charlotte's brother were all able to purchase their freedom from their masters. In fact, although not unheard of, this happened rarely. But in my story, for Charlotte's brother to plan to purchase her freedom, and for Jonathan Aiken to own even a small mill that Tabitha could inherit, she and both men had to be free people.

I offer copious thanks to the scholars whose work I depended on to write this novel, including (although not limited to) Sandie Blaise, Trevor Burnard, Emilia Viotti da Costa, Henry Louis Gates, Jr., Gad Heuman (whose generous counsel enabled me to include Eliza and Mr. Meriwether's and Penny and Jonah's marriages), Carson Holloway of Duke University Libraries, Alison Lodge, Teresa Moore, and Colleen A. Vasconcellos. For Stuart B. Schwartz's gracefully written *Sea of Storms: A History of Hurricanes in the Greater Caribbean from Columbus to Katrina*, I am enormously grateful, as well as for the Pierpont Morgan Library's gorgeous edition of *The Drake Manuscript*, which was the inspiration for the old duke's collection of natural specimens and Libby's catalogue. The title of Chapter Five, "Lords of the Ocean," comes from Ian W. Toll's engaging *Six Frigates*. And, although a tenth-century poet has no obviously direct influence on the historical events in this novel, when I came across Symeon the New Theologian's poem, it described Amarantha and Gabriel's early awakening to their love so perfectly that I could not resist borrowing from these lines for Chapter Six's title: "We awaken as the beloved / In every last part of our body." The world of the nineteenth century was an interconnected place, when ships of colonial nations and mercantile fleets connected peoples and goods across the globe. I like to imagine that some scholar whom Gabriel encountered along his sea travels introduced him to the medieval poem, and that his heart recognized the words.

For brilliant scholars Celeste-Marie Bernier, Thavolia Glymph, Martha Jones, and Adriane Lentz-Smith, who read this manuscript and offered suggestions I am especially and deeply grateful.

Borthwick Castle and the surrounding lands inspired Haiknayes, and I am very grateful to the good folks who now manage Borthwick for the tour. Kallin—which architecturally is an amalgam of several Scottish manor houses and castles that I adore—is situated in a place that I renamed for my novels: my fictional Glen Irvine is the real Glen Orchy. Just as other places in Scotland that I visited while researching this series, it is spectacularly beautiful, made all the more appealing by the wonderful people I have met throughout this gracious country.

I thank my incredible agent, Kimberly Whalen, for everything she does on my behalf. To the Lady Authors—Caroline Linden, Miranda Neville, and Maya Rodale—I am ever grateful for ideas and support. To Georgann T. Brophy, Donna Finlay, Meg Huliston, Beverly Jenkins, Mary Brophy Marcus, and Stephanie McCullough, whose reading and comments made this a much better book, and to Marcia Abercrombie, Georgie C. Brophy, Sonja Foust, and Lee Galbreath, who saved me yet again: I employ no hyperbole in saying that I could not do this without you. I offer special thanks to Mary Brophy Marcus for the delightful map of Amarantha's journeys on my website, and to Cari Gunsallus, author assistant extraordinaire. To my son and my Idaho, for patience and love and keeping me grounded in reality, thank you.

Finally, to my husband, Professor Laurent Dubois, who first introduced me to Caribbean history, and who for this series put me in touch with his colleagues, recommended books and articles, offered me ideas, helped me create a fictional network of people entirely grounded in real history, read the manuscript and gave me crucial feedback, reassured me in my worries (again and again), and pretty much lent me his entire library to research this novel, I haven't sufficient words of thanks. So I have dedicated *The Duke* to him, and to my father (in memory) and brothers and all the good men I know and have known—as friends or from afar—who work hard every day to make this world a place of justice for all.

With each novel I write, my fictional world of early nineteenth-century Britain grows. Gabriel first appears in *The Rogue* (Constance and Saint's story) and *The Earl* (Emily's story), which both take place during Part III of *The Duke*. Gabriel also has a cameo in my novella *The Pirate and I*. Amarantha first appears in *When a Scot Loves a Lady* of my Falcon Club series, and again in *The Earl*. And here and there throughout *The Duke* one can find passing mentions of characters from my other books too.

Gabriel and Amarantha now have their much-deserved happily ever after. But an intrepid lady is determined to become a member of Edinburgh's exclusively male Royal College of Surgeons—despite the delicious distractions of a certain exiled royal who requires her for another sort of project altogether. My Devil's Duke series concludes with

Libby and Ziyaeddin's love story in *The Prince*, coming in the summer of 2018 from Avon Books.

For more information about all of my books and series, and for bonus scenes, timelines, and family trees, I hope you will visit my website at www.KatharineAshe.com. I love hearing from readers.

Keep reading for a sneak peek from

The Prince

Coming Summer 2018

"*M*y knowledge of anatomy is lacking. Male anatomy, in particular," she clarified.

A single brow lifted. "Is it?"

"When the other students trade puerile banter, I am conspicuously silent. My studies on the subject are proving insufficient for the pretense of manhood I am living."

"I see." He glanced at her books stacked all over his parlor, about which he had said nothing for weeks. He was a generous host. She was depending on that now.

"Haven't you been examining male cadavers?" he said.

"Those do not *move*, of course." She looked squarely into his eyes. In the candlelight they were the color of coal and, as always, very beautiful. "But you do."

"Ah," he said, smiling slightly. "I begin to see the direction of this conversation."

"Will you help me with this?"

"Your studies would continue to suffer." The knuckles wrapped around the end of his walking stick were stretched tight. "I, as you know, am not a whole man."

She stepped forward. It was unwise, especially now that she knew what she was capable of in his proximity. But she could allow nothing to hinder her project, not even memories of his breathtaking musculature.

"If I am to succeed in this charade, I must know everything about being a man," she said. "And it is not male *legs* that interest me now."

His gaze snapped to hers, and in that moment it occurred to Libby that this man, who had agreed to her terms for living in his house, was neither celibate by nature nor inclined to remain so for much longer.

Next month, don't miss these exciting new love stories only from Avon Books

A Daring Arrangement by Joanna Shupe

Lady Honora Parker must get engaged as soon as possible, and only a particular type of man will do. Nora seeks a mate so abhorrent, so completely unacceptable, that her father will reject the match— leaving her free to marry the artist she loves. Who then is the most appalling man in Manhattan? The wealthy, devilishly handsome financier, Julius Hatcher, of course.

Ride Wild by Laura Kaye

Recently freed from a bad situation by the Raven Riders, Cora Campbell is determined to bury the past. When Slider, a member of the Ravens, offers her a nanny position, she accepts, needing time to figure out what she wants from life. Cora adores his sweet boys, but never expected the red-hot attraction to their brooding, sexy father. If only he would notice her . . .

The Sea King by C.L. Wilson

Seafaring prince Dilys Merimydion has been invited to court the three magical princesses of Summerlea. To secure the power of the Sea Throne, Dilys vows to return home with a fierce warrior-queen as his bride. But politics has nothing to do with the unexpected temptation of the weathermage, Gabriella Coruscate. She knows better than to risk her heart—until the Sealord jolts her awake with a thunderclap of desire.

REL 1017

THE SMYTHE-SMITH QUARTET BY
#1 *NEW YORK TIMES*
BESTSELLING AUTHOR

JUST LIKE HEAVEN
978-0-06-149190-0

Honoria Smythe-Smith is to play the violin (badly) in the annual musicale performed by the Smythe-Smith quartet. But first she's determined to marry by the end of the season. When her advances are spurned, can Marcus Holroyd, her brother Daniel's best friend, swoop in and steal her heart in time for the musicale?

A NIGHT LIKE THIS
978-0-06-207290-0

Anne Wynter is not who she says she is, but she's managing quite well as a governess to three highborn young ladies. Daniel Smythe-Smith might be in mortal danger, but that's not going to stop the young earl from falling in love. And when he spies a mysterious woman at his family's annual musicale, he vows to pursue her.

THE SUM OF ALL KISSES
978-0-06-207292-4

Hugh Prentice has never had patience for dramatic females, and Lady Sarah Pleinsworth has never been acquainted with the words *shy* or *retiring*. Besides, a reckless duel has left Hugh with a ruined leg, and now he could never court a woman like Sarah, much less dream of marrying her.

THE SECRETS OF SIR RICHARD KENWORTHY
978-0-06-207294-8

Sir Richard Kenworthy has less than a month to find a bride, and when he sees Iris Smythe-Smith hiding behind her cello at her family's infamous musicale, he thinks he might have struck gold. Iris is used to blending into the background, so when Richard courts her, she can't quite believe it's true.

JQ4 0916

The Casebook of Barnaby Adair novels from
#1 *New York Times* bestselling author

Stephanie LAURENS

WHERE THE HEART LEADS
978-0-06-124338-7

Handsome, enigmatic, and deliciously dangerous, Barnaby
Adair has made his name by solving crimes within the
ton. When Penelope Ashford appeals for his aid in solving
the mystery of the disappearing orphans in her care, he is
moved by her plight—and captivated by her beauty.

THE MASTERFUL MR. MONTAGUE
978-0-06-206866-8

When Lady Halstead is murdered, Barnaby Adair helps her
devoted lady-companion, Miss Violet Matcham, and her
financial adviser, Montague, expose a cunning killer. But will
Montague and Violet learn the shocking truth too late to
seize their chance at enduring love?

LOVING ROSE
978-0-06-206867-5

Rose has a plausible explanation for why she and her children are residing in Thomas Glendower's secluded manor.
Revealing the truth would be impossibly dangerous, yet day
by day he wins her trust, and then her heart. But when her
enemy closes in, Rose must turn to Thomas to protect her
and her children.

LAU6 0814

At Avon Books, we know your passion for romance—once you finish one of our novels, you find yourself wanting more.

May we tempt you with . . .

- **Excerpts** from our upcoming releases.

- Entertaining **extras**, including authors' personal photo albums and book lists.

- Behind-the-scenes **scoop** on your favorite characters and series.

- **Sweepstakes** for the chance to win free books, romantic getaways, and other fun prizes.

- Writing **tips** from our authors and editors.

- **Blog** with our authors and find out why they love to write romance.

- **Exclusive content** that's not contained within the pages of our novels.

Join us at
www.avonbooks.com

AVON
An Imprint of HarperCollins*Publishers*
www.avonromance.com